A stolen kiss . . .
an embrace on the dance floor

It was all only a game—a game of outwitting the vigilant sisters. Another fling with freedom. Of course it had to come to an end. Every group has its Judas, and Notre Dame was no exception: one Isabelle Bertrand, a fat, plain, pimply faced prig . . . She could hardly wait to report our secret excursions to Mother Superior.

Adrienne and I were called into the office to be sternly reprimanded and apprenticed out to Madame Natalie Boulanger, the notoriously stingy owner of the local bridal shop.

"Don't worry, Adrienne," I said as we walked out of the convent gates for the last time with our valises in hand. "I know it is all my fault, but I promise to always look after you. If there's one thing you must know about me by now, it's that I'm a survivor. I've had to be."

COCO

The Novel

PATRICIA B. SOLIMAN

HarperPaperbacks
A Division of HarperCollinsPublishers

HarperPaperbacks *A Division of* HarperCollins*Publishers*
10 East 53rd Street, New York, N.Y. 10022

This book is published by arrangement with G.P. Putnam's Sons, a division of The Putnam Berkley Group, Inc.

Cover photography by Herman Estevez

First HarperPaperbacks printing: October 1991

Printed in the United States of America

HarperPaperbacks and colophon are trademarks of HarperCollins*Publishers*

10 9 8 7 6 5 4 3 2 1

DEDICATON

For my mother,
Winnifred Gatehouse Brehaut,
and my father,
Colonel Ernest H. Brehaut—
on either side of "the door."
And for my godmother,
Philomene Tifrère.

Acknowledgments

Love and thanks to Sue Pollock, who showed me this new wire to walk, and to Al Lowman, my warrior agent, who elegantly set me on it.

To Phyllis Grann, my extraordinary friend and publisher, and E. Stacy Creamer, whose deftness Coco would have admired.

And to my extended family who believed: Richard Stein, Risa Kaufman, Carole Laquercia, Anwar Soliman, Carole Baron, Jonathan Dolger, Jane Isay, Rob Fitz, Helen Brann, Betty Prashker, William Reilly, Jackie Collins, Rona Jaffe, Cathy Cash Spellman, Yvone Lenard, Wayne Rowe, Carol Smith, Clyde Taylor, Claire Smith, George Nicholson, Paul Fedorko, Patrice Clay, Joanna Martine Woolfolk, Page Ashley, Elaine Marion, Gloria Nagy, Harriet Pilpel, Eve Frank.

"GREAT loves, too, must be endured."

— Coco Chanel

Prologue

Brive-la-Gaillarde, France
February 16, 1815

Prologue

*I*t was bitterly cold in the room. The fierce February wind howled down the chimney and iced over the windows. The fire in the grate had burned out hours before and there was no money for more wood. No money for the local doctor. And no money for medicine.

She sat alone with her mother. She had told the other children to kiss maman good night and sent them down to the kitchen of the inn, where at least they would be warm and the cook might be charmed into giving them some soup and scraps of bread.

The only sound in the room besides the wind was the harsh rasping of breath. The asthma had grown steadily worse as her mother followed him from market town to market town, vainly deluding herself that here he would stop his endless, aimless wandering . . . here he would make a home for her and their five children.

She knew better. Her father could never rest. Secretly she watched the way his eyes were always turned toward the road leading out of town, always scanning the distance for that bright will-o'-the-wisp, prosperity, that always eluded him. Now he had left them again, abandoning them with no money even to pay for this single, barren room.

The breathing grew even more labored. Frantically,

she gasped for air. Her mother was strangling, and there was nothing she could do to save her. Sitting beside her on the bed, the tears pouring down her face, she watched her die. Gently, she pried her mother's terror-clenched hands away from her blocked throat. Gently, she closed her eyelids.

"Goodbye, maman. It's all right. You can rest now. Your only fault was loving too much. It is one mistake I promise you I will not make."

ONE

Gabrielle/Coco
(1900-1905)

ONE

ONE

I stood in front of Mother Superior's desk in the dark, wood-paneled office, shifting restlessly from one foot to the other while she read the long letter I had brought with me from Aubazine. Not even the serene, smiling terra-cotta Virgin beneath the stained-glass window, glowing with the late afternoon light, could reassure me.

"So, Mademoiselle Chanel, my good friend Sister Anselme tells me you have decided that you have no vocation to become a nun."

How could I tell her the truth—that after my father's desertion of my mother and her lonely, terrible death, after his depositing me and my sisters at the orphanage door like so much excess baggage and virtually selling my brothers as cheap labor to the local farmers, I had very little faith left in me. Certainly not the commitment required to become a bride of Christ. How cynical I would seem if I told her I had no faith in marriage of any kind.

"That is true, Mother Superior," I said as piously as I could. "I have prayed earnestly for guidance, but no call ever came to me." Only the clear call to get away from that grim orphanage, smelling of carbolic soap and poverty, from the good sisters and their endless exhortations to cleanliness, godliness, and complete obedience. . . . Only the call to escape that black-and-white banishment before I was buried alive at seventeen.

"You know, Mademoiselle Chanel, that your Aunt Adrienne is also here at Notre Dame, but as a boarder. The convent's regulations stipulate that our paying boarders live in separate dormitories from our scholarship students and orphans."

How sharply that stung. "I am *not* an orphan, Mother Superior. It's true I come to you from Aubazine, but my sisters and I were only lodged there while my father went to America to expand his wine export business. He has never really recovered from the shock of my mother's untimely death, you understand. He loved her to distraction." Never would anyone hear the real story of that shameful abandonment from me.

"Perhaps, Mademoiselle Chanel," she said gently, "my information *is* incorrect. For now, though, until I have further instructions from your father, I'm afraid you will have to sleep in the dormitory for non-paying students."

There was a light tapping on the door that opened to admit a tall, slender young woman. Adrienne. Even in my agitation I could see that she was lovely—fair where I am dark, with a long, heavy blonde plait dropping down the back of her grey-and-white woolen uniform, a sweet smile, and warm, guileless blue eyes.

"Gabrielle," she held out her arms to me. "My mother wrote to say you would be joining me at Notre Dame. How happy I am to meet you at last. It seems impossible to have a niece who's only two years younger than me. And such a beautiful one at that."

Her welcome seemed genuine enough, but I could

not bring myself to return her embrace. I was too wary of what her mother might have told her about me and all too painfully conscious of the contrast between us— her air of gracious prosperity and my threadbare, box-pleated black skirt, the cheap white cotton blouse laundered nearly to transparency, and the scuffed and battered valise on the floor beside me.

Mother Superior must have sensed my discomfort, as she put her hand on my rigid shoulder and led us to the door.

"Fortunately, your Aunt Adrienne's dormitory is just down the hall from yours, and she has promised to look after you in the early days and help orient you to your new life with us. Sister Anselme writes that you are an accomplished seamstress. A lucky coincidence—so is your Aunt—and I'm certain I can find you challenging work to do together." She smiled kindly down at me. "I hope very much, Mademoiselle Chanel, that you will be happy with us here at Notre Dame."

We were no sooner alone in the shadowy corridor than I turned to Adrienne. I could feel my cheeks burning. I had to begin as I intended to go on.

"I am *not* an orphan, Adrienne, and I trust that you at least, as blood kin, will help me put an end to this vicious canard that has followed me since poor maman's death."

When she hesitated—so it was true, her mother *had* told her the whole shabby story—I simply hurtled on. "But Mother Superior is right about one thing. I am an excellent seamstress, though if you think for one moment that's how I mean to spend the rest of my life, you're dead wrong. I've already been locked away far too long. Five endless years—I counted every single day. Aubazine's in the middle of nowhere—in a *forest*, mind you. I felt like an exile." Dramatically, I dropped my valise on the floor, unbuckled it, and pulled out a copy of one of Monsieur Decourcelle's popular romances. It was tattered from repeated readings.

"If it weren't for my novels, Adrienne, I'd have perished of boredom ages ago. Now, tell me what *you* do for amusement here in Moulins."

"Well, ma petite Gabrielle," she said with that charming smile, "I can see you'll be delighted to know that the 10th Light-Cavalry is quartered here, only just across the river from the convent. It's a very chic regiment. And there are religious processions through town nearly every week where we can watch for the best-looking officers."

Suddenly the prospect of Notre Dame—even as a "non-paying student"—looked considerably brighter.

"No, no, my dear 'Aunt' Adrienne," I teased her, "processions where the very best-looking officers can watch for *us.*"

After the austerity and rigorous discipline of Aubazine, I longed passionately for freedom. I was forever in trouble with the sisters for rule-breaking, and I quickly recruited Adrienne as my accomplice. It was clear to me that nineteen years of bourgeois respectability and doing precisely what was expected of her had left her as ready to kick over the traces as I was.

Regulations were a direct challenge and I could always find a new way to get around them. My demerit book was as long as any of the cherished romance novels I slipped between the covers of my Latin texts. Because I somehow always finished my studies faster than my classmates, I had plenty of time on my hands to devote to what I called my personal "projects."

How I loathed those dreadful, drab, scratchy grey woolen uniforms—and as a "non-paying student" mine were of an even cheaper grade of cloth than Adrienne's—so I decided to design an alternative. It was easy enough, whenever Sister left us alone in the sewing room, to steal hours from the time we were meant to spend decorating altar cloths and chasubles with intricate needlework for Monsignor, and instead make dresses for the two of us from bedsheets stolen from the convent's linen closets. My inspiration, of course, came from the romantic heroines of my novels. I would drape and cut them on Adrienne, whose patience made her the perfect model for the light, airy, delicately embroidered dresses I created.

Once we had the wardrobe, curfew existed only to be broken. I'd learned the art of escape at Aubazine— where I took long, solitary walks in the surrounding woods—so it took me only a few warm summer days to find a drainpipe we could shinny down after lights-out, wearing my white linen creations, and a spot where the gnarled limbs of an ancient apple tree gave us an easy way up and over the convent wall.

On the other side would be eagerly waiting the latest in a long line of dashing young cavalry officers—with a friend brought along for my older "sister." I would allow my officer a quick kiss before letting him settle me in front of him on his bicycle. Then the four of us would pedal off to an evening of dancing and flirting at the Alcazar—a place most definitely off-bounds to good convent girls.

I'll admit I'd been an honor student in Monsieur Decourcelle's school of romance. Every one of those elaborate, solemn religious processions through the sleepy little town, with our pompous Monsignor leading his flock—a bevy of the brides of Christ, then a contingent of convent girls, and an escort of splendidly uniformed young officers of the 10th Light-Cavalry—provided what the nuns would have called an "occasion of sin." Not once did we return through the convent gates without my excitedly drawing Adrienne aside to show her a note slipped to me in secret by an old or new admirer setting a rendezvous.

Flirt was all I ever did—a stolen kiss, an embrace on the dance floor. Nothing serious. It was all only a game—a game of outwitting the vigilant sisters. Another fling with freedom. Of course it had to come to an end. Every group has its Judas and Notre Dame was no exception. One Isabelle Bertrand, a fat, plain, pimply faced prig who was the mayor's daughter, the school bully, and who I knew had taken an instant dislike to me. Adrienne told me Isabelle's hatred was mere jealousy—I had half a cavalry regiment chasing after me—but I knew it went deeper than that. Like most bullies, Isabelle was essentially a coward who felt threatened by my independence. Behind my back she might call me *"paysanne"* or *"bâtarde"* (how she'd found *that* out I didn't know—probably inspired guessing), but she never dared repeat any of her taunts to my face. Instead she resorted to spying on Adrienne and me. She could hardly wait to report our secret excursions to Mother Superior.

Adrienne and I were called into the same office where we had met less than a year before to be sternly reprimanded and apprenticed out to Madame Natalie

Boulanger, the notoriously stingy owner of the local bridal shop.

Goodbye to shapeless uniforms and endless rules and regulations! I was infinitely relieved to be out on my own at last. My only concern was for Adrienne. She was so much more conventional than me—so completely family-minded. I know she was afraid her parents would be furious with her and she was probably right.

"Don't worry, Adrienne," I said as we walked out the convent gates for the last time with our valises in hand. "I know it was all my fault, but I promise to always look after you. If there's one thing you must know about me by now, it's that I'm a survivor. I've had to be."

TWO

We were sitting in the back room of Monsieur Redon's Modern Tailleur, patiently stitching back torn *passementerie* and tacking on loose braid to jackets. The sun filtering through the motes of dust and onto the gold braid and Adrienne's pale gold hair made the room seem to sparkle.

I caught her eye and laughed mockingly. " 'Modern Tailleur,' indeed. If the dashing young gentlemen of the

10th Light-Cavalry knew their precious uniforms were being repaired by mere girls, they'd *never* pay Redon's outrageous bills!"

Whenever her commissions for layettes or trousseaux fell off, Madame Boulanger "generously" loaned us out, at a handsome fee I'd be willing to guess, to Monsieur Redon to do piecework in his small, dusty tailor shop just down the way from her bridal shop on the rue de l'Horloge. Piecework was all he had to do. No proper young dandy would ever consider having his uniforms made outside of Paris.

"You know, Adrienne," I said dreamily, setting my work aside, "I've been thinking that if we have a great success at La Rotonde, we ought to set our sights higher and try for a season in Vichy. The *café concerts* there are filled with managers down from Paris to take the waters—*and* to look for local talent. Who knows, I might become the next Yvette Guilbert."

"Vichy? Gabrielle, you have such big dreams." She shook her head. "If you don't finish that jacket, ma chère, you won't have the money for the rent, never mind for the costumes and singing lessons you'll need if you're going to storm the music halls of Vichy."

I laughed and went reluctantly back to repairing the glittering braid. There was a sudden commotion in the front of the shop, and we could hear Monsieur Redon trying nervously to pacify an irate customer.

"But, cher Capitaine, I have promised that the jacket will be ready by five. Here, look at my pocket watch. It's barely three."

"Not good enough, Redon. I need it right now. I have an appointment for tea with an enchanting blonde who doesn't like me to keep her waiting."

The curtains closing us off from the front of the shop were yanked apart and in strode a tall, stocky, red-faced young man with a thick, dark moustache. He was very angry—and very good-looking.

"Well, and what have we here, Redon? Child labor? Pretty children at that, but hardly experienced enough to work on a uniform from Paris." He moved to take the jacket from my hands, but I was too quick for him. I would not be patronized.

Leaping to my feet, my eyes flashing jet fire, I challenged him. "Pardon, Capitaine, but have you examined my work?" I thrust the repaired sleeve under his nose. "I doubt you will find finer stitchery anywhere on the rue de Richelieu, Monsieur. Now," I said as haughtily as I could, "if you will kindly retire and let me complete the job, you will have your precious jacket in plenty of time not to disappoint that enchanting blonde." The last was said with what I hoped was withering scorn.

The captain made an undignified retreat through the curtains. Adrienne and I doubled over in silent laughter.

"Did you see his face, Adrienne?" I asked. "He looked like a bewildered little boy."

"A little boy who's very used to having his way," she replied. "And you should have seen yourself. You looked like an avenging angel with the sun turning that blue-black hair of yours into a halo. He was thoroughly dazzled. I doubt you've seen the last of him."

Of course she was right. As we were leaving the shop at six, there he was, lounging against a shopfront. When he saw us, he came striding across the cobblestoned street and held out his hand to me with an engaging smile. He certainly was handsome.

"Mademoiselle, my deepest apologies for my insufferable rudeness. Your workmanship is superb. May I make amends by taking you and your companion to dinner?"

"I regret, Capitaine, that I do not make a habit of dining with gentlemen to whom I have not been introduced." But I smiled up at him nonetheless.

"Étienne Balsan, Captain of the 90th Infantry, entirely at your command, Mademoiselle."

"Well, Adrienne, you'll have to admit he's a refreshing change from all those cavalry types. If I had to listen to one more account of frozen pasterns I'd have stabbed myself with my sewing shears!"

We were sitting on a sun-warmed wrought-iron bench in the little park beside the pavilion of La Rotonde—the object of all my *true* desires—sharing a baguette and some delicious chèvre in the brief lunch break Madame Boulanger grudgingly gave her overworked staff.

"Gabrielle," Adrienne said exasperatedly, "I can hardly believe my ears. You can't be that self-centered. Haven't you even been *listening* to Étienne? I've been along with the two of you for weeks now, because you asked me to—as 'sister,' 'aunt,' 'chaperone' whatever you like—and all he *ever* talks about besides your dark eyes is horses. Étienne Balsan may be with the infantry, after all, it's the commission his family bought him, but his heart, if you'll forgive me, is in the stables. He's as passionate about horses and horse breeding as you are about becoming a music-hall star. That's what I worry about when I think of the two of you together—not the difference in backgrounds, but the difference in ambitions."

"What's wrong with ambition, Adrienne?"

"Do you honestly think in your heart of hearts that anyone as conventional as Étienne Balsan, who's as desperate to break down the barriers to château Society as he is, could ever afford to marry a woman who sings at the Casino de Paris—who's a star on the *Grands Boulevards?* You want celebrity. He wants respectability. The two don't go hand in hand."

"Adrienne, ma chère," I told her patiently, "you're the one who keeps coming back to the institution of marriage. It's what *you* want and need, and what I'll wager you'll ultimately have. Trust me, dear 'Aunt,' it's not for me. You come from a warm, happy, loving family. You believe in that. You should. It shines out all over you. Your mother has even taken in Antoinette and Julia-Berthe. At least I know my sisters are being looked after. *That's* family loyalty. My own example was quite different." I tried to smile, but I couldn't keep the sadness from my eyes.

And then I saw Étienne coming toward us across the little park, his arms full of roses—peach, yellow, scarlet, mauve—there must have been six dozen of them.

"Well met, Mesdemoiselles Chanel. Here I was, wandering aimlessly through this rural paradise wondering what I should do with all of summer's bounty and, *voilà,* there you are . . . two young goddesses of summer, the perfect beauties for whom the Gods intended this floral tribute." With a flourish he divided his riches and piled dozens upon dozens of roses into our arms— the lion's share going to me.

Try as I might, I couldn't help laughing and blushing all at once. Étienne's openhearted boyishness was his most appealing quality.

"Étienne, what on earth are you playing at?" I asked. "These must have cost you your month's allowance at the very least."

"A tribute to perfect beauty is never measured in francs," he reproached me gently. "Now, say you'll both agree to dine with me tonight."

"Oh, Étienne, we can't tonight," I said ruefully. "We're going to audition for Monsieur Bernard. It's terribly important." I gestured in the direction of La Rotonde.

Étienne's face fell, but he recovered quickly. He was not a campaigner for nothing. "Then a late supper after the audition—to celebrate your becoming the two loveliest *poseuses* Moulins has ever seen."

As usual, in our endless push-pull of proud wills, Étienne had won. Or had he? This was only a skirmish. The stakes were higher in our larger war.

THREE

We had worked for two weeks on our costumes. Whenever Madame Boulanger was preoccupied with a customer in the front of the shop, we would drop the veils and satin nightdresses we were embroidering for the blushing brides of Moulins and take up the outfits I had designed for our debut.

Adrienne's was pale-blue silk with a tightly fitted bodice and a drop waist that flared out into a bell-shaped skirt. I absolutely forbid her to add the border of tulle bows I knew she was planning to shyly conceal what she considered an immodestly low-cut neckline.

"It must be simple, Adrienne. The lines of the gown are everything. Don't clutter it with those foolish bows. You have a superb figure, ma chère. Show it. The blue sets off your blonde hair and blue-violet eyes to perfection."

Mine was even more daring—a feminized version of the dress uniform worn by the 10th Light-Cavalry. Our experience with Redon had come in handy. I'd replaced the trousers with a slim, scarlet skirt I knew would add inches to my height. I had cut the closely molded white tunic to artfully disguise my unfashionably small breasts. The effect, I thought, was extremely provocative.

I had somehow managed to persuade the manager, Monsieur Bernard, to let us join the *poseuses* who sat primly in chairs at the back of the stage. He hadn't actually bothered to audition us after all. What did it matter if you could carry a tune? The wealthy officers who were La Rotonde's principal customers were satisfied if you were young and pretty. And as the evening unfolded and the wine and champagne flowed, simply making yourself heard above the din was talent enough. Besides, only the principal artistes down from Paris got a salary. As *poseuses* we only made what we could collect after our songs, less the manager's commission. The money didn't matter. It was the opportunity I had been dreaming of for so long—the chance to be noticed.

As the night of our first appearance drew near, I was afire with nerves.

"Imagine, Adrienne, there might be managers of *café concerts* up from Vichy. Even from Paris! Étienne has promised to invite all of his friends and to bring the house down when I sing."

"Étienne will promise you the sun and stars, Gabrielle. He's completely infatuated. I wouldn't count on more than that, though. I'm sure his family already has a titled bride with a substantial dowry picked out for him."

"Don't be absurd, Adrienne. How many times do I have to tell you I'm not thinking of marrying Étienne— or anyone else for that matter. My singing career comes first. La Rotonde is just the jumping-off point for Paris."

"Then you had better concentrate on practicing your repertoire," she said calmly. "Your delivery of

'Co-Co-Ri-Co' is still a little shaky. I don't delude myself, Gabrielle, ma chère. My own voice is pleasant enough, but hardly the stuff music-hall stars are made of. I know you, though—in your mind you're already the toast of *tout* Paris."

At last the night came. It was a glorious late-summer evening, a crescent moon reflecting in the little pond beside the pavilion and silvering the birches. La Rotonde was packed to capacity with an almost exclusively male, exclusively military audience. Clouds of smoke from expensive cigars hung thick in the air and the noise was deafening.

I had braided my long, heavy black hair and tucked it up under a kepi. Even before I started singing, Étienne and his friends began applauding and cheering. From the moment the "star," Mademoiselle Reger, left the stage and I got up from my chair and came to the front, it was clear my costume's homage to the cavalry had succeeded.

I began with *"Qui qu'a vu Coco,"* that sentimental ballad of the absentminded shopgirl who loses her poodle in the Trocadéro. By the time I finished my energetic if slightly off-key rendition of *"Co-Co-Ri-Co"* the audience was on its feet, clapping wildly and chanting, "Co-Co . . . Co-Co . . . Co-Co . . . !"

After the performance we joined Étienne and his friends at their table. I felt giddy from the applause. This was the beginning of my new life, I was sure of it. Stardom on the *Grands Boulevards,* money, fame, independence, security—I would have it all. Étienne ordered yet another bottle of Cordon Rouge and lifted his glass.

"To the darling of the 90th Infantry, the darling of the

10th Light-Cavalry—to my *own* darling . . . Coco Chanel."

"Coco" . . . yes why not? This was to be my destiny.

FOUR

"All right, Coco, today is the day." Étienne burst into the bridal shop with his usual exuberance, paying no attention to the fluttering of scandalized brides-to-be or Madame Boulanger's obvious displeasure. "Put down that endless embroidery and you and Adrienne come with me. It's high time the mascots of the regiment learned how to ride."

"Mon cher Capitaine," Madame Boulanger drew herself up to her full five-foot-two, her copious bosom in tight brown silk puffed out like an affronted mourning dove. "I have a business to conduct here. I cannot possibly spare my two best seamstresses on a whim of yours."

Adrienne and I exchanged amused glances. This was the first we'd heard of our high standing with Madame. Her style was constant criticism. She wielded her sarcasm as deftly as I did my shears.

Étienne was not to be denied. All charm, he reassured her, "Chère Madame Boulanger, of course I intend to compensate you for the loss of these two invaluable apprentices to your high art." He pulled out his wallet and heaped such a substantial pile of notes on the counter that Madame Boulanger's greedy eyes gleamed.

"Well, mon Capitaine, put that way I suppose I could spare the Mesdemoiselles Chanel for the rest of the day." Madame was not immune to Étienne's appeal. No one was. "But," she actually rapped his wrist playfully with the measuring stick she always carried, "you must not make a practice of disrupting my operations." Madame was formidable where her business interests were concerned.

"You have my word on it as an officer and a gentleman," Étienne bowed formally. "I have always had, chère Madame, the highest regard for the sacred institution of marriage." He swept us out of the shop leaving an astonished bevy of brides and bridesmaids-to-be gossiping feverishly in our wake.

I collapsed laughing onto the red leather seat of the open carriage. "*Dieu*, Étienne. You *are* priceless. For someone with such 'high regard' for that 'sacred institution' you certainly have managed to elude it. Every one of those bourgeois mamans back there considers you a prime catch. Did you see the outraged look on their faces when you kidnapped *us* instead of one of their spoilt darlings?"

"You mistake me, Coco. I do have a very high regard for marriage—to the right woman."

I decided not to pursue that dangerous line of discussion. It led too far away from freedom.

The day was glorious as we bowled along the sparkling river, over the bridge through the stone archway to the Quartier Villars where the 10th Light-Cavalry was billeted. I'd finally had to agree that Adrienne was right. Étienne's *second* passion was horsemanship. He spent every moment away from me or his infantry regiment with his cavalry friends, either on horseback or at the races, and he was determined that I share his enthusiasm. He had even confided in me that he eventually meant to resign his commission and take up horse breeding somewhere in Compiègne, the vital heart of France's horse country where all the great racing champions were bred.

Now Adrienne and I were about to be initiated into Étienne's charmed circle. The regiment was off on maneuvers and Étienne had bribed one of the grooms to smuggle us in to the riding school.

I was the first to mount, and from the moment Étienne handed me up into the saddle and showed me how to hold the reins, I felt utterly at home. Instead of riding sidesaddle as I'd planned to do, I simply hitched my skirts up around my waist and mounted astride.

Adrienne was appalled. Étienne was delighted. "That's it, Coco, ma chère, you're a natural . . . heels down, hands light on the reins, elbows in and feel your mount's intentions with your legs. Remember your seat—your seat bones have to exert a perfectly even pressure in the middle of the saddle."

This was freedom as I'd never experienced it before. I was all fierce concentration. Étienne had me on a longeing rein as he put me through the basics of the walk, trot, and canter around the ring. But the rein was hardly necessary. Small and slight as I was, I still felt an immediate, almost uncanny oneness with my mount, a huge chestnut called Mars who was as full of fire as the war god he was named for. His strong body communicated his desires to me and I found it infinitely easy to answer.

"That's it, Coco—the balance is everything . . . the equilibrium. Mars will find his own balance and you flow with him. Control him with delicacy. Ride him as if you had a precious pair of balls between those beautiful legs of yours."

Adrienne blushed to the roots of her hair. She thought Étienne had clearly been carried away by my unexpected success.

I, on the other hand, burst out laughing and lost my concentration. Mars seized the advantage and started to buck, arching his back like a giant cat.

"Raise the head, Coco," Étienne shouted. "Raise the head!"

Obediently, I raised my head at Étienne's command, but the chestnut went on bucking, jumping straight up and down in place with all four feet in the air. I couldn't control him.

"Raise the head, Coco," Étienne shouted again, and I shouted back, "But Étienne my head *is* raised!" just as I flew out of the saddle and landed with a thud on my back on the tanbark. Étienne rushed to my side, but I was only winded and was already on my feet dusting myself off.

"What went wrong, Étienne? I did exactly what you told me to. I raised my head, but he just went on jumping."

Étienne took me in his arms and hugged me tight. "Oh Coco, ma chère, you are priceless. I meant raise *his* head. When your mount decides to buck, he has to lower his head and arch his back first. If you raise his head, he can't do it."

"Well, then," I looked cheerfully up at him, "let's get my 'precious balls' back in the saddle and proceed with my education. This is turning out to be more fun than I even imagined."

When Adrienne's turn came, she managed a sedate trot and canter on a small, docile bay mare and under Étienne's close supervision. By the end of the afternoon he was satisfied he had accomplished his mission. Adrienne would be able to acquit herself reasonably enough in a ladylike sidesaddle, but I was absolutely determined to become a horsewoman—and a superb one, if I could.

As we drove back into town in the gathering darkness, Étienne, the reins of the carriage in one hand and his other arm holding me close against him, told me I had that God-given affinity for my mount, the gift the experts call "equestrienne tact."

"Well, Étienne mon cher, then—considering this afternoon's display of *your* tact—you must admit that once again I have a certain advantage over you."

"For sheer nerve, Coco my dearest," Étienne laughed and leaned to kiss me quickly on the lips, "you always do."

FIVE

s the train pulled into the station, I could tell Adrienne was full of doubts. I knew she was wondering why on earth she had allowed me to talk her into joining me on what she'd told me more than once was a wild-goose chase. True, she'd had to admit, that over the past months at La Rotonde I'd become something of a local sensation, had even eclipsed Mademoiselle Reger, the star down from the *Grands Boulevards.* I knew that privately she believed my popularity had less to do with the quality of my voice than with my connection to Étienne who turned up faithfully, night after night, with his band of fellow officers.

They could be counted on to pour endless amounts of champagne down their throats and coins into the plate Adrienne passed after my solo turns. From the start, she said she'd realistically confined her *own* aspirations to looking picturesque. Now here we were, arriving in Vichy at the height of the summer Season, our suitcases crammed with our hastily assembled wardrobes, and I could barely contain my excitement.

"Look, Adrienne, over there . . . there's a poster for the revue at the Élysée Palace. *That's* the first place where we're going to audition."

She set her heavy valise down on the station platform with a thump. "Precisely how do you plan to arrange that? We don't know the manager of the Élysée Palace or of the Grand Casino or the Alcazar for that matter. We don't know anyone in Vichy. We don't even know where we're going to *sleep* tonight."

"Oh Adrienne, you always worry so over *details*. You're as bad as Étienne. When I told him I had my heart set on Vichy, we had our first real quarrel. 'I didn't have the proper contacts . . . I didn't realize how easily I might be taken advantage of . . . I didn't understand the difference between a provincial manager like Monsieur Bernard at La Rotonde and the unscrupulous lechers of Vichy.' He made it sound as though we were going on the *streets* not the boards. It was jealousy, impure and simple, Adrienne. He's just nervous of letting me out of his sight."

"That may be, Coco, but there's probably more truth to his suspicions than either of us wants to admit. Ever since we set out this morning, I've been regretting letting myself be swept up again by one of your whims of iron."

"Mon dieu, Adrienne, look around you—it's such a glorious day. Where's your sense of adventure? Of course I know you don't share my serious ambition to be a singer—I've always known that." I gave her my most seductive grin. "But we're young, we're beautiful and we're in *Vichy,* not stuck in that hot, drowsy backwater embroidering trousseaux we'll never get to wear."

She had to admit I had a point. The charms of Moulins, even of its most attractive but determinedly bachelor officers had definitely begun to wear thin.

"Besides," I told her, "once he'd cooled off and realized I was resolved to go no matter what, Étienne gave me a small *cadeau* to tide us over until we get established for the Season."

"Hopefully, that will be well before it ends," she said tartly.

"If worse comes to worse, not that it ever will, Adrienne, we can always find work as attendants at the hot springs at La Grande Grille or La Source de l'Hôpital. Look at it this way, ma chère, *tout* Paris comes to Vichy for the cure—and so have we. The cure for perishing of provincial boredom." With that, I picked up her bulging valise along with mine and marched off down the platform to the hackstand, the ribbons of my straw boater streaming jauntily out behind me. And Adrienne, *dieu merci,* trailed obediently in my wake.

Thanks to my shameless flirtation with our handsome young cabdriver, who was a mine of information on Vichy and its summer visitors, we found ourselves settled by teatime, in a small room at an equally modest rent out on the fringes of the city. It was in a pretty, quiet street lined with elm trees and, according to our driver, a neighborhood of office workers, students, and a few struggling "actress and models," he said with a suggestive wink.

Not even the sour, rail-thin landlady could dim my enthusiasm. Equally suspicious of our being unchaperoned and of our claim to be professional singers down from Moulins for the Season, she lectured us sternly, "No gentlemen in the room after ten, Mesdemoiselles. I run a clean, respectable house and I expect you to abide by the rules." With that, she huffed off down a narrow wooden staircase smelling of lavender oil and *blanquette de veau.*

Helpless with laughter, I fell onto the huge mahogany bed which took up most of the space not already filled by a giant highly carved armoire.

"And *we* thought we were escaping the Madame Boulangers of this world, Adrienne. Flouting convention is going to be far harder work than we suspected."

Perhaps it was her empty stomach or an overdose of my optimism, but she was not amused.

"I think she actually believes we are *irrégulières* or something worse," she said quietly.

I was genuinely shocked. She had hit a nerve, my secret terror of being owned, of being used and then heartlessly abandoned the way maman had been.

"Irrégulières, Adrienne, how can you even think that, never mind say it? If I had wished to be kept, my dearest Aunt," my tone was icy, "I had only to indicate that to Étienne. He would be overly eager to make such an arrangement. You of all people know how determined I am to make my way on my own. I thought we *shared* that ambition. I thought that was why we were here."

She realized immediately she'd gone too far. Adrienne's essential kindness made her incapable of hurting anyone. She was determined to restore my high spirits.

"Oh, but Coco ma chère, don't you remember what you told me back at the station? You are here out of ambition, but *I* have come along simply for the adventure of it and, of course, to watch you blossom from the humble *poseuse* of La Rotonde to the most glamorous *gommeuse* in all Vichy!"

It worked. I could never stay angry at Adrienne. I managed a fragile smile, reminded her that after all *gommeuse* even at its most glamorous, really meant "beginner." And by the time we had finished unpacking—and managed to fill the tall armoire to overflowing with the daydresses and evening gowns I had designed and we had stitched so lovingly back in Moulins—I was full of plans for taking the city and its influential theatrical managers by storm. Our luck, I felt in my heart, was ours to make.

Vichy in the Season was a city *en fête!* Cabinet ministers and their haughty, overdressed wives from the *Seiziéme Arrondissement* mingled with sensual, potbellied, golden-eyed sultans from Egypt, Lebanon, and the Sudan—their exotic ladies *never* in evidence—and tall, fierce, aristocratic veterans of the court of the Tsar of all the Russias. It was a scene straight out of the pages of my beloved Monsieur Decourcelle.

What they had in common was their limitless bank accounts and the healthy remorse that always set in after a year of elegant dining and dalliance in Paris, Beirut, St. Petersburg, or Alexandria—a remorse that had brought them together here at vast expense to take the healing mineral waters that had made the spa famous.

Then there was the younger set, the pale, wan, and listless heirs to France's greatest fortunes, posted back from their regiments at their parents' urgent, influential requests from the outposts of empire in Egypt or Africa where they had ignored their military pursuits in favor of what I—out of my wealth of experience with the fantasies of Monsieur D.—assured Adrienne were passionate romances with exquisite Moorish dancing girls and the hot, dangerous pursuits "of the flesh."

It was an incredibly exciting, challenging city, and I could hardly wait to take it on.

I was up at dawn, urging a grumpy Adrienne into one of the deceptively simple suits I'd designed back in Moulins, a mauve mousseline de soie with a graceful skirt that flared gently out above her ankles and a jacket subtly trimmed with arabesques of raised braid that fell below the hip but was tightly belted to emphasize the curve of her full breasts and the hand-span waist of which I knew she was secretly proud.

My own outfit was yet another homage to the Cavalry, cut far more severely than Adrienne's, in a dove-grey silk that set off the black and white of my skin and eyes and hair. The jacket was short and close-fitting, making light once again of my insignificant bosom, and the skirt was a startlingly slim triangle that stopped as hers did, daringly just above the boot tops to show off a neatly turned ankle.

But our triumph was a surprise. It came as we sipped our morning coffee (it had taken us until fashionable eleven to dress and then to walk what seemed miles into the center of town) at the Restauration Café. It was the place where the ladies who traveled to Vichy to take the waters or new lovers—or, perhaps, I teased Adrienne, the waters *and* new lovers—met every day.

Amazingly, we were the focus of all eyes, not just for the freshness of our youth and beauty, for there were certainly some great beauties there, including, I pointed out to Adrienne's dazzled eyes, some "professional beauties" from the ranks of Maxim's most notorious cocottes and courtesans, but for our *hats*.

Instead of the ridiculous, five-pound bird cages— vast constructions of braces of stuffed pigeons, yards of satin ribbon and stifling veiling, bravely borne up in this humid heat by the very slenderest of aristocratic necks—we wore the simple but dashing hats I had made for us in those hours stolen from Madame Boulanger's bourgeois brides. They were soft straw forms that I'd flipped flirtatiously up at one side of the brim and trimmed only with ostrich feathers to echo the colors of our costumes—pure white on black straw for me, and a mauve deeper than the mousseline of her suit that darkened the blue of Adrienne's eyes to violet.

I looked up from my coffee as one of the loveliest women I had ever seen approached our table. She was tall and willow-slim, wearing an elaborately tucked and pleated morning dress of white lawn and Valenciennes lace with a matching parasol, all frills and ruffles, and an immense hat of white organza cabbage roses and billows of tulle veiling that looked like a ship under full sail. She had a natural elegance and an inner radiance that made her stand out immediately from the bouquet of beauties crowding the café.

"Good morning, Mesdemoiselles," she said in a light but carrying voice. "I couldn't help but admire your hats. As I was saying to my companions," she gestured to three extremely elegant young dandies hovering adoringly behind her, "only last week in Paris I was complaining bitterly to my milliner, Mademoiselle Reboux, that she had shown me *nothing* appropriate to the costumes for my new role. And then—here in Vichy of all places—I saw the two of you and was immediately struck by the absolute rightness of the hats you are wearing. Their inspired simplicity makes these clumsy contraptions look like the travesties they are."

I laughed delightedly. A woman after my own heart. "How very right you are, Mademoiselle. It has always appalled me that an independent woman should be asked to support the extravagant weight of her hats, never mind the extravagance of their cost."

"Ah, but you see, Mademoiselle, that is the irony of it—we are *not* independent women at all. We're slaves to the tyranny of the rue de la Paix." From her beaded reticule she took a calling card and handed it to me. "I wonder if you might do me the kindness of recommending me to your milliner?"

"Of course, Mademoiselle," I said. "I would be enchanted to do you that favor."

The beauty nodded in adieu and swept out of the café, her trio of handsome admirers following close in her regal wake.

Adrienne was totally bewildered. "Coco, whatever are you playing at? Why didn't you tell her *you* made our hats?"

"Simply because I am *not* in the millinery business. My métier is the very same as hers." Smiling wickedly I passed her the card. On the creamy vellum was embossed in flowing gold, MADEMOISELLE GABRIELLE DORZIAT.

"But, Coco, Gabrielle Dorziat is the toast of the Paris stage."

"Precisely, Adrienne, and *this,*" I flourished the small card triumphantly, "this is the passe-partout that will open the door for us to the most intransigeant theatrical manager in Vichy."

"You mean you plan to imply a relationship with Gabrielle Dorziat when we haven't even had a formal introduction? I'm amazed at your nerve."

"Don't you understand it yet, ma chère Adrienne? I will do *anything* to advance my career."

That night as we lay in the big mahogany bedstead, exhausted after a day of exploring the wonders of the bustling city, I was reminded of the many nights back in the convent when I would slip out of the charity boarders' dormitory, while the Sister on night duty drowsed over her missal, and creep into Adrienne's bed, longing for comfort and reassurance. She would put her arms around me and stroke my long black hair to soothe away the night terrors and the lingering traces of my terrible recurring nightmares of loss and loneliness. She had always been there for me.

"You do know, Adrienne," I said confidingly now in the warm, close darkness of the little room, "why it's so very important for me to succeed here in Vichy?"

"I think I do, Coco. You've surely told me often enough. You want to be a great star—a star like Yvette Guilbert—and live in Paris and appear at the Olympia and the Casino de Paris and dine every night at Maxim's and have closets full of couturier clothes and jewels and dozens of rich admirers breaking their hearts and bankrupting themselves over you."

"That's part of it, Adrienne, but it's so much more. I want to be able to send money to Antoinette and Julia-Berthe and my brothers to help look after them as I promised maman I would. And I want to be free and on my own—just like Dorziat today. I don't want to have to go back to Étienne and admit defeat—to have to tell him he was right and put myself under his protection. I want to be able to depend on myself—on the power of my own talent."

Adrienne nodded, but I wondered if she could really understand. How could my sweet aunt, who had never known desertion or deprivation of any sort, ever comprehend my darkest fears and deep determination. Could she begin to know how desperately I hoped my talent was equal to my boldest dreams?

SIX

The next few weeks were a whirlwind. I had been right about Dorziat's card. The implied connection opened the doors of even the crustiest managers. It was still not enough. We were turned down as too inexperienced at one theatre and *café concert* after another—the Eden, the Restauration, the Alcazar, even the Grand Casino itself, that proud iron-and-glass survivor of the days of Napoleon III which was the heart of the spa's extravagant nightlife.

The only faintly promising audition was with Monsieur Didier of the Élysée Palace. After running us through our entire repertoires, capped off by my spirited rendition of my old crowd-pleaser, *"Qui qu'a vu Coco,"* he leaned dangerously far back in his seat in the first row of the gloomy, deserted theatre.

"Well, Mademoiselle," he pointed his fat cigar at me, "you have *something*. I wouldn't call it a voice, to be sure. Your pal can carry a tune better than you can—

a crow could! But you're not altogether hopeless. You have a certain style. What you need is some coaching. I'll give you the name of the voice teacher all my girls use. She's a tough old bird. Probably taught singing to Madame de Pompadour, but damned good at her trade. Used to be on the *Grands Boulevards* herself."

He pulled a tattered notebook from the pocket of his gravy-stained vest. "And both you and your beautiful blonde friend," he winked theatrically in Adrienne's direction, "could do with some dance lessons. Those provincial costumes will definitely have to go. This isn't Paris . . . but it's not a nunnery either. Pick up your skirts, ladies, so I can get a look at your legs!"

Adrienne blushed scarlet. This was hardly the fatherly style of Monsieur Bernard. Étienne's suspicions were right—the man probably was a lecher. But I cheerfully complied and Adrienne reluctantly followed my lead.

"Now, turn around so I can see you in profile. *Merde,* Mademoiselle Coco, you have absolutely no tits at all. How in the name of God do you expect to hold up your costume?"

"Leave the logistics to me, Monsieur." I flashed him a grin. "Just tell me you're willing to give us a chance."

"Well, Mesdemoiselles, it's a difficult call. Pretty *gommeuses* are so easily available at this time of year." His leer was unmistakable. "Why don't you come back and see me in two weeks, after you've had some coaching and pulled together a reasonable wardrobe, and I'll make my decision then."

The moment we were outside the gaudy façade of the theatre, I hugged Adrienne ecstatically. As far as I was concerned, the jobs were ours.

"I knew it all along, Adrienne. Remember when we got off the train and the first thing we saw was that poster? It was an omen. I told you we would be appearing at the Élysée Palace, and we will be. I'll show Étienne—we'll show them *all*. Now let's go find the satin and tulle and spangles for our costumes. I picked up a program from the floor backstage and I can easily copy the flashy style Didier fancies!"

I took her arm and hurried her off down the tree-lined promenade under the iron filigree arches of the Galerie des Machines, trucked here from Paris after the World's Fair. I was so preoccupied with visions of dazzling gowns, I barely noticed the amused smiles of Vichy's corseted, bejeweled dowagers and the obvious interest of gentlemen young and old.

For the next ten days I was possessed. In spite of herself, Adrienne was caught up in the heat of my obsession. In the early morning, before anyone in the house stirred, we would quickly dress, snatch a café au lait at the little place on the corner, and walk the several miles into the city centre for our voice coaching with Madame Remarque.

Her tiny, airless flat was crammed with overstuffed red-velvet furniture, and every available surface was crowded with programs, maribou fans, and silver-framed photographs and sketches of Madame at each stage in her glorious international career.

Monsieur Didier had not exaggerated—she was a martinet. With her outmoded morning dress straining over her ample bosom and strands of grey escaping from her untidy chignon, she would look up coldly at me, standing nervously beside the upright practice piano, songsheet in hand, and hiss at me, *"Mais,* Mademoiselle, an A-flat is not indicated anywhere in this passage. Shall we attempt it again?"

I would struggle gamely to stay perfectly on pitch for the next several bars, until she brought me up short.

"Mademoiselle, are you absolutely determined on this course? I understand the urge to escape from the constraints of the provinces. *Le bon dieu* knows, I did so myself when you both were mere infants. But it requires more than the will to succeed. The talent must be there as well."

I clutched the songsheet, my hands clammy with nerves.

"To be brutally honest, Mademoiselle, I must tell you your friend possesses at least the rudiments of a professional instrument. She can be trained. You, *non*—all I can do with you is to concentrate on your technique, your delivery, to refine your natural dramatic flair so that the audience may be beguiled into ignoring the unfortunate fact that you have no voice at all."

"No voice at all" . . . *"No tits at all"* . . . Deaf to everything but my own inner voices urging me on, I defied the growing weight of professional opinion.

"Then *that* is the aspect on which I shall concentrate, Madame, technique," I said boldly. And concentrate I did—hour after hour, day after day, until I think Adrienne was as impatient with me as Madame Remarque.

That was only the beginning. From there we moved on at eleven to the dancing master, Monsieur Chernov, an ancient Russian émigré, eking out a living teaching the principles of Pavlova to Vichy's would-be ballerinas and the earthier elements of the Can-can to Monsieur Didier's eager referrals. From eleven to one we struggled with our extensions, our turn-outs, and with mastering the flamboyant gymnastics of the full split.

"But Coco," Adrienne whispered desperately on the morning she was convinced she would never walk again, "your challenge is to be the next Yvette Guilbert—not the next *La Goulue.*"

"No, Adrienne ma chère," I said determinedly from my undignified—and very painful—position on the splintery rehearsal floor, "our challenge is to prove to Étienne that I have the capacity to become a music-hall sensation, and then to prove it to *tout* Paris on the *Grands Boulevards.*"

Of course, the *petit cadeau* Étienne had given me to finance our experiment ran out in the first few weeks. Between our travel, our rent, the voice and dance lessons, and the expensive materials for our theatrical wardrobe, our funds were exhausted even before I had the time to put spangle to satin to create the vitally important costumes *à la gommeuse.*

I was stubborn. Money couldn't be allowed to defeat me now. The morning after I'd had to face the fact that we were out of funds, I set off in the early hours, leaving Adrienne to the welcome luxury of a long, drowsy *grasse matinée,* and returned triumphant, the trophies of my victory in hand.

"You see, Adrienne, I told you that if one spring ran dry, we could always tap the headwaters." Laughingly, I held up two long, frilled white aprons with matching caps and pairs of boots. "As of tomorrow we are afternoon spa attendants at La Grande Grille in the Parc des Sources."

"But, Coco, we have no training in nursing," Adrienne protested.

"We don't need any training. It's a lark compared to La Rotonde. All we have to do is look fresh and pretty, pass out draughts of mineral water, and avoid the occasional pinch on the derriere from the miraculously recovered, and we can easily support ourselves until the end of next week when we meet Monsieur Didier again to become his newest stars."

Though I never would have admitted it to Adrienne, we were glorified barmaids, simply standing beside the Grande Grille's rank of sterling silver spigots and serving cup after cup of the metallic-tasting Vichy water. The worst we could complain about were sore feet and the steamy, choking heat. And it gave us the chance to meet some of the spa's more eccentric residents.

There was the one-eyed Pasha with the hawklike profile and romantic, scimitar-scarred brow, who was waited on hand and foot by his heavily veiled wives, only allowed to be seen outside their seraglio of suites in the Pavillon de Sévigné on these healing afternoons. There was the hugely fat Viennese billionaire banker, his left foot propped on an ornately carved and velvet-cushioned ebony gout stool, attended with slavish care by his very effeminate valet and his hugely fat Pekinese. And then there was Maud Mazuel.

That night back in our hot, stuffy room, as we worked feverishly against time on our costumes, Adrienne asked me about "Maud," as she'd insisted on Adrienne's calling her.

"It seems strange to me, Coco, that such a stout, plain, ordinary woman . . . entirely unfashionable with that *directoire* style and that mannish cravat . . . would be surrounded by a circle of exquisite young women. I was even more puzzled by the interest she took in me. Do you think she's a relation of the Demarchelier sisters who joined her for tea?"

"What am I to do with you, Adrienne?" I laughed at her. "You're hopelessly naive. Maud Mazuel is *nobody's* relation . . . simply the talk of Vichy."

"A woman of her age, and so dowdy, what possible scandal could involve her? Is she an *androgyne?*"

"It's not that dark, chérie, just a trifle shady. Maud Mazuel is a sort of convenience."

"Convenience? Really, Coco, you *can* be maddening sometimes."

"Maud provides a very important commodity, Adrienne—respectability. Since she has no visible wealth of her own but a very proper *bonne bourgeoisie* background, she acts both as duenna and go-between to young women, with beauty but no money or connections, and the local aristocrats."

"You can't mean she arranges liaisons?" She was genuinely shocked.

" 'Arranges' is too precise a term, Adrienne. And don't look so thunderstruck. How do you imagine that someone like me—or you for that matter—with neither background nor dowry is going to gain entrée to château Society? It was you who originally warned me that Étienne and I were highly unlikely ever to marry."

"Well then, just what *does* she do?"

"She offers the opportunity, either here in Vichy or in Paris or at her so-called 'château' in Souvigny, for a woman of looks and charm to meet a man of wealth and pedigree under strictly social auspices. If they should strike up a friendship, or an even greater intimacy, it's to both their and Maud's advantage."

"You don't mean the man actually *pays* her for the introduction?"

"Whether money ever moves from hand to hand, or whether the medium of exchange is more discreet—a share in a racing stud, a tip on the Bourse, a gift of a painting or an important piece of jewelry—is something only Maud's banker knows."

"Where does love come into it, then, Coco? It all sounds terribly cold-blooded to me."

"And you accuse *me* of being addicted to Monsieur Decourcelle's fantasies, Adrienne! You're incurably romantic. If it consoles you, there actually have been cases—not many, mind you—where one of Maud's 'matches' did end in marriage." I dismissed the world of the demimonde from my thoughts and returned with total concentration to the tricky task of stitching paillettes to the silk of Adrienne's costume.

The costumes were astonishing. At least, I knew nothing I had done so far came near them for audacity. I had taken the cast-off program from the theatre floor, with its rough charcoal sketch of Monsieur Didier's current star in her cheap music-hall finery, and set out to transform it.

I had ransacked Vichy's theatrical supply houses to find precisely the right fabrics. And I had stuck fiercely to my basic precept—let the gown express the nature of the woman, let it embody and reveal her unique and particular magic. So for Adrienne I'd chosen silver—silver watered-silk to shimmer off the white-blonde cascade of her hair, with a bodice of silver paillettes that tightly hugged the opulent curves of her high, full breasts, cinched her tiny waist, and then fell to mid-calf where it flared out in a foam of silver, sequin-starred tulle. It had taken hours—hours of patient fine stitchery and painfully pricked fingers that could not be allowed to bleed onto the silk—to appliqué the thousands of paillettes and sequins onto the fragile silver.

Now, as she stood in front of the cracked, discolored cheval glass in the backstreet boardinghouse, I saw her catch her breath in wonder.

"I can't believe it, Coco. I look like an Ondine—you know, one of those sirens who lured the sailors to wrack and ruin in those myths the nuns were always making us translate back in the convent."

The costume spoke of a secret about her. Adrienne *was* like quicksilver—calm and transparent at first glance but with subtly shifting currents that ran just below her seemingly tranquil, placid surface. That was what our close, precious friendship had taught me about her nature. And I realized now I had succeeded in designing a gown that frankly revealed to her the secret of her allure.

For myself, I chose coal black—a slender column of rich satin completely covered with a surface of brilliant jet beading. Into the bodice I'd inserted triangular panels of jet, sewn reversed and in opposition to the beading and expertly padded beneath to create the illusion of ample, rounded breasts where only small, pointed ones existed. So much for Monsieur Didier's contempt for the meager size of my breasts!

The gown fell to mid-calf as Adrienne's did, but the skirt was split in the center, in an echo of the seductive triangles of the bodice, to a point daringly high on my thigh. A cloud of midnight-black, jet-spangled tulle sprang from that provocative triangle, revealing, then concealing as I moved what I considered my best feature after my coloring, my slim legs and shapely ankles.

As I eagerly took my turn in front of the cheval glass, what I saw was *another* mirror—a dark, glittering trick mirror of onyx—revealing just what I'd intended, my own disguise, the illusion of a fashionably voluptuous, sensuous cocotte.

The night before our second audition with Monsieur Didier, I lay beside Adrienne in the big double-bed, tossing and turning so restlessly under the worn linen sheet that I knew at this rate neither of us was going to close an eye until morning.

"Coco," she finally said softly, "let me rub your back for you the way I used to do in the convent. You're so tense your muscles are coiled like wire. You've been driving yourself too hard, rehearsing for hours on end, working at the baths, then up sewing all night, every night until dawn. You need to rest and store up your energies for tomorrow. We both do."

As she massaged the taut muscles of my back and I felt the tension begin to release, I could not stop my shoulders from shaking. In all our time together at Notre Dame I'd never let Adrienne—or anyone—see me cry. I'd managed to ignore the Isabelle Bertrands who'd humiliated me by calling me *"bâtarde."* Or if the supervising nun's back was turned, I'd fly at my tormentor like a silent fury, wrestle her to the ground, grab her by the braids and bang her head in the gravel of the schoolyard until I made the bully take back her insults and beg for mercy. I had never shed a single tear, though. Not till now.

"What is it Coco, ma chère? Why are you crying?"

The words came out of me in a rush. "Oh, Adrienne, sometimes I think I'm going to die of longing. You want such simple things . . . a man to love and look after you, a home, a garden, children, friends around you. But me, what's wrong with me? Why can't *I* be content with simple dreams? Why am I so very different from you—so different from all the rest?"

Gently, still lightly stroking the soft skin of my back, she tried to reason with me. "But Coco, you have Étienne—certainly a good, kind, openhearted man and one who adores you. Though I would never have said so before, I've even come to think that he may one day have the courage to defy his family and marry you."

"That's just it, Adrienne, I don't want marriage. I don't love Étienne Balsan . . . I never will. I like him enormously. He's handsome, he's generous, he's a terror on the polo field, and he can always make me laugh. I think soon I'll even let him make love to me. He's certainly been patient enough. But love him . . . trust him . . . let him determine my destiny. I don't know if I'll ever be able to give that to a man. I think love and trust were burnt out of me long ago and that I'll never get them back."

"What will content you then, Coco ma chère?"

"Money, that's what I've got to have—money and the security it brings. Most of all Adrienne, money and the freedom it brings from ever having to love. *That's* why tomorrow is so important to me."

Long after Adrienne had fallen asleep, I lay staring into the darkness. I talked so coolly of "letting" Étienne make love to me. Where did passion come into it? Or desire? Or was I being ruthlessly honest in acknowledg-

ing that Étienne was more playmate to me than potential lover? When we sparred and feinted in our
prolonged flirtation, I had to admit there *was* more
playfulness to it than passion. If it was true, as I told
Adrienne, that I had decided to allow Étienne to relieve
me of the inconvenient burden of virginity so that I
could get on with my *real* life, what would happen if
someone someday came along who awakened what I
knew was my ardent nature?

What would happen then to all my bold vows of independence and freedom from the killing bonds of love?

SEVEN

hen the day finally came, I awoke with a
mixture of hope and pure panic. I had
pinned so very much on this single afternoon. Somehow I got through the hours that dragged
at my skirts like small lead dressmaker's weights,
though I must admit I was totally distracted. I sleep-
walked my way through our last coaching sessions with
Madame Remarque and Monsieur Chernov. And pity
the poor spa patron who received most of his draught
of mineral water down his shirtfront due to my trembling hand and wandering thoughts.

Adrienne knew that I was acting suspiciously carefree, flirting gaily with the eye-patched Pasha and teasing the gouty banker about the dangers of excess, as
though in my mind our names were already heading
the billing on that colorful poster that had lured me,
moth to flame, to the Élysée Palace and the judgment
of Monsieur Didier.

Why did it have to be Didier? There was something
dark and lurking, something sinister about the man, for
all his free career advice and coarse jokes—something
I sensed and disliked and couldn't quite put a name to.
I know I didn't imagine the furtive hand that had
slipped familiarly down Adrienne's back as he'd shown
us out the narrow shadowy backstage corridor at that
first audition. As I told her the day we walked out the
convent gates, Adrienne was my responsibility and I
would never allow anyone to harm her.

We arrived at the theatre precisely at five, Adrienne
carrying the battered, second-hand portfolio with our
sheet music for the accompanist, and me the valise
with our precious costumes. A white-haired porter
showed us to a dressing room with a tarnished tinsel
star tacked to the door.

"You see, Adrienne, what did I tell you," I whispered
excitedly behind the porter's back. "They've already
given us the star's quarters."

I know Adrienne thought I was whistling in the dark.
She was so jumpy she could barely manage the hundreds of tiny hooks and eyes that welded the silver
sheath to her body. This time the mirror did nothing
to reassure her.

"Look, Coco, you can actually see my nipples rising
under the silk from nerves. Tell me it's just an effect

of light! Why did I look like a water sprite back at the boardinghouse and a woman of the streets in this freezing-cold dressing room?"

Unlike Adrienne, I was completely unconscious of the tawdriness of our surroundings. To me, we might as well have been enjoying Guilbert's luxurious accommodations at the Casino de Paris. The only sign of my own anxiety was my inability to deal with the intricate fastenings of my costume. After several failed attempts, I cursed savagely under my breath, then turned laughingly to Adrienne.

"Do me up, ma chère. I've made these underpinnings so complex even *I* can't seem to work my way into them."

After she'd gotten me into the spectacular sliver of onyx, I insisted on applying a little lip rouge to her lips and some additional color to her already flaming cheeks. When she volunteered to do the same for me, I declined.

"Merci Adrienne, my coloring is perfect as it is. It's the single advantage I have over you." My tone was so light she couldn't tell if I was serious. It was, in fact, the very first time I'd admitted the rivalry between us, even to myself.

When we stepped out onto the bare stage, the glare of the gas footlights was so bright I couldn't see beyond them into the darkened cavern of the theatre where Monsieur Didier waited. His disembodied voice came at us like an assault.

"All right, ladies. Now why don't you show me how much you've improved since last time."

I turned to the accompanist seated at the scarred upright piano and handed him our music. I went first, with the wildly sentimental ballad on which Yvette Guilbert had made her reputation. But Madame Remarque's coaching had helped me give the old clichés of love and betrayal a wry, bittersweet twist that made them somehow new. I was counting on the technique to disguise the unfortunate fact that my voice wobbled badly in the verse. I quickly followed that up with a rousing rendition of *"Les Cuirassiers de Reichshoffen,"* a flagrantly patriotic favorite that would be bound to bring every military man in the audience cheering to his feet. At least it always had back at La Rotonde . . .

When it was Adrienne's turn, I had to gently shove her toward the piano. She was practically frozen with nerves. She raced through her two offerings—both simple love songs of the Auvergne—so quickly I was certain she had left out several verses. It seemed to make no difference to Monsieur Didier.

"Right . . . thank you, ladies. Now let's have the two of you in the Can-can," he called out of the echoing blackness.

It was easier for me with my dramatically slashed skirt to manage the final split. I heard the ominous sound of delicate fabric tearing when Adrienne joined me on the floor. We got up and took our bows bravely to the sound of silence. Then, Didier's voice of command again, ordering us to change and meet him in his office.

Back in the dressing room I was frantic for reassurance.

"What do you think, Adrienne, he *must* have loved us? I know he didn't applaud—but, then, that would have been unprofessional. I'm *sure* he must have loved us . . ."

We struggled into our afternoon dresses, packed up our costumes, and hurried through the darkened lobby to the office with MANAGER, M. ALPHONSE DIDIER, lettered in faded gilt on the cracked glass pane.

The office was filthy, littered with old programs, torn posters, and handbills. Monsieur Didier, leaning dangerously back again in a split leather chair behind a desk strewn with papers and half-empty wine glasses, was little better. His tie and vest, gaping over his fat belly, had increased in stains and grease blossoms in direct ratio to the number of days we'd been rehearsing. Suddenly, I could hardly believe we'd worked such agonizing hours to please this arrogant little man. Loathe him or not, he still held the key to my future.

He got up from behind the desk and drew himself up to his full height of five-foot-four.

"Let's be frank, Mesdemoiselles. We're all professionals here, so I'm sure you understand that the standards of performance in Vichy are higher than what you've come across in the provinces."

Quel idiot! He spoke as though Vichy were *not* in the provinces. Had he never heard of Paris?

"I'm afraid, Mademoiselle Coco, that no amount of coaching is ever going to change the unfortunate fact that you can't sing worth a damn." Ignoring my stricken look, he continued headlong. "But the theatre management didn't give me this job for nothing, Mesdemoiselles, you can be sure. I've got a real nose for talent—a *bec fin*. Why the very first time I laid eyes on you two green girls, I said to myself, 'Alphonse, the beauty can always have a place in the chorus line. But the one with no voice and no tits has got it—she's got real style.' "

I shot a sidelong glance at Adrienne. I was thoroughly bewildered.

"You ask me what I mean by style. Well, mes chères demoiselles, I mean *theatrical* style. I mean costumes. Even those jumped-up pinafores you wore at the first audition were enough to let a connoisseur like myself know there was real style there. I mean *theatrical* style. And the costumes you wore tonight—I assume, of course, that you designed them." He pointed his cigar at me and I nodded like a mesmerized doe. "No one in Vichy could have done it."

What on earth was he driving at?

"Well, Mademoiselle Coco, it seems that you turned up at just the right moment with just the right talent and accordingly, I'm prepared to make you a *very* significant offer."

I felt a surge of hope. He *was* going to hire us. I would sing at the Élysée Palace, after all.

"Yes indeed, Mademoiselle Coco Chanel, a *very* significant offer. As luck would have it my wardrobe mistress has handed in her notice—knocked up by her gentleman friend, I've no doubt. These young girls have no sense. At any rate, she's going right now—at the height of the Season—and I said to myself, 'Alphonse, *le bon dieu* works mysteriously. He's taken away Denise, but he brought you Coco. You can give this talented amateur from the provinces the once in a lifetime chance—the chance to design the costumes for your revues.' "

He stood back waiting for my ecstatic response. When I looked down at a spot on the filthy floor and said nothing, he rushed on, "Of course, I wouldn't expect you to do it simply for the experience—though many a girl would be glad of the opportunity. There'd be a comfortable salary and a flat for you and your friend in a building I happen to own only a few blocks from the theatre. So when your friend has time off and you're hard at work on the designs for my next show, you won't have to worry. I'll be right there to entertain her." The gleam in his eye was only slightly less obvious than the bulge in his pants.

Time seemed to me to stand still. Then I looked Alphonse Didier straight in the eye and said coldly, "Monsieur, you are a pig, not a theatrical manager, and this place is a pigsty. I am a singer, not a dress designer, and if I were what you think I am which, *dieu merci,* I am not, the only thing I would be willing to design for you would be a garotte."

With as much dignity as I could muster, I took Adrienne's arm, picked up the valise and swept out of the theatre.

The next morning when Adrienne woke up after a restless night, she found me sitting at the foot of the bed, our cases standing completely packed on the floor beside me.

"Bonjour, Adrienne chérie. I suppose our holiday is over. It's time we returned to Moulins, don't you think? I'm afraid Étienne will be concerned that we've stayed away this long. He'll think I took this singing business seriously." I laughed wryly.

But as we were leaving the little room, I lingered to pretend to check that we'd left nothing behind—lingered for one last look at the ruins of my exquisite black onyx gown hanging in the abandoned armoire, slashed to glittering ribbons. I felt tears come to my eyes for the death of dreams.

We never spoke of the *Grands Boulevards* again.

EIGHT

*A*drienne met him one afternoon at Maud Mazuel's. She and I had gotten to know Maud when we were spa attendants at La Grande Grille, before what I'd privately come to think of as the "Didier disaster." When I finally had to admit to myself that, for all my determined efforts, I was not about to replace Yvette Guilbert on the music-hall boards, we had left Vichy, returned to Moulins and taken modest rooms near our old lodgings in the rue de l'Horloge.

I suppose I was not completely surprised when Maud followed up on our brief acquaintance with a letter inviting Adrienne to spend some time at her château in Souvigny. She was, after all, in the business of pretty women. What *did* surprise me was that Adrienne accepted. Perhaps it was that she had had enough of pleasant, pointless flirtations with cavalry officers. Perhaps it was the lingering shadow of our encounter with Didier. Very probably it was more the awareness that she was over twenty now and, with her only dowry the perishable one the mirror reflected, she knew it was time she made a serious alliance.

I was altogether in favor of her going. I would miss her terribly, but I knew it was time for her to fly free. We all deserved the chance to shape our own destinies. I swore to her that only my attachment to Étienne prevented me from tagging along, invited or no. I even designed a few very fetching additions to her wardrobe.

She wrote me that life at Souvigny was certainly pleasant enough. Between musical evenings chez Maud, impromptu picnics, and trips to the races at Vichy or St. Cloud or Longchamp, the days, she said, passed almost imperceptibly.

She had one or two suitors she found amusing, especially the rakehell Comte de Beynac who had broken hearts from Paris to St. Petersburg. Because she took none of them seriously, she must have seemed aloof and distant and all the more desirable. It was clear from her letters that Maud considered her the current star in her personal heaven. Adrienne was never allowed to plead a headache or the vapors to avoid an outing.

So it was on a sparkling Sunday, lying on a chaise on one of the wide, daisy-dotted lawns where a spirited croquet match was in progress, that she looked up from under her white lace parasol into the dark, serious eyes of the man she knew she would love unqualifiedly for the rest of her life—the Baron Édouard de Nexon. He asked her name, sat down on the chaise beside her, took her hand in both of his and told her she was going to be his wife.

Her letters were full of the innocent joy of first love. So effortlessly, so completely had Édouard taken over her life since that first meeting, she told me, she had almost lost track of existence outside of the small, private world of their love—a fantasy world they had built to defy reality and one they both protected fiercely because it was so badly threatened by his powerful family.

To the Nexons, with a title as old as the stones of Paris itself, she was the hated outsider. Adrienne Chanel, daughter of the smallest of the *petite bourgeoisie,* with no gilt-edged pedigree, not a drop of blue blood running in her veins, with no dowry to speak of . . . no rich, fertile lands that might one day be joined to their own. In their eyes she meant ruin to their adored eldest son.

How much more comfortable if Édouard had chosen a mistress from the ranks of the courtesans who thronged the pink silk and mirrored mahogany splendor of Maxim's—a beauty who could laughingly be described by the city's roués as "the special of the day," but a professional beauty nonetheless. *That* was a situation they might have been prepared to accept. A discreet allowance for gowns and millinery, a carriage and pair, and the occasional gift of a pearl necklace and earrings or a diamond brooch, a modest pension for that inevitable moment when Édouard would wish to be rid of her. *That* they could have dealt with. What they refused to countenance was the intensity of their love and Édouard's absolute determination to marry her.

They had become lovers, she confided, on that first magical, ordinary day they met, in the shady serenity of her small room at Maud's with the white eyelet curtains billowing out onto the tiny terrace and the white linen sheets cool beneath them as freely, eagerly she gave Édouard her innocence. And they had been lovers ever since, she said, whenever he could find the excuse to slip away from Paris and come to her.

In this daring conspiracy against all things traditional, Maud had proved their staunchest ally, probably, the cynics would say, because of her superb nose for long-term profit. But I think it went beyond that into genuine affection for them . . . for her. Adrienne was entirely lovable. Everyone who met her fell into her gentle thrall. Of all the belles Maud had "placed" in "suitable" arrangements over the years, Adrienne, I suspect, was the one who had somehow touched the crusty heart that beat beneath the ironclad whaleboning of her stays.

Whether she reminded Maud of herself in her younger days when the freshness of her youth made up for her plainness and she dreamt the same dreams as her protégée, dreams of love that lasts and home and security, or whether she saw her as the daughter she had never had, I don't know. What I do know is that Adrienne swore Maud was as firm in her support of their love and their commitment to marry as she could have been if Adrienne had been her own true blood.

I was reluctant to interrupt their idyll, but I posted my enigmatic letter anyway. I had to. *Come back to Moulins at once. Urgently need your presence here . . . Coco.*

When she arrived at the rue de l'Horloge two days later, she found me on my knees on the floor in the midst of chaos. Open suitcases stood everywhere, and around me were my clothes, my hatboxes, my shoes, my sewing kit—all my belongings. When I saw her, I jumped to my feet and rushed into her arms.

"Adrienne, *dieu merci,* you're here. I knew you'd come. I've been beside myself . . . saying 'yes' to myself one moment and 'no' the next. For the first time in my life I can't seem to make a decision."

"A decision about *what,* Coco? Your letter was so mysterious. When I showed it to Maud, she agreed with me that I should spare no time to write for an explanation but leave at once. So I packed a valise, left a note for Édouard and took the afternoon train. I thought you were in some kind of trouble."

"A decision about Étienne. About what I'm to do with the rest of my life. And I *am* in trouble. You see, Adrienne," I drew her down on the chaise beside me, "Étienne has finally done what he's been threatening for ages—he's resigned his infantry commission and bought a breeding farm up in Compiègne, the Château de Royallieu, and he wants me to come with him. Oh, it's a beautiful place, Adrienne, you'd love it. I know you would. It's an old abbey, fourteenth-century, I think, with grey stone walls and tall narrow windows. And *vast* stables with acres and acres of paddocks and grazing land for the horses. Étienne says it's ideal for breeding racing champions."

"At last, Coco, he'll get the chance to make his dream come true," she said. "He's longed for it ever since you met him."

"I've never seen him so happy, Adrienne. He wants me to do it up for him—*all* the decorations on an unlimited budget. Would you believe the name of the first abbess was Gabrielle? We found a portrait up in the attics. A formidable old thing . . . reminded me of that horrid Mother Superior at Aubazine. But just imagine, Adrienne. I think it's an omen, don't you?"

"You and your signs and portents, Coco," she smiled at me and took my hand. "So, my small niece, you and Étienne are going to marry. Coco Chanel will become Madame Étienne Balsan of Paris and Royallieu. I'm so very happy for you, though in all honesty I must admit to some jealousy. What an irony. You who have always been so scornful of marriage will have it, while Édouard and I who want it so desperately . . ."

"Not exactly, Adrienne." I smiled wistfully. "That's why I wanted to see you. I need your advice. I told you I would never marry Étienne even if we could—and we can't. His family forbids it. Even though his brother Jacques took our part. *He* likes me, I know he does." I couldn't let my hurt at their rejection of me show even to her. "But the rest of the family is adamant. Conventional to a fault. 'No title, no dowry—no marriage.' "

"By the look of things, Coco," she gestured at the mayhem around me, "it seems you're going anyway. You've agreed to let him keep you, then. I thought that was against your principles."

"It is, Adrienne, and that's just why I needed to talk to you. I'm not going to Royallieu as Étienne's mistress. If I go, I'm going as his friend, his comrade. He calls me his 'apprentice.' I share all his interests."

"But do you share his bed, Coco? *That's* all Society will want to know. And it won't matter whether you tell them 'yes' or 'no,' they'll assume you do anyway."

"Oh, Adrienne, sometimes you're hopelessly naive. Étienne and I have been sleeping together for months. Ever since we came back from Vichy. I *told* you I was bored with my virginity. Étienne seemed the logical choice to rid me of it."

"How very clinical you sound. It's certainly different from the heat lightning that flared up between Édouard and me the first time our eyes met . . . Well, if neither his family's nor Society's disapproval bothers you, why the hesitation? Étienne's an honorable man. Even if he can't marry you, he'll see to it that all your needs are taken care of. I'm certain he'll give you a generous allowance—enough to maintain your wardrobe in the style he intends to keep at Royallieu."

"And in return, I'm to give him *what*? My body? He already has that. My loyalty? He has that, too. My independence? No, I can't do it, Adrienne. I won't be kept. I want to go with him, but I'll simply have to find some way to support myself at Royallieu."

"How do you propose to do that, Coco? Somehow I can't quite see you taking in hand laundry for the neighboring *châtelaines.*" She laughed gently.

I jumped up from the chaise and began pacing. "I know what I'll do, Adrienne. That's why I needed you to come. You're always my inspiration. I'm going to make *hats.* You remember that actress, Gabrielle Dorziat at the café in Vichy. She said our hats were more stylish than her own milliner's. And, God knows, she was right. *That's* what I'll do, Adrienne, I'll make hats and sell them to Étienne's houseguests at bargain prices. Most of them are struggling showgirls from Paris who could never afford the prices on the rue de la Paix. They'll be delighted, and I'll be able to pay my own way." I was flushed with the heat of discovery.

"How do you think Étienne will feel about your taking money from his guests, Coco? For all his so-called rebellion, deep down he's as conventional as the rest of the Balsans. And he's particularly sensitive to money because his own family is in trade."

"What Étienne doesn't know, he won't know. It will be a secret between me and my customers. I'll tell him I'm doing it to express my creativity."

"How will you explain your profits then? Étienne knows you have no independent income."

"Precisely," I smiled like a particularly satisfied cat, "that's where *you'll* come in, Adrienne. You'll be here in Moulins or at Maud's in Souvigny, and you'll forward me a monthly 'letter' from Papa in America. Clearly, I couldn't let *him* know I was living in sin. And I'll tell Étienne my father's sending me a share of the fruits of his American triumphs."

Adrienne looked deeply doubtful. "Oh dear, Coco, it's all so elaborate. It reminds me of the old proverb about the beautiful spider caught in her own web of lies."

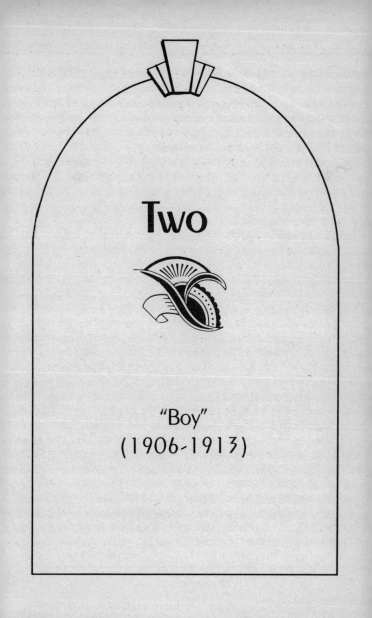

Two

"Boy"
(1906-1913)

ONE

They burst from the fringe of the woods and came galloping full-tilt across the fields and up the drive to the forecourt where I was waiting with Mademoiselle Émilienne and Alec.

"By God, lad, you have a damned fine seat," he called out to the small, dark-haired rider.

"Alec," Émilienne said, "you're right about the seat. It's the sex that's confusing you. That *lad* is Coco Chanel, Balsan's latest protégée. In Paris they're saying he found her in a tailor shop in Moulins and brought her to Royallieu to be his playmate—in the saddle, of course. She and her sister, Adrienne, were said to be the mascots of the 10th Light-Cavalry." She laughed wickedly.

What struck me as I watched her lightly dismount and hand the reins of her sweated horse to one of the grooms was her style. Where Émilienne d'Alençon was all curved, dimpled blondeness—the complete *cocotte* who had captured Balsan's fancy for five years before he passed her along to his friend, Alec Carter, France's reigning jockey—this little Coco was *quite* another matter. She and Balsan came striding toward us and, damnit, you had to admire the girl's audacity. Instead of the usual elaborate riding habit from Redfern, she was wearing men's breeches . . . damned well-cut breeches at that. Showed off her slim legs and tight little bottom to excellent advantage.

"Boy, delighted to see you," Étienne boomed. "Alec and Émilienne got here this morning, and the rest of the mob should turn up by teatime. Weather's perfect for the races, and I've got a number of diversions—not the least being the lovely Mesdemoiselles Dorziat, Orlandi, and Léry—planned for the weekend." Then, suddenly remembering his manners, "Oh, and may I present Mademoiselle Gabrielle Chanel, Arthur Capel—but everyone calls him 'Boy.' Mademoiselle Chanel is my apprentice. I've been teaching her the rudiments of horsemanship and, as you can see, she's proving an apt pupil." He winked broadly.

Through all this Coco simply stood quietly, her black eyes amused, a half-smile on her wide, sensual mouth. Then she held out her hand and grasped mine firmly.

"Enchanted to know you, Monsieur Capel. Étienne tells me you are one of England's premier polo players. Perhaps one day, if my skills improve sufficiently, I may join you in a chukka."

While the others laughed at her cheek, I found myself unable to let go of her hand. I had the sudden, absolute conviction that I had known and loved this beautiful gamine in another place and time. Probably too much reading in reincarnation and Eastern thought, one of my secret vices. Before the moment could become awkward, Émilienne deftly broke the tension.

"Why Monsieur Capel, I do believe you have experienced the *coup de foudre*. Remember, Monsieur, that Mademoiselle Coco is *Étienne's* apprentice."

Throughout that first long weekend, I found myself secretly observing her. Her status at Royallieu was ambiguous, and it soon became evident to me that she wanted it that way. Unlike Jeanne Léry or Suzanne Orlandi, she had no "cover" profession. There were no allusions to her career on the *Grands Boulevards* or her burgeoning stardom as an actress. And she was certainly not a professional courtesan like her predecessor, Émilienne. Everything, from the simplicity of her dress to her complete absence of coyness, spoke of fierce iconoclasm.

Still, Émilienne had called her Balsan's protégée. Étienne *had* to be keeping her. She had no visible income and no discernible family connections. She was clearly a Royallieu fixture, equally at ease with everyone, from Étienne's aristocratic houseguests like Léon de Laborde and Baron Foy and their ladies, to Alec and the other jockeys and grooms and stablemen whose company she obviously enjoyed.

In fact, I discovered that she far preferred the steamy warmth of the stables with their rich tang of saddle soap on leather tack and ripe horse dung, and the intent discussion of stud fees and bloodlines to the perfumed boudoirs and chilly drawing rooms of the château where all the talk was of amorous intrigues and who was keeping whom.

She and Alec Carter had hit it off from that first moment on the terrace when he complimented her on the excellence of her seat. So I took to joining up with them when they slipped away from the bridge or backgammon tables for their frequent forays to the stables.

Alec grinned at her story of ordering riding breeches from an ancient tailor in La Croix-St.-Ouen. "You must have given the old chap quite a turn, Coco. I doubt he's ever had a female customer."

"You're right, Alec, mon cher. When I told him what I wanted, he went pale. But when he saw I was completely serious he shrugged, told me, 'Mademoiselle, you are an *originale*,' got out his tape, and measured my inseam. He's been making my breeches ever since."

Well done, Coco, I thought to myself, saving the considerable expense of a lady's equipage from Redfern. If she was accepting Étienne's protection only at the loosest level of room and board, without assuming the full status—and obligations—of mistress, she'd cleverly made a virtue of necessity. The old tailor was right. She *was* an *originale* and I was fascinated by her. Royallieu was going to see a great deal of me that fall.

TWO

B y my third and fourth visit, I would have done anything to be alone with her. Life at the château was so bloody public. Between the race meets, the Hunt, visits to nearby studs to survey potential blood-stock, the lavish dinners and card games and dancing that lasted till dawn, every hour of these "relaxing" country house parties was accounted for. Balsan was, hands down, the most generous host I'd ever come across. He never stinted when it came to pleasing his comrades in arms, on or off the polo fields, and their surpassingly beautiful ladies.

To his credit he had none of the *snobbisme* that fettered so many men in Compiègne's stratified, elitist microcosm. At Royallieu, excellence of horsemanship, beauty, and talent carried the day, precisely because Balsan wanted it that way. And devil take the prudes who smiled behind their fans at the newness of his money or sat in judgment of the fact that the beauties who graced the arms of his titled weekend guests were seldom their wives.

When Coco drew me aside conspiratorially and asked if I would motor up to Paris with her to help track down the costumes for the weekend's "entertainment," I told her I was her willing slave.

As we raced through the countryside in my Austin-Lagonda, she was an enchanting study in contradictions, first deploring the boyishness of Étienne's penchant for pranks and games and charades, then devising a way to delight him—and herself in the bargain.

"Can you imagine anything more ironic, Boy," she said laughingly, touching my thigh with an innocent intimacy that nearly had me send the car spinning out of control off the road. "Étienne's decreed that the theme of tomorrow night's tableau is to be 'a country wedding.' It's true that here we are deep in the countryside. And it's true that country weddings are steeped in rural tradition. But the odds on any of Étienne's guests marrying his *belle amie* are a million to one. So what *we* must do is to mock the venerable institution of bourgeois marriage. Then we can hope that even one of our 'players' sees the absurdity of the convention clearly enough to resolve to take a gamble for once in his over-privileged life—a gamble on authentic living."

I was so bowled over by the remarkable accuracy of her insight I had all I could do not to pull the car over to the roadside and take her in my arms and make love to her right there.

"Just consider the cast of characters I've drawn up, Boy," she continued. Again that electrifying hand on my leg . . . "Jeanne Léry is to play 'the bride.' And it's less than a month since Grand Duke Boris turned her out of his bed, cancelled all her dressmakers' and milliners' accounts and even asked for the return of the emeralds and diamonds he'd given her. These Russians are as cold and barbarous as the steppes they come from."

"But, petite Coco, wasn't there the question of her being seen at Maxim's three nights running in intense conversation with her leading man?"

"Dieu, Boy, you sound like the rest of them! Jeanne and Maurice are friends. Imagining anything more would be as absurd as Étienne's assuming you and I were lovers."

She was right, of course. Then why did that sting so? I glanced over at her. As soon as we were out of sight of Royallieu, she had torn off her hat with its confining driving veil. Now her long black hair had escaped from the knot at her neck and blew free in the wind like a glossy banner. My God, she was beautiful. And damned intelligent. I wondered if Étienne realized how fortunate he was.

"Then," she continued running down the cast, "there's Léon de Laborde as 'the Baby'—born considerably in advance of the nuptials. That's the country way, after all. My own father neglected the formalities until I was a toddler. You must admit, Boy, that bit of casting is positively inspired. Léon is so *very* young he's still firmly attached to his mother, the Vicomtesses's leading strings. Pity the demoiselle who sets her cap for him! Certainly he's handsome and there's a fortune there, but whoever catches Léon will have his formidable maman to contend with."

So Coco was illegitimate. What amazed me was the way she would suddenly drop her guard and allow me to glimpse a piece of her past that must have caused her great pain. I know the secret of my own birth shadowed too many of my early days before I came to grips with it. Was she unconscious of these moments of revelation or was she, as I hoped, beginning to trust me just a little, beginning to let me in to the fiercely protected world of her privacy?

"And what about you, petite Coco? What role have you chosen for yourself?"

She completely ignored the double edge to my question.

"Another triumph of casting, Boy. My new friend the actress Gabrielle Dorziat, who I met in Vichy, and I will be the 'Maid of Honor' and the 'Best Man.' The delicious thing about that is neither Gabrielle nor I have the slightest intention of *ever* marrying. So she'll play the Maid as slightly retarded, and I'll be the village simpleton. . . . Two young women with no ambition for marriage *must* be crazy." She laughed delightedly.

"What role do you have in mind for Étienne?" I

couldn't resist my jealous impulse. The question, once again, had a double meaning that she carefully ignored.

"Étienne, of course, will be 'the Groom'—the man determined never to marry, yet probably destined to be the first of us to do it. As for you, cher Boy . . . *you* will be the 'Mother-in-Law,' forever finding fault, forever disapproving of us all."

That wasn't fair. "You know damned well that isn't true, Coco. Why would I spend so much time at Royallieu if I felt that way? Étienne is my closest friend—one of the finest men I've ever met. I'll admit his lack of serious ambition troubles me, but only because I believe he's wasting himself burying himself in the country to breed horses. He's so much more than the perfect country gentleman he longs to be. Probably, if I examine it, it's also because I'm so driven to succeed by my own personal demons."

We covered the last miles to Paris in an uneasy silence. Clearly both of us had revealed more than we intended. As we drove through the porte du Nord, Coco roused herself from her reverie.

"You know, Boy, all I've ever really seen of Paris is the outskirts and the gates, as Étienne and I and our friends roar through them on the way to Longchamp or Enghien or one of the other high-stakes horse races . . . the gates and the Galeries Lafayette where we're going now, because that's where I buy the forms for the hats I make for my friends and the costumes for Étienne's weekend theatricals. Papa Bader, the owner, has been like a second father to me. He keeps trying to convince me to create a line of hats for the Galeries."

"Why don't you do it, Coco? It would be a challenge?"

"I'm not a professional designer, Boy, and besides, Étienne would never permit it. So," she smiled wistfully at me, "the gates and the Galeries—that's all I know of the city, though, I've heard and read and dreamed about it for so long, by now Paris lives in my heart."

Once again I was touched by her essential innocence—and by the strange resemblance between us.

"Someday, petite Coco, you must let me show you the city."

"I'd love that, Boy." Her dark eyes were glowing.

"I grew up in London, but Paris has always been my place, from the very first time I came here as a schoolboy on holiday. I'm certain I've lived here in a past life, and I've been coming back as often as I could ever since. Now that the management of my family's coal interests is in my hands, I do a great deal of business in France. So I keep a flat in the Boulevard Malesherbes and I have a very capable second-in-command in our London offices in the City. That way, I get to spend the better part of every year here."

Again that wistful look in her fathomless eyes.

"How I envy you, Boy. I've never admitted it to anyone, but I'm dying of boredom at Royallieu. Oh, I love to ride and the Hunt—and we *do* go to the races nearly every day. But it's all horses and horse talk there. Sometimes I feel like a prisoner. If only you could convince Étienne to come up from the country now and then. He keeps a flat here, too, though I've never even seen it. He hasn't said so, but I sense his reluctance. It's almost as if he's afraid of losing me to Paris."

Papa Bader was delighted to see her. He enveloped her in an enthusiastic hug, then held her out at arm's length for a long, deliberate inventory.

"Well, Coco chérie, has that idiot Balsan been looking after you properly? You look a little pale to me, a little too thin . . . *especially* for the fashion."

He gave me a conspiratorial wink. "So, Balsan's still hiding you in horse country, eh? I thought he had more sense than that. He has to know a treasure like you can't be concealed forever."

How right the old man was! The very same thing had occurred to me as we came through the doors of his flourishing emporium and I watched Coco's face light up.

She tried valiantly to deflect his scrutiny.

"Mon dieu, Papa Bader, while I've been attending to country matters, you've only been expanding. Every time I get up to see you, I find that the Galeries has gobbled up yet another hectare of valuable land."

Respect for the land. Like a benign Père Noël he glowed in the warmth of her approval. But he was still too shrewd to let her elude him. Their shared peasant roots were stronger than that.

"So, Coco chérie, you have finally seen the light and agreed to create hats for me. That's it . . . *that's* why you're here! Am I right, Monsieur?" Graciously he included me in their old game. "Ah, *non.* I see it's more serious than that. You've thrown Balsan over. You know I've never thought he was your equal. And this dashing young fellow has had the incredible good fortune to be there at the strategic moment."

I understood then why she loved this canny old merchant. He was a priceless amalgam of courtly gallantry and earthy common sense. I only wished she was listening to his excellent advice.

The next evening over dinner, with the post-race excitement and gaiety surging all around us, Alec Carter having ridden Étienne's two-year-old champion Centime to a splendid victory at St. Cloud, I was completely preoccupied. Though Léon and Émilienne made countless toasts—to the jockey, to Étienne, to Centime's peerless bloodlines—for me there was only Coco . . . only the two of us at that long, polished mahogany table with the warm candlelight reflecting in her eyes and the stern portraits of Étienne's purchased "ancestors" watching us disapprovingly from the walls.

Now and then, I caught her stealing a glance at me—a glance that was frankly bewildered. Then she would bring herself up short and devote her rapt attention to her fortunate dinner partner, Baron Foy. Foy and I had done some good business together and the gossips had it that he was deeply involved in a passionate affair with Coco's friend, the lovely Suzanne Orlandi. But as I saw him casually put his hand on Coco's bare arm to emphasize some point of racing protocol, I could cheerfully have strangled the man.

The "country wedding" went off without a hitch. Jeanne Léry was the perfect bride in a yellowed antique satin gown Coco had found in a trunk in the château's labyrinthine attics. Hard to tell if the tears in Jeanne's eyes were an actress's trick of glycerine or the result of real regret for the loss of Grand Duke Boris. Étienne made a suitably nervous groom, fumbling for the ring and muffing his responses, unwittingly in practice for the ceremony Coco had predicted for him. And the two Gabrielles—Coco and la Dorziat—were suitably addled.

The entire evening would have been another Royallieu triumph if it hadn't been for the aftermath. At some ungodly hour near dawn, I was roused by a hand shaking me out of my troubled dreams of mismatched marriages. It was Coco, wearing only a modest, high-necked cotton nightshirt and with her hair tumbling darkly around her shoulders. For a moment, hope surged. Had she come to me?

"Wake up, Boy," she whispered urgently. "I need your help. Jeanne has swallowed an overdose of laudanum."

I was instantly out of bed, hastily pulling on my trousers and fumbling in the dark to button my flies.

"Étienne's gone for the local doctor. I need you to help me keep her awake. I've made some strong coffee, but we have to walk her out in the cold air until they get here."

The October night was crisp and still, the wind rustling the dry chestnut leaves like paper, as we paced the terrace back and forth, supporting a resentful Jeanne between us.

"Let me go, *mes amis,*" she begged us. "Let me go back to sleep. You don't know what it's like. It's not that I loved Boris. I did or I didn't—I hardly remember now. That's not the point. It's tomorrow that frightens me. Tomorrow and what will happen to me."

"Don't be foolish, Jeanne," Coco told her, "you have your entire life in front of you."

"I have my youth and my looks to bargain with now. But what I see in front of me is only a long line of

Borises, until time catches up with me and my beauty fades. Without real talent, without something of my own what do you honestly see in store for me? That's why, if you were truly my friends, you would let me go now."

Coco and I exchanged glances. How could we argue with the truth. The life of an *irrégulière* was as precarious as the fidelity of the men who kept her. We were saved by the arrival of the doctor and Étienne who half-carried the unresisting girl back into the château, leaving the two of us alone under a silver scatter of stars blazing indifferently in the cloudless sky.

THREE

The wind whipped her hair and turned her cheeks scarlet as we raced across the open meadowland and drew up at the high stone wall that marked the château's boundary. She jumped down from her horse.

"I told you I'd beat you, Boy." She laughed up at me. "Centime is invincible today!"

How ravishing she looked in her tight jodhpurs and boots and open-necked shirt. How different she was from all the others. Defying their vapid, silken, ruffled prettiness, she dressed like a groom or a wild gypsy lad. And she could ride all day, and in any weather, without a word of complaint.

"I let you win, petite Coco. I held Étoile back."

"Merde, Boy. You never *let* anyone win. Centime left you in the dust. From the moment I mounted him, I was certain we would beat you." It was stunningly hot in the field. The meadow grass shimmered in waves stretching back toward Royallieu and a warm wind reversed the birch leaves, turning them to silver. A sure sign, my governess used to say, of a storm coming up.

"Well then, petite Coco. Come and claim your wager." I produced the silver flask of brandy from my pocket and we tethered the horses to a tree and wandered out into the meadow.

I took her hand. The closeness of the night before had not left us.

"You know where this is leading, Coco. I've tried to convince myself that you belong to Étienne, but damnit you know I can't take my eyes off you. He must have noticed—they all must know by now."

"I don't *belong* to anyone, Boy. I don't intend to, ever. My father betrayed my mother and left her to die. Then he turned his back on me and my sisters and brothers. I've seen what possession is. All those women back at Royallieu—Émilienne and Suzanne and Jeanne—all of them are owned."

"Isn't that a little harsh, Coco?"

"No—just truthful. Their lovers pay for their jewels and carriages and their dressmakers' bills. They install them in pretty dollhouses in the Plaine Monceau where they visit them at their convenience. When they grow bored with the charms of one, they move on to another. If you play the game with calculation like Émilienne does, you survive, but if you ever make the mistake of taking it seriously, you're lost. Jeanne came close to death last night. I intend to make my way by myself, Boy. No one will ever own me."

She turned away and stared off across the fields toward the château.

"Where have you gone, Coco? I'm always afraid that somehow I'm going to offend that proud spirit of yours in some clumsy way. Don't you know my life is all *about* freedom? My father abandoned me, too. I've been alone since I was a boy. Our bargain would be a bargain for pleasure—the pleasure of equals."

We lay in the deep, dry, whispering grass. A strong scent of clover and thyme. I reached out and traced the line of her lovely profile.

She turned to me and then sat up and very slowly began unbuttoning her silk shirt. Drops of moisture glistened in the sweet hollow of her neck. I took her in my arms and licked the sweat away. Her slim body shivered uncontrollably against mine. She took my hands and drew them to her small, firm breasts. Her skin was slick and shining.

"You know, if we do this, Boy, we can't turn back. All these weeks of being near you . . . all the long nights of wanting you . . . trying so very hard *not* to want you."

I covered her lovely mouth with my own.

FOUR

*I*f I hadn't liked the man so much I would probably have gloated over the fact that our bachelor
establishments in Paris were, by what I can only
regard as a cosmic coincidence, both located in the
Boulevard Malesherbes.

So when he reluctantly allowed her to open a modest
milliner's shop in his flat at No. 160, the convenience
of the thing was almost embarrassing. Since Royallieu,
Coco and I had tried our damndest to turn our backs
on the spontaneous attraction that had ignited between us. It was no use. There was no way we could
keep away from each other.

All she had to do was place her small, competent
hand on my thigh . . . all I had to do was to take that
hand and place it where I longed to feel her touch, and
it would begin between us again. It was unquenchable,
that was the extraordinary thing.

At any hour of the day or night, when Étienne was
at Royallieu or visiting with his very proper family
where she would never be welcome, Coco would slip
away to me where she was always welcome. When she
came I would pretend that I had been engrossed in my
reading or the research for my book instead of counting the endless hours, hopelessly distracted and long-

ing for that light tapping on my door. I would open to her and wrap her in my arms.

What frightened me was the very force of our coming together. So many times when we were one, I felt the riptide of our passion would carry us too far away. I was sure we would die to the world . . . that we could not possibly come back from that far, fine place we had reached together—the place I believed we had been before in past lives. If I feared anything it was abandoning control, losing my very self in her.

As the weeks of stolen pleasure went by, we knew there had to be a reckoning. Coco wanted to tell Étienne the truth, felt she owed it to him for the care and protection he'd given her. I argued that it would be less hurtful to him if I pretended to regard it as simply the "gentleman's way" out of an awkward but familiar situation. God knows what he would have done if he knew the intensity of feeling that existed between us.

When I told Coco I would be willing to finance her expansion into more important premises, a shop that would be more than the "little hobby" of a rich man's mistress—that would become "Chanel Modes"—she looked at me with that cool, considering gaze I'd come to recognize long before I knew her, when I practiced it myself while shaving each morning in front of my mirror.

We were lying in front of the library fire when I made her my proposition. Unspoken was the understanding that it would also provide the occasion for her to leave Étienne with both their pride intact.

"Only as a loan, Boy, and at the current rate of interest," she said, as though I'd made an inappropriate suggestion.

"Well, petite Coco, if as a loan, then against what collateral and on what terms of repayment?"

For a brief moment she hesitated, then she gave me that reckless hoyden's grin. "Against my heart and my entire worldly estate—and payable on demand."

I gathered her into my arms, secretly and shamefully hoping she would be forced to default to her only creditor.

Coco haunted me. She had taken possession of my imagination so completely I could not remember that I had ever loved before. It was the very elusiveness of her that endlessly enticed me. The more she seemed to let me know her—the tantalizing glimpses she gave me of the intensely private world she inhabited behind that mask of democratic charm—the less I knew and the more I hungered to know.

In so many ways she was my double, equal in energy and drive, equal in the ability to compose herself like one of her own deceptively simple designs out of scraps of truth and fabrication, equal in the sturdy gambler's heart that made her take risks that would have made most men quail.

It was the Russians—Dostoyevsky I think—who believed it was bad luck to so much as *see* your double. How much more dangerous to fall headlong in love. But that was what I had ambushed myself by doing and it was time for me to own up to it.

Étienne would have to be told. Discreet as we had tried to be, I was sure some gossip had seen us at the local flower stall or walking hand in hand along the

Seine in the magical *l'heure bleue* as we loved to do. Paris was a small town that way. He deserved better than to hear it from some smirking houseguest, drinking his vintage port while he shattered the simple certainties of Étienne's world.

Besides, our mutual guilt over hurting the man who trusted us so completely was beginning to poison even our brief, stolen hours together. So I drove down to the château myself at mid-week, confident I'd have a chance to see him alone and tell him about my plans to launch Coco as a serious couturière.

It was a glorious day, cold and clear without a cloud in the skies. Royallieu spread out before me in all the splendor of its sprawling stables and paddocks. It looked timeless, as peaceful and welcoming under the pale winter sun as it must have done to weary fourteenth-century travelers who visited it when it was an abbey. How many of them, I wondered, came there seeking absolution for a guilt as heavy as mine?

I found Étienne in the stables where I'd guessed he would be, surrounded by grooms, his steward, and the local veterinarian. They were involved in assisting a mare in a particularly difficult breach birth. A February foal sired last April. As I watched, the doctor pulled on a pair of rubber gloves and reached right up inside the straining, sweating mare. Braced by two stablemen, he turned the foal and drew it down through the birth canal by main force. The labor that had probably gone on for hours was over in a few bloody minutes. The mare lay exhausted in the straw while her foal struggled up on its spindly legs and regarded its new surroundings with dazed wonder.

Étienne produced a flask of cognac, passed it to the

veterinarian, took a deep swig himself, then handed it round to the rest of his men. It was only then that he saw me leaning on the stall-gate.

"Boy, *quel plaisir!* On a weekday, too. What the devil has lured you out of the temples of mammon? It's clearly not women—you know Coco's up in Paris during the week now. She's actually selling those preposterous hats she makes. Can you credit it?"

I felt the heat of embarrassment flame in my face, but Étienne took no notice and hurtled on. "Not women, *non,* then it must be horseflesh. I'd offer you this young contender who's just made such a dramatic entrance into this sorry old world, but Foy's already spoken for him. A shame. Look at the depth of that chest, Boy. Look at those long legs—he'll stand sixteen hands at the very least. This one's a certain winner!" He beamed with paternalistic pride. "He won't carry the turquoise and black Balsan colors—but he's bound to be a champion, just the same. It's written all over him."

Full of hearty goodwill, he shepherded me up to his study where, as so many times before, we sat in the comfortable, cracked-leather wing chairs in front of a blazing fire that drove out the February chill but did little enough to melt the ice I felt in the marrow of my bones.

"Well, Boy, out with it. If it's not a question of women or horses or business, what *does* bring you down here so unexpectedly?"

Why did I sense that he instinctively knew the purpose of my visit and was doing all he possibly could to forestall acknowledging it?

"Actually, Étienne, it *is* a matter of business. Coco

told me you'd let her requisition your *garçonnière* for her millinery shop. But she's suddenly caught on with the ladies of the Faubourg St.-Germain, and she has more custom than she can comfortably handle in your flat."

" '*Custom,*' Boy, don't be a horse's ass. You know I let Coco play at this hat-making foolishness for her demimonde friends because it gives her something to do with her energies. As you can imagine, her energies are prodigious!" He gave me a brotherly nudge that made me wince. "But *custom* . . . a business . . . you must be joking. It's one thing to indulge Coco in an amusing hobby, quite another to have a mistress who's in trade. That wouldn't do at all." He threw back his brandy and poured himself another liberal jolt.

"I thought you'd probably feel that way about it, Étienne, but it seems that Gabrielle and Marthe Davelli and Geneviève Vix and a number of her other theatrical friends have been trying to persuade her to move into couture proper."

"Ridiculous." He was turning dangerously red.

"Not really, Étienne. They've seen some of the clothes she designed for Jeanne Léry and Suzanne Orlandi who can't afford their own couturiers, and they're telling her she could easily give Doucet—even Worth and Poiret—a run for the money. I think they're right."

"Come off it, Boy. Stick to coal futures where you know what you're talking about. The only thing you and I understand about women's clothes is how damnably complicated they are to get off them." He laughed a little too heartily and tried to change the subject. "What do you think of these two new Stubbs studies I got through my man in London? Cost me a bloody fortune, I can tell you."

"They're magnificent, Étienne. Well worth whatever you paid for them. Take my word for it, though, an investment in Coco's future as a designer would be just as sound. She's told me she's determined to expand, and I've encouraged her to feel confident that the money to back her would be easy enough to raise."

"Since when have you appointed yourself Coco's business adviser, Boy? Hell will freeze over before I put another franc into her so-called 'business.' Why, I'd be the laughing stock of my club and in every paddock from St. Cloud to Longchamp."

His face had gone from angry red to purple and he was throwing back brandy after brandy. "Frankly, I have to tell you I don't appreciate your encouraging my mistress in something you know damned well I can't possibly go along with."

Now we were coming to it.

"She's always been too bloody independent for my taste, but I've put up with it because you know I'm damned fond of her . . ." He fell silent and stared broodingly into the dancing blue and green flames of the applewood fire. The tension between us was palpable.

"That's a real problem, too, Étienne," I said, "Coco's independence. The best part of her is the part you're least happy with. A mistress like Émilienne d'Alençon is one thing—expensive but predictable, and certainly comfortable. You're never going to be able to put a bridle on Coco and turn her into someone tame and docile."

"And I suppose *you* know a better way to handle such a high-spirited creature, Boy. Is that it? That's the real reason you're here, isn't it—to tell me you're ready to become Coco's new handler . . . to finance her across the boards. And that *she's* ready to be financed . . . or should I say, to be handled by you? You're altogether too shrewd a gambler to have approached me with anything less than a full hand."

Suddenly I was ashamed at the transparency of my tactics.

"I'm sorry, Étienne. It was never my intent—or Coco's—to have this happen between us . . . for us to hurt you in any way. She's deeply loyal to you . . . and so am I. I tried hard not to violate that loyalty."

"Well, that was damned decent of you, Boy . . . damned decent to share my friendship, my trust, and my hospitality—*and* my mistress." He hurled his heavy crystal brandy snifter across the room at one of the paintings, and the cognac ran down the priceless Stubbs. "Now, why don't you get out of here before I take a riding crop to you."

I left him sitting slumped in the wing chair in front of the dying fire and drove back to Paris, full of pain and regret and explanations about the fundamental difference between himself and rogues like Coco and me—explanations he would never understand, even if he had had the uncommon tolerance to let me make them.

I found Coco waiting anxiously in my study, pacing the worn turkey rug in front of the fire.

"What happened, Boy? Did you see him? Did you tell him? Did you make him understand why I *have* to leave him, that it's really a matter of my business . . ." Seldom had I seen her so agitated.

"Balsan's anything but a fool, Coco. He understood all too well. About the business and everything else. I think he's known all along, just hoped that if he left it alone—ignored it—our attraction would wear itself out. That was his gamble, and he lost and he knows it now and he's in pain. He does love you, you know."

"But I'm the absolutely wrong woman for a man like Étienne. In the long run, I would make him miserable."

"He recognizes your genius *and* your ambition, Coco. And you're right, they *would* make him miserable. That's his dilemma. Genius, ambition, and independence. Those are the very things Étienne could never tolerate in a woman—not comfortably in a mistress, *never* in a wife. That's what threatens him. That and the fact that he knows I'm in love with you."

"And *you* can tolerate it, Boy—tolerate a woman who lives for something more than you? Whose hours are not always yours to command. Whose commitments are divided between you and the work. Whose challenge is larger than love?"

Never had she seemed as beautiful as she did at that moment, standing there blazing at me, confronting me with everything she already was and everything she could be.

"No, Coco, I couldn't tolerate that either. What I could and can tolerate—what I *need* in my life—is a woman who finds work and love equally challenging and equally rigorously demanding. That's why you and I belong together. And that's why you're going to stop examining your convent-girl conscience and go back to Number 160, pack your things, and come to me tonight."

"All right, Boy," she said quietly.

"This is not the right place for us ultimately. Our guilt over what we've done here, over what we've had to do to Étienne—would tarnish it for us both. For now though, until we can find you new premises for the work and us, new premises for our love, you're going to have to make the best of it." I pulled her to me, kissed her fiercely on the mouth, and turned her toward the door and our future together.

FIVE

Coco's official entrance into my life was not an alteration of my well-ordered bachelor's existence. It was an explosion.

For someone whose cardinal rule of style was simplicity, she traveled like a maharanee. Between the supplies for her flourishing millinery business and her new tentative venture into couture, and her own by-now considerable wardrobe—since she was her own advertisement—Coco had turned my once-serene drawing room and library into a nightmare vision out of Hieronymus Bosch.

Decapitated mannequin heads, some sporting half-finished hats, some bald as billiard balls, stared blankly at me from the mantel over the fireplace, the end tables, from every available surface—even my sacro-sanct writing desk.

"Just be glad I cut my dresses on live models, Boy," Coco said gaily, "otherwise there'd be a troupe of head-less torsos, too!"

I opened a bottle of Veuve Clicquot and toasted my new tenants.

"Welcome to my home and heart, chère Mademoi-selle Chanel and friends. As you can see, our first prior-ity tomorrow will have to be real estate. Tonight, though, if you will forgive me, Mesdemoiselles," I bowed to the silent company and swept Coco up into my arms, "we have more pressing business to attend to."

I carried her, laughing helplessly, into my bedroom where we made love until the dawn light crept palely around the edges of the heavy green velvet drapes and found her sleeping like an exhausted child, her improb-ably long, dark eyelashes feathered on her ivory cheeks.

I could have happily stayed there in our tumbled bed, watching her sleep, guarding her, if I could, from her dark dreams. No one in my strange untethered life had ever touched me in quite the way this brave, beau-tiful orphan had. I knew in my heart that no one else ever would.

She stirred sleepily and opened her eyes.

"Boy. I can't believe it's you. How many times I've imagined waking up here in your bed . . . in your arms! She drew me down to her and all my good resolutions about getting an early start on the morning were gone. If it hadn't been for the insistent rapping on the door, we probably would have spent the day right there, exploring the wonders of this bold new intimacy.

"Mon dieu." She jumped out of bed and began searching frantically for her underclothes. "That must be Antoinette. I told the concierge to send her here when she arrived for work." She tossed on one of my silk dressing robes and hurried off to let her in to the flat.

When Coco first opened her millinery shop, she'd written to her sister to ask her to come up to Paris from Varennes where she'd been staying with an elderly aunt. Four years younger than Coco, Antoinette was brash, jealous, and full of herself. She and I had taken an instant dislike to one another on the single occasion when we'd met at No. 160. But Antoinette was a hard worker and Coco needed help.

The commissions were coming in hot and heavy. Her first choice to assist her had been her beautiful, soft-spoken "Aunt" Adrienne who I'd met on a number of Royallieu weekends with her lover, Baron Édouard de Nexon. Adrienne was a constant source of worry to Coco. Against all her advice—and the bold example of her own new career—Adrienne had chosen to embrace the shadow world of the unacknowledged mistress and was traveling now with her lover in Africa, as far from the icy disapproval of his arrogant, *ancien régime* family as his allowance could put them.

So it had to be Antoinette. Well, that gave me one more good reason to devote all my energies to the search for new premises. I could always breakfast at my club. By the time I had shaved and dressed and walked quietly past the library door, they were already totally absorbed in the hard work of creating beautiful tomfoolery.

I caught Coco's eye, blew her a kiss and stepped cheerfully out into the brilliant Paris morning.

Finding No. 21 rue Cambon was a stroke of the sheerest good fortune—or good Karma, if you subscribed as I did to the teachings of the Eastern masters who believed your good deeds, even your good intentions, bore fruit in this and later lifetimes.

I'd been hurrying back to her along the Faubourg St.-Honoré on my way home from a highly promising meeting with Georges Clémenceau, the upcoming Minister of Finance. Beyond his obvious interest—with rumblings of war with the Kaiser sounding louder in our ears every day—in forging a tighter coal connection with London and Newcastle, he seemed determined, for reasons of his own unorthodox temperament and self-made background, to make me his personal protégé.

I had left the meeting in a celebratory mood and was thinking idly of picking up a gift for Coco to commemorate our own joining forces when I absentmindedly turned off the St.-Honoré into the rue Cambon instead of taking my usual route home along the rue Duphot past the silvery, weathered pillars of the lovely church of the Madeleine.

There, on this short, bustling street of elegant shops catering to Paris' most profligate spenders, I saw a hand-lettered sign in a second-story window, LOCAUX COMMERCIAUX À LOUER, with an agent's number listed beneath. I nearly ran the rest of the way along the Boulevard Malesherbes and astonished the fat, sleepy concierge by taking the marble steps three at a time. I burst into the flat and found Coco alone, struggling exasperatedly with a stubborn length of tulle veiling.

"I've found it, petite Coco! The perfect spot for your new enterprise . . . that is, of course, if you agree. Drop what you're doing and come with me to have a look. We can't get in to see the interior this evening—it's too late. If you agree with me that the location's perfect, though, you can be in touch with the agent first thing tomorrow."

She smiled up radiantly at me and rushed inside to get her wrap. That was one of the things I loved most about her—her trust in the absolute oneness of our business instincts. She knew anything that appealed to me would almost certainly coincide with her own highly ambitious vision of her future.

As we stood outside No. 21 in the empty street, deserted now in the aftermath of the day's frenetic trade, she gripped my hand tightly in hers and stared raptly up at the darkened windows.

"Oh yes, mon cher," she said with quiet assurance, "yes, this is the place. This is the place I will make my own. I love you for finding it for me, for knowing it was meant to be mine."

She stood on tiptoe and kissed me deeply, sweetly, lingeringly in the peaceful shadows of the rue Cambon.

Coco was a woman possessed. She was on the agent's doorstep early the next morning. And as I watched her cannily manipulate the wiry little *agent immobilier,* Monsieur Le Brun, my respect for her grew by leaps and bounds.

She was a master negotiator. Shrewd and persuasive,

flattering and threatening by turns, she kept poor Le Brun constantly off-guard. First she got him to reduce the monthly rent by 5,000f on the grounds of the extensive renovations she'd be forced to make.

"After all, Monsieur," she gave him her most eloquent Gallic shrug. *"Look* at this place. It's a shambles. Your previous tenant, whoever he was, took terrible advantage of you. It will cost me my first year's profit—should I be lucky enough to make one—simply to restore the premises to attract the sort of clientele who buy my designs."

She brushed aside his feeble attempts at hinting at the existence of other eager bidders.

"Anyone, cher Monsieur Le Brun, anyone at all who rents from you will face the same challenge." She gestured dismissively at the shabby state of the small, cramped rooms. "You might as well allow me to be the one to pick it up. I come from the Auvergne where property is taken seriously. You can trust me to maintain yours—perhaps even," she smiled at him provocatively, "to improve it for you!"

Le Brun shrugged and surrendered. He had lost the first round—the rent reduction. Her next target, a longer-term lease than the one he was proposing, was achieved despite his skepticism at her going up against the established masters of the business.

Coco was magnificent. "I guarantee you this, Monsieur Le Brun," she told him coolly. "If I fail—which I do not for a moment believe I will—I will do so so dramatically that you will be able to say to the next tenant, 'Here Mademoiselle Coco Chanel went into battle against the giants of couture—Doucet . . . Poiret . . . Vionnet . . . Worth . . . and here she was defeated. The place is famous—the Waterloo of fashion.' You'll be able to *treble* the rent in that sad eventuality. But you must give me five years to wage my war. Three years barely allows me time to recruit my troops."

Le Brun was completely vanquished. We left No. 21 with the signed five-year lease at a remarkably reasonable rent clutched firmly in Coco's hand and the key tucked in her reticule.

"How would you like to negotiate the lease on the new coal port I plan to establish in Casablanca, Mademoiselle Chanel?" I asked her teasingly as we strolled arm and arm down the rue Cambon.

"Ordinarily, for the proper commission, I would certainly consider it, cher Monsieur Capel. At the moment, however, I am caught up in a small business of my own that I am launching. I fear it will take up whatever hours I can spare from my major avocation—the great love of my life."

The shop was an overnight success—a sensation not just because of Coco's startlingly simple, revolutionary millinery and dress designs, but because from the very beginning it had that priceless element, cachet.

All Paris was talking about "Chanel Modes" and its beautiful owner. Customers who came initially out of curiosity about this "little milliner" who'd dared to defy the giants of the fashion establishment were so impressed by her bold new style that they stayed to buy and buy . . . and to recommend her to their friends.

I knew my hunch in backing her had been right. "Chanel Modes" was a gold mine. All the tangled strands of Coco's young life came brilliantly together at No. 21. Her old friends from Balsan's horsey set—Suzanne and Jeanne, Marthe and Gabrielle—were her first customers. Even Émilienne d'Alençon came in to browse, though her overblown style was firmly frozen in the winter of the *belle époque*. I told Coco she was probably there as Étienne's spy.

Coco had confided that she'd been getting increasingly desperate letters from him, letters ignoring my existence, ignoring her success, and begging her to return to Royallieu.

Soon music-hall stars from the *Grands Boulevards* and divas from the Opéra were rubbing shoulders with grandes dames from the forbidding mansions of the Faubourg St.-Germain in Coco's sunny, black-and-white shop.

The only dicey moment, she told me laughingly over a late supper at Larue's, had come one afternoon when a vicomte's fat, spoiled, aging wife and his beautiful, spoiled young mistress crossed paths on the way to a fitting room.

But Coco had not been a careful student of fashionable society at Vichy and Royallieu for nothing. With her ear close to the gossip circuit thanks to Marthe and Gabrielle and Jeanne, and the innate diplomacy of a Richelieu, from that point on she had had Antoinette schedule the intricate gavotte of her appointments so that such an awkward collision would never happen again.

Coco was in her element.

SIX

W hy did I think that dailiness would make me tire of her? Because it always had with others in the past. Instead, my feeling for her only grew.

She had become an obsession. At completely unexpected moments during the day—in the middle of complex discussions of the new coal port in Casablanca, or dining with some fat, self-important banker at my club, or exercising one of my string of polo ponies in the Bois—she would suddenly be there in my mind and body with an incredible erotic immediacy.

I would think of the way she had of drawing herself slowly, infinitely slowly away from me to tantalizingly delay the moment of our mutual climax. I would see the uplift of her perfect pointed breasts with the firelight flicking her golden nipples as she raised up to offer them to my hungry mouth.

I would feel the satin of her blue-black hair as she wound it playfully like a ribbon around my aroused member. How I loved that long, heavy hair that hung to the sweet cleft of her ass. And I would imagine the times when her own urgency overtook her and she rode me as relentlessly—even ruthlessly—as any other mount.

She was a perpetual source of erotic delight because

everything new we did together pleased her so much. The day I had led her up the stairs at 21 rue Cambon and showed her the simple brass plaque I had had installed on the door to surprise her—the plaque that announced CHANEL MODES—she had said nothing. She simply took the key from her reticule, led me inside the light, airy premises she had transformed from dark shabbiness, undressed me and herself with indecent haste, and drew me down on top of her on the newly varnished floor.

When our endless need for one another's bodies had been temporarily assuaged, she had smiled languidly up at me.

"Voilà, Monsieur Capel. You may consider that the first installment on your loan."

I was in so damn deep it frightened me. Marriage to her was out of the question. I had spent too many years steadily, carefully accruing power and influence. An important marriage of wealth, connections, and convenience—my convenience—was an integral part of that master plan. Coco had neither the money nor the proper family lines. Not for a minute did I believe the elaborate fantasies she spun of her father the heartbroken wine merchant in America. Her background was even murkier than mine.

At least I had evidence of the rumors that my father had been an international financier—evidence in the form of the blind trust he had established that had paid for my governesses as a child, sent me to exclusive English public schools and university, and then enabled me to buy my first coal works in Newcastle. It was not entirely a lie that coal was my "family business." Coal was the foundation on which I was building my security. The next step would be to acquire an influential political mentor, hopefully Clémenceau himself, and a very proper bride. No, I certainly couldn't marry Coco Chanel.

On the other hand, she was fused so completely in my blood and my being that I could not imagine a life without her.

Of course, the underside of erotic obsession is jealousy—the dark, sick, corrosive emotion that had never touched my earlier affairs because, frankly, I had never been able to give myself to anyone as I did to Coco. Totally. Holding nothing back. Nothing in reserve. No safety net. Exposed. Rendering myself vulnerable in a way I had always considered foolhardy in business or in love.

I'd suffered its first insidious whisperings as early as those weekends at Royallieu when she'd displayed her affection for Alec Carter, a man no one could fail to like, or when she'd listened patiently to Léon de Laborde's endless tales of unrequited love, or appeared to encourage what I knew very well were the practiced, meaningless attentions of Baron Foy. But it took Paris, and our moving in together into the wonderful new flat we found on the Quai de Tokyo overlooking our beloved Seine, to bring things to the boil.

Worse—and it kills me to have to admit it—my jealousy was not confined to the many men who flocked around the jet flame of her intensity. I was as threatened by the brilliant women who were drawn into her orbit. Coco was a universal magnet.

Not long after she had opened 21 rue Cambon to what all Paris perceived as a triumph—right on the heels, in fact, of the powerful fashion journal, *Les Modes,* declaring her the shining new star in the millinery firmament—she was ambushed by one of her old demons, insomnia.

I would wake with a start from the drowsy languor of sexual fulfillment to find her gone from our bed. I would discover her, wrapped in my dressing robe, pacing the length of the drawing room, staring forlornly out over the silver ribbon of the moonlit Seine.

"Come back to bed, petite Coco," I would say gently. You're going to wear yourself out without sleep. You'll end by making yourself sick."

"Don't you understand, Boy, I want to sleep. I need to rest. I know it better than you do. But I can't." The look of helpless panic on her face tore at my heart. "I can't turn off my mind. The images come one after another—designs I want to make, mistakes I see now in the designs I've already made. Call it madness. Call it whip-wiring, like an electrical circuit run wild. Call it whatever you wish. It won't let me be. It never has—it never will."

So when Marthe Davelli, who suffered the same torments of sleeplessness, told her she might get some relief from regular exercise and recommended her own dance teacher, I was all for it.

"Marthe is right, petite Coco. You're being vampirized by your customers *and* your staff. This—what did she call it . . . 'eurythmic dance'—might well be the perfect way to burn off your anxieties. After all," I tried to joke her out of her depression, "it did wonders for Isadora Duncan. *She* certainly seems relaxed. At least, all her lovers say so."

What I hadn't counted on was Caryathis.

Coco came home from her first session with the dancer as thoroughly intoxicated as if she'd drunk an entire bottle of champagne. She had discovered a whole new world, *la vie de bohème,* and had conceived what amounted to an intense schoolgirl crush on its high priestess. Or that was how I saw it at first.

"You won't *believe* her studio, Boy. It's right at the very top of Montmartre on the rue Lamarck, overlooking all Paris. I was so out of breath by the time I'd climbed up there I thought I would faint, never mind dance. Caryathis was splendid, though. She settled me on a beautiful silk paisley cushion—her studio is like a Turkish seraglio—and made me a cup of herb tea."

"Sounds like a good businesswoman to me, Coco. She didn't want to lose a new pupil before you even had your ballet slippers on."

"Oh no, Boy," she was genuinely shocked. "No ballet slippers. No shoes at all! We dance barefoot. As nature intended it. Eurythmics is all about freedom . . . freedom from constraint . . . expression of the inner being through body movement. Oh, it's truly marvelous, Boy. So liberating. So energizing. Carya told me it relates directly to the spirit of my *own* work—simplicity, naturalness, freedom from convention."

Coco was glowing, her dark eyes shining and her cheeks flushed that hectic scarlet they always did after we made love. Suddenly I had an intense urge to demythicize this young earth goddess, Caryathis.

"Next she'll be asking you to design costumes for her. That's happened before," I said, not so subtly conjuring up the image of the lecherous theatre manager in Vichy—the one Coco told me had wanted to make her his mistress.

But she was in full flight, totally oblivious of my irony. "How did you guess, Boy? That's *just* what she wants me to do. Imagine. She's only been costumed by artists up till now—Larionov for Jean Cocteau's production of *Le Jongleur,* and Larionov's wife, Nathalie Gontcharova, for Carya's variations on the music of Granados."

She smiled dreamily. "Think of it, Boy. Only artists. She knows *all* of them—Gris, Modigliani, Picasso. They all live in Montmartre or Montparnasse and go to the Rotonde or the Dôme where they stay up talking until dawn. And they all drop in to her studio to drink wine and sketch the dancers. Cocteau even smokes opium with her, she told me. Of course, she doesn't do *that* often."

"I hate to dampen your enthusiasm, Coco my darling, but struggling painters and writers are notorious freeloaders."

"Oh, Boy, don't play the bourgeois with me. It doesn't work. You'd *love* Caryathis and her 'special friend' Charles Dullin. He's quite the most beautiful man I think I've ever seen." This time she realized she'd definitely gone too far and backtracked hastily.

"I mean beautiful the way a great dancer is—eloquent and poetic—not dark and dashing like certain Anglo-French financiers."

"Nice recovery, petite Coco," I managed a laugh. Inside I was seething.

"The three of us danced a spontaneous *pas de trois* to the most amazing music by that new Russian composer, Stravinsky. Cocteau, who was watching, said we were 'eroticism incarnate.' You *have* to come the next time and see how good we are together."

"I'm frankly proud that voyeurism isn't one of my vices, Coco," I said with as much dignity as I could muster, which wasn't considerable given the circumstances, and buried myself in that day's edition of the financial *Times*.

SEVEN

Over the next few weeks, Coco's absorption with Caryathis and her circle was complete. She neglected the business. She neglected me. All her conversation was about Carya and Charles . . . their defiance of conventional morality, the daring boldness of their style of life, and the constant parade of genius through the studio.

Carya was coaching the young writer, Colette, who'd left her husband, Willy, who was stealing her royalties, and was trying to support herself by dancing on the music-hall stage. Carya was encouraging Pierre Reverdy, the brilliant poet and founder of *Nord-Sud,* the controversial literary review that was shocking the Paris bourgeoisie to its rotten core. Carya was lending money to the gloriously handsome Modigliani to keep him in paint and absinthe. The rue Lamarck was Eden and Olympus and Xanadu all rolled into one.

"You can't imagine how brave she is, Boy, living so intensely and entirely by her own rules."

We were leaning on the stone balustrade of the stately Pont Alexandre, watching the *bateaux-mouches* ply their trade, the candles on the diners' white-clothed tables fireflies in the gathering darkness.

"I thought you told me she lives with this choreographer fellow, Dullin."

"Of course she does," she said patiently, gently, as if instructing a particularly backward child. "He's her grand passion. The main source, she says, like you are for me, of *all* her creative inspiration. He takes other lovers, though. And she does, too. In fact, *she* chooses the ones she wants to sleep with. She picks them out and approaches them—almost like a man."

Coco's eyes were shining suspiciously. Had Carya singled her out for special attention? Were her lovers always men? Some self-protective instinct stopped me from asking.

"She's even cut her hair short like a man's—bobbed it so that with her amazing, luminous eyes she looks just like Jeanne d'Arc."

"Promise me you'll never follow her example, petite Coco. I can't imagine waking up in the morning and not seeing your glorious hair spread out over our pillows." *And none of her other examples, either,* I said superstitiously to myself.

"Not unless you give me cause, Boy," Coco said laughing. "Carya told me she'd cut off her hair to punish a lover who refused her his bed. Tied it with a ribbon and hung it on a hook on his door. So as long as you don't deny me access to our bed, my hair is safe."

"If that's all that's required, your raven tresses will

soon reach down to your ankles, Mademoiselle," I said boastfully as I took her in my arms.

But the serenity of the evening and our perfect rapport had been subtly jangled. My worst admission is that, for the first time, I empathized with Étienne. How ironic, given the worldly ambitions that meant I could never marry her, that in his most recent letters to her Étienne had said he actually intended to defy his parents and ask Coco to let him make her his wife. How very well I understood the hammerlock she had on his simple, straightforward heart. It was the same one she had on my own byzantine one.

Now I knew what it was to watch the single woman who had ever occupied my body and my mind and soul in the grip of what I could only hope was a temporary infatuation . . . one of Coco's passionate enthusiasms . . . the quality of spirit I'd always liked most about her.

How many times Étienne must have repeated the same humble prayer that I found on my lips at the most likely and unlikely hours of the night or day. *"Please, don't let her leave."*

But unlike Étienne, I believed—and it might have been arrogance on my part—that I understood her better. Coco could not tolerate someone who tried to own her. The man (or, God forbid, the woman) who truly deserved her exceptional loyalty would have to understand that the secret to loving someone as wild as Coco was to free her utterly and trust her utterly. She would return that trust in full. I was convinced of it. So then why was I torn by dark, gut-destroying suspicions of Caryathis?

Finally I couldn't stand it any longer. I had to exorcise the demon of my jealousy, and it seemed to me that the best way, the businesslike way was to confront it head on. I would meet this phenomenon who had so thoroughly captured my lover's imagination, and by doing so reduce her in my mind, then in Coco's to human dimensions.

I decided my single strategic advantage would be surprise, so I said nothing about it to Coco. I simply left my office late one Thursday afternoon when I knew she was having a lesson, and climbed the steep hill of Montmartre to rue Lamarck.

A young man, naked except for what looked to me like a loincloth, let me into the studio where a class was in progress. The light was dim and thick with some musky incense. Along one wall cushions were piled where a number of men and women—some dancers, some wearing the denim overalls affected by the painters of the district, some in street clothes—sat drinking wine and smoking. The only evidence that this was a professional dance studio at all was the wall of mirrors and the brass barre running the length of the far side of the room.

In the center of the floor two women, barefoot and wearing brief, filmy tunics, were dancing to the accompaniment of drums and a wailing sitar. This "eurythmic dance" looked to me more like a bastardized version of the temple dancing I'd seen on my travels in the East than anything you'd see on the slanting boards of the Maryinsky.

There was a great deal of flourishing of the silk veils they carried, winding them sinuously, lingeringly around one another's bodies. The taller of the two, beautiful in a sleek, angular way with short, blonde, mannishly cropped hair, was clearly Caryathis. She set the pace of the dance and drew her partner steadily into the orbit of her desire. Then they were joined by a tall, slender blond man.

Dullin. It had to be. Lithe and with oiled, sculpted muscles gleaming, he insinuated himself into their dance—enticing first one woman, then the other, then submitting as the two caressed him, caressed each other. The beat of the drums was insistent, compelling. They were an erotic temple frieze come to stunning, vibrant life. I felt as if I couldn't breathe.

The sexuality was almost as explicit as any of the "exhibitions" I'd ever seen in the smoky, crowded after-hours *bôites* tucked away in the city's backstreets.

And their partner was Coco. My heart hammered so hard in my chest I was sure she must sense it over the drumbeat. Rapt in her fantasy of pursuit and conquest by this gorgeous man, this gorgeous woman, these two perfect animals, she did not even notice my presence—not my arrival nor my frantic departure as I escaped from the stifling studio into the welcome night air and found my way to the closest café where I ordered a double brandy.

By the time I got back to the Quai de Tokyo it was long after midnight and I had had too much time to brood and drink.

I couldn't bear the thought of losing her, but the thought of sharing her with anyone else was just as intolerable. With every cognac I drank, new visions of the three of them intertwined in their erotic dance—her darkness against their athletic blondness, her white, white skin against theirs gleaming gold—burned behind my eyelids, closed against the pain and the images that would not stop coming even then.

I let myself in to the flat determined to confront her. The drawing room was empty, only a faint glow of embers in the grate, and her workroom was deserted.

I found myself picking up a scrap of satin ribbon from her worktable and running its cool length across my burning mouth. "Dear God, don't tell me she has stayed with them," I said aloud in the quiet little room, usually so intensely alive with her presence.

Had she left me, then? At that moment I knew what Étienne knew—that the loss of her was unendurable. I stumbled down the long, narrow hallway to our bedroom and opened the door.

She was there. A shaft of moonlight sliced through the drapes and fell across the white satin comforter. She was sleeping. Sleeping the deep, peaceful sleep of an innocent child. But her beautiful hair—her wild gypsy hair was gone. She had broken her promise to me and cropped it short just like her newest idol. Damn her.

I sat down on the foot of the bed and watched her sleep while the first tears I had risked since my lonely boyhood ran down my face.

EIGHT

or what remained of that interminable night I stayed there watching while Coco slept, and by morning I had made up my mind. I would not confront her after all. It was not cowardice on my part but selfishness. Confrontation would be the surest way to lose her.

When I'd theorized to myself about why I was the better match for her than Étienne—all those lofty sentiments about giving her her freedom and trusting her utterly—I had been grandiose and remarkably naive. I had also been right. I just hadn't known how much the gift of freedom and trust could cost the giver.

The same instincts that had made me a shrewd judge of business antagonists told me the best way to deal with a poacher like Caryathis was to sit back and wait her out. These passionate enthusiasms of Coco's were like brushfires—they blazed up spontaneously, but without real fuel to stoke them they could die down just as quickly.

Caryathis had no real substance, no real originality like Coco. Even her dancing was derivative. She was a rebel for rebellion's sake. Empty rebellion and self-indulgence—qualities Coco with her peasant pride and dedication to hard, disciplined work would have to see through and disdain.

For the first time in hours I could even laugh at the image of the three of them and their ridiculous veils. I would not join Caryathis's dance. That would be what she was counting on. Triangles and manipulating men into joining them as bait for the women she really wanted was probably her obsession. I would refuse to be manipulated. I wouldn't be the one to try to lift the veil of infatuation from Coco's eyes. If I left her to it, she would be compelled by her essential honesty to do it for herself.

How I survived the next few months I'm still not sure. I began to make more frequent trips to London, as the talk of war escalated. Coal would be the dark lifeblood of both sides in any conflict, whatever its outcome. Cynically, I knew that war would only work to my advantage. And cynicism was my defensive mode—the only thing, to be frank, that was saving me from madness.

On those evenings when I was in Paris, I was incapable of doing anything but return home early from the office and install myself in my study with the brandy bottle close at hand and the files of research for my book piled haphazardly around me.

Of course, the files remained unopened as I drank and stared abstractedly into the flames, seeing lovers grappling passionately in their writhing—two women and a man . . . two women together . . . every possible permutation of lust and heat and twisted desire—and waiting with all my senses alert for the sound of her key in the lock and her light step along the hall.

She would burst in to the study like an eager child and come to sit on my lap, winding her arms around my neck, her eyes sparkling, her cheeks flushed and the evening chill still clinging to her short, curly hair. How I mourned the glossy jet banner that had come to me to symbolize those first, perfect, heart-whole days of our love, before betrayals—real or imaginary—had begun to complicate it.

Secretly, I think she knew how I felt, though I had never given her the satisfaction of acknowledging the havoc she'd wrought with her shears, beyond telling her I thought the new boyish bob "suited her." Let her try to puzzle that one out.

She would be full of gossip—gossip from the shop, where business was booming. Proudly she assured me that she'd be clearing her indebtedness to me well before the note came due. And gossip from the studio, where all the talk was of the upcoming premiere of the Russian impresario Serge Diaghilev's revolutionary ballet, *Le Sacre du printemps,* with choreography by Diaghilev's young lover, Nijinsky, and an iconoclastic score by Caryathis's favorite composer—and thus Coco's favorite—Igor Stravinsky.

Le Sacre du printemps, the rite of spring. What a splendid irony. All I could feel was the bleak iron chill of winter in my heart.

On that May night of the premiere there was an air of barely suppressed excitement in the brilliantly dressed throng milling in front of the new Théâtre des Champs-Élysées. It was a wildly eclectic crowd, drawn from Paris's Society, the lions and lionesses of Montmartre and Montparnasse, and, of course, the press who had gotten wind that they were in for something far more newsworthy than the opening of one more obscure ballet.

Coco had prevailed on me, against my better judgment, to join her for the first time with Caryathis and Charles who had taken a box. When I opened the velvet-draped door and saw that she and Carya had conspired to dress alike in black and white gowns of Coco's design with exotic touches of Russian embroidery as *hommage* to the evening, I was even more uneasy. I resolved to steel myself and sit on my jealousy for this one evening at least. It touched me to see that, even after all the months in Paris and her success, Coco still had the air of a star-struck provincial.

She kept tugging excitedly at my sleeve to point out her titled or famous or notorious customers in the audience—the lovely Comtesse Greffulhe, one of Proust's patronesses, the Baronne de Rothschild, the all-powerful Society hostess Comtesse Édith de Beaumont.

"Look, Boy—no *don't* look until I tell you. All right . . . *now* you can look . . . in the box to our left. The beautiful red-haired woman with the amazing pink pearls and the ostrich aigrette."

She was right. The woman *was* stunning in pink satin, with a radiant voluptuousness.

"That's Misia Sert, Diaghilev's confidante and patron. Carya says it's only because of her that *Le Sacre* is premiering at all."

"Why? Did she put up the money? She certainly looks as if she could afford to. Those pearls alone could have footed the bill for the performance—for an entire season for that matter. There must be ten yards of them."

"Dieu, Boy," Carya interrupted us. "It's no wonder

you and Coco are together. You're exactly alike. For you money always comes first."

When Coco, hurt, tried to protest, she swept on. "Misia Sert saved *Le Sacre.* Diaghilev, that fat, crass impresario, and my darling Igor were at daggers drawn over the cuts he wanted to make in Igor's brilliant score—and all for his temperamental lover, Nijinsky. Igor absolutely refused to accept them."

"Yet here we are tonight," I said. The woman's arrogant assumption that art and money were antithetical offended me almost as much as the slender arm she had draped around the back of Coco's chair. "Was it, perhaps," I asked, "Madame Sert's healthy contribution to the production that changed his mind?"

"She acted as the *artistic* mediator between them, *Boy."* Never had I heard my nickname used with such contempt. "I'm certain money had nothing to do with their compromise."

We were saved from further sparring by the dimming of the houselights. Coco's small hand found mine in the darkness.

Fifteen minutes into the ballet and the theatre was in total pandemonium. Even these sophisticated Parisians were unprepared for the primal power of Stravinsky's iconoclastic score with its intricate, driving, pounding rhythms celebrating the explosive force of spring, and the stylized sexuality of Nijinsky's tribal dances. In the middle of the *Danse des adolescents,* the audience erupted into violence.

From boxes around us and the orchestra seats below, loud cheers and "bravos" warred with catcalls, hissing, and shouts of *"hérétiques" . . . "sauvages" . . . "assassins" . . . "barbares."*

In a box nearby us a fistfight broke out between two elegant men in evening clothes who had to be separated by a burly usher. I could see Misia Sert in her box, her beautiful face flaming the color of her hair, clearly distressed and trying to silence the people around her.

Coco was gripping my arm so tightly it hurt, but her eyes were blazing with excitement.

Caryathis, of course, was ecstatic. *Any opportunity for self-dramatization,* I thought cynically. Like a fury, she climbed up on her chair and began hurling insults at the protestors, calling them *"imbéciles"* and *"espèces d'idiots."* Charles had to physically restrain her from pitching over the rail of the box in her frenzy.

"Look, Charles," she pointed across the tier of boxes, "there's Ravel himself, on his feet and cheering. What's the matter with these bourgeois idiots? Ravel recognizes true genius when he hears it!"

Then a man in the loge next to Ravel's shouted at him, *"Sale juif!"* and an usher quickly intervened before blood was shed.

Diaghilev must have given desperate orders to the stage manager, because the houselights started blinking on and off in a vain attempt to quiet the crowd.

Onstage, the dancers struggled gamely on with the sacrifice of the exquisite virgin to the Sun . . . with Nijinsky's complex, hieratic movements that Carya had told us required over a hundred rehearsals for this single performance. As a businessman, I realized it would take a triumph for Diaghilev to so much as break even.

But the crescendo of passion onstage and in the music was drowned by the crescendo of outrage. As the curtain fell, the audience that had become a mob exploded out into the avenue, still trading insults and obscenities.

The glittering crowd that poured through the etched-glass and mahogany portals of Maxim's in the rue Royale was still caught up in *Le Sacre* fever.

Henri, the distinguished, silver-haired mâitre d'hôtel, greeted us at the desk. "Good evening, Mademoiselle Chanel, Monsieur Capel. And *what* an evening. . . . Historic wouldn't you agree, Mademoiselle Caryathis and Monsieur Dullin? Your world . . . the world of dance has suffered an earthquake."

Word of the near-riot at the Champs-Élysées had reached him with the excited arrival of the after-theatre diners. Henri was always the first to know the inside story of any and all of the city's intrigues—financial, political, artistic, or amorous—and the most discreet keeper of its secrets.

"Will Diaghilev survive this debacle, do you think?" he asked us as he led us to a prominent banquette in the rear dining room where all Paris Society dined while unwary tourists were banished to the restaurant's long, narrow front room.

"Of course he will, Henri," Caryathis said indignantly. "He's a visionary in a world of philistines." *What, I wondered, had become of the 'crass impresario'?* "And besides, controversy always stimulates ticket sales. *Le Sacre* will ultimately be a triumph, mark my words. All of them—Diaghilev, Stravinsky, and Nijinsky—will be vindicated."

Though Henri had asked them both, Charles as usual was not allowed to get a word in edgewise. Carya was one of the most infuriatingly domineering women I'd ever met—and one of the loveliest. I'd secretly observed heads turn all over the dining room as we walked in. Coco and Carya were a brilliant contrast of dark and light with their daringly bobbed hair, Coco's matching black and white gowns in the Russian style, and their frankly sensual beauty. Charles and I were the envy of every man from violin player to vicomte in Maxim's that night.

The elegant room with its etched-glass mirrors swirled with dark mahogany in the style critics had dubbed "Art Nouveau," and the soft glow of the pink silk lampshades on the pink tablecloths was humming with an even greater electricity than its usual high voltage.

I ordered a jereboam of Cordon Rouge from the captain and counted on the very publicness of the place to diffuse the erotic tension I could feel building at our table. Coco, I could see, was almost sick with excitement, still in the grip of Stravinsky's raw, primal rhythms and bewildered by the torrent of conflicting passions they'd unleashed in that supposedly worldly audience—and in her.

How incredibly innocent she was, and how protective I felt toward her at that moment! She needed protection. Caryathis was clearly past mistress of manipulation. With the beluga caviar arrived her hand under the table, unbuttoning my flies, while with the other she coolly stroked the nape of Coco's swanlike neck and gently flicked an imaginary speck from her small, perfect breasts.

To someone used to assessing rivals, I knew Charles posed no threat. He had clearly been a willing party to Carya's sexual games before—it was probably the glue that bound them together. And I, with my gambler's instinct, was clinically curious as to just how far Carya's lust and jealous greed would take her.

So I allowed her to free my stiff penis and stroke it steadily, surreptitiously, while Charles fed her belon oysters and we spoke of the politics of the arts and the many ways the financial community might prove helpful to genius.

Ironically, through Carya's determined assault on my senses, all I could think of . . . all I could see and feel was Coco. At one point she and Charles got up from the table and delighted Maxim's veteran and seriously jaded orchestra with a brilliantly executed tango. Coco was as graceful and assured on the small, square floor as she was on horseback. When they resumed their seats the other diners burst into applause.

How very beautiful she was and how much I desired her. I would never let Caryathis have her.

When Coco excused herself to repair her makeup, I left Carya and Charles at the table on the pretense of needing some air and followed her up the red-carpeted stairway to the *"Dames"* where I tipped the attendant lavishly to disappear for a while.

Coco stood in front of the tall, pink-lit glass, flushed and overheated from the tango, with tiny drops of sweat beading the curve of that wide, sensual mouth. So intent was she on her own image, she was unaware of my presence.

I came up behind her and pressed my body against hers, my hands clasping her breasts, my hardness pushing into her. She gasped and turned into my embrace.

"Boy, what are you doing in here? Have you gone

mad? Someone will come in and see you and there will be a scandal that will titillate all my customers and your backers and make *Le Sacre* yesterday's news."

"I can't help it, Coco. I couldn't stand to watch that damned woman tease you for another moment. The intimate way she touches you at every opportunity. The way she caresses your hair, your neck, your wrist. The sick, twisted games she plays. You didn't know she was touching me under the table at the same time, did you? I won't let her take you from me, Coco. I have to have you for myself."

Silencing her protests with my demanding mouth, I pushed her back against the dressing table and lifted the skirt of her gown. Frantically unbuttoning my flies—clumsy in my urgency as Carya hadn't been—I freed myself, pulled down Coco's cool satin drawers and thrust up inside her.

She arched to me and uttered a single half-smothered cry.

We moved in that hot, precise, perfect dance of our own, and when we came it was together like it always had been with us since the first time.

As she rested in my arms and I tenderly brushed the black satin of her hair back from her lovely face, I made a silent promise. Somehow I would get Coco out of Paris—out of Carya's seductive orbit . . . out of the predator's reach. Coco Chanel, after all, was mine.

THREE

Coco
(1913-1915)

ONE

When Boy first suggested my opening a second salon outside of Paris, I was hesitant. We were doing so well in the rue Cambon. Gabrielle had generously given me programme credit for the two velvet tricorne hats I'd created for her leading role in *Bel Ami* right below Doucet *(mon dieu, Doucet!)* for the costumes, and that had influential new customers turning up on my doorstep every day.

I'd already had to expand into three more workrooms and I had close to a hundred seamstresses and assistants working for me, with Lucienne, the veteran milliner I had lured away from Caroline Reboux, happily tyrannizing the hatmakers, allowing me to concentrate my energies on the couture.

I was still using Adrienne and Antoinette as my models, with an occasional turn by Marthe Davelli, when she was between roles at the Opéra Comique. At the rate things were moving I knew I'd soon have to employ professional mannequins as well.

Even skeptical little Monsieur Le Brun had cheerfully admitted that "Chanel Modes" looked more like Trafalgar than Waterloo, after all. I'd negotiated an extension on the lease on most favorable terms and was well into paying off Boy's initial investment. I had never been so content as I was at rue Cambon.

Besides, I was reluctant to leave my friends—Gabrielle and Marthe and Suzanne and Jeanne, Cocteau and Charles, and that brooding young Basque poet Pierre Reverdy whom I'd met one afternoon at Carya's. He'd been sending me his newest verses and copies of his little review that he'd named *Nord-Sud* for the tramline between Montmartre and Montparnasse.

And of course there was Carya. How could I give up, even temporarily, the exhilaration of those amazing afternoons at the rue Lamarck? She had opened up a whole new world of ideas and experience to me.

Secretly, I wondered if Carya wasn't the real reason behind Boy's suggestion. Ever since that electrifying night of *Le Sacre,* he'd been openly disapproving of our close friendship. I couldn't seem to convince him it was nothing more than that—perhaps because I hadn't completely convinced myself.

As usual, Boy was infinitely persuasive. Any business in order to live *had* to grow, he argued. Look at his own example. From a single coal mine in Newcastle to an international enterprise spanning three continents. His initial faith in me, he reminded me only half teasingly, was not as a gifted amateur with a clever little hobby, but as a potential rival to the great giants of couture.

Vichy, he thought, with its flourishing spa, was a good growth opportunity. But I declined it immediately on the grounds of its being too far from Paris—too far from my suppliers. I couldn't let him know the real reason—sheer peasant superstition overruling the business judgment he admired. The hair on the back of my neck actually rose. To go within a country mile of the scene of the Didier debacle would so put me off my stride I'd probably never be able to design another dress. Only Adrienne knew how badly I had been wounded in Vichy. And only Adrienne would ever know.

Finally, we settled on Deauville, chic seaside resort of international Society, safely close to my suppliers and close enough to Paris for Boy to travel back and forth easily when he wasn't in London or Casablanca on business. Adrienne and Antoinette could come down to join me to help set up the new salon as soon as Boy and I found the most likely site. After the rue Cambon, I trusted his nose for real estate utterly. I'd estimated it would take six months or so to get established and that Lucienne could probably deputize for me in Paris for that long.

We hadn't been in Deauville for a fortnight before I was forced to admit to myself that, once again, Boy's instincts had been right. It *was* time for me to get away from Paris for a while. I had let the suddenness of my success there go straight to my head. I'd begun to lose track of my true priorities—my love for Boy and the work. Only at a distance could I see the strain my infatuation with Carya and her set—no, to be fair, with Carya—had put on our relationship. Small wonder Boy had been traveling so much. Small wonder he'd neglected his work on the book for the brandy bottle.

The stiff sea breezes blowing across the beaches of Deauville cleared my mind of the cobwebs of worldliness and confused loyalties.

Carya didn't love me. She hadn't seemed even slightly upset by the news of my departure, hadn't tried to persuade me to stay. She'd been amused and flattered by my wide-eyed adoration of her Bohemian lifestyle, her independence—the quality that always drew me.

Now, away from her influence, I understood that Carya was not independent at all. She was addicted—addicted to conquest. She was a collector of pretty prizes and, with my notoriety as the little provincial who'd dared to defy the fashion establishment, I had been her favor of that particular season. Had Boy not had the determination and the strength to rescue me from her—from myself, really—I would most certainly have been replaced by the next pretty face to take Paris by storm. Thank God for that strength of Boy's. Thank God for his love. It had been a narrow escape.

Alone with him in Deauville I would regain my bearings.

For the first week we did nothing but spend long, sweet sensual mornings under the eiderdown comforter of our bed in the lovely old wood-gabled Normandy Hôtel, reaffirming that incredible physical connection we had had from the start.

My desire for him had never been more intense. I was avid for him. When we had been together a lifetime, I would still not have had enough of his finely chiseled mouth on mine, those powerful hands that could demand wanton response from my willing body at one moment, then gentle me down with slow, steady caresses until I lay quietly beside him in the big four-poster bed listening to the Atlantic rollers receding down the shingle outside and to the receding thunder of my heart.

In the afternoons we would walk along the sand, following the curve of the beach and watching the bathers in their ridiculous costumes. I wore a pair of loose silk pants I'd designed after the style of Boy's pajamas and a cotton singlet of his that reached down to my mid-thighs, with one of his sweaters tied loosely around my neck. I was forever stealing his comfortable clothes. Heads were certainly swiveling in our wake.

"It's hard to believe, Boy, that women feel compelled to dress almost as elaborately for the ocean as they do for a day at the races. Here at the shore I want to be free to feel the sun and the sea on my bare skin—not shrouded in a long dress, wearing shoes and stockings and carrying a parasol, to boot. It's ludicrous."

"Well, they've taken off their stays at least, Coco, you have to give them that."

"I'm frankly surprised they make even that small concession, they're so hopelessly manipulated by the rue de la Paix."

"Make Deauville your beachhead then, if you'll forgive the god-awful pun." He laughed. "Start your revolution here and bring it back to Paris. You've certainly got a rich and influential enough constituency here to do it. I've been watching the women watch you walk down the beach, Coco. Believe me, their heads are spinning."

It was those beach walks that gave me the inspiration for my first Deauville collection. Not the aristocratic bathers, God knows, but the fishermen.

I loved their loose, simple long-sleeved sweaters, knit from local woolens, and their flat caps. Easy enough for me to adapt my signature boater hats to their slightly smaller dimensions, make them up in navy straw to match the knit tunics, and trim them with navy or white ribbons the way the fishermen of Normandy had worn them for centuries.

And a matching silk scarf, rolled and tied loosely around the waist of the tunic to serve as a belt. And a straight, simple, ankle-length skirt dropping down to short boots like the comfortable ones Adrienne and I had worn as spa attendants at Vichy. That was it. Short, simple ankle-high boots instead of the elaborate high-buttoned mid-calf contraptions that required an hour with patience and a buttonhook even to put on. I was sure Deauville would have a cobbler who could work to my design.

My mind was racing with new ideas. All that was required now was a place to execute and sell them. I could count on Boy for that. Within the week he had discovered an ideal and available space for me equidistant from the city's most fashionable hotel and the Casino. I was almost unsurprised. Boy had never let me down.

TWO

"*I* don't care *what* you say, Coco. It's simply unfair the way you try to run our lives." Antoinette was flushed with defiance.

Used to her moodiness by now, I continued calmly arranging the navy sailors' tunics and flat navy boater hats in the show window overlooking the sunny rue Gontaut-Biron. How well they'd turned out. The shop had been crowded from the first day I opened the door.

"Why do *you* put up with it, Adrienne?" She couldn't contain herself. "I know I'm four years younger and on her deathbed maman made us promise to do what she says, but *you* aren't even her sister. You're her aunt and you're two years older than she is. Besides, you're blonde and much more beautiful, and your gentleman is a Baron—even if he can't marry you. But you let her wind you around her little finger just like she does the rest of us. I, for one, am thoroughly sick of it."

Adrienne, ever the peacemaker, tried to calm her down. "Coco has our best interests at heart, Toinette. Look how she rescued you from the provinces and brought you up from Varennes to live in Paris."

"That's right, Adrienne," she retorted, "and I was having *fun* in Paris for the first time in my life. I had my own flat and my friends. I was even having a flirtation with the most adorable gendarme on my street. Now look at us. Can't you see the way she manipulates us all. Dragging us down here to Deauville on this wild scheme of Boy Capel's. All because the hats we made during the Season for his horsey set were a *succès fou* and that snooty Gabrielle Dorziat wore them in *Bel Ami*. Well, it's gone straight to her head and here we are at the seashore—only *not* on holiday like everybody else."

Toinette's jealous resentment of Boy had begun the first day they met. I could endure her sulks and tantrums, but I had no patience with her irrational attacks on him.

"Boy thinks Deauville is a splendid opportunity for

me—for all of us," I told her. "A way to consolidate the reputation I've made in Paris and expand my custom to the international set. They come here every summer for the racing."

"Easy for *him* to say, Coco! He only puts up the money—and he's got pots of it. We're the ones who have to do the sewing, the embroidery, the trimming, the pressing, the selling—*and* provide free modeling services for your creations on the Boardwalk every morning."

"You're always at your prettiest when you're angry, little Toinette," Adrienne said cheerfully, rearranging the drape of a pale, ankle-length woolen skirt on a wax mannequin. "Coco may tire your feet and try your patience, but she certainly picks up your color. Why, only yesterday morning on the Boardwalk I overheard one of the Russian grand duchesses refer to us as 'the three Graces.' *You* may not consider your sister a beauty, Toinette, but with that raven hair and those magnificent eyes it's my opinion Coco puts both of us blondes in the shade."

I understood Antoinette's chagrin. How hard it must be to be the younger—with a bossy big sister. Adrienne was never so infuriating to her as when she was being *fair* about me.

But even Toinette had to admit that the new salon was elegant, with its sparkling white awning and GABRIELLE CHANEL in simple, bold black letters. The customers had taken to sitting outside between fittings in the shade of the awning in white wicker chairs. They sipped *citron pressé* and gossiped scandalously about last night's gambling losses at the Casino and how Grand Duke Serge had installed his exquisite young mistress in a suite near our own in the Normandy across the way.

As Boy had predicted, "Gabrielle Chanel" had quickly become the meeting place for Deauville's idle Society beauties and their lovers and would-be lovers. If only Antoinette could curb her impatience with me, I might even put her in the way of a far more advantageous marriage than to her "adorable" gendarme.

Certainly I was at my wit's end over Adrienne's status with her baron. Once the Nexons got wind of Édouard's intention to marry her, they threatened to disinherit him. And Adrienne lives in a state of fond hope that they'll come to change their minds. Not in *our* lifetime, I'm afraid. I worry so about her.

At least I'm more realistic about my own situation with Boy. I know all too well that an outsider like Boy will eventually have to make a proper marriage. Clémenceau may have taken him up, but only the right heiress to the right title will put an end to those persistent rumors about Boy's shadowy parentage.

No, my beloved Boy could *never* marry an itinerant peddler's illegitimate daughter. It strikes much too close to home. Thank God I'm wise enough to understand that!

THREE

The highlight of the summer Season was the Grand Prix de Deauville, run for a purse of 100 thousand francs and considered by afficionados the equal of Ascot. As the end of August and the race approached, owners, breeders, jockeys, trainers, odds-makers—and their retinues of wives and marriageable daughters and mistresses—poured into the already crowded resort from all over France, from England, from as far off as Casablanca and Cairo and St. Petersburg, wherever the cult of equestrian speed and heart and stamina flourished. Not even the threat of war could dim the excitement of the annual ritual.

The Casino was packed every night with dinner-jacketed high-stakes gamblers. Kings' ransoms were won and lost at the tables. Kings' ransoms were worn by their gorgeously gowned and bejeweled ladies. Doucets . . . Worths . . . Poirets . . . I could pick them out at a hundred paces. Only Biarritz, Boy told me, could rival Deauville in carats of diamonds per millimetre of perfumed, pampered flesh.

In the evening after dinner the small, smoky hotel bar was full to capacity with vicomtes, barons, grand dukes, and pashas, and I lost Boy entirely to endless analyses of bloodlines, jockey weights, and past racing records from the studbooks.

While the gentlemen spent every day at the track, clocking the trials of the cream of their own studs or preparing to pick their favorites, their ladies shopped, shopped, shopped. Not for nothing was Deauville called the "21st Arrondissement." Even with Adrienne and Antoinette's full-time help and Marthe's welcome arrival for the race month, I had all I could do to keep up with the orders that were flowing in.

The knitted fisherman's tunics and matching boaters were an instant sensation with the *beau monde*. They loved what they laughingly christened my "rich poor look." In humble grey-shingled cottages dotted up and down the shorefront I had *actual* fishermen's wives knitting furiously on consignment to my designs.

The simple bathing dress in black trimmed with white, with its cap sleeves, mid-thigh tunic, and knee-length knickers, had been snapped up by legions of grateful bathers. I was frankly curious to know if "Chanel" would be recognized as having made an impact on the fashions in the stands and paddock on Grand Prix day.

What I hadn't counted on—or perhaps I'd allowed the press of work to push to the back of my mind—was Étienne. Of course he would be there. I'd already heard that his two-year-old filly Tout d'Accord, by the great D'Accord out of Allaway, was one of the two favorites. And when I saw his close friends the Chavagnacs and the St.-Sauveurs in the Casino—and found myself frigidly cut by them—I should have known Étienne could not be far behind.

It had been two years since I'd seen him, and I'd finally had to begin returning his letters unopened, as much to save him the embarrassment of my reading his blunt, agonized, and obsessive declarations as to assuage my own guilt at not being able to love him— at loving his best friend.

So when I looked up from the pale satin evening cape I was on my knees pinning on Adrienne and saw him standing there, his back to the dazzling sunlight coming from the shop door, I experienced an uncanny sense of *déjà vu*. For a moment I was that young, green convent girl again, mending uniforms for pennies, full of foolish dreams and unfocused longings. Before I knew there was a beautiful rogue called "Boy" Capel . . . before my own obsession began.

"Coco," he said quietly into the dimness of the shop, "more beautiful than ever."

I managed to get to my feet with some semblance of dignity. "How very good to see you, Étienne. I'm told I should have all my Deauville profits riding on your filly, Tout d'Accord, for the Prix."

"With Alec Carter up, how can she fail?" he said with a wry smile. "Alec sends you his warmest regards and memories of those golden times at Royallieu . . . as I do."

"Oh, Étienne," I moved forward and took both his hands in mine, "we were so very young then . . . such dreamers . . . not knowing what it was we really wanted." Adrienne had discreetly vanished into the back of the shop.

"Not true, Coco," he said, "I always knew it precisely. From the moment I parted the curtains in that godforsaken tailor shop in Moulins and looked into your astonishing eyes, I knew very well what I wanted . . . what I had to have. I just wasn't brave enough to go after it."

"Whatever happened to that 'enchanting blonde,' I wonder," I said teasingly, trying to keep the atmosphere light. "Still having tea with eligible officers, or married by now with two or three children tugging at her leading strings?"

"Don't toy with me, Coco," he said, his dark eyes serious. "You've had my letters—the ones before you stopped reading them. You know you're the only woman I've ever truly loved. You know it was only fear of my father's disapproval that held me back. Well, your absence has taught me that doesn't matter. My father lives his life according to his own notions of what's 'proper.' My own are different."

"Are they *truly*, Étienne?" I doubted it.

"I've defied him at every turn, Coco. Resigning my commission. Not going into the family business. Buying Royallieu and breeding thoroughbreds. Keeping company with rakes and gamblers and what he'd call 'loose' women. And falling wildly in love with a beautiful maverick with no title and not a franc in her dowry. My life could not be more different from the safe, predictable existence my father has in mind for me. But for it to work for me, for it to mean anything at all to me, I've realized that it has to include you. I want you, Coco. I need you in my life. I want to marry you."

I didn't know whether to laugh or cry. This honest, generous, openhearted man was risking his father's love, risking disinheritance to propose to me.

What a splendid irony. I knew the pain of rejection too well. My dreams still echoed to that slammed door at Aubazine when my own father turned his back on me. How could I do this without hurting him too badly? I was still holding tight to his strong hands.

"Étienne, you were my first lover and the first man who was ever a true friend to me. But I told you when I came to you at Royallieu, and I tell you again now, I am not made for marriage. My mother's experience has prejudiced me terribly against it. My temperament is wrong for it—I'm far too strong-willed to be ruled by a husband. Believe me, Étienne, as your wife I would make both our lives actively miserable."

"I *don't* believe you, Coco. We were happy at Royallieu. *You* were happy. I know it. I can still see you galloping across the fields with the wind in your hair or dreaming over one of your foolish novels by the library fire. We were perfectly happy there until that unscrupulous bastard abused my friendship and my trust and took you away from me. *That's* the reason you won't accept my proposal—it's still Boy with you, isn't it Coco?"

I looked straight into his honest eyes. "Étienne, I promise you one thing. I will never marry Boy Capel." It was not strictly a lie. The only man I would ever think of marrying would never ask me.

The next time I saw him was at the Grand Prix. As the locals said it had historically, the day dawned bright and beautiful. The banners of the various studs with their vivid racing colors snapping in the stiff Atlantic breeze made the stands and track look like the lists in a medieval jousting tournament out of one of the old costume books I'd studied in the Louvre.

There was a full field—fourteen promising two-year-olds—the finest horseflesh to be found within a five-thousand-mile radius, and ridden by the pride of international jockeys.

I recognized Étienne's turquoise-and-black colors right away and saw Alec backing a nervous, dancing Tout d'Accord into the starting gate. What a spectacular filly! A deep bay with a white blaze and white socks on her prancing hoofs. Étienne must be so proud. Breeding champions was clearly what he was born to do.

I hadn't seen him since that awkward moment in the shop. I'd made it my business to stay clear of the places where we were bound to meet—the Casino, the track, the Boardwalk. I had enough commissions to finish before the race and Grand Prix ball to preoccupy me and allow me to make my excuses to Boy in the evenings on the grounds of exhaustion. I didn't want him to know about our encounter. He'd felt more than enough remorse for Étienne after their ugly confrontation at Royallieu.

The horses were in the starting gate now, chafing to be away, and just as we took our seats in Boy's private box with Édouard de Nexon who'd managed to get leave from his regiment and a radiant Adrienne, the starter fired his pistol.

The fourteen leapt from the gate, and the other favorite, Pasha's Pride, from the stud of the Sultan of Muscat and Oman, took an immediate lead. Wearing the Sultan's scarlet-and-white silks, Adam Connaught—one of the reigning English jockeys the Arabs favored—let the big black have his head. He was running a furlong in front, followed by Grand Duke Dmitri's chestnut, Champagne Cognac, another big horse but more barrel-chested and shorter in the legs, with Franc Cardinale up.

Nose to nose with Champagne Cognac was Victoire,

another magnificent chestnut who must have stood seventeen hands. She was owned by the Baron de Rothschild and ridden by one of France's premier jockeys, George Le Mair. Rothschild's amethyst and gold colors flashed in the brilliant sunlight.

Where was Étienne's Tout d'Accord, the other favorite? Oh, there she was . . . quite far back in the pack as they thundered around the third turn. Why was Alec holding her in, I wondered? As they pulled out of the turn, I suddenly saw his strategy.

"Look Boy," I tugged at his sleeve, "Alec's been waiting until the pack thinned out to get the inside track. *Dieu,* look at her flying up the rail. She's amazing!"

"Did you put any money on her, petite, for *old* times' sake?" Boy asked wryly. "Mine's all on Pasha's Pride. She's clocked spectacular times in the trials and she's won her last two times out at Auteil and Enghien."

Tout d'Accord was gaining steadily on the two chestnuts. Alec had that remarkable telepathic communion a superb jockey enjoys with his mounts. He would simply indicate his intention and they would invariably give him passionate response. Tout d'Accord had come up on the inside and drawn even with Champagne Cognac and Victoire. It was definitely going to be a four-horse race. The other ten riders were eating dust.

The elegant crowd was electrified. The thudding of hoofs. The shimmering silks. The jockeys crouched low, asking the maximum from their splendid mounts. Everyone in the stands was on their feet as the four thundered toward the stretch. I was clutching Adrienne in my excitement and we were jumping up and down—all ladylike restraint abandoned.

Then something unprecedented happened. As they rounded the fourth turn into the stretch there was one of those horrifying collisions that haunt every jockey's nightmares.

Ferdinand Le Beau used his crop on Victoire who came over on Champagne Cognac who stumbled and forced Tout d'Accord to take up, jarring Alec loose from his seat. The two big chestnuts crashed to the ground in an agonizing tangle of flailing legs and leather.

But Tout d'Accord shot on ahead, with Alec clinging to her mane from below, his boots wrapped tight around her neck. In the stretch she pulled even with the front-runner, challenging Pasha's Pride with a final burst of speed born of equal parts heart and terror. As they crossed the finish line—Alec still clinging tight to her neck—Tout d'Accord was the winner by half a head. The stands erupted into wild cheering.

"What a performance, Boy," I cried. "I've never seen anything like it. Alec hung on like a burr on a jackrabbit!"

"But will the stewards allow the win?" Boy asked. "What do you think, Édouard? This must be one for the racing books."

"Look at the stewards' table," Édouard pointed. You could see the consternation among the grey-haired gentlemen of the Jockey Club. Then the chief steward rose to his feet, turned and addressed the crowd.

"The Grand Prix de Deauville has been won in a record time of two minutes, thirty-three seconds by Tout d'Accord, by D'Accord out of Allaway, owned by Monsieur Étienne Balsan of Royallieu stables, with Monsieur Alec Carter up. The stewards have ruled that because Monsieur Carter's feet did not at any point touch the ground and the weight, therefore, remained constant, Tout d'Accord is the clear winner of the race."

The stands went wild all over again. Top hats and boaters were flung into the air and flowers and lacy handkerchiefs rained down on the track.

After the ceremony in the Winner's Circle where the mayor of Deauville presented the heavy silver cup to Étienne, and the mayor's pretty wife placed a wreath of crimson and white roses around the neck of a sweated Tout d'Accord, we made our way back to the jockeys' room.

Miraculously, neither horses nor riders had been seriously injured in the smash-up in the stretch, so the atmosphere was celebratory. Champagne was flowing. I threaded my way through the mob with Boy trailing behind me. I could hardly wait to see Alec again and congratulate him on his astonishing ride.

When Boy and I finally got to his side, I threw my arms around him and kissed him hard on the mouth. *"Magnifique, magnifique!* I've never seen riding to touch it. How on earth did you manage to hang on?"

"Well, Coco," he said wickedly, "I kept thinking of the times when Émilienne and I have been in roughly that same position and how bloody embarrassing it would be for me to disengage."

At that moment Étienne, whose back had been to us while he gave an interview to the racing journalist from *L'Excelsior,* turned and came face to face with Boy for the first time since that wintry afternoon at Royallieu.

"Mes félicitations, Étienne," I said quickly, hoping to break the tension between them. "What a filly. They'll

be toasting her courage in every paddock from here
to St. Petersburg!"

"Thank you, Coco," he said gravely, taking my hands
and looking deep into my eyes as though we were the
only two people in the room. "And have you given further thought to my proposal. I do not intend to withdraw it."

Boy interrupted him, trying to rescue me from the
awkwardness. "And you have *my* best congratulations,
too, Étienne. She's a superb filly—bound to be the
mother of a whole line of Royallieu champions."

"I don't want your congratulations, Capel," Étienne
said curtly. In the sudden silence that had fallen over
the crowd I knew every man and woman in the room
was waiting, breath bated, for what would happen next.
The racing world was an incestuous microcosm and
everybody in it knew the intimate business of everybody else.

"Besides, what would you know of breeding, Capel?"
Étienne continued icily. "Your own bloodlines are so
clouded you don't even know the name of the mare
who threw you. We all know at least something of your
father, though don't we, Capel? If there's any truth to
the rumors, I'd be willing to make a considerable wager
that you're *circoncis.*"

His savage sarcasm was not lost on the gossips. *Cir-
cumcised.* He was giving public credence to the old
rumor that Boy was a Jew.

Boy paled visibly and slowly drew off one of his
suede gloves. For an endless moment I was afraid he
was going to call Étienne out. I had to do something.

Flushed with fury, I confronted Étienne. "It's true neither Boy nor I have impeccable bloodlines, Étienne.

Both of us, as you well know, are bastards. But neither one of us has ever done anything except wish you well. I only hope someday you'll have the wisdom and compassion to realize that." I turned my back, took Boy's arm in mine and swept through the curious crowd out of the jockeys' room.

FOUR

That night for the Grand Prix ball I was determined to look as spectacular as I ever had—as part of my continuing campaign to advertise "Gabrielle Chanel," even more to show the flag for Boy, to demonstrate to all the prying eyes and wagging tongues of international Society that neither of us had been even slightly damaged by that awful moment in the jockeys' room that afternoon.

Boy had not said a word about it but I knew and shared his fierce pride and his defensiveness when it came to origins. Étienne could not have chosen a more cruel—or efficient—way to get at him. Any lingering warmth I'd felt for my first protector died at the moment he'd stooped to low tactics I knew Boy, however desperate, would never even entertain.

Now he came up behind me where I stood in front

of the cheval glass adjusting the diamond earrings he'd given me.

The slim sheath of ivory silk skimmed my body, making a very great virtue of slenderness. And the matching triangular silk scarf I'd designed to accompany it was caught up on one shoulder with a gold and diamond clasp in the shape of a prowling lioness that Boy had brought me from Asprey after his last trip to London.

He put his arms around me and breathed into my hair. "Ravishing, petite Coco. There won't be a woman in the ballroom tonight to touch you. You know," he murmured, "I'd just as soon stay here in the suite and order up champagne and caviar and make love to you all night long." Tantalizingly he slid his hands down my back to cup me and draw me to him.

I knew Boy too well. Knew precisely what he was doing. Though he would never admit it, especially not to himself, he was reluctant to face the smirks and snickers of everyone who had heard of his encounter with Étienne.

All the more reason to be there. Gently I disengaged his hands from the place where I longed to keep them and slipped my arm through his.

"Lovemaking later, Monsieur Capel. Right now I have two burning desires. To show off this dress I designed for myself between commissions, and to dance the tango with you while all those ancient duchesses break their diamond-studded hearts with envy."

The ballroom of the seaside Casino was full of life and gaiety. The stud banners had been requisitioned by the decorations committee and hung from the ceiling, turning the prisms of the huge central chandelier into a kaleidoscope as they caught the vivid colors of the racing silks.

The bandstand was banked with flowers—mimosa, gardenias, lilacs, peonies—and the elderly gentlemen of the Deauville Chamber Orchestra, for whom this evening was an annual triumph, had carnations in the buttonholes of their shiny, threadbare dinner jackets or, in the case of the more dashing, behind their ears.

By the doors opening onto the terrace, close enough to the sea air to preclude the possibility of a swoon, were the resident dowagers on brocaded sofas, the opulent Russian grandes duchesses, the lofty vicomtesses and marquises, imposing in their *belle époque* armor of whaleboning and lace. A fortress of propriety. Only their vigilance, they knew, would prevent the sort of misalliances the warm sea breezes, the heady scent of mimosa and gardenia, and the rhythms of the tango were bound to inspire in their flowerlike, infinitely marriageable, dangerously seducible daughters and granddaughters.

When Boy and I came into the ballroom there was a distinct disapproving flutter of fans from the dowager brigade. We were unmarried, in love, living in sin—notorious. To my very great relief the first people we met were Adrienne and Édouard. How exquisite she looked in my lilac silk chiffon, her pale-blonde hair piled high on her head and threaded with violets and amethyst satin ribbons.

Édouard had the most extraordinary effect on her. Adrienne had always been a beauty, but a cool, composed one. In his presence she came blazingly alive with the force of her passion for him. As we crossed the floor, arms linked, Édouard and Boy following behind, every man in the room turned to watch her and every woman but me probably wished her dead.

We were quickly surrounded by admirers. Édouard had taken the precaution of pre-empting Adrienne's dance card and tucking it into his dinner jacket. Excuses to escape the surveillance of his family were few and far between, but the Grand Prix was one of them and he was taking no chance of sacrificing a single moment with her.

My own card was quickly filled in. Speculation among the idle rich about a woman with the audacity to go into trade, combined with rumors of the confrontation at the track, made me an intriguing curiosity. I only just managed to save two waltzes and a tango for Boy.

There was a ceremonial drumroll and the doors opened again to welcome the guests of honor. The mayor and his prettily dowdy wife led the way, followed by the runners-up for the Prix, a regal, towering Grand Duke Dmitri Pavlovich, the Tsar's handsome young cousin, resplendent in the uniform of the Imperial Horse Guards, the swarthy Sultan of Muscat and Oman, shining in his gold-brocaded djellaba like the sun on the Sahara, and the tall, slender epicene Baron de Rothschild, an eloquent testament to Paris's most expensive tailoring.

Then a shyly smiling Alec Carter, wearing the Royallieu silks of turquoise and black, dwarfed by a voluptuous, beaming Émilienne who looked more like his mother than his mistress. And finally the day's victor, Étienne, the proud winner of one of France's premier equestrian prizes. I could feel Boy freeze by my side.

The flowery speeches of congratulation were made, praising owner, horse, and rider in that order. . . . The ritual champagne toasts were drunk. Boy excused himself during the toasts to "get some air" on the terrace, and while he was gone the orchestra tuned up and the dancing began.

As I was whirled around the ballroom in the arms of yet one more bored, jaded marquis, I secretly counted the gratifying number of "Chanels" on the floor and gave one ear to yet another conversation limited strictly to horses, which I enjoyed, and a sort of obligatory compulsion to try to seduce me, which I did not.

Boy danced by me, the loveliest of the blonde, vapid princesses de Polignac in his arms. Over her slender shoulder he gave me a theatrical wink. I was struck all over again by the difference between my lover and these vain, arrogant, empty men.

Looking around that crowded room, full of youth and beauty and the music of money, I saw no one besides Boy who could possibly afford me. Oh, there were a number of men there who could buy and sell him many times over, but that didn't mean they could afford me. I was expensive in a way none of them with their blinkered, conventional vision of a woman's purely decorative role, could possibly understand or support. My intensity of feeling, my drive for perfection, my determination to succeed in the world on worldly terms would simply terrify them.

I had come from nothing and I was damned if I would leave this world in the sad, helpless, invisible way my mother had, without making my mark on it.

How had I found a man wise enough to accept me just as I was? With his Eastern sense of fate, Boy would probably tell me it was "written" . . . destined that we meet. Not the simple random chance of his being a friend of Étienne's—of his turning up there on the terrace that miraculous unexpected morning at Royallieu.

Just at that moment, as though I'd summoned him up, I felt a tap on my shoulder and turned to find myself face-to-face with Étienne. All the fury of the afternoon's bitter exchange was gone. Étienne could not afford me, and deep in his heart he knew it. His refusal to accept defeat . . . his continuing struggle to deny the truth of the situation was what had turned him ugly and provoked his cruelty to his closest friend.

"I'm sorry, Coco," he said with quiet dignity. "You and Boy have every right to despise me. I despise myself right now. You were the only woman I have ever wanted and I couldn't bear losing you to him. I don't know if I can bear it now, but I do know I have to try. Will you have one last dance with me, Coco, for forgiveness' sake?"

"For friendship's sake, Étienne," I said as I stepped forward into his arms. If Boy saw us out on the dance floor, with all Deauville Society watching and wondering, I knew that he would understand. Boy could easily afford me. He was strong enough to let me be strong.

FIVE

I knew when he proposed a holiday in Biarritz that Boy was trying to make up to me for his increasingly frequent trips to Paris and London.

"You've pushed yourself so hard opening the new salon, petite Coco. Now that it's the triumph I knew it would be—now that all the Grand Prix commissions are behind you—you deserve a proper rest."

I was lying warm in his arms, drowsy from early-morning lovemaking, in the ornate carved bed in our suite in the Normandy.

Smoothing the damp curls back from my forehead, he kissed me gently, lingeringly, then lightly traced the curve of my throat with the tip of his tongue. "Besides," he breathed softly into my ear, "I'm tired of all the customers, the suppliers, even Adrienne and Antoinette and Marthe . . . everybody vying for your attention. I never get to see you alone. I practically have to make an appointment. I know you'll tell me the whole thing was my idea, but it's consuming you. I want to have you to myself for a change. I *miss* you, Coco."

He sounded like a forlorn little boy. That was the heart of his endless attraction for me—the contrast between the commanding maleness he showed to the world and the secret depths of need and vulnerability he trusted me enough to let me see.

"All right, Boy." I slipped out of his embrace and wrapped myself, as I loved to do, in his paisley dressing robe because it carried a faint scent of his skin in the silk. "Let's pack and go today—right now. Before I have time to feel guilty about the shop. I've always wanted to see the 'Beach of Kings.' It's ironic that all I've done since we arrived in this resort town is work . . . work . . . work. I actually think I've worked harder here than I *ever* did in Paris."

Less than an hour later, a disgruntled Antoinette left in charge of the salon, we were speeding along the hair-pin curls of the coastal route in the brilliant afternoon sunshine down to Biarritz in Boy's new Hispano-Suiza.

After me and horses, Boy loved fast cars best, and this sleek silver beauty with its soft pale-grey glove-leather interior and its high-powered engine evoked the same direct sensual identification he made with his thoroughbred mounts. Boy was a brilliant driver. He and the car were one. Even though we were driving at speeds more appropriate to Le Mans, and he had one arm around me holding me close, I felt entirely safe with him. Boy was invulnerable, so I was too.

As we swept down the roadway into Biarritz, I laughed out loud. "This isn't a city, Boy, it's a *pâtisserie!* Look at those villas up in the hills and along the bluffs— pink and yellow and lime green—and decorated with all that rococo molding. *Petits fours!* And what's that in-credible blue-and-white fantasy in the middle—a wed-ding cake?"

"That, chère Coco, is the Casino where I am going to take you tonight, looking ravishing as usual, and win millions of frivolous francs at the baccarat table so I can buy you a pair of emerald and gold earrings to catch the green and gold glints in those hypnotic black eyes of yours."

We stayed at the lovely red-brick Hôtel du Palais, once the villa of Napoleon III and his gorgeous Empress Eugénie, in another opulent suite looking out over the manicured lawn to the golden sands of the Grande Plage and the wild, curling surf of the Atlantic.

In September the hotel was half empty, but it was still warm enough for us to dare the breakers and explore the serpentine walks carved into the face of the cliffs. At every turn, like a cocotte with a fan, they revealed another breathtaking glimpse of the sea crashing ceaselessly against the rocks below.

It was a time out of time—stolen from the work and the lengthening shadow of war—in a fantasy city by the sea.

The old magic between us was as strong as ever. Waiting for him to join me in the hotel bar, I would tease myself by sitting with my back to the door till he came up behind me and kissed the nape of my neck, blowing gently on my short-cropped hair. I would always know the precise moment he came into the room, my sensual awareness of him was so acute.

He was the same. We couldn't stop touching each other. Any excuse would do. No sooner had the door of the ornate cage-lift closed behind us and the little car begun its creaky climb to our third-floor suite than he would back me against the mahogany paneling, pressing the full length of his strong slender athlete's body hard against mine, while his mouth explored mine as hungrily as though he had never tasted me before. His hands moved possessively over my body, claiming me again, leaving fire wherever they touched. By the time we reached our floor, I would be actually trembling with desire for him.

Strange, that sensual shivering. I had never felt it with Étienne—only seen it in the paddocks when a nervy high-strung mare in heat waited braced and shivering for the first thrust. Boy had that effect on me. He had from the beginning. He always would.

We were sitting in a dockside café in the ramshackle little Port des Pêcheurs, the old fishing village backed defensively away from the ocean right up against the cliff face. We were drinking a sharp local red wine and eating that fiery fish soup the Basques call *ttoro,* and Boy was telling me the legend of the cave beneath the stone lighthouse that towered two hundred feet above the harbor, keeping it safe from marauding pirates—and now, surely, from the invading *Boches.*

"An old fisherman told me they call it 'La Grotte de la Chambre d'Amour,' because a reckless young nobleman and a fisherman's daughter would risk the incoming tide to make love there, in hiding from the fury of their families."

"And what happened to them, Boy?" I asked, a sudden shiver of premonition running through me. "Did they eventually persuade their families to accept their love?"

"They never had the chance. The tides here are treacherous, and one night they were so rapt in their love they forgot time altogether. The tide swept in and they drowned. Some locals still say it was a suicide pact. Do you want to try it with me tonight, petite Coco? To make love in the 'Grotte d'Amour?' The tide's out now. I'm willing to risk everything for a single night in your arms. Are you?"

"Don't tease me, Boy," I said, suddenly serious. "It reminds me too much of Adrienne and Édouard. How will their story end? I can't imagine."

"All right then, petite," he refused to let me slip into melancholy, "come riding with me instead. We can hire horses and ride along the Plage de la Côte des Basques. It's much rockier and more untamed than that sandbox in front of the hotel."

His high spirits were contagious. We made our way, laughing and light-headed from the wine, to the local stable where we hired what Boy told me would inevitably be a couple of hacks reserved for the "romantic moonlight beach ride." Far from it. We'd forgotten the Basques' reverence for horseflesh.

They were splendid animals. Mine was a silver-grey mare whose dish face, proudly curved neck, and compact body spoke of an Arab somewhere in her blood. Boy had a coal-black stallion that must have stood close to seventeen hands. He was so headstrong, Boy had all he could do to hold him in as we picked our way down the winding path to the *plage.* At the foot of the cliffs, he dismounted and set about unsaddling the black.

"Come on, Coco, we'll take off the saddles and our clothes and ride this beach bare-arsed and free the way God intended us to!"

I could never resist him when he was in one of his daredevil moods. We piled our clothes and the saddles behind a boulder and bareback, using only the bridles to guide us, galloped naked and strong and utterly abandoned down the pale stretch of sand, Boy and the black rocketing ahead, but my game little mare keeping the pace not far behind.

The full September moon lit the sand and picked out the boulders standing like dark sentinels watching our black and silver shadows—pagan centaurs, half-horse and only half-human—hurtling along the water's edge as the tide swept toward us.

At the end of the beach, Boy leaped from his mount, secured the reins under a rock and turned to lift me down from mine.

Even with the stiff breeze coming off the sea, it was surprisingly warm on the sand. Boy pulled me down on top of him, the night and the wildness of our ride beating in him—panting, silent, ruthless in his first urgency to take me.

The second time he was tenderness itself, turning me so that I lay beneath him on the sand, using his deft hands and his mouth, he slowly took possession of my entire body, licking my closed eyelids, my lips, the sweat from my breasts as he did that first day at Royallieu, burying his face between my legs and teasing my senses with his tongue until I was tense and trembling and crying out for satisfaction.

"First this, petite Coco." He rose over me, his beautiful manhood throbbing in his hands, and began gently rubbing it between my breasts, teasing my nipples with the tip until I felt my climax begin to build again inside me. Then, as he reached his own, he controlled himself so that the droplets fell one by one around my neck until they formed a perfect strand of iridescent pearls, shimmering in the moonlight.

"A gift of night magic to match your peerless beauty,

chère Coco," he said and then he plunged into me and the tides of our reckless passion swirled unchecked within me. Our wild cries, as we came together, drowned in the crashing surf.

SIX

"*I* won't do it, Coco. And nothing you can say will make me change my mind. So don't even bother to try out your usual repertoire of bribes and threats and flattery."

"But Toinette, you'll *adore* Biarritz." Boy and I had fallen in love with the fantasy city the year before the war broke out and had just stolen another delicious, idyllic week there when he got leave from his service with Sir John French's British forces. "We could hardly bear to cut short our holiday when Boy was called back to London."

I could never admit to wondering what—or even worse *who*—might have so urgently summoned him away from my side. Was I more afraid of the war or of another deeper threat to our security that I felt in my peasant bones but couldn't name?

"It's the last bastion of international Society . . . the Russians are there, the whole Spanish court," I rushed on. "You won't believe the nightlife at the Casino, Toinette. You'd scarcely know there was a war going on."

"That's just it, Coco. There *is* a war on. This is no time to be thinking of something as frivolous as opening another fashion salon."

"You haven't seen the Villa Larralde, Toinette," I persisted. "It's exquisite—the perfect site for the third salon. It will make this place seem shabby by comparison. You must admit Boy was right about our staying on here when everyone else went racing back to Paris. He predicted the German advance would inevitably drive our customers back to Deauville, and it did. We've seldom been so busy. He's right about Biarritz, too. It's a golden opportunity to expand!"

"Expand . . . expand . . . Coco, it's *wartime.*" Antoinette was wild with exasperation. She'd never shared my vision. "Where will you get the fabrics? You don't even know the Basque importers."

"I'll devote one of the Paris workrooms entirely to meeting the orders you forward from Biarritz."

"Coco, you're not listening to me. I will *not* go to be your directrice in Biarritz. If you're set on this lunatic scheme, send Adrienne. She's much more biddable than I am."

"More biddable, perhaps, but not such a capable administrator. Her mind is forever on Édouard. All she lives for are his letters from the Front. She has the concentration of a butterfly. I couldn't trust her to manage the accounts, let alone the entire salon."

"Why this obsession with expansion, Coco? Paris is flourishing and we're doing very well here. Why not wait until the war is over? It could get worse, you know. The battle reports from the north are grim."

"I *must* expand, Toinette. The business *must* grow. There *must* be new revenues. You don't understand, I promised maman I would look after you. And I need to send money to Julia-Berthe and the boys. Besides, there's no sign of the *Boches* here in Deauville. Please, ma chère, you simply have to help me. Maman would have wanted it."

Antoinette understood my absolute terror of poverty. She could identify with it. Even though she was much younger, she could remember those bleak years of following papa from dream to dream to nightmare . . . too many times of bed without dinner and cold rooms with no fire on the hearth. The gnawing insecurity that would never entirely leave us.

"All right, Coco, I surrender as usual," she said resignedly. "I'll go to Biarritz as soon as we finish fulfilling the orders from the collection here. But damnit, at some point you're going to have to admit that you can't arrange *everything* . . . that life won't always conform to your precious ideals of beauty and cleanliness and order."

SEVEN

"Take these uniforms down to the depot, Toinette." I thrust the bulky, hastily wrapped parcels into her arms.

"Why can't *you* take them, Coco? Or at least come with me? They're too heavy for me to manage alone."

We'd been up all night, cutting and stitching furiously, dispatching to the dustbin ruffles and bows—any and all fripperies—to turn the chambermaids' aprons from the Normandy across the way to nurses' uniforms. I'd used all my charm, and Boy's influence, to persuade the hotel manager to give us the aprons, then driven the four of us relentlessly to convert them.

The first morning light filtering in through the show window found Adrienne and Marthe, who'd come to join us when the government closed all the theatres and cafés for the duration, sound asleep at the worktable, their heads cradled on their arms.

Only Antoinette and I had managed to keep our eyes open, and now she was accusing *me* of deserting her.

"Oh, Coco, why is it that *I* always end up with the donkey work?"

Reluctantly, I helped her wrestle the packages out the salon door onto the rue Gontaut-Biron. The street was deserted, only an occasional light in the window of an early riser. We made our way through town, enveloped in sea-mist and eerie silence.

Only as we approached the depot did I begin to see signs of life—or, more accurately, of death. My heart nearly stopped. The station that had, till then, seen only aristocratic holidaymakers in their silks and lace and Paris finery was a scene out of nightmare. Smoke rose from the engines of two trains shunted onto sidings. A third was just pulling into the depot. On flatcars strewn with rough coverings of hay and straw, and on filthy, bloodied blankets spread hastily along the station platform, lay row upon row of wounded *poilus*—hundreds of them—the first casualties of the battle of Charleroi.

Where were the army doctors? Where were the nurses? Clumsily we felt our way down the platform. I was terrified of stepping on an outstretched limb. The stench was terrible—blood and pus and gangrene. All around us were muttered prayers and curses and cries of agony.

"Mademoiselle, Mademoiselle . . ." a young private, half his chest shot away, pulled at my skirt. "Help me, please . . . it hurts, Mademoiselle . . ."

Just as I was about to drop my bundle and run back to the shop in terror, I saw a doctor and two young women, the princesses de Polignac, bending over one of the wounded.

"Docteur," I touched his sleeve. "I am Mademoiselle Chanel. I have brought the nurses' uniforms."

He straightened up and glared at me. "And not the nurses. Why are you wasting *my* time? As you see I am one of the few doctors here. Distribute them, Mademoiselle, give one to your friend and put one on yourself.

Until more doctors or the Red Cross arrives, we need every pair of hands we can get."

Struggling against an overpowering wave of nausea, I unwrapped my package and gave a uniform to Antoinette and to the young princesses.

"Thank you, Mademoiselle," said one with a wry smile, tying on the apron, "but I fear you come too late to save this gown." Her exquisite morning dress of embroidered white lawn was soaked with blood.

Somehow, I made myself continue down the platform and across to the sidings. Antoinette and I passed out nursing aprons to the cream of Deauville Society— the duchesses and grandes duchesses, the vicomtesses and marquises—young and middle-aged, some in their seventies who had rallied to help save the victims of the *sales boches*.

What seemed hours later I was helping a harried young doctor, who looked little more than a boy himself, vainly trying to save a group of infantrymen who had been gassed in the trenches and were strangling on their own vomit. Over the harsh, terrible retching, I heard familiar voices.

"Adrienne," I called out, "over here. We need your help."

Adrienne and Marthe hurried to our side.

"Mon dieu, Coco," Adrienne said, "this is ghastly. How long have you been here? You look so tired and pale." She smoothed back the sweat-soaked hair from my face.

"I don't know how long, Adrienne . . . hours, forever. But I do know one thing. Anyone who can apply a bandage or administer chloroform is needed."

Adrienne and Marthe hastily tied on aprons and the

white cotton bands I had fashioned to hold back my own unruly curls. We moved off beside the young doctor, helping him change dressings, tying tourniquets on crudely amputated limbs, carefully doling out the pathetically small amount of morphine that remained to staunch a tidal wave of pain. For every one we were able to save, three were carried off on blanket-shrouded stretchers.

I was like an automaton. The old habit of command had taken me over and I was tireless, bossy, ordering the three of them to fetch and carry ... fresh bedding and bandages and clean slop basins ... impatient when they were clumsy, scolding when they were slow, just as though we were back in the workroom during an endless fitting.

At one point I was sponging the forehead of a cavalry officer with a raging fever.

"Maman, you're so very beautiful. Please take my hand. I won't be afraid to die, if you'll just hold onto my hand."

My eyes met Antoinette's in dismay. Both his arms had been blown away when his horse stepped on a landmine. What else was there to do? "Of course, *mon pauvre petit.* There now, I'm holding on tight," I said calmly. "You don't need to be afraid anymore."

"Goodnight, maman," he said in a sigh. A moment later I reached out and gently closed his eyelids.

Until dawn ... until we were dropping with exhaustion, the four of us tried to do what little we could in that charnel house of carnage and pain. As we made our way, filthy and sweated and bone-weary, back along the rue Gontaut-Biron, Antoinette took my hand.

"Thank you, ma chère Coco. I know what staying there must have cost you."

"No, little Toinette, you were right after all. I thought of Boy and Édouard and our brothers Alphonse and Lucien—and of all those other brave, foolish young men rushing to their death, chanting *'Le mort n'est rien . . . Vive la tombe,'* and I *had* to stay."

EIGHT

*L*ike most of my decisions, the one to go back to Paris was made on pure instinct. The original six-months' estimate I'd done when we came to set up shop in Deauville had been extended by the war to nearly two years. Even though Lucienne's regular reports on the good health of the business reassured me, I was eager to be back in the rue Cambon again.

Besides, since the grim days of nursing the dreadfully wounded survivors of Charleroi, Deauville had become a haunted place to me. My old insomnia had returned with a vengeance, and the few restless hours I could manage were filled with graphic nightmares of the loss of Boy—Boy with his limbs blown off like that poor *poilu* who'd died in my arms . . . Boy in the trenches with the deadly hail of artillery shells marching closer and closer to him. Worst of all, Boy being comforted in the embrace of a young woman whose curtain of pale-blonde hair hid her face from me.

In the sane light of day I knew these for what they were—night terrors brought on by being separated from him for too long and by the lurking sense I had that the perfection of our love somehow tempted Boy's old ally, Fate. But they were sufficiently disturbing for me to decide to pack up and make my way back to Paris.

A still-protesting Antoinette had been dispatched to Biarritz, and Adrienne and I gathered our things, left a responsible local seamstress in charge of whatever trade there might be until the next Season, and had our bags carried to the station.

What I hadn't counted on was the herd instinct of the aristocrats. The platform was mobbed with whole families of Rothschilds, Sauvignys, and Greffulhes who had made their usual joint decision that, with the fighting concentrated now in the bloody trenches to the north, it was probably safe enough to return to the capital.

I had to bribe a porter substantially to get us on the afternoon train at all, and we ended by sitting on our cases out in the smoky corridor, with all the compartments jammed to overflowing. *Dieu merci,* I had even-tempered Adrienne as my traveling companion. Antoinette would have been in hysterics by now.

The only signs of war we saw as we crossed the wintry countryside were the occasional troop convoys driving north along the empty roadways. There was little or no gasoline available for private travel, and periodically we were shunted onto sidings so that hospital trains with red crosses painted on their sides and roofs could pass on the way to the Front to collect the casualties of the terrible slaughter we knew was going on there.

As darkness fell and the ink-blue blackout curtains were drawn, the atmosphere on the train grew almost festive. Bottles of wine were produced and passed hand to hand. Someone broke out an accordion and soon we were singing the popular ballads of Mistinguett and Yvonne Printemps, *"Mon Homme"* and *"Parlez-moi d'amour,"* as though the horrors of war could somehow be kept at bay by the love of a good woman for her man.

Four

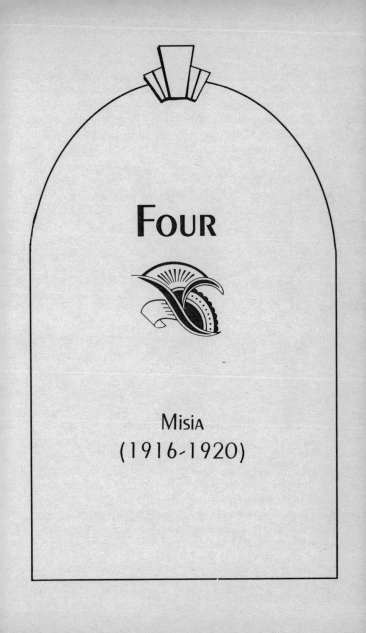

Misia
(1916-1920)

ONE

Could I possibly have known on that first evening the profound impact she would make on my life? Could I have envisioned that for more than thirty years our destinies would intertwine and, between us, we would weave that intricate web of love and hate, support and rivalry, tenderness and treachery that is an intimate friendship between one strong, manipulative woman and another?

All I *am* sure of is that, as I watched her down Cécile Sorel's long, candlelit dining table on that evening late in May—watched her with her graceful swan's neck and carbon-black eyes—I knew she was secretly observing *us* and calculating how she might best gain entrée to our magic circle of revolutionary music and painting and dance that was setting Paris ablaze.

And more, I knew with a terrible certainty I had already fallen under the spell of the silent sorceress whose irresistible charm and shocking *style masculin* had transformed a little milliner up from the provinces on the arm of a rich protector into the new force in fashion.

In only two years she had expanded her premises into five workrooms employing three hundred seamstresses, had been hailed in America by *Harper's Bazaar* for the charmingly simple chemise dress that was the highlight of her Biarritz collection, and had become the first one audacious enough to challenge the undisputed reign of that fat fantasist, Paul Poiret. In place of his ridiculous Turkish harem dresses, she had given us freedom of movement, elegance of line, and a delicious androgyny that perfectly matched the mood of Montmartre.

And I knew that as eager as she was to know us, I was equally determined to penetrate that artful disguise and come to know *her*, the source of her sure instinct for survival, the essence of her genius.

For, as all Paris knows, I have always been a collector of genius. By the time of our meeting, I had already survived two marriages. The first, the marriage of my girlhood, was to gentle, scholarly Thadée Natanson who had turned our Paris apartment in the rue St.-Florentin and our country house at Valvins into twin sanctuaries of art and literature.

There the poets of Thadée's beloved *Revue Blanche,* Valéry, Verlaine, and Mallarmé, would gather to read their new works and drink our very old wine late into the night. And at Valvins on the banks of the sunshot Seine I had been painted so many times—by Vuillard, who hoped I would return his passion; by impetuous, roguish Bonnard; and that tragic cripple Toulouse-Lautrec, who burnt himself alive in the flame of his own genius.

Although I would prefer to forget my second marriage, I cannot seem to. Alfred Edwards, impresario and all-powerful owner of *Le Matin*—that huge, coarse coprophiliac whose obsession with me cost first my marriage to Thadée, and nearly my sanity as I was drawn into destructive thrall to his dark passions. Strangely, the portraits—were there eight of them?—that the dying Auguste Renoir painted of me in that period show only my unchanged surface beauty (though I *did* make him weep by refusing to let him paint my breasts) and fail to reflect the decay I felt consuming me from within.

That rainy afternoon when my jealous madness drove me to go to Alfred's mistress, the voluptuously beautiful, bisexual actress Geneviève Lantelme, to beg her for the return of my husband's affections, she demanded as the price one million francs, the pearl necklace I wore—and *me* in her bed. That was the low point in my life, and neither my divorce from Edwards nor Lantèlme's mysterious drowning off the *Aimée,* the yacht he bought for me in the first hours of his infatuation, entirely freed me from the shadows of that time of terrible debauchery.

So this is the Misia, enjoying a pleasant dalliance with yet another fashionable painter, José-Maria Sert, infinitely more worldly and ten years older than the "little milliner" sitting four places down at Cécile's glittering table . . . This is the Misia who believed she could never love again, yet who is about to be caught up in one of the two great passions of her life—both for women, the first for Mademoiselle Coco Chanel . . .

José, of course, sensed it before I did.

"You know, Tosche," he said, laughing slyly as he took my wrap, "I've seen these instant intimacies of yours blaze up before. Remember Colette? That time when the two of you danced the *Rêve d'Égypte* at the Moulin Rouge? Even Diaghilev was scandalized which takes some doing. Only that sublime fool, Willy, was oblivious of the sapphic overtones . . . but then, I suppose he's unaware of anything beyond collecting Colette's royalties."

"I can't imagine *what* you're referring to, Jojo." If he could call me by my pet name while mocking me, I could pay him back in kind. "You know Colette and I only did it as a lark."

"Of course, Tosche my darling, as you say. Perhaps you're forgetting the gold pendant she gave you, engraved . . . now, what was it . . . ?"

"Engraved, *'I belong to Missy,'* as I recall. I think I've lost it," I said lightly, attempting to put him off whatever scent he thought he was following. "Besides, I only did it because I knew you secretly enjoy having two notorious women on your arm. After all, you have to live up to your reputation—that your appetites are as immense as your frescoes."

Quelled, but surely not vanquished, he poured us a conciliatory cognac.

This time what he, or perhaps both of us, failed entirely to take into account was the intensity of my burgeoning obsession with Coco. Colette *had* been a lark—my endless temptation to walk the wire, balancing precariously between adulation and infamy. This, I knew in my Eastern soul, was something altogether different, something far more dangerous.

In the weeks that followed that significant encounter at Cécile's I took Coco up with a vengeance. It was easy enough. She wanted it so very badly. And her wartime triumph in Deauville, when the theatres closed and the actors and artists and set designers followed their fleeing patrons south out of the line of fire, had already spun her into the orbit of that elite circle where I stood unchallenged as fixed star and center.

Now, night after night, she would rendezvous with us at the Meurice, pretending to admire my pink Venetian shot-silk draperies, my pink quartz ming trees, my mother-of-pearl fans, and Jojo's gilt, rococo studies for the massive frescoes for the Waldorf in New York, when I knew very well her taste ran to the simple, the linear, if not the monastic and austere.

At first her lover, Boy Capel, Clémenceau's protégé, the English arriviste who had set Coco up in business and was said to be keeping her in his flat on the Quai de Tokyo, would join us, and we would make the evening's round—a vernissage, the ballet with my darling Diaghilev, who, to my slight chagrin was clearly taken with Coco. Then dinner at Maxim's or Larue's where— after enough champagne—Nijinsky and his sister Bronislava could easily be persuaded to dance on the tables, then a prowl until first light through the smoky *boîtes* of Montmartre.

Coco was tireless. When even Jojo was about to fall in the traces, she would gaily urge us on.

"Come on, *mes amis particuliers,* it's not even daylight! Have you spent too much time in the atelier, Jojo *mon semblable?* And you, Boy, worn out from increasing your holdings on the Bourse?"

Boy knew her well and even tried to warn us. "You take up her challenge at your peril, my friends . . . until you've seen Coco on horseback. She can ride the most ardent polo players or hunt the Francport hounds into the dust and then dance until dawn. *Petite* Coco is a woman of compleat stamina."

Of completely compelling beauty, too, I added to myself. We made a dashing band, the three of them dark and dazzling: José with his swarthy, bearded grandee charm, Boy with his burning blue eyes and jet hair and moustache—black-Irish ("Jewish," some whispered maliciously behind his back), certainly one of the most magnificent young men my collector's eyes had ever beheld—and Coco with her wild gypsy beauty. All setting off my red-gold radiance to perfection.

Coco and I vied as to who would be the most outrageous. Sometimes we played at dressing to the outer limits of her own *style masculin,* in white tie and tails to match our escorts, like four spendthrift dandies out on the town. I'd learned from my childhood tutor, Franz Liszt's formidable mistress, George Sand, the indiscreet charm of cross-dressing.

It did not take long, though, for Boy to recognize the powerful undercurrents coursing between us. Surprisingly—perhaps because of the rumors that had come to my ears of his *own* infidelities—he felt threatened by me, uncertain of his once-secure hold on Coco.

She and I were forever exchanging confidences. At every turn, as new women friends inevitably do, we looked for correspondences between our lives. And at every turn we found them.

For her father the "wine merchant" who had, in Coco's telling, forsaken his homeland, stunned by grief, but had probably deserted his dying wife and his children and was still chasing skirt in some market town, I had my own. My father, the second-rank sculptor Cyprien Godebski, had run off with my seductive Aunt Olga. He left my three-month-pregnant mother to follow him three-thousand kilometres where, in a blinding blizzard, she beat brokenheartedly on the door of his mistress's house. Ultimately she died giving birth to me in St. Petersburg.

We both understood too clearly the powerful fascination of charming, domineering, and abandoning men.

For Coco's lonely years at Aubazine that left her wedded to nunlike notions of thrift and regular bathing, I had my own eight-year incarceration in the Convent of the Sacred Heart. We'd even shared a benighted passion for the stage—Coco's imaginary rivalry with Yvette Guilbert, my own feeble challenge to Sarah Bernhardt.

And, without ever articulating it precisely, we hinted at our attraction to beautiful women . . . those hot, breathless early infatuations. My schoolgirl crush on my glorious stepmother, Catherine; Coco's on her dance mistress, the bohemian Caryathis, one of my own admirers and much addicted to art and beauty wherever she found it in young men—and especially in young women.

Oh, *yes,* we were the best of friends, though neither of us wished, or dared to acknowledge, the strong subtext of sexuality flickering like the city's summer heat-lightning between us and charging our every exchange.

It had, inevitably, to come to flashpoint. The occasion was the Beaumont's *Bal des dieux et des déesses,* a gathering of Paris's most fashionable gods and goddesses and all their attendant minor dieties.

It was the most coveted invitation of the Season. This was to be Coco's debut into the closed society of the Faubourg St.-Germain. We arrived on the rue Duroc at the height of the evening. Hundreds of flambeaux blazed, illuminating the facade of the beautiful eighteenth-century mansion and lighting the winding pathways of the lavish gardens.

At the very heart of the long, mirrored ballroom with its fifty Lalique chandeliers, blatantly designed by its owner to rival—if not to dwarf—Versailles, stood Comte Étienne de Beaumont, tall, slender with the aquiline nose and sharply pointed chin my dear friend Cocteau so affectionately caricatured. At his side, his darkly beautiful Comtesse Édith.

They were dressed as Zeus and Hera, the ultimate arbiters of elegance and talent, Étienne holding a stylized silver thunderbolt, Édith in a gorgeous gown of blue and green satin, its skirt made of layer upon layer of irridescent, golden-eyed feathers of the peacock, Hera's emblem, and holding two live and extremely restless peacocks on satin leashes.

Zeus and Hera. What could have been more appropriate? For twenty years they had reigned undisputed over Paris Society. None had the sheer audacity, or the sheer wealth, to achieve the splendor of the Beaumonts' "entertainments." They had met and vanquished challengers as ambitious as poor Poiret who had bankrupted himself on his *Bal Shéhérezade* in a vain attempt to unseat them. After that, no one wished to risk the social oblivion that would follow a thunderbolt from our own Zeus. The Beaumonts' approval was tantamount to a passkey to every aristocratic drawing room in the Faubourg, and I knew my adorable orphan was desperate to possess it.

When Coco first learned Boy would not be able to accompany her to the ball—another summons to London on business—she was beside herself. He reminded her gently that that was why Clémenceau had gotten him transferred from Sir John French's British forces to the Franco-English Coal Commission—there was, after all, a war on.

She retorted that the Beaumonts knew it well enough. Hadn't the Count designed and funded those invaluable mobile first-aid stations and manned one himself at the Front? And wasn't war-weary Paris entitled to *some* diversion?

When he ignored her arguments and left anyway, Coco was disconsolate, but she recovered quickly enough when I revealed my scheme. She could still go to the ball. Jojo and I would take her. We would portray one of the immortal, immoral triangles: Aphrodite, Eros, and Psyche.

"Perfection, Misia ma chère," Coco smiled wickedly. "Who better-qualified than you to play the goddess of the act of love?"

Of course, we had no trouble persuading José to play the god of love. He'd always assumed the role was his by birthright.

What the two of them couldn't know was that it would also give me the opportunity to compete in Étienne's plan for the highpoint of the evening—that Olympian beauty contest "The Judgment of Paris." I knew because Diaghilev had delightedly told me Étienne had chosen him to play the role of Paris, that ultimate impresario of beauty.

My rivals would be formidable—the lesbian Princesse Edmond de Polignac as (what an irony!) Athena, the chaste goddess of wisdom, and our hostess Édith as Hera. I knew how the legend turned out, though. And I was secretly counting on my friendship with Diaghilev—not to mention my still-abundant charms or my mythological role as Aphrodite—to be the beauty who carried off the golden apple.

Now we were announced by a trumpet-bearing Mercury to the four hundred divinities assembled in the vast ballroom. José made a flamboyantly erotic Eros, naked to the waist—the Beaumonts' dictum had been that each guest display the most fascinating aspect of their anatomy—his golden bow and arrow perpetually cocked and ready. I wore a diaphanous pink tunic, artfully draped to half-reveal one breast, my long, curly red-gold hair threaded with pink rosebuds. I carried Aphrodite's emblem, a snow-white dove, heavily sedated thanks to José's ever-present supply of morphine from the Front.

And Coco, surely the most beguiling Psyche since the original, wore a seductively simple silk toga of the purest white, a white silk bandeau of her own design confining that wild, curly hair I yearned to run my fingers through . . . that I imagined glossy black against my pink satin pillows. In her hand she held the multifaceted crystal jar of beauty ointment—how prophetic I could not then have dreamed!—that in the legend an envious Aphrodite had sent her down to Hades to procure. Its intoxicating vapors were said to induce a sensual trance in any unwary mortal or immortal who came near her.

Of course, the first immortal to fall under Coco's spell was Picasso, my confidant and fellow brigand, appropriately disguised as Dionysus, the god of wine and revelry.

Behind him trailed his ever-vigilant, ever-socially ambitious mistress, Olga, dressed as the rainbow goddess,

Iris. Not even Picasso's genius, displayed in Olga's glorious tunic that was truly a rainbow of subtly shimmering hues, could transform her essential, freckle-faced plainness. Playing the debauched Dionysus to the hilt, Picasso simply ignored her and turned his burning attention on me and my remarkable protégée.

Picasso and I had reached détente early on in regard to my alliance with José. As long as I was willing to acknowledge Picasso's superiority to my lover's artistry, he would cheerfully concede my contention that José's true talents lay in bed. That never stopped him, though, from trying to lure me into his.

"Aphrodite incarnate," he roared approvingly, throwing his arm around me and letting his strong hand slip down to fondle my exposed breast. "But who is this ravishing Psyche, Misia, and why have you been keeping her from me?" His wreath of vine leaves tilted drunkenly over one eye.

"For the very best of reasons, Picasso mon cher— her own safety! Besides, Mademoiselle Chanel already has a rich, handsome young lover. What could she possibly want with a wild Spanish bull like you?"

"Are you absolutely certain you're not saving her for yourself, Misia?" he asked with a broad leer. "You know what Philippe Berthelot said about you, 'Here comes the cat, hide your birds.' "

"This lovely black-and-white swan is far too independent for even *you* to cage, my friend," Jojo observed wryly.

Once again I was struck by my lover's ability to cut to the heart of the matter. Picasso only wanted women he could tyrannize like poor martyred Olga. It was why he never entirely abandoned his pursuit of me. Predator that he was, he had sniffed out my self-destructive compulsion to tame the untamable.

All through the laughing exchange Coco was looking increasingly nervous, while Olga writhed with jealousy. Only the appearance of my darling Cocteau broke the tension. At the height of his arresting beauty Cocteau made a dazzling Apollo, tall and slim, his curly hair rinsed electric blue, a golden miter on his head radiating the sun's rays, a lyre in his hand, and on his arm his latest boy, Raymond Radiguet, a bored, petulant, monocled Hyacinthus.

"Greetings, bold gods and lovely goddesses," Cocteau said regally, drawing his long fingers caressingly across his lyre, "and you *cher Magnifique Dionysus,*" deferring, as he always seemed to feel the need to do, to Picasso. "What an amazing assembly. Those poor, benighted souls who weren't invited must feel they've been banished straight to the Underworld."

"They've all either fled to the country or are at home, lurking behind closed draperies with all the chandeliers dimmed, pretending not to be there," said Radiguet mockingly.

Coco took the occasion of Cocteau's arrival to whisper urgently, "You must get me away from him, Misia. Picasso frightens me."

I loved the feeling of her soft, slender arm trembling in mine as I led her away from Apollo's impromptu court.

"He's like a sparrowhawk," she whispered. "I feel powerless when he looks at me with those devouring eyes. No wonder all the women break their hearts over him. Even you are drawn to him, Misia, I can tell."

"Drawn to him, yes, Coco ma chère, but not to *do*

anything about it. Picasso is one of the few geniuses I've met who I know is altogether too dangerous for me."

"I'm glad Boy will be back soon, Misia." She said it softly, as if reassuring herself. I could sense her confusion, and I loved it.

All around us and against Picasso's vividly painted backcloths of Delphi and Delos, the party swirled, a riot of noise and heat and color. Another Beaumont triumph.

Orpheus and Eurydice, a blood-chilling, snake-haired Medusa, Neptune with his trident, a pale-skinned Artemis with the moon a diamond crescent in her hair and led by two greyhounds, a poisonous-looking red-haired homosexual spider Arachne— every recognizable member of the Pantheon danced and flirted abandonedly to the music of a sixty-piece orchestra of satyrs playing pipes and lyres.

Silken divans inviting lusty young nymphs and centaurs to seduction lined the walls. Buffets laden with mountains of caviar and oysters and truffled goose and peacock pies provoked an orgy of gluttony in those elder dieties who had lost their other appetites. The champagne flowed endlessly, even splashing from the fountains out in the moonlit gardens.

We stood on the terrace in the still center of our intense mutual attraction. I put out my hand to touch her heart. I could feel it beating frantically through the silk.

"Coco, forget them all. Picasso, José—even Boy. Men think only of their own desires not of ours. Come with me now . . ."

Before she could reply, the trumpets blared and Mercury announced the Judgment of Paris. I already knew that, this time, the winner had lost.

TWO

I was determined to make up for having let her slip through my fingers at the Beaumonts'. Terrible timing that wretched beauty contest. Now Boy was back in Paris and they were inseparable again. I needed another occasion to drive a wedge in their closeness, to impress her with my potent influence— my absolute power, really—in that intense electric world of the arts she coveted so fiercely. Wasn't power, after all, the ultimate aphrodisiac?

She'd confided that the first time she'd ever seen me was at the premiere of *Le Sacre*—that bonfire of a night! She confessed how beautiful she'd thought I was, like a queen in pink satin and those amazing pink pearls I'd once foolishly offered to Lantelme to buy back my worthless husband. Ironically, those same pearls had been the occasion of Boy's slighting remark that Coco told me had sparked a quarrel with Carya. He must have been aware even back then of Coco's enormous appeal to a certain sort of worldly woman— aware of it and defending against it.

By my standards, Carya was *hardly* a formidable adversary, but Boy must have thought differently. He'd taken Coco out of Paris into a two-year exile in Deauville in a successful bid to end that particular infatuation. Of course, Coco wouldn't see it that way. He'd probably convinced her it was good business to leave Paris, with the storm clouds of war gathering fast. And in fact it had been, especially when the *Boches* moved south and began laying waste to the château country around the Meuse, the Aisne, and the Ardennes, driving their terrified, burnt-out owners straight to Deauville.

Our detractors called us "unpatriotic" . . . "frivolous" for staging an enchanting ballet like *Parade* to try to light up even a corner of the dark night of war. They should have seen Étienne and Édith de Beaumont driving their ambulance at freezing midnight along the Yser, slaloming between incoming artillery shells and the huge craters left by exploding mines. One of his team said Étienne "remains the same under shrapnel as under the chandelier of a ballroom."

They should have seen Cocteau on Christmas Eve on the Belgian Front carrying wounded men twice his weight out of the trenches on his slender shoulders, depriving rats as big as lapdogs of their dinner.

That was the incongruous quality of our war. The terrible slaughter at the Front . . . the dreadful, bloody war of attrition waged over ten miles of trenches for three years that cost nearly a million young lives . . . and the rich burst of creativity back in Paris.

Gallantry and artistry went hand in hand as usual. Those pompous bourgeois who equated genius with frivolity would never understand the consummate bravery of the artist, compelled to live always on the edge—testing the vision the way an athlete or a dancer tests the muscle, coordinating the vision and the execution just the way an athlete or a dancer does—walking the wire like the beautiful acrobats who were a part of Cocteau's amazing scenario for *Parade.*

Diaghilev had said to Jean, *"Étonnez-moi,"* and Cocteau had gone ahead and done it against all odds, traveling from Paris to Rome to work with Picasso and Massine and the company, shuttling back and forth from his brutal ambulance corps stints at the Front, dealing with the conflicts that inevitably surround an act of theatrical alchemy.

Had it not been for *my* intervention, though, those conflicts would never have been resolved. *Parade* would have died stillborn. It was *Le Sacre* all over again. First I had to convince Diaghilev that Cocteau could, in fact, "astonish him" with the scenario and that that brilliant misogynist Erik Satie, with his fastidious wing-collars, his bowler hats, and precisely furled umbrellas, could actually stay sober long enough to compose the score. A score so bright, so glittering, so completely unexpected that it would inspire Massine to revolutionary heights of choreography.

Then, in production, when Satie conceived a gigantic crush on Picasso and his spectacular New York "cubist" skyscraper sets and decided he knew far more about the ballet than Cocteau, I had to work my usual magic. Soothing the badly ruffled feathers of *four* Icaruses, I convinced them all to work in harmony to produce the sparkling gift they wished to offer the wartime world—the gift I secretly longed to lay at the feet of my "little milliner."

Now at last it was ready, and as Coco and Boy and Jojo and I sat in our box waiting for Picasso's magical drop curtain, with its banqueting harlequins, its silvery

Pegasus ridden by a beautiful winged bareback rider, its trained monkey scaling a ladder to nowhere, to rise on Cocteau's inspired fantasy of a circus sideshow, I could see Coco had already fallen under its spell. As the houselights dimmed, I felt her small, cool hand slip into mine and grasp it tightly. She was sitting on the edge of her chair, holding her breath like a delighted schoolgirl waiting to be surprised.

And it *was* surprising, or "sur-real" as Apollinaire called it in the program notes, as surreal as our strange wartime lives divided between the carnage of the trenches and this glittering spectacle here in the Théâtre du Châtelet. *Parade* was a brave, lighthearted *jeu d'esprit* flung in the face of the *Boche* war machine and reflecting the courage and bravura of its creators.

Afterward, ignoring the jeers and boos of our super-nationalist critics—hadn't we survived *Le Sacre?*—we convened at the Restaurant Weber for a victory celebration. Though the government had boringly decreed that evening wear was banned from the theatres for the duration, I knew I was looking splendid in a tightly fitted Worth ensemble of a creamy crepe that showed off my still remarkably high, firm breasts, and my emerald choker and earrings. I sat at the head of the table matching wits with Cocteau and Diag over toast after toast, queening it over my devoted court. Just as I wanted her to see me.

I'd placed Coco to my right, crown princess of my heart, looking stunning in a simple suit of black satin and a spray of diamonds in her ink-black hair. José was on my left and Boy was just as far down the table as my subtle maneuvering could manage to put him, next to Satie who was glowering into his cognac and meditating violent revenge on his critics.

The troupe had taken over the restaurant, along with their White Russian émigré friends who'd poured into Paris over the past two months since the Tsar's abdication. Balalaika players roamed the tables, caviar was consumed by the pound, and icy vodka and champagne were flowing free.

Hours later Diaghilev rose unsteadily to his vast height for one more toast. He lifted his glass. "To the Tsar of all the Russias . . . the Little Father . . . and to his beloved family. May God keep them safe. I fear they need His protection now."

The room fell suddenly silent, as everyone rose to their feet, solemnly raising their glasses and, in a single voice, toasted "the Tsar!"

I felt the mood of the evening darkening—that characteristic Russian plummet from joy to despair—and I whispered to Jojo that a drive along the moonlit Seine would be a good way to clear our heads.

In the cloakroom I found Coco sitting at the vanity table, her head propped in her hands, staring disconsolately at her beautiful image in the mirror.

"Dieu but I look dreadful. I'm afraid I've had far too much champagne. The whole room is spinning. However do you manage it, Misia?"

"It must be my Polish blood. Poles are as stalwart drinkers as the Russians. And there's one other thing my stepmother Catherine taught me. Never look in the mirror when you've had too much champagne. You'll see what you're going to look like when you're old."

Gently I raised her from the little velvet stool and put my arms around her. I knew I was taking terribly unfair advantage, but I couldn't stop myself. I kissed her full on her wide sensual mouth, as I had longed to do from the first time I saw her. For one wondrous moment she responded to my embrace, pressing against me and opening her mouth on mine. Then she drew back, shaking her head bewilderedly as though roused from a trance.

"But Misia, there's José . . . there's Boy . . ."

"Of course there is, chère Coco," I said reassuringly, "and there always will be." Taking her by the hand I led her downstairs where the men were waiting with our wraps against the chill Paris night.

THREE

*W*hen the butler announced Mademoiselle Chanel, I was astonished. It was mid-afternoon, the time she always spent at the rue Cambon evolving new designs or overseeing the fittings of her most important clients. The hours between one and five were inviolable, devoted to the work she always insisted was not art, but a craft. None of our friends—not even Boy—could lure her out to lunch. Whatever had happened to disrupt her routine and bring her here to the Meurice must be serious.

I found her in the drawing room, standing in front of the fire with her back to me. The tension in her small figure was palpable. When she turned to face me, she was white with rage.

"It's happened, Misia. He's done it. Why did I believe he never would? What a fool he is. What a fool *I've* been."

"Done what, Coco? You're not making sense."

She began pacing back and forth. I had never seen her so agitated.

"He's married that infant, Diana. Lady Abdy was in for a fitting, and she told me she'd had a letter from a friend in London who'd attended the wedding at Lord Lovat's private chapel in Inverness. Of course, she thought I knew. 'Everyone always said he would have to make a marriage of convenience, Coco chérie,' she told me. 'And what could be more convenient for *you* than a child-bride. No real competition there. He'll tire of her in a few months' time.' She actually had the nerve to laugh."

She threw herself down on the sofa and began distractedly rearranging the pink silk pillows.

"But Coco, you told me yourself you knew he was seeing Diana on his Coal Commission trips to London."

"Not *seeing* her, Misia. He said he had met her at the Duchess of Sutherland's and they had dined together once or twice, that he'd felt sorry for her, only twenty-one and losing both her husband and brother at the Front. He said she needed someone to confide in— someone to take her out of herself and back into Society." She laughed bitterly. "Little did she know it was *he* who wanted to be taken into Society. Wanted it so badly he would even deceive an innocent child to get there." She leapt up and resumed her frantic pacing. Never had she seemed to me so much the Leo of her birth sign.

"Coco, please listen to me. Ia Abdy may have seemed cynical, but she's right. It *is* only a convenience. You know Clémenceau's been urging him to form a closer alliance with the banking interests in London. As a parvenu himself, Georges Clémenceau can hardly afford to back a protégé with the same conspicuous lack of status."

"Well, Misia," she said savagely, "then with his infallible instincts Boy's certainly picked the ultimate insider. Baron Ribblesdale's daughter—there could *hardly* be a tighter connection than that."

It was her controlled rage that frightened me. If she had broken down, I could have tried to comfort her. This icy anger made her unapproachable.

"And what does he imagine, Misia?" she said. "Does he think I'll stay docilely on here in his flat and count the hours until his visits? Or now that he's so very respectably married, will he want an even more discreet arrangement? A cozy little house out in Neuilly where he can drop in for a weekend now and then when he feels the need for the consolations of a *mature* woman? He knows very well I will never agree to be kept. The money he gave me for the shop was a loan—one I repaid well before it came due."

How could I argue with her cold-eyed assessment of the all-too-predictable future?

"I can't believe it, Misia. He told me the very first time he saw me at Étienne's he knew our love was predestined. He said we had been lovers before in another lifetime. He swore nothing—not even death—could separate us. He told me he was inside my soul as I was in his."

"Coco, ma chère, I know you can't accept it right now, but I believe he meant what he said. Boy loves you as much as he can love anyone. He always will. No child like Diana . . . not any other woman will ever touch him in quite the way you do. But Boy puts himself first."

"All men do, Misia," she said quietly.

"I won't quarrel with you, Coco, but you must understand. You and Boy are so very much alike. You're almost his double. Both outsiders. In your own way both orphans. Both driven to prove something to what you think are others but really to yourselves. That you are *worthy.* If you can understand that, you can understand what he's done in this marriage."

"All right, Misia, you win. As usual your logic is unassailable. I suppose I always knew it was inevitable. I only wish to God it didn't hurt so much."

I put my arm protectively around her as I walked her to the door. Though I would never have admitted it, because I felt the intensity of Coco's pain, I was secretly pleased. Boy married! Very probably he would spend most of his time in London from now on. The major rival for Coco's affections eliminated. As I turned away from the door I caught a glimpse of myself in the Venetian-glass mirror. I was still very beautiful and I was smiling.

FOUR

*É*dith de Beaumont and I were sitting in my sunny morning room drinking mint tea in front of the fire and absorbed in our favorite pastime, dismantling reputations. We knew very well that all Paris considered us the reigning Empresses of gossip—hers from the white-and-gold salons of the Faubourg St.-Germain, mine from the vivid, kaleidoscopic world of the Ballets Russes and the studios of Montmartre. Not so secretly reveling in our reputations, we strove to outdo one another with the newest, the choicest stories of seduction and betrayal. It was our own chess game and we were grand masters at it.

That morning, Édith moved first—her queen—with a racy tale of the lesbian Princesse de Polignac who had stolen the young wife of a prominent cabinet minister right from under his pompous nose.

I countered with my knight—the news of Cocteau's having taken a new lover.

"His name is Raymond Radiguet—a mere boy really, Édith, only eighteen and an aspiring poet. You remember, Jean brought him to your Olympus ball. He was dressed as Hyacinthus. You *must* remember, it was priceless—Hyacinthus wet behind the ears and wearing a monocle! Well, Jean tells me he's been giving his protégé more than instruction in the intricacies of rhyme and meter. He says the child is remarkably endowed. 'Don't let his small stature deceive you, Misia,' he told me, 'his cock is as prodigious as his brain.' "

"My dear Misia," Édith said laughingly, "if only you could see yourself right now. You look precisely like the cat Philippe called you." Then, with one bold move, she proceeded to checkmate me.

"On the subject of protégées, ma chère," her dark eyes gleamed, "did you know that your own Mademoiselle Chanel is dressing the wife of her lover? I was in the rue Cambon for a fitting the other afternoon and I saw it with my own eyes or I would never have believed it. When it comes to Monsieur Capel, Mademoiselle Chanel is not known for tolerating rivals."

Coco dressing Diana Capel. Even though I was certain Édith had heard rumors of my infatuation with Coco and was watching hungrily for my reaction to add one more malicious tidbit to her repertoire, I couldn't help myself. All I could do was attempt an air of casualness.

"What an extraordinary situation, Édith. How very *English*. And what does the new Madame Capel look like?"

"Another child, Misia—but a ravishing one. She can't be more than twenty, blonde, startling sapphire eyes, and one of those glorious English complexions. Actually the first one I've seen in Paris that equals your own." She couldn't resist that final jab.

The rest of the hour was endless. As soon as Joseph had shown her out, I threw on a cloak and hurried to the rue Cambon. I had to know what Coco was feeling.

I found her in her office going over the details of a design with one of her supervisors. It had always fascinated me that Coco never entered the workrooms herself—only the fitting rooms and then only for her most influential clients. When I'd asked her why, she told me she believed the only way to instill respect in her employees was to keep her distance from them. "Familiarity leads all too quickly to insubordination, Misia," she'd told me loftily.

I wasn't convinced. Perhaps the cutters and pressers and seamstresses reminded her too directly of her own modest beginnings. She was sufficiently familiar with her mannequins that I believe she intentionally played favorites and set up jealous rivalries between them. Certainly it was jealousy that had brought me there now.

When she'd dismissed the supervisor, she sent an assistant for tea.

"What a lovely surprise, Misia. You must be clairvoyant. Only this morning I made a note to myself to call you. I have such wonderful news."

"It must be spectacular, Coco. You look radiant." She did. The high color in her cheeks was echoed in the scarlet of the crepe chemise dress with the pristine white collar and cuffs, and her black eyes with their strange flecks of green and gold were glowing.

"He's come back to me, Misia. I always knew he would. That's why I kept the flat on the Quai de Tokyo, no matter how painful it was to go on living there alone without him. I kept it because he *had* to come back . . . because we belong together and I knew he'd eventually have to recognize it. I knew she couldn't hold him."

"But Coco, she's in Paris *with* him. And Édith de

Beaumont told me she saw Diana here—that you were actually *designing* for her. What's happened to your pride?"

She looked as though I'd slapped her. "Oh, Misia, I thought you of all people would understand and be happy for me. Boy brought her to me himself because he needed a way to see me. I wouldn't read his letters—I sent them back unopened. I wouldn't take his calls. So ten days ago he simply turned up here with Diana on his arm and insisted that I take her on as a client—'as a favor to your first backer,' he said. She certainly needs me, Misia. She's pretty enough in a porcelain-doll sort of way, but you know the English have absolutely no chic. The child was expensively dowdy when she arrived. I'm making up an entire wardrobe for her, and Boy comes to all the fittings. But it's *me* he comes to see."

I couldn't resist puncturing her ridiculous balloon. "How can you do it, Coco? How can you bear to make her look even more beautiful—and, whatever you may think, Édith de Beaumont says she *is* a beauty—and then know she's going to spend the night, all her nights in his arms?" I knew I was being terribly cruel, but the extent of her self-delusion appalled me. "Coco, don't you see what he's doing? He's using you, just as he does everyone . . . Étienne for entree into château Society . . . Clémenceau for his political connections . . . José and me for our social influence . . . Diana for her family lines. *You* most of all. Boy is what he is, and you know it—a supremely beautiful user."

Her eyes filled with tears. I was instantly ashamed of myself. In my own way I was a more calculating manipulator than Boy Capel could ever be.

"That's simply not true, Misia," she said with quiet dignity. "Boy has come back because he loves me. He always will."

For the next few months Boy and his bride stayed on in Paris in a magnificent suite at the Ritz. During the day, while Boy attended meetings of the Supreme Inter-allied Council at Versailles or saw to vital wartime coal business in his Paris office, Diana shopped endlessly, like the frivolous, openhanded, spendthrift child she was. Millions of francs went for gems at Cartier, for furs at Jacques Heim, at Charvet for dozens upon dozens of exquisitely handmade shirts for Boy.

In the evenings they entertained lavishly at the Ritz, where Boy presented his impeccably bred young wife to everyone of consequence, from his mentor Clémenceau and the press lord Léon Bailby, to the crème de la crème of the Seventh Arrondissement, the Greffulhes, the Beaumonts, the Chauvignys, and the Rothschilds.

Of course, José and I were invited and urged by Boy to bring along Diaghilev, Stravinsky, Picasso, Poulenc, Cocteau—any and all of the current stars in my constellation. I continued to tender our regrets on the grounds of José's preoccupation with his work on the gigantic frescoes for the cathedral at Vich. I'm quite sure he saw through my excuses, but I refused absolutely to be a party to what I still regarded as Boy's flagrant opportunism.

Not so, Coco. She was generosity itself, personally overseeing the endless hours of fittings on Diana's stunning new wardrobe—from subtly simple tea dresses in a rainbow of soft hues and suits of pale Scottish woolens to sumptuous ball gowns of satin and Valenciennes lace in black and white, Coco's signature colors.

She appeared as a frequent guest at their "evenings" at the Ritz, sometimes on the arm of Diaghilev or Cocteau which made my blood boil when I heard it, as I'd, in effect, declined the invitations on their behalf. Didn't she *know* all Paris was talking about the irregularity of the situation? Didn't she know there was avid speculation in gilded drawing rooms and Montmartre's smoky cafés that she and Boy and Diana were enjoying a ménage à trois?

She did not, and they were not. She told me so in no uncertain terms when I finally faced her with the gossip over Sunday lunch on the terrace of the lacy iron-and-glass Grande Cascade under the chestnut trees of the Bois.

"Don't you understand, Misia, Boy belongs to me. Yes, he *had* to make this marriage. I refused to accept it at first, but he's finally convinced me his career and his financial security depended on it. No one knows more poignantly than I do how desperately an orphan seeks security. My business, all my creative energies— my whole life up till now has been driven by that same impulse. Money and the security it brings."

"Security from what, Coco?" I was still unwilling to let Boy slip so easily off the hook. "From betrayal? From abandonment? From the loss of love?"

"I *haven't* lost his love, Misia, why can't I make you see that? He doesn't love Diana. He's fond of the child—and so, for that matter, am I. She's so open-hearted it would be hard *not* to be. But the rumors of a ménage à trois are ridiculous. Believe me, Misia, if

Carya with all her sophisticated wiles and all her determination failed to seduce us into an erotic triangle, Diana never would. Her very innocence is her protection."

"He *must* be sleeping with her, Coco. Even your adroit tailoring can't disguise her pregnancy."

"That's right. Boy has fulfilled his marital obligations to her. He wants an heir so badly. You remember, Misia, when my poor sister Julia-Berthe died. Boy virtually adopted my nephew, André Pallasse and sponsored him at his own public school in England. André was already an adolescent, though, and Boy wants the chance to be the close, loving father he never had. He and Diana have asked me to stand as godmother to their child, and I've agreed." I was horrified to see that she actually smiled proudly. "He still comes to me, though, at every opportunity at the Quai de Tokyo. Our lovemaking is more ardent than it was in our very first days together. Our connection has never been stronger. Diana has Boy's affection and his family loyalty, Misia, but I have his soul as he has mine."

Was it the late afternoon breeze, springing up to rustle the chestnut leaves like ominous whispers, that suddenly chilled me to the bone, or was it my love and fear for my darling, my brave, my vulnerable friend?

Despite Coco's passionate reassurances, the whispers did not stop. If anything, as Diana's pregnancy advanced they only grew in currency and flamboyance. Behind the fan, they were referred to as the *"trio à l'anglaise"* as if France had not had more than its share of notorious love triangles. I was increasingly concerned for Coco's emotional state. Was she deeply deluding herself?

I'll admit the prolonged emotional and physical abuse I had suffered at the hands of Alfred Edwards had left its scars—left me distrustful of men in general and, to be frank, of ambitious, plausible arrivistes like Boy Capel in particular.

Finally, I could hear no more of it, and I resolved to confront Boy with the rumors myself. I had Joseph take a note round to him at the Ritz, not so much inviting him as summoning him to tea with me at the Meurice that afternoon on a matter of some urgency.

As I sat waiting in the blue-and-gold splendor of the tearoom on a discreet banquette, well-screened by kentia palms, I tried to compose myself and sort out my own tangled motives. I knew in the byzantine depths of my soul that a part of me wanted to discredit Boy Capel—wanted to ruin him in her eyes and drive him once and forever out of Coco's life. Whether it was concern for her well-being or my own possessive longing to have her for myself I could not honestly say.

I watched from my concealment as Boy came into the tearoom and looked around for me. Even after all the hours spent together, I was struck once again by his animal magnetism. My God, he was a perfect specimen . . . so tall and tautly muscled with that thick, coal-black hair and moustache and those blazing ice-blue eyes. An aura of sensuality radiated from him. Any woman would want to be in Coco's shoes or Diana's—or both. No wonder there was so much conjecture about him. He was entirely beautiful, entirely dangerous, untamable man.

The captain led him to my table, and he greeted me

with his usual gallantry, "Misia, how incredibly lovely you are. José is a fortunate man. If I were not already committed elsewhere, I would owe it to my masculinity to attempt to seduce you." He kissed my hand and I was embarrassed to find myself blushing like a green girl. I tried to recover the advantage.

"Committed elsewhere—the very subject I have invited you to discuss this afternoon, Boy. Precisely where *are* you committed? All Paris is speculating that your commitments are either recklessly divided between your surpassingly beautiful, very pregnant girl-wife and your surpassingly beautiful, very womanly mistress who also happens to be my closest friend. Or worse, that you're sharing your precious commitment between them."

" 'All Paris is speculating,' Misia," he said coolly. "And what about *you?* Would I be presumptuous to suspect that your concern for Coco is somehow excessive, particular . . . that it goes beyond the straightforward parameters of friendship, even the very 'closest' friendship?"

Oh, well-matched indeed, and this looked to be a fight to the finish.

"My concern for Coco is based on love, Boy, and on my very real fear that you and your vaulting ambition will end by breaking her strong, honest heart."

Suddenly all our worldly games were set aside and the arrogant man before me vanished to be replaced by a small, forlorn boy—the orphan boy who looked out at me from eyes as wary, as desolate as Coco's own.

"Never, Misia, I promise you on whatever honor this knockabout life has left me . . . I will never abandon her or break her heart. Don't you understand? Coco and I are inseparable—the same infinitely fallible flesh, the same wild gypsy hearts, the same restless, unsatisfied souls."

And I did understand then. And I forgave him. And I forgave myself. Secretly, I prayed for us all. But God must not have been listening.

FIVE

*W*hy is it we are never adequately prepared for the tragedies of our loved friends? When Léon de Laborde telephoned to give me the news of Boy's death, all I could think of was Coco. Boy had lived consummately for himself. Coco had broken her own vow of independence. She had lived for him.

Bad enough that Boy had fulfilled his own premonition—that he would survive the war . . . would stand triumphantly at Clémenceau's side at Versailles when the peace was signed—only to die a violent death. Worse, that the fiery car crash that consumed him had happened not en route to Paris and Coco but on the way to a Christmas rendezvous with Diana in Cannes. Worst of all was that, according to Léon, Coco had immediately set out for the south of France. The odds that she could reach Fréjus before his burial were astronomical. She was in shock, like so many of the brave *poilus* I had seen when I drove an ambulance at the Front, wandering dazed and bloodied, oblivious of the fact that they had been mortally wounded.

José wisely advised that we not try to follow her but wait in Paris to be here for her when she got back and the insulating veil of shock lifted.

The moment I heard of her return, I hurried to her little retreat, the Villa Milanaise in St. Cucufa. In her absence, she had instructed that the bedroom be painted black—walls, ceiling, floor—as though light and life were intolerable to her.

Coco had always been energy incarnate. Her sheer vitality, her direct identification with all things sensual had been what originally attracted Boy and what drew the rest of us. Now I found her sitting in the darkness, wrapped in Boy's worn silk dressing gown, frozen in a terrible stillness, as though her own life had stopped at the moment his had and all that remained was a beautiful carapace.

I took her cold hand in my own. She didn't resist. She did not even look at me.

"Coco, ma chère, listen to me. *None* of it makes sense. I know what you're thinking. None of it. Not his foolish, vain ambition . . . not Diana . . . not the marriage . . . not this pointless death. All that does matter is your love for each other. *That* was the reality. It still is. It's all right, Coco, you can cry for him."

Slowly, like a stunned child, she turned to me and tried to focus on my face.

"Misia . . . it's you. What are you doing here in Fréjus? It's the wrong time of year. Do you know what's happened, Misia? He's gone. He's left me. He promised me he never would. And I'm so cold . . ." She was shaking.

"My darling, it's not Fréjus. You're back in Paris and I'm with you."

"I went to find him, Misia. I drove down the auto-route to meet him. When I got there, he was gone. I sat for hours on a stone, looking out over the sea waiting for him. He must have got the time wrong. All that was left was his beautiful car—how he loved driving that car! But it was all burnt, Misia—all the lovely silver black and blistered. I looked for him in it. I touched it and tried to find him there, but it was empty and cold and my hands were covered with ashes." Her eyes were cinders. "Then I went to the church and there was a box in front of the altar. They told me he was in it. But Boy would never let them close him in. He told me once his governess used to punish him by locking him in an armoire. He hated the dark. He would never have let anyone lock him in the dark."

"Coco, Boy is dead. What they told you is true. But that doesn't mean he has left you. Remember all those books he gave you—the books about reincarnation, about the next dimension."

She looked hard at me, struggling for comprehension. "The next dimension, where we would meet . . . where our love would defeat death . . . Where we would always be together. He really did believe that, Misia. He almost made *me* believe it." The first tears tracked down her face.

SIX

From the window of our suite in the Cipriani I watched her aimlessly cross and recross the *terrazzo* below. My beautiful sleepwalker. José and I had brought her with us to Venice. It had been Jojo's idea. I was frantic at my inability to help her . . . even to reach her in the isolation of her terrible grief.

More than six months had gone by since Boy's death and Coco showed no signs of recovering. True, the first disbelieving agony that had sent her reeling down to Fréjus and then left her virtually paralyzed in her darkened villa had passed, and she had come back to the fashion house and got on with the work. She supervised her staff, attended important fittings, dealt with her suppliers and made certain the flood of orders from Antoinette in Biarritz was fulfilled.

To her models and assistants and customers, used to seeing her all in black and with that certain aloofness she cultivated, she was the Mademoiselle Chanel of old. But to anyone who loved her, as José and I did, the charade this time was less than brilliant. The light in those eloquent eyes had been utterly extinguished. Those small, competent hands that I had loved to watch sketch a dazzlingly new gown for me in the air were still in her lap. That roguish gypsy smile that had seduced us all was gone—and there were no new designs being born in the rue Cambon.

When José suggested Venice, I knew intuitively that he was right. Venice, *La Serenissima,* floating in splendid improbability on its mist-swirled lagoon. City of mirrors and masks and lighthearted flirtations, far from demanding, passionate Paris and memories of Boy lying in wait to ambush her in every café and flower stall that had witnessed their love.

Venice was a dream city made for forgetfulness and healing. Here, if anywhere, Coco could put on the mask of wellness and hopefully, in time, come to believe in the reality of her new disguise.

José was in his element as tour guide and patient tutor. If Coco required a magician to distract her from her pain, José would twirl his cape and spread the glories of this artists' mecca before her like a wily conjurer. Never had I loved Jojo more than I did now. The incredible generosity of spirit that made him envision his huge frescoes, the monumental paintings Picasso scoffed at as "gilt and *merde,*" was what he offered now to Coco in an attempt to draw her back to the world in this most worldly of cities. Not once did he reveal the slightest jealousy of the intense, obsessive love he knew I felt for her.

Day after warm July day, with the heat-haze shimmering off the lagoon and reflecting on the white and gold ceiling of our suite and the unforgettably pungent aroma rising from the canals, he had led us from church to church, museum to museum—the vast Ca' Rezzonico and the treasure house of the Doges' Palace, the more intimate collections of the Correr, the Ca' d'Oro, and the Querini-Stampaglia—teaching us the

evolution of centuries of Venetian art until we were
both dizzy with whole families of Bellinis, Longhis, Tie-
polos, Canalettos, Guardis.

An entire day in the claustrophobic Scuola di San
Rocco was devoted to Jojo's patron saint, Tintoretto,
that fertile god of productivity whose output was as
staggering as Jojo's own. More than fifty scenes from
biblical life, culminating in his agonizing *Crucifixion* series, married the dailiness of homely peasant madon-
nas and farmhand disciples to the supernatural and
sublime. But I think Coco's wounded spirit was more
in tune with the hint of melancholy in Veronese's wise,
sad-eyed courtiers and queens that we saw in the Acad-
emy.

It was Jojo's special genius to know that Coco the designer, even in her trance of grief, would be compelled
to respond to the stuff—to the *material* at the heart of
the Venetian school of painters: the sables and richly
figured brocades, the damasks and glowing satins, the
lush velvets, the watered silks, the gorgeous colors, ver-
millions, ice-blues, moss-greens, crimsons, and gold . . .
gold everywhere.

As I watched her move dreamlike from gallery to gallery, I knew she was mentally cataloguing—because
she couldn't help herself—this saffron taffeta, this silver
shot-silk, and the yards and yards of lustrous pearls
wound round the creamy throat of the painted courtesan teetering on her twelve-inch, bejeweled wooden
zoccoli. Whether Coco was conscious of it or not, I
knew the seeds of future collections were beginning to
germinate. I was confident now that the impulse to
create would drive her back to life.

I joined Coco on the terrace after asking the concierge to order us a gondola. Today we were giving our guide and teacher the afternoon off to attend to some business affairs while we paid a visit to the Scuola dei Merletti, the famous lace school of Burano. This was the only official "sight" Coco had expressed any desire to see, and I had seized on it as a hopeful sign of awakening interest.

Now as we were poled across the glittering water I tried for our old teasing rapport.

"Do you suppose, Coco ma chère, that the Ministry of Tourism gives a bonus to every Venetian family who encourages their handsomest sons to become gondoliers—the scholars for the Church, the beauties for the oar?"

I glimpsed the ghost of her old smile. "You may be right, Misia, I hadn't really noticed. Beautiful young men are so thick on the ground in Venice that after a while you don't really see them anymore."

"You may not see them, but I for one would not mind it one bit if we got marooned out here on the water with that glorious young specimen behind us."

"It's strange, Misia," Coco's eyes looked far-off into the haze rising from the lagoon. "Somehow I don't really *see* men anymore, or if I do it's because something about one of them—some telltale gesture or way of walking into a room reminds me of Boy. The other afternoon in the hotel bar I saw a tall, slender, black-haired man come in and pause in front of the mirror to adjust his tie the way Boy always did, and my heart nearly stopped beating. Of course when he came closer he was nothing like him. Do you think I'll go on looking for Boy for the rest of my life, Misia? I don't know if I can bear it." She looked so lost I had all I could do not to wrap her in my arms.

"Not forever, Coco ma chère. I would be lying to you, though, if I told you you would ultimately forget him. It may be my Eastern blood, but I don't believe that anyone you truly love is ever lost to you. Alive or dead, they're just offstage somewhere. You still hear them speak to you in your heart. They still come to you in your dreams. And when you love again—and you will, Coco, believe me, even if not in the same, wild, head-long way you loved Boy—that new love will be touched by the gifts of openness and proud, free sensuality he gave you."

"How wise you are, Misia—and how kind. Without you and José I don't believe I would ever have found my way back to life. I will always love you for it." She leaned over and kissed me lightly on the cheek. It felt like a burn.

SEVEN

On the day of the surprise I planned for Coco, I awoke to find the city swathed in *la nebbia,* the sea-mist—the single day in our stay so far when the sun had failed to gild the five grey domes of

San Marco, set alight the agate eyes of the winged lion, proud on his pillar in the piazza, and shimmer off the fretwork of canals.

The fog seemed somehow appropriate to our mission. I'd sent José the day before, while Coco and I were visiting the little lacemakers, with the necessary details of date and time and place that Johanna would require for her work. And this morning we had left him behind at the Cipriani, happily immersed in the international papers that had been piling up unread since our arrival.

Coco and I crossed the damp-silvered stones of the old Ponte di Ghetto Vecchio and entered a microcosmic fantasy within the larger fantasy of Venice itself—the ancient Jewish ghetto with its tall houses, crowding up and up when they were forbidden by the Doge to expand out beyond the ghetto walls, and laced with a maze of winding passageways.

"But Misia," Coco had already protested our venturing out at all into the strange spectral mist. "I don't understand why we couldn't postpone this till another day. Why does Diaghilev insist on a menorah from Venice for the ballet, anyway? I thought he'd abandoned his plans for the *David*. Besides, there *must* be shops in Paris that specialize in Judaica."

Fortunately, her rebellion at my ruse coincided with our arrival at the massive wooden door of Johanna's narrow stone house with its guardian mezuzah. A man-servant opened to our knocking and led us into an opulent drawing room in direct contrast to the house's austere facade, furnished with dark, ornately carved mahogany and rich crimson velvet upholstery and somber paintings of bearded patriarchs on flocked velvet walls. He offered us tea in glasses with raspberry jam instead of sugar.

I could see Coco's impatience and curiosity growing in equal bounds, when the velvet draperies at the end of the room parted to admit a tall, slender woman with a mane of dark, curly hair, pale ivory skin, and remarkable, opalescent eyes.

"Johanna, ma chère," I jumped up to embrace her fondly, "far too long between meetings. You only grow more beautiful with time. How old *are* you now? It's impossible for me to tell."

"Nor will I, Misia my dear. An astrologer must have *some* secrets from her clients."

By now Coco was looking thoroughly bewildered.

"Johanna, may I present my very closest, most beloved friend, Mademoiselle Coco Chanel. As José told you yesterday, Mademoiselle Chanel has recently suffered a bereavement, and he and I thought your insights might be helpful to her."

"An astrologer . . ." Coco's astonishment overrode her usual politeness. "Misia, how *could* you? You know how very superstitious I am. I'm terrified of witchcraft . . . of astrology!"

Johanna smiled that warm, radiant, utterly open smile that had drawn me to her years before when we met on my first trip to Venice in the terrible aftermath of Alfred Edwards. She had helped me so much then.

"Witchcraft and astrology are rather far apart, Mademoiselle Chanel," she said, "though I do number some white witches among my friends. Astrology is, in fact, a science. The science of the stars. I can't claim to be able to weave spells or concoct love potions for you, but I can, with the help of your birth chart, tell you something of your dreams, your difficulties in realizing them . . . your destiny. Something, I hope, about yourself."

Though Coco was still clearly uncomfortable, I could sense her insatiable curiosity overcoming her fear.

"Besides, Coco," I reassured her, "astrology is certainly a science Boy would have respected, with all his reading in reincarnation and Karma. With his own firm belief in Destiny." It was unfair, I know, but invoking Boy would break down any lingering resistance.

"Your chart is such a strange one, Mademoiselle Chanel," Johanna added with her engaging candor, "one of the most compelling I've ever done. Since José gave me your date and time and place of birth yesterday, I've thought of nothing else. I was so caught up in it I even canceled a dinner engagement to complete it for you. There is so much here . . ." she held out a sheet of creamy vellum with a circle drawn on it, divided into equal wedges and covered with dozens of arcane symbols, "so much I would like to share with you. Things you need to know."

She motioned us to chairs around a low table, placing the birth chart in the center, and Coco was drawn to it. She could never resist her fascination with a skill she did not possess.

Johanna looked at the paper, then smiled encouragingly up at Coco. "Your astrological chart is a map of where the planets stood at the moment of your birth. First I'm going to tell you something of the basic influences in your chart that determine your destiny or, as I prefer to call it, your 'journey.'" She pointed to the circle. "The strongest planets are at the top of your chart, indicating that you are being pulled into public life . . . that you have an enormous responsibility to magnify your talent . . . to make a very strong mark in the world. You have important planets in the House of Fame, which means you were born with a destiny to be noticed. And they are also very strong in your House of Freedom. May I take it, Mademoiselle Chanel, that you are an independent sort of person?"

Coco's eyes widened and I couldn't stifle a laugh. "Independent doesn't begin to describe it, Johanna," I said. "Coco carries independence to the point of rebelliousness . . . in her life, in her work. Ask any of the more 'traditional' designers in Paris. Ask poor Poiret or Doucet . . . or even Worth about Coco Chanel's 'independence.' They'd give you an earful."

Johanna laughed, too, then grew more serious. "Unfortunately, Mademoiselle, the planets of self and love fall in the House of Endings and Sadness. It appears you must work through various trials and times of pain to become stronger and fulfill your destiny. The Moon in your chart, for instance, falls in the House of Work. That means, I'm afraid, that you are not meant to find total and complete fulfillment in your relationships but in the work you are doing, the work you will do."

"I suspect I have always known that, Mademoiselle Johanna. Even when I've tried to deny it to myself," Coco said quietly.

Johanna turned thoughtfully back to the chart, her dark hair falling around her face like a cloud. "Now, to be more specific, you were born on August 19th when the Sun was in Leo, and so your journey is to become the perfect Leo—the perfect public person with tremendous feeling, great fire, and passion for doing something in the world. The sign of Leo represents the heart, people whose feelings start in the heart and *then* are made visible. You cannot enter a relationship or begin a piece of work unless you *feel* it first."

I, who had so many times watched Coco's amazing identification with the fabrics themselves as she draped and shaped and pinned them into her unique, revolutionary designs, could certainly attest to that. Coco was directly connected to things of the earth.

And I knew, to my own pain and jealousy, that in her friendships and loves—her instant infatuations—her heart always spoke first.

"Sun in Leo is a *demanding* sign, Mademoiselle Chanel," Johanna continued, her oddly beautiful eyes holding Coco's own. "You need to feel that you are in control within your own domain and that you are respected. Your Moon in Pisces is not an easy configuration either. Pisces is a difficult sign to begin with— concerned with intense feeling, emotion, spirituality, creativity, and sacrifice. It's a troublesome sign in which to have *any* major planet—and you have your Moon there. Your chart tells me you have recently made a terrible sacrifice—been through a time of agonizing pain. You feel your life has ended . . . that there is no reason to move on or to continue your existence. Am I right, Mademoiselle Chanel?"

Johanna looked up questioningly, and Coco nodded silently, transfixed by that pure, opalescent gaze.

"When I look at the difficulties in your chart, I see that Pluto, the planet of death, sits in the House of Freedom and close to Neptune and Saturn."

"But what does it all mean, Mademoiselle Johanna?" Coco was completely caught up in the mystery of her chart.

"What it means is that you were destined to live through a major, sudden, and totally life-transforming death—the death of someone dear to you." Johanna ran a hand abstractedly through her heavy mane of hair. "When I say 'life-transforming,' I mean that the placement of these three planets speaks not only of death but shows you where you must go."

Coco exchanged a frankly bewildered glance with me.

"What seems to you now like a hurricane—sweeping away everything you depended on, counted on—so that you're laid waste and bare, like a hurricane sweeping through the country, leaving nothing in its wake except what can be rebuilt—shows that not till you came to a place where everything was laid waste . . . everything was taken from you, could you begin to use that intense creativity and authority you have within you to rebuild a bold new life on top of the devastation."

Coco was sitting still as a statue, but the tears poured unchecked down her lovely face. Johanna was equally rapt in the chart. Her pale, almost translucent skin glowed with her inner vision, her inner fire.

"What you have endured, Mademoiselle Chanel, has been a turning point. Without the devastation you could not have gone on to do all the things your chart reveals."

When Coco looked skeptical, Johanna took her small hand in both of hers.

"Of course, sitting here as you are now, feeling that you cannot move, cannot make a plan . . . I know none of this makes sense to you. All you have to fall back on is your Leo courage and sense of survival. That is the strongest influence I see in your chart."

Her fiery opalescent eyes held the jet flame of Coco's.

"It's very rare, my dearest Mademoiselle Chanel," the intensity of her *own* feeling—of her own pain at the dark side of the influences the chart required her to reveal—had the tears flowing down Johanna's exquisite face as well, "to have both Venus and Leo together as you do in the twelfth House. The twelfth House is not only the House of Sorrow, Sacrifice and Death, but is ultimately called the House of Wisdom, of self-wisdom."

She stood up and raised Coco to her feet, gazing steadily into her eyes. "Over the next months, perhaps the next year, you will come to some conclusion about what you've been through and what that relationship represented. For the first time in your life you gave someone else a great deal of power. You did so willingly. You did so out of love. Now, because of circumstance, you must take that power back into yourself."

Coco shook herself, as though rousing from a trance.

"The iceberg of your pain that has frozen you into paralysis will inevitably melt. Little by little, you will make small steps out of the clutch of pain into health, productivity, new relationships, and the work."

A small, tremulous smile began at the corners of Coco's mobile mouth.

"As a Leo you are first and last a survivor. Your spirit, I promise you Mademoiselle Chanel, whatever you think right now, will not be killed by what you've been through. You can go and do something with your life that will astonish everyone, perhaps even yourself."

Johanna picked up the chart from the table, rolled it up, and put it into Coco's hand.

"Because of this, I've waited until this moment to tell you that your Rising Sign . . . your ascending sign . . . the sign that denotes who you were when you separated from your mother and started life as an individual is Virgo, the sign of work, service, perfectionism, utilization—the sign of *using yourself.* And that, my very dear Mademoiselle Chanel, is what I know you will do. Use yourself fully to make your significant mark in the world."

EIGHT

*A*fter that afternoon with Johanna, Jojo and I noticed a real change in Coco. The sadness was still there in her give-away eyes, perhaps it always would be, making her seem older somehow—not the reckless fun-loving innocent provincial of our madcap Paris nights—but deeper, wiser and, if possible, even more beautiful in my eyes.

As Johanna had foreseen in her chart, Coco began taking small, halting steps back toward life. I saw it for the first time one evening in Harry's Bar, even more crowded than usual with the infusion of tourists—the Germans, the Russians, our own countrymen—assembling for Sunday's Feast of the Redentore, the annual celebration of the city's miraculous relief from the plague four centuries before.

The three of us were sitting at a table in the corner, drinking Bellinis, that golden concoction of champagne and peaches honoring the painter and born at the hands of Harry's inspired bartender.

"You know, Tosche . . . Coco," José said, raising his glass to us, his black eyes gleaming. "From this moment on, whenever I drink a Bellini—even in Paris in the dead of winter—I'll be back in summertime Venice with the two most beautiful women in the world."

Coco, smiling warmly, answered his toast. "And whenever I do, I will remember my two dearest friends in the world who conjured up an imaginary floating paradise of beauty and art to remind me of the things of this world and then produced a celestial astrologer to make me the gift of a future."

Through the smoke I saw a familiar figure making his way toward us in the crowd, stopped at every table by someone he knew. Who could fail to recognize him, huge as he was and with that signature streak of white hair, the monocle, and those protruding front teeth that had made Cocteau call him "the chinchilla," a name he hated but that had unfortunately stuck.

"Misia," Diaghilev boomed, nearly lifting me out of my chair in an enormous bear hug. "Of *course* you would be here. Wherever there's a spectacle in the making, expect the goddess of the spectacular to be there, too!" He clapped José on the back and made a courtly half-bow to Coco.

"And Mademoiselle Chanel. Paris is not at all the same without you. When are you coming back to us?

Your customers are pining, your rivals are licking their chops."

Coco laughed in spite of herself.

"And all those lovers are in terror of the return of the corset, those tiresome whalebone ones Cocteau said made undressing a woman almost as difficult as moving house. Not that *he'd* know very much about it."

Before she could reply he turned to introduce her to the handsome young man trailing in his wake.

"My friends, may I present Luchino Visconti, heir to a title as old as the bridges of Venice. But we will forgive him that because, where his noble father expects a reactionary, mark my words, this young man has a visionary cast of mind that will astound the old order in our lifetime!"

High praise indeed from a man whose entire career had been devoted to the discovery and fostering of genius.

Visconti was dazzling. Dark, slim, and intense, with the worldliness of a Veronese courtier, he was clearly not one of Diag's "young men." From the moment he raised Coco's small hand to his lips, and turned it palm-up to kiss, it was obvious he had been badly smitten.

Coco's pale cheeks flamed scarlet at his touch. So much for "not noticing" the beauty of Venetian men. I fought down the familiar demon of corrosive jealousy because I truly welcomed that blush. It was the first sign of what Johanna had called the "iceberg" melting—the first indication there might be feeling life again for Coco after Boy Capel.

Throughout the evening Visconti hung on Coco's every word, asking her a hundred questions about her work . . . where she drew her inspiration . . . her favorite painters here in Venice . . . her plans for a new collection, making any excuse to brush her hand while reaching for his drink or lighting her cigarette.

Coco was animated and talkative for the first time in more than half a year, her gypsy eyes sparkling again—lightly flirting with Visconti and Diaghilev, even Jojo—looking closer, I'm sure in the *very* young Visconti's eyes, to twenty than her thirty-seven years.

When we left Harry's Bar at closing time, having agreed to accept the hospitality of Visconti's *palazzo* to watch the spectacle of the Redentore, I linked my arm in Coco's and drew her close to my side as we crossed the deserted Piazza di San Marco.

"See the winged lion—high up there on his pillar? They say he was originally a chimera stolen from the Assyrians like so many of the treasures in this pirates' city. But here he is, lording it over his would-be conquerors. Leo—a survivor like you are, Coco—and I love you for it."

"And I love you, Misia," she said, "more than I think you even know."

Sunday evening found us assembled on the balcony of the splendid Visconti *palazzo* with its sweeping marble staircases leading to the piano nobile, its collection of Titians and Veronese nobility on the walls and its magnificent Tiepolo ceilings where cherubs took flagrant advantage of languid, sloe-eyed Venetian ladies, as I knew Luchino longed to do with Coco.

He was the most gallant of hosts, offering wine, champagne, cognac, cannoli, spun-sugar cookies, fine cigars for the gentlemen, and lace shawls for the ladies against any possible chill in the night air. He was attentive to his aloof, elegant mother . . . to me . . . to everyone. But it was obvious he could barely take his eyes from Coco. He kept trying to tempt her with candied violets, with a Bellini which he swore Harry's barman had taught him to make perfectly—with himself.

The spectacle was as brilliant this August as it had been for the past several hundred. Thrown casually across the Guidecca canal to Palladio's stately Church of the Redeemer was a string of every sort of seagoing craft imaginable—and in Venice the variety was almost infinite.

Gondolas, fishing boats, trading vessels, garbage scows, rowboats, even an old wooden galleon with a faded Crusaders' cross emblazoned on its sails. Garlanded with roses and hung at the bows and sterns with Japanese lanterns, the entire motley flotilla sparkled like a gimcrack necklace around the throat of a particularly gaudy courtesan.

Every few minutes the boom of exploding fireworks launched from the Piazzale Roma would drown out the strains of Vivaldi's "Summer" played by the entire sixty-piece orchestra of the Fenice Theatre from its float in the center of the fragile chain.

Venice that night was a city of a thousand mirrors— the lagoon, the canals, the tall, dark windows of the *palazzi*—all reflecting the flaming colors of the fireworks. It was as though in this final week of our stay, the city was offering up one last burst of unbridled vitality against the paralysis of Coco's pain—one last challenge to her to move toward life out of the prison of memory.

"You know, Misia," she confided when Luchino had

left to order up one of his family's gondolas so we could follow the pageant to the island of San Giorgio, "I've been thinking about what Serge said last night. And about Johanna. It probably is time for me to get back to Paris—back to the work. It would be so easy to stay here in Venice . . . so easy to keep my back turned to reality. Luchino has offered me his family's hospitality if I decide to stay on after you and Jojo leave."

"Will you accept, then, Coco?" I tried to keep my voice steady. The prospect of Paris without her was unutterably bleak.

"It would be unfair to him, Misia. He wants more than my friendship. He deserves more. He's kind and sensitive and wonderfully intelligent. But he's still really just a boy . . ." she stopped short, horrified at her own slip, "I mean a very young man. I'm not ready yet to love again, Misia. I don't know if I ever will be. I would only end by hurting him, and I've gone through too much pain to risk inflicting it on anyone else."

On another innocent, you mean, I said to myself. Our conversation was interrupted by the return of a beaming Luchino, full of his youth and the happiness of what I'm sure he was confident was his conquest of Coco.

"Beautiful ladies," he swept us a bow, "your gondola awaits. Let me show you yet one more trick of my wily city of mirrors and mystification. You thought the fireworks were finished, but now we'll go to the opposite end of the canal, and the entire display will be perfectly duplicated for your special pleasure. A mirror image."

When the last part of the spectacle was over—when the final rocket had been fired and its shower of burning petals drifted down on to the dark surface of the water, when even the full moon had drowned itself in the lagoon, Luchino told his gondolier to pole us out to the Lido.

"Oh Luchino," I protested, "have pity on us. We've been up all night and I, for one, am longing for bed. I know Jojo and Serge are, too, though they're too proud to admit it. Tell the truth. You only want another hour of Coco's company."

He was sitting close beside her in the gondola, holding tight to her hand as if she might vanish if he let go for even a moment.

"You are half-right, *Signora bella,*" he said, "but it is also a tradition of the Redentore. All evening we have watched the most elaborate display of *illuminati* that man can devise. But we are only men not gods after all, despite our pretensions. So now we must go to watch the sun rise and pay tribute to the master illuminator of them all."

The conceit was so charming I couldn't deny him— even if he *was* only inventing it on the spur of the moment to buy more time with Coco. Where these silver-tongued Venetians were concerned, you could never quite be sure.

Jojo had actually fallen asleep and was snoring loudly by the time we reached the Lido. Serge, his already-heavy eyelids drooping, was nodding over yet one more glorious bottle of pinot grigio. Coco's head had dropped to Luzhino's shoulder—a burden that was clearly no hardship to him. I had drifted into a half-dream in which Coco and I were rocked gently, lying in each other's arms, in a narrow, gleaming mahogany cradle.

The thud of wood on wood as we docked at the landing stage shook everyone out of sleep or reverie.

Over the sea the night began to dim, and bands of misty color appeared on the rim of the horizon—amethyst, fuchsia, salmon—and then bright, burnished Venetian gold as the sun began its fiery climb up the pale dawn sky.

The five of us sat silent, transfixed by a spectacle no artist . . . no conjurer could perfectly reproduce.

NINE

I wonder whether history will ever give me credit—should I be fortunate enough to be remembered at all—for being anything more than an attendant Muse, a catalyst to others' genius.

Ironically, my most enduring contribution may turn out not to be to my own world of the arts but to the world of fashion, the domain of my best-loved friend and fiercest rival.

What was to prove my opportunity came in the form of a gift. Shortly after the three of us got back to Paris, an admirer gave me yet another elaborate flacon of one of Poiret's popular scents. I'm not sure whether I should have been flattered or appalled that his choice was "Lucrece Borgia" (God knows, Cocteau and Picasso and Diag have often called me worse!). Instead, I was simply bored, bored by the overpowering, stifling floral perfumes that were all the rage.

Over lunch at the Ritz, I complained bitterly to Coco that I was tired of smelling like a gardenia or a cypress tree. I'd just been reading a fascinating little volume called *The Secrets of the Medici* that included an obscure recipe for a "Medici" scent, and I told Coco that if the dukes of *cinquecento* Florence had their signature essence, so should she.

Since her return from Venice, leaving a crestfallen Visconti behind her with the empty promise of returning before another *signorina bella* captured his heart, Coco had actively been looking for new outlets for her talent. Even so, she laughed at me at first.

"A woman should smell like a woman, Misia. Above all, she should smell fresh and clean. Those cloying floral scents are made to cover up the fact that women don't bathe nearly often enough. Why sometimes in the fitting room it's almost more than one can bear. Princesses, baronesses, marquises—never mind their titles—they could all do with more regular baths."

I knew this was an old idée fixe of Coco's born in her orphan days at Aubazine where the good sisters drummed the virtues of cleanliness and purity into the heads of their rebellious charges.

"I know that, Coco, but there's more to it than soap and water. A woman wants a special fragrance . . . something uniquely her own . . . something to leave a trace on her lover's skin to remind him of the moments when they've been closest together—something to stir his desire for more."

She looked at me consideringly. "You know, Misia, you might just be right. An eau de Chanel. With all my major customers still out of Paris till the end of the month, and Jojo involved in that endless cathedral fresco, what better time for you and me to motor down through Provence? We could make a sentimental pilgrimmage to Moulins—the scene of my girlhood music-hall triumph."

She laughed ironically. But why did she leave out Vichy? Boy had told me she'd tried her hand there, too.

"And we could stop at all those marvelous artisans' shops to get ideas for accessories for the February collection. Of course our target would be Grasse. If I intend to create a unique fragrance, I'll have to go to the foremost perfume chemist in France—Ernest Beaux."

Why did I feel Coco was always one jump ahead of me? "How do you know about Beaux?"

"One of the émigrée grand duchesses told me about him. His father was perfumer to the court of the Tsar. Everyone knows Russians have been the premier *parfumeurs* for centuries. Beaux is said to have the finest 'nose' in France."

Poor Ernest Beaux. Little did he know what was about to descend on him. By the time we arrived on his doorstep, Coco had become totally committed to creating the most expensive perfume in the world. Johanna's prediction that she would find salvation by throwing herself into the work was coming dramatically true.

As we drove down through the early autumn countryside of Provence, the gold and pinks of peaches and apricots ripening all along the roadside, she talked of nothing else. On the margins of the maps we carried, on the back of menus or on tablecloths in the country inns where we dined, she drew sketch after sketch, in search of the perfect container for a perfume that was still to be invented.

"The bottle's only function is to display its contents. *Simple,* Misia. It must be simple like my dresses. Simple and new and bold. Something like this . . ."

On a cocktail napkin in a few strong strokes she drew a plain, unadorned, square bottle with beveled corners and a small rectangular stopper—utterly different from the ornate, multifaceted crystal flacons women bought as much for decoration as for the fragrance inside. Simplicity and uniqueness itself. Her signature.

The road to Grasse ran through fields of flowers—a glorious tapestry of lavender and jasmine and roses. It amused me to imagine that the essence of hundreds of thousands of these blossoms would end in the cleavage of countesses and kept women and shopgirls in every city and town in France.

The door to Beaux's modest shop was opened by a pretty young assistant who led us into an Aladdin's cave. Flacon after flacon of various fragrances stood on the floor-to-ceiling shelves, reflecting the late afternoon sunlight like so many gemstones—topaz, canary diamonds, amber, carnelian.

"May I be of help, Mesdemoiselles?"

"Please tell Monsieur Beaux that Mademoiselle Coco Chanel has arrived from Paris to consult with him."

Looking flustered, the girl disappeared into the back of the shop. A few minutes later a small, prematurely grey, middle-aged man wearing a wildly stained overall came out and grasped Coco's hand.

"Mademoiselle Chanel, what a pleasure to welcome you to my establishment. Even down here in provincial Grasse we've seen examples of the revolution you are creating for women. At last we gentlemen are privileged to openly admire a pretty ankle! We are forever in your debt."

Laughing, Coco introduced me to the wiry little chemist.

"Well, Monsieur, you are about to have the opportunity to repay that debt. I wish to commission a perfume that will reveal a woman's essence as precisely and unforgettably as the finest dress I have ever designed reveals her body. *That* is to be your challenge."

For the next two weeks Beaux worked valiantly to meet that challenge—or rather, Coco drove him to it. As soon as we'd finished our morning coffee at the little country inn just outside Grasse, we would join him in his evil-smelling laboratory behind the shop.

Donning overalls like his own, Coco would work at Beaux's side for hour after hour, delegating the humble tasks like petal-picking or beaker-scrubbing to me and his young assistant as casually as if we all worked for her.

"No heavy floral essences, Beaux," she ordered, rejecting the second sample he'd spent days in concocting. "That's the very thing we've been trying to avoid."

"Mademoiselle Chanel," Beaux said patiently, masking his growing exasperation behind his natural courtesy, "you must have *some* sort of important floral note. Otherwise you're going to smell like a civet cat or a musk deer, and that will defeat your purpose."

"Unless, Coco ma chère," I couldn't resist, "you're planning to take up with that civet cat Caryathis again."

She stuck out her tongue at me. "You should know, Misia. After a day in the studio, I seem to recall, Jojo has a distinct odor of civet about him. The rest of the time it's pure musk when he's trying to lure you back into his bed again."

"Ladies . . . ladies . . ." Monsieur Beaux was clearly not used to the gutter tactics of two Parisienne street fighters. "If you'll let me explain. The unadulterated animal oils are just as cloying as the pure florals, perhaps even more so. What we want here is a balance between them—but we *must* have a floral note."

Coco unstoppered yet another of the hundreds of vials, this one labelled "Jasmine" in Beaux's spidery handwriting, and sniffed it. "Then try this one," she commanded, "at least *it* has a spicy scent . . . lighter than that dreadful 'Chypre.'"

"Of course, Mademoiselle Chanel—and a good choice at that. You *do* understand that jasmine is the single most expensive floral you could employ? It takes eight-million jasmine blossoms to produce a single kilogram of the essential oil. And I would combine it with tuberose. But that, too, is quite literally worth its weight in gold. The blossoms are picked by hand at dawn, wrapped in damp cloths and processed with solvents while the dew is still on them. The labor alone is costly."

"As I said when we met, Monsieur," this time it was Coco's turn to be patient, "cost is not the issue here. My sole aim is to create a unique and unforgettable fragrance. My customers can well afford it. You're the alchemist here. All you have to do is discover it for me."

As the deadline for our return to Paris approached and we still did not have our eau de Chanel, tempers began to fray. We were all exhausted, especially poor little Monsieur Beaux who looked as though he'd aged ten years in as many days.

We had tried every combination imaginable of natural oils and essences and, Beaux's specialty, chemical fixatives to anchor and hold the scent in place and make it resonate on the air. Still, in Coco's opinion, the perfect, *un*-platonic fragrance had yet to be found. Now I understood where she had gotten her reputation among her girls as a martinet. She was a fierce, finicky perfectionist.

Finally even Beaux's apparently endless fund of patience ran out, and when we arrived in the morning to work, as courteously as possible he ordered us out of his laboratory.

Taking Coco's hands in his permanently stained ones, he told her earnestly, "Chère Mademoiselle Coco, you are going to have to trust me. We've been at this for ten days now, and my gut—and my nose— tell me I am very close to the solution you seek. Forgive me, Mademoiselle, but I will never be able to find it with you breathing down my neck, watching my every move, checking my calculations." He gestured exasperatedly at the workbench.

"I am rapidly approaching the paralysis of a schoolboy with an implacable headmaster. If you want your fragrance, I beg you to leave me alone for twenty-four hours with my work—and a little room for inspiration. Come back tomorrow afternoon and I will give you what you want or," he smiled wryly, "finish where this whole perfume business began by annointing my body

with resins and immolating myself with my bunsen
burner as a sacrifice to your divine vision."

He succeeded. When we returned the following afternoon he had ten two-ounce samples, labeled only
by number, lined up on his scarred workbench for her
review.

Imperious as a general, she moved down the line, un-
stoppering, sniffing, dismissing with a shake of her
head. When she came to the fifth sample, she sniffed,
paused, and sniffed again. After continuing along
through all ten, she came directly back to the middle
and picked up the fifth again. Then she touched a drop
of it to her wrist and raised it to her nose. She held the
vial out to me.

"Try it, Misia."

I put a touch of it on my own wrist, sniffed, and
smiled silently into her glowing, confident eyes.

"Perfection itself, Monsieur Beaux. Subtle, spicy, unforgettable. Precisely what I always knew you were capable of. Precisely why I came to you."

"It *should* be perfect, Mademoiselle," the little chemist said with quiet pride. "It has over eighty ingredients.
And I've used my own formula for aldehyde—deoxyge-
nated alcohol, that is—as a fixative to hold the floral
notes of jasmine and tuberose. This is a perfume, I
promise you, that time will not fade."

"Then it will last longer than most love affairs, Monsieur," I said. The mood was becoming altogether too
solemn for my taste. "Well, Coco, now that you have
it at last, what will you call it . . . 'Jasmin de Chanel' or
'Jardin de Chanel'?"

"No, Misia, I don't think so. Something much simpler.

Those sound too much like everything else that's gone before." She eyed the little bottle speculatively.

"The fifth sample . . . the halfway mark . . . five out of ten . . . number five. . . . *That's* it, Misia," she smiled triumphantly at us, " 'Chanel Numéro Five.' "

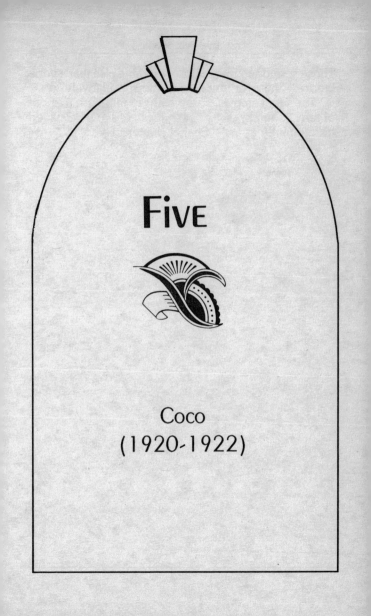

Five

Coco
(1920-1922)

ONE

*C*oming back to Biarritz so soon was a mistake and I knew it. In spite of Misia and José's best efforts and the very real exhilaration I'd felt at the creation of my new fragrance, the dark shadow of Boy's death still hung over my heart. And Biarritz, where he'd branded my soul with his love, held too many memories.

I'd had no choice. Antoinette had bolted. I should have seen it coming. She'd always rebelled against my authority, and an inappropriate marriage was the ultimate defiance.

Not that Lieutenant Fleming was unattractive, quite the opposite. He was a Canadian, flying fiery dogfights against the *Boches* over France and Belgium for the RAF in the last days of the war, one of those courageous young daredevils who'd plundered the hearts of countless Parisiennes. Antoinette hadn't stood a chance against the sheer force of his glamour.

His whirlwind courtship had begun when she came up to Paris to discuss the next Biarritz collection with me. They'd met one evening at the Boeuf sur le Toit, the new club in the rue Boissy d'Anglas that was all the rage where that gloriously beautiful black singer, Josephine Baker, was appearing to ecstatic crowds drunk on the bold syncopations of American "jazz."

Before I knew it—before I'd even had time to read the obvious signs in the bed unslept-in and the sensual languor that had softened Antoinette's sharp edges— they were married and on their way to his family in Windsor, Ontario.

She'd regret it, I told her. No self-respecting Chanel would willingly bury herself in provincial obscurity in the wilds of Canada where they probably didn't even bother to dress. I regretted it even more because it left me without a directrice for the flourishing Biarritz salon and meant a trip I knew I was emotionally unprepared to take.

Fortunately, I was spared the torment of nights spent alone in that cold, empty bed in our old suite at the Hôtel du Palais. Marthe Davelli, between roles at the Opéra Comique, had rented a villa in the hills outside the city and insisted I stay with her while I found my new directrice. It was a lilac stucco confection, lavishly decorated in the Moorish style with pierced wall screens and arched windows looking out over the sea—one of those *"petits fours"* I'd pointed out to Boy on our first drive into the city.

Marthe was tact and warmth and concerned friendship itself, leaving me when my morning's interviewing of candidates was over to the peaceful solitude of the villa where the only sounds were the subdued laughter of the young Basque maids, the whirring of white doves in the sunny courtyard, and the soothing plash of fountains on brightly painted tiles.

Marthe spent her days golfing, swimming, and watching the polo matches with her hectic circle of theatrical friends and international playboys and only came back late in the afternoon to oversee the series of intimate dinners she was determined to give for me to take me out of myself.

While I couldn't offend her hospitality by refusing, even those small dinners were an ordeal. I was still too fragile and, though I smiled and drank champagne and feigned attention to my dinner partners, the fragments of their bright, brittle conversation fell around me, locked in the still, aching void of my loneliness, like so many shards of glass.

"I said, Mademoiselle, that you have traveled so far away from this table I feel I am calling out to you across the *taiga.*"

"Excuse me, Monsieur," I roused myself from a waking dream of Boy and me and a moonlit beach. "I realize that I am being insufferably rude."

"Not rude so much as preoccupied . . . absent . . . wandering somewhere in the past, far away from all this inconsequential chatter. I understand that, Mademoiselle. I spend much of my own time these days walking with ghosts."

I shivered. Ghosts. So he had them, too. How had he managed to read my thoughts? I looked with renewed interest at the aristocratic profile of Grand Duke Dmitri Pavlovich.

"And now that you have returned to me, Mademoiselle Chanel, I am struck by the absolute certainty that I have seen you before. Have you been in St. Petersburg?"

"Never, Monsieur. Venice has been the far extent of my travels."

He turned and looked intently at me. "I have it," he said, "Deauville—it must be seven years ago. The Grand Prix . . . where my Champagne Cognac and

Baron de Rothschild's Victoire had that unfortunate collision. Afterward in the jockeys' room, when Monsieur Balsan insulted your . . . your friend. You were magnificent, Mademoiselle. I admire spirit—in a thoroughbred . . . especially in a woman."

"I was only trying to avert a second unfortunate collision, Monsieur. It seemed to me there had already been more than enough mayhem for one afternoon."

"Where is your friend now, Mademoiselle? Is he with you in Biarritz? I don't see him at the table this evening. He looked inquiringly around at the handsome, wealthy, dinner-jacketed men Marthe had produced as potential diversions for me.

"Monsieur Capel died in an automobile accident last December," I answered quietly, saying it aloud for the first time, embarrassed at the catch in my voice. "I am here in Biarritz on business. Quite alone—as I prefer to be." Why had I added that? There was something in the Grand Duke's steady, grave regard that unsettled me. Visconti, with his polished compliments and Venetian commitment to seduction for seduction's sake had been, after all, a boy. This was something different.

Marthe's announcement of port and cigars for the gentlemen in the library came at a welcome moment. I escaped the ladies, settling in for serious gossip in Marthe's frilly boudoir, and stepped out onto the terrace under the clear night sky, thousands of stars sparkling like paillettes on jet velvet.

At the far end of the terrace I saw the red glow of a cigar and gravitated toward it. The Grand Duke was leaning on the balustrade, staring out over the restless sea. He did not look at me.

"So, chère Mademoiselle Chanel," he said into the

darkness, "you find society as difficult as I do these days."

Once again he had succeeded in reading my mind. What was it about this complete stranger that inspired such confidence in me—made me feel safe enough with him to want to tell him the secrets I'd hidden even from myself?

"I'm not fit yet for polite company," I said. "I wonder if I ever will be again. Marthe's been an angel, letting me stay with her, arranging these dinners, worrying about me—all my friends have. They think that if I just keep busy enough, keep meeting new people, working on new projects I'll forget Boy and get on with my life. What they don't understand is that I feel so unmoored, so badly displaced from the center of my feelings, so cut off from 'normal' life—so lost."

He reached out, brushed back the curls from my forehead that the sea breeze had disarranged, and looked deep into my eyes.

"My dear Mademoiselle Chanel, only someone who has lost whatever held real meaning for them can understand what you've experienced." His grey eyes were unutterably sad.

"Three years ago I wouldn't have understood it myself. But when I was forced to leave my country, to leave Russia—not for one more high-stakes race meet, but for good—because of something my honor, my deepest loyalties required me to do, I became an exile from my homeland . . . from my loved ones . . . from my heart. That's why I knew you tonight the first moment I saw you. Not because of Deauville. Not because of what Society says about you, but because I recog-

nized a fellow exile." Gently, he took my hand, raised
it to his lips and kissed it.

For the rest of my stay in Biarritz, Dmitri and I were
often together. He would come to the villa in the afternoons, driven by his man, Piotr, who'd left Russia with
him and who, doubling as valet and chauffeur, observed the rigid Romanov protocols of master and
servant as precisely as if they were still in St. Petersburg.

We would go for a drive along the wild Basque coastline or he would simply sit with me out on the sunny
mimosa-scented terrace, neither of us saying much, offering each other occasional glimpses of lives as different as though we had come from separate solar
systems which, in effect, we had.

From the start we had an easy, undemanding camaraderie. Neither of us could afford more. It was as if we
were two war veterans recovering slowly from near-
fatal wounds. Dmitri had lost his way of life. He was a
survivor of an elitist, completely privileged world that
had died in a volley of rifle shots on that terrible day
in Ekaterinburg with the assassination of his cousin—
his beloved Tsar Nicholas—and all his innocent, beautiful, hopelessly sheltered family.

"I wish I could have been there with them . . . done
something to help them . . . or just been there, Coco,"
he told me, "but my cousin Nicky had already sent me
to join the army in Persia after the incident with Yusupov."

I knew, because I remembered Misia and Diaghilev
and the others talking about it back in Paris, that he
was speaking of his part in the execution of the peasant

seer, Rasputin, who had held the Tsarina hostage to his power over the life of her hemophiliac son. All the White Russian emigrés considered him directly responsible for the fall of the dynasty. Even Kerensky was said to have admitted that "without Rasputin there would have been no Lenin."

Dmitri always referred to it obliquely as "the incident" or "the Moika Palace affair," but I knew that of all the terrible things he'd witnessed in a world splitting apart at the seams, it was the single memory that haunted him most. Someday, when he trusted me enough, he would tell me about it.

For now, just the mutual pleasure of being understood and accepted as damaged but on the mend was enough. Outside of lighting my cigarette or wrapping me in his jacket when the sun set and the evening chill moved in off the sea, Dmitri had never touched me, never kissed me. Yet once I'd hired a capable administrator as Antoinette's replacement and begun to pack for Paris, it seemed perfectly natural to ask him to join me.

Marthe had told me he had few resources, beyond the handful of jewels Piotr had sewed into the lining of Dmitri's uniform tunic when they left Russia. This proud, sensitive, lonely man needed sanctuary, and so in my own way did I.

"I'm not ready to live in Paris proper yet, Dmitri," I told him. "It still holds too many traces of Boy for me. But I've found a villa out in the suburbs in Garches, and my friend Misia is doing it up for me. If you can stand acres of pink chintz and a petrified forest of pink quartz and coral ming trees, you and Piotr are welcome to stay with me."

When he seemed to hesitate, I hurtled on. "I've let Diaghilev persuade me to give house room to our composer friend Stravinsky and his family who are having financial difficulties. So with Diaghilev and the Stravinskys and the entire Ballets Russes dropping in as they'll inevitably do, Garches is bound to become a Russian colony. I think you might be quite comfortable there."

Dmitri smiled that infrequent smile that lit up his handsome face.

"If what you're proposing, my dear Mademoiselle, is installing a tame Russian bear to protect you from the excesses of my countrymen, you may certainly have me. Just don't count on my remaining tame forever."

TWO

That's how haphazardly my "Russian period" began. No sooner did the gossip get out—one telephone call from Misia to Édith de Beaumont and *tout* Paris knew that Mademoiselle Chanel was "living" with Grand Duke Dmitri—that the rue Cambon was besieged by emigré aristocrats looking for work. Their hopes were not misplaced. Dmitri's stories of mellow, sun-struck country dachas and coldly glittering palaces along the Neva callously looted and burned by the Bolsheviks, their owners lucky to escape the country with their lives, inclined me to their predicament.

I had Prince Kutuzov as my personal assistant, Dmitri's own sister, the Grand Duchess Marie, in charge of my embroidery atelier, and the daughters of the nobility as my mannequins. How very much I respected them! The fierce determination not to be defeated by circumstance, however incomprehensible, and the very real *tendresse* they showed one another in exile. They had lost their homes, their dowries, their expectations, but they had never surrendered their dignity or their ability to love.

Contrary to the gossips, Dmitri and I were not lovers—at least, not at first. At the Villa Bel Respiro we'd continued to enjoy that sweet, strange, unlikely intimacy that had grown up between us in Biarritz. I had come to admire so many things about him—his strength, his resilience, his gallantry, his sense of privacy, and above everything else his protectiveness, the instinctive way he reached out to the innocent.

He would hold the Stravinsky children spellbound for hours with tales of wolf hunting on the snowy steppes, or midnight troika races along the frozen Neva with the horses' breath turning to crystals in the icy air and the sleigh bells chiming in the pure cold. He conjured up for them an entire world that was theirs by birthright, even if it no longer existed except in their father's music, the dances of the Ballets Russes, and the nostalgic imaginings of the exiles. He gave them a gift of their heritage and, for someone like me who had spent what seemed a lifetime longing for security, for roots, it was wonderful to watch.

And I loved the secret vulnerability he revealed only to Piotr, who had looked after him since he was a boy, and to me.

The night I awoke to hear him shouting, "No, Gregory, go back! You're dead . . . you *have* to be dead . . ." I was at his bedside even before Piotr.

Dmitri was sitting upright in bed, his eyes closed tight, drops of moisture beading his forehead, and his nightshirt drenched with sweat, but his strong hands were ice-cold as he gripped mine.

"Wake up, Dmitri, it's only a dream . . . a nightmare. You're safe here with me. It's all right, I'm with you." I told Piotr to send the frightened Stravinskys back to bed. The Grand Duke had had a bad dream.

Slowly he opened his eyes and focused on me. "Not a dream, Coco, I only wish it was. It's as real to me as it was that last night in the cellar. He always had the power, whatever anybody said. He promised vengeance and he's taking it—on all of us."

The story, held back for so long except in the dreams he could not control, poured out of him. "It was murder, Coco, and it's stained my soul. But it had to be done. Father Gregory, the peasant *starets* Rasputin, had gained so much power over my cousin Nicky that he was blind to the fact that we were on the edge of a People's revolution. Whether Rasputin was a miracleworker or a madman, I still can't say. All I *do* know is that he'd convinced the Tsarina he was the only one who could save the little Tsarevich . . . could heal the boy's terrible hemorrhaging simply by touch. And on more than one occasion he had."

The hair on the back of my neck rose. Boy had believed firmly in the power of the spirit to survive death.

If love could defy death, then hatred could, too. Suddenly my hands were as icy as Dmitri's.

"You think Paris is treacherous, Coco. St. Petersburg was a city ruled by rumor. Every new one was more vicious than the last! Rasputin was conducting orgies with Society women . . . Rasputin had been allowed to deflower my nieces, the grand duchesses . . . Rasputin was sleeping with the Tsarina herself."

"Couldn't anyone do anything to stop him, Dmitri? He was only one man after all?"

"But was he, Coco? Was he a man or a devil? Finally my friend, Prince Felix Yusupov, came to me and asked me to join a conspiracy to kill Rasputin—'like the mad dog he is,' he said. Felix knew the danger all too well. He was no angel—the richest, most beautiful, and depraved young man in Russia. He'd spent too many drunken nights in Rasputin's company. He'd felt his remarkable personal magnetism and recognized, probably out of his own perversities, that the man had an infinite capacity for evil."

I shuddered at the image.

" 'Only one man,' you say, Coco. Well, there were five of us. Even a physician, Dr. Lazoverts. Five of us— and that one man. Felix lured him to the cellar of his palace on the Moika Quay on the pretext of meeting his wife, Princess Irina, who was actually away in the Crimea. Rasputin would go anywhere to seduce a beautiful aristocrat, and Irina was considered the most exquisite woman in Russia. I was half in love with her myself."

He made me see it all. The bearded monk with the burning eyes, dressed in his best embroidered white silk peasant shirt with a scarlet sash around his waist, black-velvet trousers, and boots polished to a high sheen for the occasion of seduction. The assassin, Yusupov, in flamboyant evening dress.

"We tried everything, you know. Dr. Lazoverts had put enough potassium cyanide powder in the Madeira and sweet cakes to kill a dozen men. The 'party' went on for two endless hours while the four of us hid upstairs and Felix entertained him. Rasputin ate and drank and told lewd stories about my nieces and the Tsarina and kept demanding that Felix play him one gypsy ballad after another on his guitar. The tension was terrible. Even after Felix cracked and took his revolver and shot him in the chest, Rasputin refused to die. It took four more shots to bring him down."

"My God, Dmitri. What happened then? What did you do with the body?"

"We bound it with rope and threw it off the Petrovsky Bridge. The body *had* to be found, you see Coco, otherwise the people would never believe Rasputin could be killed by ordinary men. When they fished him out of the Neva three days later, they found he'd managed to work one of his arms free of the rope and he was holding it up—like a blessing."

Although the bedroom was warm enough, Dmitri was shaking in the grip of the macabre vision, his deep, troubled eyes far away.

"You know, Coco, the worst thing . . . the thing that torments me most to this day is not the killing. It's that I don't know whether we were right or wrong. My own father said we'd only made a martyr of Rasputin. That we'd widened the rift between the Imperial family and the people and made it fatal."

"I can't believe that's true, Dmitri," I told him. "Everyone here in Paris—Diaghilev, Stravinsky, all the émigrés—say that revolution was inevitable. What you and your friends did was to try to put out a forest fire when it was too late."

"I want to believe that, Coco, but sometimes—in the terrible dreams that come like this, night after night— I'm afraid I have the blood of Nicky and the Tsarina who, God forgive me, I never loved, and little Alexei and all my beautiful young nieces on my own hands." Tears streamed unchecked down his face.

I took his hands in mine. "No, Dmitri, these are clean, strong hands. Hands made for life not for death." I drew him to me and began the ritual I hoped with all my heart would heal us both.

THREE

My existence for the next months was divided sharply in two. On the one hand there was my very public life at the rue Cambon where the postwar buying spree had me and my entire staff swept up in a tornado of productivity. I'd even had to expand my workrooms to encompass the premises at Number 31.

I was gratified that, *force majeure,* the wartime restrictions had completed the revolution for women that I'd begun as early as Royallieu and Deauville. With only pedicabs, buses, and the Métro for transport, women had had to simplify their dress to meet their new physical freedoms—their unexpected independence. To succeed, any revolution must reach the streets, and the trim, ankle-length clothes I had designed—especially the fluid jersey creations I'd been inspired to make when Jean Rodier agreed to sell me his entire stock of the wonderfully supple new machine-knit jersey he'd failed to adapt to men's undergarments—were changing the face of Paris.

And my evening wear—with its elaborately embroidered Cossack shirts over slim, straight skirts with highly polished boots and sable-trimmed hats—was a tribute to the peerless workmanship of my embroidery atelier and a secret homage to the sweetly private, restorative life I was living at the villa.

Because Dmitri and I kept so much to ourselves, we were the object of constant speculation among my customers and friends. Not even Misia knew the truth of our relationship, though she guessed that there must be one. It drove her to a positive frenzy of mischief-making. With her own penchant for triangles, she became convinced that I was enjoying one with Dmitri and Stravinsky. Over tea at the Ritz, she put me through her own jealous version of the Inquisition.

"Of course it's true, Coco—it *has* to be. I mean there you all are, marooned together out in Garches in splendid isolation, with nothing to do in the evenings except listen to the birdsong and make love." Her topaz eyes positively glowed. "Stravinsky's on the small side for *my* taste and his hair *is* receding, but he does have those voluptuous lips and that adorable moustache. All three of you so intense . . . so wildly attractive—it would be inevitable."

" 'All three of us,' Misia. Are you forgetting Igor's wife, Catherine, and his four children? It's hardly the stuff menages are made of."

"Oh, Catherine," she said contemptuously, "Igor hasn't let her stand in his way in the past when he sees someone he really wants." She smiled slyly, her meaning unmistakable. "And as for the children, between his work and his amours, they've always considered themselves lucky to get even a glimpse of him."

Ironically, she was right on both counts, but I refused to satisfy her overheated curiosity by admitting it. Igor was a part-time father at best, totally preoccupied with his work. After finishing the *Concertino* and the *Symphonies of Wind Instruments* in Brittany before Diaghilev sent him to stay with me, he had barely drawn breath before plunging into obsessive work on the scoring for his new composition, *Les noçes villageoises,* and the plans for a retrospective evening of his work at the Salle Gaveau which I had agreed to finance. Catherine complained bitterly about his neglect, and it was Dmitri who was serving as substitute father to the small Stravinskys.

It was also true that Igor's eyes were wandering—but most definitely *not* in my direction. Igor loved me, but not in the fierce, possessive way Misia did, the only way she understood. Intuitively he knew, or Diaghilev had told him, the toll my passion for Boy had taken on my spirit. He was genuinely happy that Dmitri and I had found one another at a moment when we were both adrift, trying to make sense of the cruel, random games Fate had played with our lives.

As for himself, Misia was right, he was unfaithful. Beyond his music, though, the love of his life was not his wife, certainly not me, and not his casual mistress of the moment, the spoilt Chauve-Souris Russian dancer Katinka who kept pestering him to compose a piece in her honor. No, Igor's love was Vera de Bosset Sudeikina, the strikingly beautiful wife of the stage designer friend who had introduced him to the petulant Katinka. How did I know? The way Vera's name kept coming up again and again in our conversations. The way he always managed to include the Sudeikins in his musical evenings at Garches. The way he watched her covertly, longingly, whenever Catherine's attention was taken up by the children.

I had no intention of letting Misia know the truth so she and her gossips could dine out on it all over Paris. Misia was the friend of my heart, but I knew *au fond* that she was not to be trusted. Even happily married now to José after their twelve turbulent years together, she was still not content. Misia lived for drama. She breathed intrigue. Her overwhelming need to meddle, to play with lives—especially the lives of those she loved—made it simply impossible for her to keep secrets.

And I felt oddly protective of all the birds of passage who'd come to lodge under my roof at Garches. One way or another, we had all been dispossessed. We all needed time—time to rest and regroup. If my gentle evasions of Misia's prying bought us that time, so much the better.

As usual, I had underestimated her. Philippe Berthe-lot was right—once Misia was on the scent she was a stalking cat. Stealthy and persistent. One evening when I returned to the villa, I found Stravinsky pacing the carpet in the drawing room, his wire-rimmed glasses shoved unceremoniously up on his balding head.

"You won't believe what our perfidious Pole has got up to this time, Coco." He handed me a note on Misia's embossed stationery. It was brief and extremely provocative.

My very dear friend,
Coco is a *midinette* who prefers Grand Dukes to artists!
Your
Misia

"You and I know just how preposterous this is—innuendos and all," Igor sighed, "unfortunately, Catherine doesn't. She found it lying on the desk in my study and she's determined, as she put it, that we 'can no longer accept Mademoiselle Chanel's hospitality.' She's packing right now to take the children to a friend in Biarritz. Frankly, Coco, I'd like to wring Misia's lovely, trouble-making neck with my bare hands."

"Don't be too upset with her, Igor. It's just her way," I told him. "And, after all, the worst thing she's called me is 'a little dressmaker.' For Misia, that's letting me off easily."

"I know . . . I know, Coco, but it's damned inconvenient right now. You see how it is with me and Vera. I've known you were aware of our attachment from the beginning. I simply can't leave Paris. I've got to be near her and try to work things out somehow. But I won't be able to stay here, either. With you putting up the money for my concert, that would confirm all Catherine's worst suspicions."

"Ironic, isn't it, Igor? I think the concert is really what this is all about. Misia is just as jealous of my becoming your patroness as your mistress."

That night, lying sheltered in Dmitri's arms as the soft spring rain fell on the roof of our refuge, I told him about Misia's letter.

"I don't understand it, Dmitri. How can someone who claims to love you—who *does* love you and has demonstrated it time and again—how can they do anything as malicious as that? I pretended to Igor, because he was so upset about Catherine . . . about Vera . . . about everything, that it hadn't hurt me. But it *did*, Dmitri. Misia is my closest friend. Why would she want to hurt me?"

"She doesn't want to hurt you, Coco. She wants to own you. There's a kind of lover—and I'm not implying you and Misia have ever been together in that way—it's not my concern. Let's just say there's a kind of person who is never secure unless they can control the one they love. For someone like Misia, for whom love and ownership are one and the same, your independence is frustrating, frightening. It implies loss—that you don't belong to her. It's the fear of abandonment that's making her strike out blindly."

How wise Dmitri was. After his own sacrifices.

"Those of us who thought we'd lost everything—like you and me, Coco—and have gone on to discover that particular loss *is* permanent, but that love endures and moves on . . . we're not threatened the way Misia is.

We don't need to defend against love. We treasure it whenever we're fortunate enough to find it."

And I had been infinitely fortunate to find Dmitri. The love I felt for him was something so different from what I'd experienced before—the total abandonment of myself in Boy and to him—that it hardly seemed the same species of emotion. It was love, nonetheless, strong and steady and life-affirming.

Johanna had seen it in my birth chart. With Dmitri I had begun to rebuild.

The months we spent together alone in the villa after Igor and his family had gone and I had temporarily turned my back on Misia and Paris Society were a kind of convalescence of the soul.

Gradually, Dmitri's night terrors receded. The vengeful spirit of Father Gregory no longer rose every night from the icy waters of the Neva to accuse him. The bullet-riddled bodies of his exquisite young nieces in their white court dresses, Olga . . . Tatiana . . . Marie . . . Anastasia no longer appeared at his bedside to reproach him for stealing their hopes and dreams of love.

And I fought off my own terrible nightmares of Boy's fiery death, the flames racing through my own flesh and boiling my blood as I burnt alive in his arms, so that I would come awake pouring with sweat and crying out his name.

Dmitri would nurse me then, as if I was a child with a fever, sponging my hot, restless body, changing our soaking sheets and holding me safe in his strong embrace, telling me the fantastical folktales his own nurse had used to lull him into sleep until I drowsed off again or the first sleepy birds roused themselves in the garden and began their announcement of a new day.

Our affair couldn't last and we both knew it. We truly had come from separate galaxies. A grand duke and a peasant's daughter. Dmitri could accommodate the notion of a woman's work being of any real importance even less than Étienne. Only Boy had understood and supported my commitment to the work, and that probably because of his own completely unorthodox upbringing.

Though his love for me was not possessive like Misia's, Dmitri was ultimately jealous of the work and the time it took away from him. I could sense his growing frustration. While I spent my days in the rue Cambon, oblivious of time, happily, totally absorbed in the designs for the new collection, Dmitri remained at the villa, reading Roman history and making an attempt, at my urging, at writing a memoir of his experience of the revolution.

The crumpled pages littering the study floor and the half-finished and scratched-out paragraphs on the pad lying on the desk that I found when I came home in the evenings told the story. Dmitri was only marking time, counting the hours till my return and finding them too empty. His was the dilemma of so many of the émigrés. He was a man of action with nothing to do . . . a courtier with no monarch to serve, a soldier without a war to fight.

One day I came home to find the villa dark and empty, Dmitri and Piotr gone, and a letter in Dmitri's strong, sloping handwriting propped against a bouquet of Parma violets on the mantel—almost hidden in the green leaves of the violets, a perfect emerald as big as a postage stamp. One of the last of Dmitri's small fund of precious stones. My hands trembled as I opened the envelope, even though I knew what I would find inside.

My very dearest Coco,

This is a coward's way to say adieu, *but I knew that if I saw you—saw your dark, thoughtful eyes and that gallant smile I've come to depend on so—I would not ever be able to leave.*

And you know—we both do, no matter how hard we've tried to deny it to ourselves—that it would be wrong for us to try to stay together, that we would ultimately undo all the good we've done for one another over these blessed months.

I hope that we are wise enough to understand that love is sometimes a form of rescue—a bridge back to life from a wasteland of pain and loss. We found each other in that wasteland. We held hands tightly and crossed that bridge together. You have already recovered the strength to take up your life again—to do the work that I have finally understood is an integral part of you, as essential to your wellbeing as love. And you have recovered the strength to do that, too.

I haven't found my own challenge yet, but I must go out and look for it. If I stayed on here at Garches, in the sanctuary you openheartedly give me, and played at writing a history I still do not fully understand, I would eventually become a burden to you. I would lose respect for myself as a man—and, ultimately, I would lose your respect and your love. And that I cannot afford.

Understand, chère Coco, that I will always be in your life as you will be in mine.

Your
Dmitri

FOUR

With Dmitri and Piotr and the Stravinskys gone there seemed little point to my staying on at Garches. When I came home in the evening, worn-out by an afternoon on my knees pinning the skirt of a new design, the sound of my key in the lock echoed into emptiness.

All I had to remind me of their vital, vivid presence in my home was the antique icon Stravinsky had pressed into my hand on the day he left—"for luck, chère protectrice, we're all going to need it"—and Dmitri's proud, blunt, touching letter. The Villa Bel Respiro had been aptly named. A sweet breathing space. It had served its purpose for all of us before our lives inevitably took their new turnings.

Besides, Misia's spiteful note to Igor still rankled. Clearly, we had unfinished business between us. I knew that part of her chagrin was my affair with Dmitri and my excluding her from it. Because he and I were both so damaged—and our lovemaking as much an act of healing as an act of sex—I had felt superstitious about speaking of it, and she had felt doubly left out. She seldom saw us, and I withheld the details she longed to know.

It wasn't just Dmitri. It was as much my putting up the money to back Igor's concert that had provoked her. Like a jealous empress, she resented my slightest encroachment on the precious world of the arts she considered her private preserve.

All very well for me to come from nowhere to queen it over the couture, as the last two years had proved it looked as though I could. That was only fashion, after all—frivolous, fickle, subject to endless new vogues. (As if art didn't follow its own fashions. Look at the Dadaists like tigers at the Surrealists' throats!) But for a "little dressmaker" to presume to play even a minor role in the fate of one of *her* artists . . . "Heresy," the Empress had declared, "off with her head!"

Well, we'd see about that. High time for me to move onto her turf and give my beloved Madame Sert a run for her money. I'd have to plan my campaign like a general. After nearly thirty years of undisputed reign, Misia was certainly entrenched. If I was going to create a salon to rival hers at the Meurice, I surely couldn't do it out here in Garches. And I couldn't do it at the rue Cambon either. I had my private flat there where I could retire to lunch with the current favorites among my mannequins or one or another of my best clients. But for the writers and artists I intended to lure away from Misia, it was too closely linked to the deeply suspect, bourgeois world of trade, of commerce.

I got out my diary and looked up the telephone number of Monsieur Le Brun. He'd always served me well in the past. I was confident he'd understand precisely what was required.

29 rue du Faubourg St.-Honoré, the ground floor of an elegant *hôtel particulier,* the Hôtel Lauzun. Boy would certainly have approved. Close enough to the

rue Cambon for convenience, but in no way tied to the fashion house. *Mademoiselle Gabrielle Chanel at home*—I could see the coveted invitation on gold-embossed vellum. As I signed the lease in Le Brun's office I made another decision. I would decorate it myself, not even telling Misia until I had finished. It would be as different from her pink and gilt extravaganzas as my trained eye and cardinal belief in simplicity could make it.

Two months later—two months of hours stolen from the constant demands of the rue Cambon, two months of driving myself and my suppliers to distraction—it was done. And I was satisfied. Rich without being rococo, sumptuous without assaulting the eye. The palette I'd chosen was one of my favorites, shades of brown, from deep chocolate to cocoa for the suede couches with their quilted-suede pillows and beige for the simply patterned Savonnerie carpets, accents of white velvet to cover the Louis XVI chairs.

Antique lacquered Chinese coromandel screens I'd found in a shop in the rue du Bac had their hunting scenes amusingly brought to dimensional life in a pair of bronze miniature deer grazing on the carpet. A library of my favorite authors, Verlaine, La Bruyère, Mallarmé, Racine—even, for nostalgia, the complete works of my beloved romanceur, Monsieur Decourcelle—but with new works by Cocteau and Apollinaire and Radiguet, flatteringly handbound in soft moroccan leather and gold leaf by my friend Hervé Mille.

Mirrors and masks to remind me of my magical Venetian summer. And all the objects I'd assembled—from the pride of small, golden lions, my personal "Leos," and the crystal sphere Johanna had sent me to remember our visit, arranged on the table beside the largest of the couches—each one had a special significance for me.

The lioness had created her lair. Now, all I needed to do was attract the prey . . . Misia's artistic lions. When I finally invited her one afternoon to see the flat, she pouted prettily as only she could, complained that I'd kept yet *another* secret from her, then finally gave me the response I'd been hoping for.

"Coco, ma chère, isn't it a little somber? A little austere? I mean, all those browns and beiges. I suppose Jojo and I are used to more color . . . more drama . . . more of everything . . ." she trailed off into bewilderment.

"That's just it, Misia. It's the way I've gone with my dresses—always cutting back from excess. My assistants actually tease me, 'Don't hand Mademoiselle the shears, the poor mannequin will end up shivering in her chemise.' Well, that's what I've tried to do here— to create an environment that sets off beauty . . . genius . . . the extraordinary to perfection, just *because* the backdrop is so very simple."

Misia came over to me from the mantel where she'd been examining a ceremonial mask and put her arm around my waist, drawing me close.

"Well, perhaps it's still the influence of Aubazine and your convent days, Coco. It's certainly striking—everyone will say so. What troubles me about it is that I'm afraid it's *too* monastic. The person who's likely to feel most at home here is not a sensualist like Boy, rest his spirit, or my Jojo, or even—if there's any truth to rumor, your Dmitri—but an ascetic, someone who finds the pleasures of the flesh too demanding. Someone like my very own protégé, Pierre Reverdy."

I remembered him, the intense young Basque poet who'd sent me copies of his verses after we met that one time at Carya's. Misia must have stolen him away from her. Did Misia bring Reverdy to me out of friendship or as revenge for the act of defiance she correctly understood my creating my own salon to be? Why did the hairs along my arms rise?

My evenings were a *succès fou* from the first. Everyone came—Cocteau with Raymond Radiguet on his arm, observing us all with the clear, unforgiving eyes of extreme youth, Cocteau's old friend Georges Auric, Apollinaire, Giraudoux, Max Jacob, Satie, Picasso and, inevitably Olga, determined not to let her already-wandering husband out of her sight.

There was Diaghilev with his strikingly handsome new "secretary" Boris Kochno, Tristan Tzara, founder of the Dadaists, and his disciples André Breton and the dazzling Louis Arragon. Man Ray, that astonishing young American who was turning photography into fine art; Salvador Dali, the flamboyant crown prince of the surrealists who longed to unseat Picasso from his position as uncrowned king of Paris's painters . . .

Just what I'd intended. All the warring factions were represented. Add limitless champagne and very old cognac, and I had all the necessary elements to make a salon combustible—and famous.

And of course, Misia. How she must have hated coming, but on the other hand her not being there would have been a public admission of weakness, and she could never have permitted me that advantage. The first time she came with Jojo and stayed suspiciously close to his side all evening. But Jojo loathed salons, even Misia's—probably because he knew so many of the other artists thought he was a hack who prostituted his talents for money—so after that, her escort was Diaghilev or Cocteau or, with growing frequency, Reverdy.

What was it about him that drew me? I could understand Misia's attraction. In many ways he resembled José, a Mediterranean type, small and stocky, with olive skin, dark eyes, and a head of thick dark hair with an unruly lock that kept slipping down over one eye. I had always preferred tall, slender athletic men . . . men who dominated a room by their sheer physical presence. Gorgeous men like Boy and Dmitri. Pierre Reverdy was hardly a beauty. But there was something about him that fascinated me—his solitariness.

In a room full of posturing, self-dramatizing, rivalrous men he seemed to create an island of stillness around himself, as though he was in this gaudy, super-heated world but not of it. It was the way I had so often felt after Boy died, and even after my interlude with Dmitri—in my body but not of it, solitary, isolated with the world's busyness swirling just out of reach around me. I couldn't resist discovering his secret. I went over to him and drew him down beside me on the couch.

"Tell me, Monsieur Reverdy, what paths have you followed since we met at the rue Lamarck? How is the work progressing?"

"Ah, the work, Mademoiselle Chanel. When we met at Carya's I was an unknown poet publishing my verse myself in editions of one hundred copies through the kindness of the printer of *L'Intransigeant* where I worked as a proofreader. Now I am an unknown poet publishing my verse through the good offices of a publisher friend of Madame Sert's in editions of three hundred copies which he not-so-secretly doubts that he will sell. And he's probably right. Hundred-copy editions may well be my fate." He smiled charmingly, with just a hint of self-mockery.

"You are far too modest, Monsieur Reverdy. I treasure the editions you sent me and have had them bound for my library. I know that Picasso himself illustrated the most recent volume of your poems. And if it hadn't been for that review of yours, *Nord-Sud,* where you introduced their work, a number of the most famous artists in the room tonight would probably still be in the category of 'unknowns.'"

"Fame, obscurity . . . the world's applause or its profound indifference. What does it really matter, Mademoiselle Chanel, in the life of the spirit? I do the work for the work's sake and because I seem incapable of stopping myself from doing it. A part of me insists on celebrating the sensual things of this world—things like a woman's unique, particular beauty . . . her earthly magnificence. Madame Sert's . . . your own."

He put his small, square hand—a peasant's hand so very much like mine—on my thigh, and it was so hot I could feel it burn through the silk of my skirt. And Misia told me he was an ascetic . . .

"Then, chère Mademoiselle, I realize that all these fleshly things are endangered, ephemeral, false . . . dust in the eye of God. So with the same urgency with which I do the work, I am forced to put it aside and go back to the abbey to spend my days and nights contemplating the Eternal in humble silence."

His hot hand remained where it was. Clearly, he was

in his earthly phase. *Mon dieu*—what an odd man. Not conventionally attractive, but strangely compelling.

Misia abruptly abandoned the circle of admiring men where she was holding court and came to join us on the couch. She was looking especially lovely in an amber velvet chemise dress I'd created for her that flowed softly over her opulent curves and darkened her superb topaz eyes.

"What did I tell you, Coco? Pierre fits into your ambiance like a hand in his own 'massage glove.'" She played with the title of his newest work, *Le Gant de crin*.

Practically snatching his hand from my thigh, she held it possessively in her own. "I'm afraid he finds my decor at the Meurice altogether too comfortable . . . too corrupting for a man of his monastic turn of mind," she said. "Tell the truth, Pierre, isn't Mademoiselle Chanel better suited to your rather spartan taste? Pierre has trouble with too much comfort, you see." She ran her free hand lightly down the straight bodice of my black crepe dress. The comparison—and the challenge—was unmistakable.

He ignored the gesture completely. "Ah, but my dear Madame Sert, whenever I begin to find your 'comforts' too seductive . . . when I feel your sublime worldliness drawing me too far away from the work, I have no alternative but to make another retreat to the abbey at Solesmes."

"A retreat, Monsieur," I asked, "or a strategic withdrawal?"

He laughed ruefully. "Call it whatever you like, Mademoiselle Chanel. It's only in the isolation of the monastery that the noisy demands of my flesh recede into silence. Order and discipline are as essential to a poet as they are to a contemplative."

How well I understood his longing for order. When my own world turned upside down and spun out of control like Boy's car on the autoroute, I had found my own sanctuary in the rue Cambon—in the order and discipline of creation. I thought I understood this divided spirit—intense, passionate, torn between heaven and earth—and I knew I wanted to meet him again.

"When you have finished your retreat, Monsieur, I hope you will come to see me. I have had the audacity to attempt to write down a few *pensées* in the manner of La Bruyère, and I would welcome your help in polishing them."

"It would be my very great pleasure, Mademoiselle," he said, fixing me with that dark, almost hypnotic gaze.

I didn't dare look at Misia. I knew what I would see in her predatory cat's eyes. Outrage, jealousy, disbelief.

FIVE

ver the next months, Pierre became a sort of shuttlecock between Misia and me and God— not to mention his long-suffering wife, Henriette, the seamstress who for obvious reasons we were never to meet. Henriette, he told us proudly, labored long into the night in their modest rooms in the rue Cortot, doing the piecework that paid for his room and board at the abbey, paid for his retreats from the world—and from her. For a man who professed a determination to avoid the temptation of women, he was certainly doing a good job of keeping three of them in thrall.

From the safety of the monastery he wrote us the impassioned, seductive letters that kept us hoping he would fail in his withdrawal from sensual life. He played each of us according to what he knew of our natures. I'm sure he was confident our rivalry would force us to compare them. And he was right.

"Tell me, Misia," I asked as we sat in my drawing room in front of a cheerful fire, with the velvet drapes drawn against the twilight chill, "do we regret more losing him as a literary lion or as a potential lover?"

"Potential in your case, perhaps, Coco," she said provocatively, always determined to keep the upper hand when, in fact, Pierre had assured me they had never been intimate—at *his* reluctance.

"Just listen to what he says in his latest letter to me, Coco ma chère. Do these sound like the words of a 'potential' lover?" She had to reach into her reticule for her lorgnette. I was delighted at this reminder that she was ten years older than me. At least my eyesight was as sharp as her sarcasm. Pierre was only thirty-one, after all. She could be his mother.

She unfolded the creased and obviously much-read letter: "You are one of those whom I love to the point of pain. Often my arms, my lips, my heart long for you . . . Here in the silence some would call mortal (only the birds are heard to speak, only the monks to sing) I listen to God and I love my friends with a divine love . . . The choice was to die, to wither away, or to live in the unique light."

She smiled so smugly I wanted to slap her.

"Of course I don't mean to quibble, Misia my darling," I said, "but in fact those sentiments are *all* in potentia. He 'longs' for you. He loves you—*and* the rest of his friends—with 'a divine love.' The only way he could achieve his 'unique light' was to avoid your embraces."

I picked up my latest letter from Solesmes which just happened to be lying on the table in front of the couch. "Now he writes *me* quite differently: 'Chère Coco, I need this solitude. It is time for me to change my life if I do not want to end in complete self-contempt. Running after pleasure is like running after the wind. One loses one's breath and all that is left is a gnawing bitterness.' "

"And you think those are the sentiments of any *kind* of a lover?"

"I do. You see with me, Misia, he is more thoughtful, more philosophical. He knows how very well I understand him, knows what a serious commitment that kind of understanding represents—what a temptation *I* represent. He tells me quite plainly that he means to change his life."

"If you're right, Coco, and perhaps you are—Pierre is such a strange, guarded, lonely man—all I can say is, be careful. The one clear thing in his letters to both of us is that he's hell-bent on reform. In my experience, reformers make very uneasy lovers."

Prophetic. But then, Misia so often was. As I learned to my dismay, a saint in society is no more useful than in the desert—but far more dangerous.

Not a week later Pierre turned up on my doorstep at midnight, carrying a half-empty bottle of cognac and a folder with a sheaf of manuscript pages—the poems he'd written at Solesmes.

"Well, my dear friend," I teased him, "welcome back to Paris and the enticements of the flesh. Have the Brothers given you time off for good behavior?"

"Don't play with me, Mademoiselle. I thought you understood me better." His eyes burned with a strange black light. Was he drunk on the cognac or on prolonged abstinence?

"Don't you see, Mademoiselle, that you are all that's standing between me and a life of chastity and self-denial—a life of perfect serenity, of peaceful contemplation? Every hour out of your sight has been a lifetime. At matins . . . at noons . . . at evensong your image has been there taunting me. Fasting only sharpened my hunger for you. Celibacy only made me want you more. Prayer became the endless repetition of your name. These verses—some of the best work I've ever done—were not written for God as they should have been, but for you."

He threw the folder at my feet and the pages scattered like confetti on the drawing room carpet. Without another word, he picked me up and carried me into my bedroom.

His lovemaking was different from anything I had known before. He was skillful enough, but he made love as though he were in pain. I opened my eyes to watch him moving above me, and his face was contorted into a mask of anguish, as though every strong, determined thrust was excruciating, not pleasing to him.

He could not find release. For what seemed to me hours—until I had climaxed not once but a number of times—he continued to struggle, until at last he simply collapsed on top of my body, still erect inside me, and fell asleep.

When I told Misia about Pierre's strange nocturnal visit and that when I woke in the morning he was gone, no trace of him except for the dozen exquisite poems still lying on the carpet, she expressed no surprise.

"I warned you, Coco. Men like Reverdy are a curse on the women who care for them. Not like Picasso and his compulsive womanizing. Picasso is dangerous, but these men are worse—the cripples of the soul. They long to love, but despise their own weakness when they surrender to it. I'll admit I wanted him, too, but the healthiest part of me is relieved that Pierre's chosen you."

I recognized the honesty of her words. For once they were not tinged by our endless competition.

"So pleasure is constantly sought—never achieved," I said quietly. "That's what he meant then, Misia, by 'running after the wind.' The bitterness he speaks of was there on his face when he made love to me and couldn't be satisfied. I saw it and it frightened me. It was as though he hated me."

"Not you, Coco, himself. Pierre is a brilliant poet . . . I would go so far as to say a genius. But he's a man at war with his own flesh. The sooner he recognizes that the only logical response to the world for a man like him is to leave it and retire to Solesmes once and for all, the better for you . . . for poor Henriette . . . for any woman who has the misfortune to spark his desire."

Pierre never frequented my salon again, but he came to me three more times. Always unexpected, always after midnight, and always flushed with passion and brandy. And each time the pattern of his silent lovemaking was the same—voracious lust, followed by frustration, followed by remorse.

Despite Misia's continued warnings, I couldn't bring myself to refuse him. Part of it, I knew, was the shallowest sort of female vanity—the arrogant belief that I would be the one strong and steady and loving enough to release him from his prison of guilt and ambivalence. More than that, though, there was a part of me that knew to the last franc the cost of his pride, his isolation, his difference from all the rest—the fortunate ones, as I'd told Adrienne so long ago in Vichy, with their simple, attainable dreams and desires.

Pierre Reverdy. Another exile. But this one the loneliest of all—a man in exile from himself. When he left me the last time, to quit the world for the serenity he was determined to find at Solesmes, part of my heart went into seclusion with him.

SIX

*P*ierre's final retirement to the solitude of Solesmes left Misia and me with our old intricacy unresolved. Having "lost Pierre" to me, as she insisted on putting it, when in fact, she knew Pierre had been lost to all of us from the start, she was increasingly jealous of any attachments I made to the artists she considered her own.

So when Cocteau approached me about doing the costumes for his adaptation of Sophocles's *Antigone,* I was wary for more good reasons than one. With Cocteau doing the scenario and Picasso the set design, Misia was bound to be furious if I agreed to join them. And the producer was to be Charles Dullin, now artistic director of the Théâtre de l'Atelier and separated from Carya, but still a reminder of that strange, potent attraction that had nearly cost me Boy six years before I had had to surrender him to a more jealous lover than all the rest.

Underlying all these dark premonitions was my deep superstition about designing costumes for the stage at all, an irrational fear that I could still date directly to my girlhood encounter with Monsieur Didier in Vichy. Irrational or not, I was quite prepared to decline on the very real grounds of the pressures of my business, when Cocteau came to me on one of my evenings in the Faubourg St.-Honoré to argue his cause.

"You *can't* refuse us, chère Coco," he said, the long, eloquent fingers of his slender hands sketching the characters like his drawings that seemed to hover in midair like smoke rings. "You have to *see* them . . . the blinded monarch, his incestuous wife . . . and his loyal daughter. Frankly, Coco, I've already told the press that I can't *imagine* Oedipus's daughters as badly dressed . . . dressed by anyone less than Mademoiselle Chanel, the Empress of couture. You'll simply have to risk Misia's wrath and make an honest poet out of me."

Cocteau could always make me laugh. Though his critics accused him of bitchery, with me he revealed a gift for gentle mockery—a way of making me see the absurdity of the conflicts Misia was forever trying to create just for the joy of watching sparks fly.

Besides, it was time I put my old bogeyman, Didier, behind me once and for all. It would be a challenge to me to see if I could do the impossible . . . if I could take the purity of line that had become my signature in fashion and move it into the realm of high drama.

The curtain rose well before opening night when I was fitting Genica Athanasiou into the coarse woolen robe with its Greek key motif border in the brick-red of recently dried blood. Even her costume, I intended, would announce Antigone as victim.

Misia came backstage unannounced and interrupted us. She dispensed with any attempt at polite preliminaries. "Coco, I must talk to you. Right now. It's on a matter of extreme importance."

"I can't stop work now, Misia. Madame Athanasiou is due for a line rehearsal with Jean in half an hour, and he wants to see my preliminary conception of her costume. Why don't we meet for tea later?"

"No—this can't wait until teatime. I regret having to have this discussion in front of you, chère Madame Athanasiou, but I simply can't put it off any longer. Just what are you up to, Coco . . . you have to tell me." A hectic flush burned under her translucent skin. She looked as if she had a fever.

" 'Up to,' Misia? I don't understand."

"You know very well what I mean. First it was Igor's concert . . . then that so-called 'salon' of yours . . . then your appropriation of Pierre. Now this new charade— this ridiculous attempt to get close to Picasso and Jean. 'COCO CHANEL DESIGNS FOR THE STAGE,' the very thing you swore for reasons of your own—private reasons I've had the delicacy never to inquire into—that you'd never do. Designing for the stage. Don't think for a moment, Coco, that I'm unaware of your *larger* designs."

In all the years of our highly charged friendship, I'd never seen her so agitated . . . so vulnerable. I wondered if the wine she'd obviously drunk at lunch—that telltale scarlet flush gave her away—had released the brake on her true feelings.

" 'Get close to Picasso and Jean' . . . Misia, take hold of yourself. Jean came to *me* about doing the costumes. And you're right, I *was* reluctant at first because of an unpleasant experience I'd had with a theatre manager when I was very young and very green. But Jean prevailed over my reluctance. He'd already spoken to the press about my commitment to the production, and I couldn't embarrass him, could I, Misia?"

"No you couldn't Coco. I'll give you that—though I have a strong suspicion it's more than your concern for saving Jean's face that motivated you. You seem overly willing to have your name bandied about in the press these days."

How that stung! Unlike Poiret or Worth, I had never actively courted the press. In fact, for a very long time the French had simply ignored me. Misia knew how much that had hurt. What was the matter with her today?

"Perhaps you're right, Misia. Perhaps I *am* too often in the public eye. But for someone whose livelihood depends on attracting new custom . . . new markets, rather than depending on the generosity of a rich and doting husband, press mentions do assume a certain significance."

Poor Madame Athanasiou. As the level of our acrimony escalated, so did her discomfort. I'm afraid in my preoccupation with Misia's bizarre—and unprovoked—assault, I may have placed a pin or two painfully close to her anatomy.

Misia was pacing frantically back and forth, her redgold hair shimmering in the half-light of backstage. Knowing her for as long and as well as I had, I was certain we were on the brink of the truth—or the truth according to Misia.

"Stravinsky . . . that was nothing, Coco. I didn't believe for a moment that he was in love with you. Igor could never tolerate a woman like you who would refuse to take second place to his music. Reverdy . . . I *gave* him to you. And a lot of good it did either one of you. There he is in Solesmes, flagellating himself for what little pleasure he allowed himself with you—if he allowed himself any. But *this* . . . this is too much!

"Excuse me, Mesdames," Madame Athanasiou had had her fill of this whispered cat fight, "but I *must* meet now with Monsieur Jean to review my lines." With her intrinsic dignity she stepped down from the table I'd had her stand on to adjust her sacrificial gown. "I shall return at the soonest opportunity to complete the fitting, chère Mademoiselle." She was gone, leaving Misia and me to have whatever it was out.

I busied myself collecting scraps of material and vagrant pins from the table and the floor around it. I had to count on my silence to draw her . . .

"Don't be coy with me, Coco," she hissed. "We've known one another too long and too intimately for coyness. You understand precisely what I'm referring to—Diaghilev . . . Diaghilev and *Le Sacre.* You thought your three hundred thousand francs could buy my friend . . . one of my oldest, dearest friends. The friend I introduced you to, as I did to so many others—so *very* many others. How many of my friends *do* you intend to buy, Coco ma chère?"

So *that* was it. I'll admit I flushed scarlet, but not for the guilty conscience she thought. I blushed for Diaghilev's weakness. She must have lunched with him today and he'd broken his promise. He'd sworn the gift would be a secret between us. When I'd heard him that evening last summer in Harry's Bar in Venice, complaining bitterly to Misia that he was short the money to restage *Le Sacre,* I'd resolved at that moment to lend it to him. And—a secret between Diaghilev and me—to dedicate it to Boy and, in my heart, to the memory of the extraordinary night of the premiere . . . the night I'd finally understood in that passionate encounter in the *"Dames"* upstairs at Maxim's the full extent of Boy's love for me.

When I'd gone to Diaghilev last week at the Hôtel Continental to make him my proposition, he'd agreed enthusiastically to it all. To the first condition, that the donor be anonymous . . . that my name never appear in the press . . . that it never pass his lips at all. Knowing and loving both of them as I did, I should have foreseen that I was making an impossible demand. Secrecy between Misia and Diaghilev—two people who lived for intrigue—was a contradiction in terms.

Laughing, now that I understood what it was all about, I told her. "Oh Misia, what am I to do with you? You know your friends are loyal to you to a fault, even when you try their patience as sorely as you're trying mine right now. Diaghilev adores you. You could never lose him as a friend, any more than you could me. Will we have to be together for a thousand years before you understand that I love you for yourself and for your particular gift—your genius at recognizing and encouraging all that's new and bold and promising in the arts." By now I was addressing her turned back.

"And that you love me for myself and for *my* particular gift, which is to practice my craft, which I acknowledge to you is just that—a craft not an art. Surely, Misia, there's room in all Paris for two brazen women as avid for life as you and me?"

Laughing now, too, but with tears streaming down her face, she threw her arms around me.

"Forgive me, Coco chérie?"

"No need for forgiveness between friends, Misia," I said.

And when the curtain finally rose on Picasso's striking violet-blue pillars and his hieratic masks and shields, inspired by the potters of Delphi, and my stark robes of white and earth-toned wools, the press declared the production a success—not a popular success, but a theatrical success for Picasso's decor and my costumes that one critic observed "looked like antique garments rediscovered after centuries."

A theatrical success . . . the words carried me back in time to the cold, barren stage of that dingy theatre in Vichy . . . *Theatrical style . . . that's what you've got, Mademoiselle Coco . . . theatrical style.* More than fifteen years later I had to admit Didier probably had been right. I couldn't sing worth a damn. But I could make theatrical magic my own way.

SEVEN

J was in my office with one of my suppliers, looking at color swatches of the new silk jerseys for the spring collection when Madame Deray, my directrice whom I'd hired for her unshakable *tranquillité,* burst into the room without knocking, wringing her well-manicured hands.

"Que dieu nous aide, Mademoiselle. I don't know what on earth to do. The Comtesse Greffulhe and the Baronne de Rothschild are quarreling over the very last ounce of Chanel No. 5 in the house. I'm afraid they're going to start pulling hair at any moment."

The notion of two of the most elegant doyennes of Paris Society rolling around on the floor of my salon, fighting over a bottle of scent was so delicious I had all I could do not to laugh out loud. But she was genuinely upset.

"Don't distress yourself, Madame." I attempted to calm her. "It just so happens I keep a cache of a half-dozen bottles in my desk for precisely this sort of an emergency." I opened a drawer and handed one to her. "Go and pour jasmine and tuberose on troubled matrons, Madame."

We both laughed then, but I realized the implications were no joke. My signature fragrance had caught on like wildfire. Poor beleaguered Monsieur Beaux, working out of his modest laboratory down in Grasse, could not *begin* to keep up with the orders. My directrices in Deauville and Biarritz were pleading for shipments, and I had even had requests from buyers from some of the premier shops in America.

What an irony. Misia and my little *jeu d'esprit* was turning into a phenomenon, and I had no experience with manufacturing for sales of the volume these orders anticipated.

I concluded the meeting and sat alone at my desk with the drapes drawn, trying to puzzle it out. This was one of the times I missed Boy most. Diaghilev knew to the last centime the economics of staging a new ballet or maintaining the troupe for a season. José could give me the exact specifications and number of assistants required to create a gigantic wall fresco. But I had no one to ask about the means of mass-producing something as frivolous as a fragrance.

I felt as blank and innocent of inspiration as the plaster heads standing on the wall-shelf opposite me, waiting for new creations. Wait a minute. Of course, why hadn't I thought of him immediately? It had been such a long while since I'd seen him, it had taken the hat forms to remind me. Papa Bader. If anyone in Paris knew the answer to my dilemma it would be him. He'd built the Galeries Lafayette into one of the most successful retail empires in the world. I would telephone and invite him to lunch with me at the Ritz at his earliest convenience.

As I walked through the doors of the Espadon Grill, I saw him immediately. The years—and the expanded girth from good living—had only increased his uncanny resemblance to Père Noël. He rose from the banquette and enveloped me in a vast bear hug.

"Mademoiselle Chanel, success certainly suits you! You look radiant. Of course you'll recall that I predicted it the first time we met and you showed me those foolish little boater hats of yours. I told you you were a walking gold mine. My only regret is that you would never agree to come and design for me. Always *were* too independent for your own good, chérie."

"Probably so, Papa Bader, but you knew even then I was never intended to work in harness. I'm a rogue like you. And rogues need their freedom to fly. Look how high you've flown. The Galeries are famous all over the world."

"I'm not so old that I'm still not susceptible to blatant flattery by a pretty young woman." He winked broadly "Well, out with it! Tell me what it is you want from me, chère Coco. You haven't invited me to lunch to hear an old man reminisce over the oysters about his triumphs in the retail trade. An investment of capital in your couture house? So you can expand into new markets? Tell me and it's yours. I'm not too old to remember what a shrewd business head you have on that swan's neck of yours."

How I loved this wily old merchant. He was the only one—before Boy—to understand I was truly serious about the work . . . the first one to encourage me that I could make my dreams happen.

"I have a business problem, Papa Bader," I told him, "not with the couture house. That I deal with on a crisis-by-crisis basis, the way I'm sure you do at the Galeries . . . a supplier who fails to deliver on time, a seamstress with an ailing mother who needs financial help, a mannequin with an awkward pregnancy, a Comtesse whose account is so very delinquent I hesitate to cut another yard of cloth for her, beyond the black crepe I would gladly cut if her ancient husband finally passed on and freed her to be able to afford her dresses *and* her devoted young lover."

Papa Bader smiled wryly. "These, my dear Coco, are problems that I would call 'operational'—problems intrinsic to the business of doing business. Surely 'operationals' are not what have brought us together again after all these years?"

"No, Papa Bader, you're right. I have a completely unexpected problem . . . one I know you've experienced yourself. It's a matter of too much success."

"Trop de succès?" he laughed and motioned to the captain to open the chilled bottle of Cordon Rouge. "What could be too much success for you, Coco? Don't tell me that handsome young devil you brought to the Galeries is so jealous he's demanding you marry him and give up designing to devote yourself to raising a pack of unruly Anglo-French children?"

"No, Papa Bader, that's not quite the case. Monsieur Capel is no longer in Paris." Tears came to my eyes and he immediately sensed he'd gone too far. Taking my hand in his vast one he said, "Whatever the problem, chère Coco, if I can be of any help to you in solving it, be assured you can count on me."

"It's my perfume, Papa Bader—Chanel Numéro Five. Have you heard of it?"

" 'Heard of it' . . . false modesty doesn't become you, Coco. You know very well all Paris is wild for it. I practically face revolution every day when my shop girls have to tell their customers it's not available at the Galeries. I'm beginning to feel sympathetic to the keeper of the bastille."

I had to laugh. Papa Bader had never lost his gift for melodrama. "Well," I told him, "your problem is my own. I simply can't keep up with the demand. We're constantly out of stock at the rue Cambon. My customers swear they wear it instead of nightclothes and that a drought of Chanel No. 5 will mean the demise of countless important love affairs. My directrices in Deauville and Biarritz are threatening to mutiny. And my single supplier, Monsieur Beaux down in Grasse, admits he and his staff are completely overwhelmed. What am I to do, Papa Bader? You must help me."

By now he had downed two dozen oysters and was about to commence his assault on the *Ris de veau à la crème Dom Pérignon.* While he ate there was no conversation. Papa Bader applied himself to the practice of gastronomy with the pure concentration of a devout. All I could do was pick at what I suppose was an excellent *Salade de langoustines.* To me it tasted like paper. When he had polished off his *Selle d'agneau Maurice de Talleyrand,* followed by a *Soufflé Grand Marnier,* and settled back over his cognac and cigar, he was finally ready to turn his attention to my troubles.

"Inviting me to lunch today was inspired as usual, Coco. When it comes to instinct for the business, I've always told you that, for a woman, you have a superb gut." Satisfied, he rubbed his own ample one. "Retailing's my passion, you see. Give me something new, something unexpected to sell—something like your fragrance—and I'll sell the very devil out of it. I never involve myself on the manufacturing side, though—the nuts and bolts of it all hold no magic for me. I'm in it for the show, the glamour."

My heart sank. "Sales, as I told you, are hardly my problem, Papa Bader. Or, ironically, they are—too many of them with too little product. I couldn't let you sell Chanel No. 5 through the Galeries. I can't even keep up with the needs of my limited outlets."

"Don't look so crestfallen, chérie." He laid his huge paw over my small hand on the banquette. "Just because I don't direct the factories doesn't mean I don't know how things work. I have, in fact, the perfect solution to your problem—two gentlemen from Neuilly." He beamed at me like a benevolent Buddha.

"That sounds suspiciously like a cabaret act, Papa Bader. Precisely who are these 'gentlemen' and what makes you think they can help me?"

"The brothers Wertheimer—Pierre and Paul—proprietors of the biggest fragrance and cosmetics company in France. The blush you see on the cheeks of most of your customers over the age of nineteen is almost certainly the Wertheimers' 'Bourjois.' Their products fly out of the Galeries."

"If they're so very well-established, why would they want to take on new products?"

"For the same reason you always used to go on at me about . . . growth, expansion. For profit. The brothers have expensive hobbies—women and horses. Their stud is one of the finest in the country. Pierre's the genius in the family, inherited his father's business head and doubled Bourjois's revenues since he took over."

"But why would he be interested in me?"

"Exceptional women have always fascinated him. He's already made an arrangement with Madame Rubenstein in America to manufacture her face creams that promise to make a dowager's dewlaps feel like a baby's bum. Even set up a factory for it somewhere in New York. She's meant to be a beauty and a tough negotiator, but I'd back you against La Rubenstein any day. You, my darling Coco, would be very much to Pierre Wertheimer's taste. And, of course, I'm willing to take only a small percentage—say ten percent off the top of whatever you agree—for the privilege of putting you two talented people together."

"How selflessly generous of you, cher Papa Bader." I had to smile. His tactics were as shameless as my own.

He had decreed that the most strategic way to intrigue Pierre Wertheimer was to meet him under apparently social auspices. So that Sunday we drove out to the races at Longchamp.

Papa Bader looked aggressively prosperous in his dress coat and dove grey top hat, and I had taken more trouble than usual over my toilette to achieve an impression of complete naturalness. Over a soft, slim skirt of cream-colored jersey, I wore a navy blue blazer, an innovation I'd originally borrowed from Boy's wardrobe and feminized by the addition of a more defined waistline and a lace handkerchief in the breast pocket. A simple cream silk shirt with a matching ascot tied at the throat, several ropes of creamy pearls, pale stockings and pumps, a navy straw modeled after a gentleman's panama hat completed the costume. It had always amused me to play with the elements of Boy's wardrobe, and there was something consoling about dressing like him now on this day when I needed his business luck so very badly.

The afternoon was perfect, cloudless and blue, and the sunny paddock was surrounded by the crème of Paris Society. The men were deep in discussion of the bloodlines and trial times of the day's rivals, the women equally rapt in another form of competition—high-stakes fashion.

I greeted a number of my favorite clients who laughingly assured me that Longchamp had been "Chanelized," and, in fact, they were right. My characteristically simple tailleurs outnumbered the Vionnets and Poirets by at least two to one, and I saw that the others had followed my lead in lifting the hem to mid-calf. How much more practical than those ruffled skirts and elaborate trains that had eaten the paddocks' dust in the not-so-distant past!

I saw Papa Bader in earnest conversation with two slender, elegant, top-hatted men leaning on the paddock rail. When I caught his eye, he motioned to me to join him.

"Voilà, Pierre, the very woman I've been telling you about," he said, beaming up at the taller of the two men as though he were making him a gift of me.

"Pierre Wertheimer, may I present my dear friend, Mademoiselle Coco Chanel, the brave Jeanne d'Arc who has single-handedly liberated the women of France from the tyranny of the corset. A blessing we gentlemen count as often, I suspect, as the fair sex do." He winked broadly, and then as an afterthought, "Oh yes, and Paul Wertheimer, next in line after Pierre to the throne of Tsar of Bourjois."

"Delighted, Mademoiselle," Pierre Wertheimer said, holding onto my hand for slightly longer than was proper. "No recompense could be adequate to the favor you've done *both* sexes, Mademoiselle, but perhaps I might offer a tip on the first race? My own 'Reine Hélène,' named after my old friend Madame Rubenstein, is the favorite, but I have a side bet riding on Rothschild's 'Surpris,' and that's the horse I would recommend to you. Done splendidly in the trials. Betting against myself may seem reckless to you, Mademoiselle, but I always acknowledge talent when I meet it."

I was struck by the warm glint in his intelligent brown eyes and the charm of his slow smile. Very attractive and very sure of himself. He overshadowed his shy, gangly younger brother altogether.

"You will do me the favor of gracing our box this afternoon, Mademoiselle Chanel," he announced, brooking no argument, tucking my arm proprietarily in his and leading all of us off to the stands.

Oh, handsome Pierre Wertheimer was a player, all right—a worthy adversary. And I already knew, in that moment of mutual recognition when our eyes met, that this strong, infinitely challenging, worldly man was going to have an important part to play in my future.

No matter where I put my money this afternoon, I was going to emerge the winner.

EIGHT

I can't remember a more arctic winter. It seemed years, not months, since Pierre Wertheimer and I had sat in the sunny stands at Longchamp, working out our agreement to establish Parfums Chanel, while Surpris, the snow-white filly he'd told me to back against his own contender, went on to pay off at odds of twenty-to-one.

It was the white horses drawing the hearse that reminded me. What a macabre contrast between the exhilaration and promise of that brilliant afternoon and this dark, forbidding December twilight. The pavement seemed to crackle with the cold—vapor rising like smoke from dry ice—and the trees along the Seine and in the Bois wore slim sheaths of frost. Perhaps an appropriate setting for the funeral of the boy genius his lover, Cocteau, once described as so hard it would take a diamond to scratch his heart.

It was Raymond Radiguet's icy, incredibly precocious brilliance—a gift for social satire that might one day have rivaled Proust's—that had astounded us all. That a child of seventeen could so intimately understand and truthfully depict the lust and greed and naked ambition and fear of death that drove so many of us had made a sensation of his first novel, *Le Diable au corps.*

And the pages of his work-in-progress, *Le Bal du Comte d'Orgel,* based shamelessly on the elegant master of our revels, Étienne de Beaumont, were being avidly devoured by those few who could lay hands on them. Misia was trying desperately to get a copy. All Paris waited in fear and trembling. Would it be worse to find yourself as one of Raymond's *monstres sacrés*— or worse, to be ignored? I'm sure Misia thought the latter.

Now "Monsieur Bébé," as Jean so lovingly called him, was dead of typhus at twenty. It was the knowledge that Raymond had died alone that most tormented him. Jean had come to the Ritz, where Misia and I were dining, in the first hours of his terrible grief. He was full of guilt and remorse and self-hatred for the quarrel that had parted them. When we tried to reason with him, he was inconsolable.

"You don't understand, Coco. He knew. He warned me. The last time I visited him I remarked on how much better he was looking, and he told me he would be dead in three days. He actually said, 'I'll be executed by God's firing squad.'"

I shivered. My well-hidden peasant roots ran very deep, and I believed in the Sight. Why wouldn't I? Hadn't Boy's premonition of his violent death come tragically true six years before?

"And that's when he died, Jean?" I asked.

"Three days almost to the hour. In that bleak little room. Alone. I can't forgive myself. I was behaving like an outraged parent and a jilted lover—angry that he'd gone back to drinking and jealous that he was sleeping with women. I deserved to lose him."

"That's not true, Jean mon cher, and you know it," I told him. "It would be like my saying I deserved to lose Boy because I resented his marriage to Diana. And, believe me, I did. But love is always larger and deeper than the wounds it makes. Raymond knew you loved him."

Somehow I had penetrated his grief and touched his heart. "I simply can't endure the thought of burying him now, Coco. In the cold. It's so very cold. Monsieur Bébé worshiped the sun. He was never so happy as when we were naked and golden and romping with Georges and Marcel and Pierre on the beach at Le Piqueÿ."

"Wait a minute, Jean. What else did he like best? What were the things, the places that made him the happiest?"

Jean stopped weeping and even managed a fragile smile.

"Bébé . . . a child . . . like me. He loved the circus—the acrobats and the beautiful bareback riders who jump through burning hoops. And of course he loved cabaret . . . jazz . . . especially the 'Boeuf sur le Toit'—Vance, the black piano player, and all those incomparable *types*. He even loved it when they let me join in for a set on the drums."

"That's it!" I cried. *"That's* how you'll bury him, Jean, and we'll help you!" Appalled heads turned all over the dining room. Even Misia looked startled.

And I did it. In two days' time I managed to organize it all. Somehow it hardly mattered that the sky was dark and leaden with rain and it was so cold the white horses' breath froze in the air. What we saw were their dancing white feather plumes, and the sparkling white coach where Monsieur Bébé rested in a pure-white coffin covered entirely in white blossoms—roses, carnations, gardenias.

And what we heard was the black band from the 'Boeuf sur le Toit' leading the followers to the Père Lachaise cemetery with a joyful rendition of 'When the Saints.' All of us were there—Diaghilev, Misia, Stravinsky, Picasso, Mistinguett, Auric, Man Ray, Josephine Baker, Barbette the Texan transvestite trapeze artist . . . all the *types* who loved Raymond, loved his bright, scintillating spirit and now celebrated its transmutation into a new form.

It was at the moment when Jean turned to me and took my hand in gratitude that I realized the power had finally shifted. I had bested Misia at her own game. But my triumph was empty somehow. In my heart I knew what Jean and I really were—two lonely, heartbroken children, erecting a barricade of joyful fantasy against an adversary too wily and too earnest for us all.

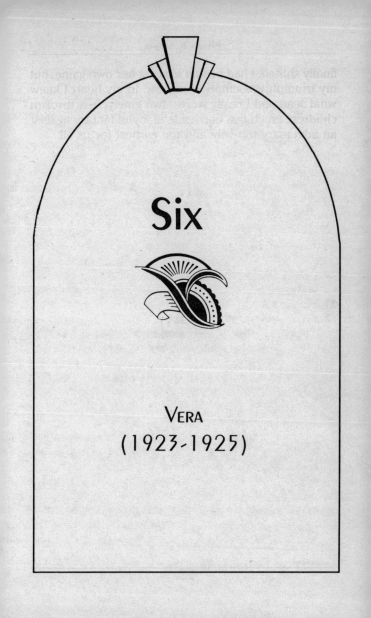

Six

VERA
(1923-1925)

ONE

*C*hristmas is always festive in Monte, and that's why I persuaded Coco to join me. She'd been driving herself much too hard on the spring collection.

I think the reason she originally took me up was not simply that she wanted to add me to the bouquet of "aristocratic" mannequins—from rebellious heiresses of the Faubourg St.-Germain to émigrée Russian princesses—who've been modeling her collections since the war, but because she sensed in me something of the same gift for self-invention she'd practiced so brilliantly herself.

My shadowy background must have intrigued her—in many ways a British drawing room version of her own. My real name is Sarah Gertrude Arkwright, but I took the name Vera Fitzgeorge years ago, until my so-called marriage left me Vera Bate.

Like Coco, I wished to forget my modest beginnings. If the rumors that eternally fly around Mademoiselle are true—and who knows if rumors *ever* are—we share the secret of our illegitimacy. Unlike my dear friend and employer, though, my origins are widely whispered to be Royal at least on *one* side—my father not the humble stonemason on my birth certificate, but a by-blow of the womanizing Duke of Cambridge.

I had always found that connection immensely helpful to me in my determined climb up through the tight ranks of English Society. By the time I came to Paris, my striking looks and Royal "uncle" had given me entrée to all the premier drawing rooms and country houses in England.

At any rate, since I've been modeling for Mademoiselle, and have had creation after creation "made" on me, I've gotten to see firsthand the incredible number of sheer agonizing hours—many of them spent on her knees adjusting a hemline or standing patiently to wrestle with an unruly sleeve, tearing it out and resetting it time and time again until it satisfies her infallible eye—the hundreds upon hundreds of hours that go into putting a successful collection together.

No matter that she has dozens of forewomen and innumerable seamstresses at her beck and call, not one gown will go down the curved staircase at the *défilé* next spring that has not had Mademoiselle's personal attention lavished on it. Creating beauty requires damned hard work.

Besides, it's been more than a year now since her affair with Grand Duke Dmitri. I wasn't the only one who felt Mademoiselle was in need of a recuperative, even better: a new flame. On both counts, Monte seemed just the place.

We were sitting in the dining room of the Hôtel de Paris, lingering over our café filtres, admiring the towering Christmas tree with its hundreds of candles and sparkling, handblown crystal ornaments and contemplating a foray to the tables of the Casino across the square. Coco was looking particularly lovely in a black chiffon evening dress with a drop waist and a softly pet-aled skirt. Her only ornament was her favorite flower, a white camellia, pinned in her blue-black hair and yards of lustrous pearls that fell below the sash of her dress.

"You were absolutely right you know, Vera, to insist on my coming," she said. "When you first proposed it I had a hundred reasons not to, but only two days away from the salon and all its tensions and I feel ten years younger."

"And look it, too, Coco, if I may be so bold," I told her, smiling. "Believe me, every man in the restaurant has taken notice. You can have your pick of the litter. What strikes your fancy—a prince, a pasha, a prime minister, an American playboy?"

"A rest, Vera—*that's* what I'm here for. The very last thing I need in my life now is another entanglement with a man. My income is more than adequate to my needs. My work is demanding—and fulfilling. My flamboyant friends with all their amorous intrigues will *never* allow me to be bored. Frankly, Vera, I wouldn't sacrifice my peace of mind for the richest man in the world."

"Don't look now, Coco," I said ruefully, "but I'm afraid you've summoned him up. He just walked in and he's headed our way. That's your luck."

"What on earth are you talking about, Vera?"

"My old friend Bend'or, the Duke of Westminster," I told her. "He may very well *be* the richest man in the world. Certainly, he's richer than the King of England. He owns half the property in London—all of Mayfair, Pimlico, Belgravia—and he probably has bids in, as we sit here, on the other half." Before I could make further explanations, Bend'or and his party had reached our table. He saw me and stopped short, motioning the others to go on ahead.

"Vera, by God, I *knew* all the professional beauties would migrate south for the holidays! That's why I decided not to have Christmas at the Hall for a change. Everyone's restless this year."

I watched his intense blue eyes move to Coco who was fitting a cigarette into her long ivory holder with elaborate unconcern. Restlessness was Bend'or's nature and his curse. But I knew the reason for his not acting as lord of the manor for Christmas at his beloved Eaton Hall, as he'd done since he took the title, was not boredom but the awkwardness of his separation from his second wife, Violet.

"Benny," I said, crossing my fingers beneath the table on *both* their accounts, "may I present my dear friend . . . my mentor . . . and my employer, Mademoiselle Coco Chanel."

"Fortune favors the inspired gambler, Mademoiselle," he said, looking straight into her ambushed eyes. "I knew there was a reason for me to come to Monte this year. If you two superlatively lovely ladies have the patience to wait, I'll make my excuses after dinner and volunteer to be your guide through the secret subterranean passageway from the hotel to the Casino." He moved on to join his table where his female guests were visibly impatient at his delay.

" 'Secret subterranean passageways . . .' *really,* Vera. He sounds like a small boy with a small boy's fantasy of hidden coves and buried pirate treasures," she said, laughing.

"Be warned, Coco," I told her, "part of Bend'or is still

a boy, a boy who longs to be a buccaneer. But he takes his plunder—and he *does* take plunder—very hard."

In half an hour he was back at our table.

"I told them my appetite for *trente et quarante* was keener than my taste for *foie gras,*" he said. "My friend Castlerosse saw straight through me, though. 'Your hunger lies due south of your stomach, Benny, and I'd put a considerable wager on that!' he told me. Blighter knows me too well." He smiled wryly and held out his arm to Coco. "Come along, ladies, the evening's young and the tables are calling."

He led us past the equestrian statue of Louis XV in the lobby, stopping to rub the horse's bronze nose. "For luck," he said, "everybody does it—that's why his nose is so shiny. Though with you two beauties on my arm, it's clear luck's already smiled on me." He took us along a narrow corridor to a bronze-finished door opening on a miniature lift that carried us down into the bowels of the hotel.

"The Casino's only just across the square," Coco said. "Why would they go to the enormous expense of installing an underground passage?"

"The official story, Mademoiselle Chanel, is that it's for heavy weather." He smiled down at her from his great height. "Its first purpose, though, is to protect the punters from the disapproving eyes of their wives. The Casino and the hotel managements have entered into an entente cordiale to make everything as easy for the high-stakes players as they can."

A short corridor beneath the cobblestones of the square led to a matching lift that delivered us straight up to the lobby. Bend'or ignored the sweeping staircases up to the Opéra and the Casino offices and turned us left into the main salon.

Despite the glittering crowds clustered around the tables at the height of the evening's play, there was an almost reverential hush. The subdued sounds were the click of the chips and plaques, the rattle of the bouncing balls in the whirring roulette wheels, the soft sough of shuffling cards.

Coco and I had taken up observer positions behind Bend'or at the roulette table. "Somehow it always reminds me of being in a cathedral, Vera," Coco said softly. "The cigar smoke rising to that lofty ceiling like incense. The croupiers like acolytes calling the numbers. The ritual movements of each different game. The tension of the devout congregation, waiting for response to prayer."

"A pretty image, Mademoiselle Chanel," Bend'or said over his shoulder as the croupier shoved a huge pile of chips in his direction. "Gambling is rather more addictive than religion, though, because your prayers are guaranteed to be answered—or denied—on the spot. Monte Carlo's a principality that lives to serve a universal obsession."

Bend'or's style of play mirrored his nature: restless, arbitrary, whimsical, quickly bored. He would stop for only a few minutes at any one table—roulette, baccarat, *chemin de fer,* or his favorite, *trente et quarante*—just long enough to place a few bets and collect his winnings. Sometimes not even that long.

Coco took to sweeping his abandoned chips into her purse and carrying them after him from table to table. Though she wouldn't admit it, even to me, her peasant thrift was obviously appalled by Bend'or's absolute indifference to money. She was mesmerized by it, too. Boy had been rich enough, but he was not in Bend'or's league. No one was.

Benny, for his part, was vastly amused by her ill-concealed horror. "You see, Vera," he said as she emptied yet another purse-full of salvaged chips onto the green baize beside him. "Mademoiselle Chanel has appointed herself my guardian angel. I suppose all my friends would agree I need one. And, by God, no man could wish for one more beautiful!"

Whenever his attention was held by the action at a particular table, I could see Coco covertly studying him. Bend'or was larger than life in every way. His grandfather, the first Duke, who loved horses better than any man he'd ever met, had recognized it early and had nicknamed him after his greatest Derby winner. "Hugh Arthur Richard Grosvenor" became "Bend'or" to his adored grandpater. And Bend'or he'd become to all the world.

He'd always reminded me of the young Henry VIII, with his reddish-gold hair, his blazing blue eyes, his aristocratic features, and his fine athletic figure. Bend'or glowed like the gold of his name. He radiated good health, vitality, and the sublime confidence that anything he wanted should be his by divine right.

But he shared the monarch's tragedy, too. He couldn't get an heir. Two marriages had produced only two daughters, Ursula and Mary, by his first wife, the brunette beauty Constance "Shelagh" Cornwallis-West. She'd given him a son, too, Edward, a perfect child who'd died at four of septicaemia following an appendectomy. Though Shelagh had had no blame in their son's death, Bend'or had never forgiven her for it and it had broken the marriage.

Watching Coco fall under the spell of his animal magnetism, her dark hair and fine dark eyes contrasting his red-gold radiance, I thought of Anne Boleyn, darkly brilliant, spirited, witty, unable to give Henry an heir . . . doomed. Although the crowded Casino was overheated, I shuddered.

After an hour or so of avid play, he suddenly tired of it and cashed in his chips, stuffing wads of ten-thousand-franc notes casually into the pockets of his dinner jacket, oblivious when a few drifted to the Casino floor and Coco hastily bent to retrieve them.

"You are shedding banknotes like a birch tree in a windstorm, Monsieur," she said tartly, holding out a handful.

"The hazard of my height and my carelessness, Mademoiselle." He laughed. "Do me the favor of guarding them for me while we repair to the bar for a cognac. Winning always leaves me with an unslakable thirst." He shepherded us onto a banquette and ordered a bottle of Cordon Rouge for Coco and me and a decanter of Hennessy for himself.

The next morning we received an invitation, delivered by an adorable young crewman wearing a jersey with the ducal crest, completely hidden behind a massive bouquet of six-dozen white camellias. It was addressed, "To my guardian angel and our mutual friend." I'll admit it made me feel quite the indispensable go-between. We were invited to dine that evening on board Bend'or's four-masted schooner, *The Flying Cloud,* moored in the Monte Carlo harbor.

Coco was reluctant. I wondered if she was overawed by his vast wealth. Nearly every one of the unmarried and titled Society beauties in London, I told her, had set their tiaras for Bend'or when his separation from Violet became public.

"That's just it, Vera," she said. "Englishwomen regard men as quarry. You're a nation of huntresses. You're bred to it from the cradle. Now he's free of his wife, it's open season on Bend'or . . . the richest prize of all. And *he's* equally committed to being the huntsman. How very confusing! I barely know the man, but I feel a certain sympathy for him."

"You should." I laughed. "Just imagine all that amazonian English energy directed at bagging Bend'or. Why don't you outwit them and bag him yourself?"

"I told you when I agreed to join you for the holiday Vera, I'm in Monte Carlo to escape pressures of any kind. If it will do your own cause good, I'll agree to dine with your handsome, arrogant 'lord of all he surveys.' But in the words of my beloved co-conspirator, Misia Sert—on the subject of another giant, Picasso—our 'mutual friend' Bend'or appears far too dangerous . . . too all-consuming for a woman like me."

That didn't stop her, however, from looking completely ravishing when Bend'or's driver arrived at the hotel to collect us. Every head in the lobby turned. Coco was wearing *pants.* That's the only way I can describe it—simple pants of white silk, softly flared at the ankle, with a strapless bodice of black crepe de chine and a white bandeau in her hair, anchored with one of Bend'or's camellias.

A woman in pants. Unheard of! You could hear the flutter of outraged fans from all sides as we crossed the crowded lobby. Though I'm a head taller than Coco and had long ago mastered the eye-catching "mannequin's walk," I felt invisible beside her.

As we approached the harbor, the first thing—the only thing really—that we saw was *The Flying Cloud* lying at anchor, her rigging hung with thousands of red and green fairy lights winking against the black velvet sky.

"Dieu, Vera," Coco murmured beside me, sunk in the comfort of the soft leather seats of the Rolls limousine. "It looks like a ruby and emerald parure from Cartier. It must be two-hundred feet long."

"Two-hundred-and-three feet, Coco, to be precise. Bend'or was determined to have the biggest of the lot."

"He's certainly succeeded, Vera. It makes the rest of the yachts in the marina look like children's sailboats in the pond in the Tuileries."

*"Flying Cloud'*s certainly no toy to Bend'or. She can make twelve knots under sail. Sailing's one of his major passions—and the dirtier the weather, the better he likes it. Poor Violet spent most of their marriage alternately heartsick and seasick. If you have a queasy stomach, Coco, forget our mutual friend!"

"My sea legs are remarkably steady, Vera, and as for my heart, I have no intention of giving that away ever again. Especially not to a man who collects hearts like hunting trophies."

We were met at the dockside by one of *Flying Cloud'*s launches and carried out to the yacht. Even from a distance, we could hear the strains of violin music drifting toward us across the water. Bend'or himself was waiting at the top of the gangway, dressed in full regalia— navy blazer with *Flying Cloud'*s insignia on the pocket,

slim white flannel trousers, and a yachting cap heavy
with gold braid.

"Welcome aboard my privateer, ladies," he said. "At
your command, Mademoiselle Chanel, we'll run up the
skull and bones and put to sea to take whatever rich,
unwary prize strikes your fancy."

He had eyes only for Coco. For the second time that
evening I felt totally invisible. I had to keep reminding
myself this was meant to be Coco's opportunity, not
mine. Besides, I'd be mad to think I could manage him.

Coco got it just right, letting him take us on a guided
tour of what was, in effect, a floating country house, designed by Benny's resident architect, Detmar Blow, in
the Queen Anne style and fitted with every comfort for
guests used to having just that—from elaborate arrangements of fresh orchids and gardenias in each of
the eight, wood-paneled staterooms, to antique chased-
silver and crystal containers for mineral water on the
bedside tables.

She was suitably impressed but far from bowled
over, implying by her occasional perceptive comment
on the hand-blocked drapery fabrics or the Stubbs
studies of Bend'or's racing champions in the library
that she was no stranger to luxury, even on such a magnificent scale.

When we got to the master stateroom with its pine-
paneled walls, its delicate embroidered curtains of
white Florentine silk, and its small Gainsborough over
the bureau, Benny suddenly swept Coco up in his arms
and deposited her unceremoniously in the middle of
the four-poster bed.

"Now, Mademoiselle Coco, I think I shall instruct the
captain and crew to raise sail and run with the tide. You

look altogether too tempting in those foolish pajamas or whatever you call them."

She laughed up at him. "Piracy, Milord, is still a capital crime, punishable by hanging. Besides, my faithful friend Vera would be honor-bound to leap over the rail, swim to shore, and raise the alarm."

"Pity," he said, "I suppose in that case we shall have to settle for supper."

Out on the afterdeck under the sparkling Christmas lights, where an eight-piece gypsy orchestra was playing, we found a candlelit table spread with cold lobsters on beds of ice and seaweed, heaps of pearly oysters, mountains of beluga caviar with blinis. Silver buckets of Cordon Rouge and icy vodka stood alongside.

"I ordered the vodka and blinis on your account," Mademoiselle Chanel," Bend'or said. "I understand you are partial to things in the Russian style."

Touché, I thought, but Coco was imperturbable. She loved nothing better than a duel of wits. For all their difference, I suddenly saw that she and Bend'or were a match. Despite his pursuit of—and by—England's most eligible young heiresses, he'd never come up against a woman of Coco's beauty and mettle before.

" 'Things *à la Russe'* . . . I suppose you could say so, Monsieur." She threw back her small crystal glass of vodka, neat. I was astonished. Coco drank spirits seldom, if ever. "I have recently become a patroness of Monsieur Diaghilev's troupe—you must come to Paris to watch the rehearsals of his new ballet, *Le Train bleu.* I've done the costumes for my darling Serge . . . based them on the sporting clothes from my Deauville collection. And Stravinsky, yes, I recently sponsored a retrospective of his work at the Salle Gaveau. There *is* something in me that responds to his primitive rhythms. You're right, Milord. How very sensitive of you. I *do* have a predilection for those splendid exiles."

As surely as if he'd been piped on board, the image of Grand Duke Dmitri Pavlovich—impoverished and most splendid of all her exiles—had joined us at Coco's side at Bend'or's opulent table.

He hurried to change the subject.

The rest of the evening passed in a dream—or perhaps it was just blurred by all the champagne we drank. I remember watching Coco in Bend'or's arms, circling the deck in a waltz while the gypsy violins played, her head thrown back on her slender swan's neck as she laughed up at one of his jokes. How small and fragile she looked next to him!

I knew better. Bend'or would do well not to underestimate Mademoiselle. He'd never seen her, as I had, wielding her sarcasm like a whip when one of her forewomen dared to try to add a small personal detail to one of Coco's designs thinking it would go undetected. Or lying on her side on the salon floor as the mannequins filed past in the pre-collection review, checking one last time to make certain every one of her new creations hung perfectly at the hem, only to order that an offending gown be remade overnight. Coco was made of tungsten and Bend'or would discover it soon enough.

As the night surrendered to the dawn, with only a few stubborn stars still hanging in the pale sky, the supper was cleared away by a retinue of silent stewards and replaced by Georgian silver chafing dishes containing a lavish English breakfast.

Coco declined to stay. "I will never forget the delight of this unexpected evening, Monsieur." She smiled up at him. "Vera and I must return to the hotel, though, and get at least a few hours sleep before we pack for our return to Paris."

"You're going back to Paris?" Benny had his small-boy look again—the shocked disbelief of a child whose shiny Christmas plaything has just been snatched away. "Why back to Paris now when the festivities are only beginning? When we've only just *met?*" He took her hands in his as though he could hold her in place. "There's still New Year's to come—the black-and-white ball at the Casino . . . and a superb fireworks display that I have to admit rivals the ones I commission at Eaton Hall. You'll have a ringside seat for it here on *Flying Cloud* . . . or a cruise along the coast up to Biarritz for New Year's there, if you'd prefer it . . . or a run over to Morocco. . . . *Anything* that would amuse you."

Trying to forestall her departure, he pulled elaborate pleasures out of his hat like a magician frantic at losing his audience.

"How very much I wish we *could* stay, but the February collection feels to me only minutes away. So many small but crucial details to be seen to. You can't imagine."

Of course he couldn't. While Bend'or, like a great general, plotted out the grand strategies of expanding and protecting the vast Grosvenor empire he'd inherited from his grandfather, the daily details of its management were delegated to his trusted lieutenants, leaving him free to follow his most extravagant whims wherever they led him. Coco's brand of hands-on entrepreneurship would be bound to baffle him—especially when the hands belonged to a woman.

"Surely, chère Mademoiselle Coco, those pesky details can be attended to by your managers—that's what you pay them for, after all. It's only a week till New Year's. Say you'll stay and keep a lonely man company."

Bend'or pleading was particularly appealing, especially when I'd never seen him do anything but issue orders before.

Coco was politely adamant. "I hope you will not think me arrogant, Monsieur, but the preparation of a Chanel collection absolutely requires the presence of Mademoiselle Chanel."

"Arrogant, no . . . beautiful, yes, chère Coco," he said, taking her arm in his to help her down the narrow gangway to the waiting launch. "You leave me no alternative than to spend the rest of the holiday devising some compelling means by which *I* can 'absolutely require' your presence."

TWO

We weren't back in Paris for a fortnight when Bend'or's courtship—or should I call it his siege of Coco—began in earnest.

He was a veteran campaigner. He'd served in the Boer War with his old friend—and mine—Winston Churchill. And once during the recent war he'd even raised a private army from the grooms and valets of Eaton Hall to liberate a hundred British soldiers being held prisoner in some godforsaken hole in the Egyptian desert. On the race course . . . on the Hunt . . . in the bedroom, Bend'or lived for a challenge. Coco was one he couldn't resist.

I was in the showroom modeling a charming pale-grey satin tea gown inset with panels of darker grey velvet for the Baronne de Rothschild when Coco drew me aside.

"Vera, you will never believe what that Englishman has done now. He's completely *fou.*"

"After the four-dozen orchids that arrived yesterday along with the sapphire and amethyst spray from Asprey . . . after today's offering—daisies he swears he picked at first light from the meadows of the Hall . . . daisies with diamond hair-clips under the petals and that letter describing how he longs to pin them in your 'raven' hair—it would take a great deal to surprise me, Coco. Bend'or is known to be a superb tactician."

"Well, it's my conviction he's gone mad. Joseph, the butler I stole from Misia, just telephoned to say that three *more* letters had been hand-delivered."

"That makes more than thirty in a fortnight!"

"He told me the messenger was such a presentable, unassuming young man—and he said he'd driven all night from Calais on Bend'or's urgent instructions— that Joseph invited him into the kitchen for a cup of tea. They talked about everything from horses to politics to the franc against the pound. I suspect Joseph was starting to contemplate seduction." She laughed wickedly. "Then, as he was leaving, he gave Joseph his calling card. FOR THE ENCHANTING MADEMOISELLE CHANEL, it said. It was the Prince of Wales."

"My God, Coco. This is becoming serious. I'm not sure *what* I've got you into. Do you fancy being the next Duchess of Westminster?"

"Don't be foolish, Vera. You know his reputation. Two duchesses in the divorce courts already and countless mistresses from Anna Pavlova to that music-hall star, Gertie Millar."

"The Normans didn't call his family the *gros veneurs* for nothing, Coco. He's positively atavistic—a born hunter. It's the chase Bend'or loves," I told her. "He always tires very quickly of the prize."

She reached out and began agitatedly tugging the grey skirt around my hips. She plucked pin after pin from the cushion that was an extension of her wrist and began assaulting the offending satin.

"The *drape!* I can never convince those fitters that they must get the drape right or the gown is ruined.

The skirt is the heart of any garment. I've told them so too many times."

She beckoned to one of the lovely young comtesses who was working as an assistant. "Take Madame Bate up to the workroom and show the forewoman how I've ripped out and pinned this drape. Tell her to begin again."

The gown had seemed perfect to me when I put it on, but I sensed right away as we went up the staircase that Coco's subtle readjustment of the fabric had made it flow in absolute harmony with my body. Perfect elegance and perfect comfort. That was her greatest gift—making her dresses a second skin for the women who wore them.

At the curve in the stair I looked back and saw her staring abstractedly into the wall of mirrors. What was troubling her now? Perhaps a suspicion that Bend'or would want only to display her as the ultimate huntsman's trophy?

What she failed to grasp, for all her native shrewdness, was that this was not the cliché of the duke and the peddler's daughter, but the meeting of a man of the highest rank with a woman of the highest sensibility. Somehow, no matter how many times she looked into the mirror, Coco could not seem to see herself.

Her "dear friend" Misia professed to be all for it. Why not? For one thing, a liaison with Bend'or would very probably take Coco out of Paris where, since the success of her artistic salon, she'd begun to come uncomfortably close to unseating Misia from her throne of Empress of the arts.

For another, from what I could see, Misia was one

of those women who lived through the dramas of her friends. God knows, her own life had been drama enough. If you listened to gossip—which, of course, I could hardly *not* do in the perfumed claustrophobia of the mannequins' *cabine* where love affairs, high and low, were dissected daily with surgical precision— Misia had had more than her share of "important" lovers. Artists, composers, writers, press lords.

Having watched her at close range, though, because of my special relationship with Mademoiselle, I sensed that Misia was beginning to feel her age. Coco had a ten-year advantage over her and, for the first time in a life of brilliant notoriety, I believe Misia felt threatened by Coco at every level, threatened by the woman she loved.

That much was clear. Coco and Misia loved each other, loved in the way only women can—sympathetically, empathetically, each one knowing on her own pulses what the other is living through. Each one supporting the other through the labyrinth of broken promises and broken dreams and broken hearts that make up a woman's life . . . and probably a man's as well, if any one of them would ever be brave enough to admit it.

Misia came to tea at the rue Cambon, shortly after our return from the south of France. Coco included me in the party as much, I suspected, to provide a buffer against Misia's shameless curiosity as anything else.

She certainly was compelling. In her fifties, I knew it, but surpassingly beautiful and not looking a day over thirty-five. Dressed for their "reunion," not by Coco, but as provocatively as possible by Madeleine Vionnet, in a closely cut suit of fawn jersey. Amazing how all the other designers like Vionnet were now copying Chanel! She could hardly wait for the door to close on the assistant who brought our tea.

"You've done it this time, Coco ma chère. The Duke of Westminster. *Mon dieu,* what a catch! Jojo says his income is conservatively estimated at a guinea a minute. He has houses every where—England, Scotland, the Landes, Dalmatia. And two major yachts—one a *destroyer* actually. Anywhere you go, no matter *how* late the hour, you'll find a full staff, abruptly awakened like the court of Sleeping Beauty, just waiting to do your bidding." She was so excited she was out of breath.

"You must feel as though you'd died and gone to Paradise. Tell me, Coco, as your closest friend, how *did* you manage it? I've always admired your gift for self-invention . . . but the next Duchess of Westminster? You exceed even my most exaggerated notions of the possible!"

"Vera, ma chère, please give Madame Sert another cup of herb tea. She appears to be overstimulated." She laughed wryly. "Whatever your gossips have been telling you, Misia, I have absolutely no interest in becoming the third Duchess. The fate of the first two is warning enough that, in Bend'or's case, the tiara sits very uneasily on the head of any woman who fails to give him an heir."

"An heir . . . that should be easy for you, Coco, with your hardy stock."

Ignoring the dig, Coco continued calmly. "We both know, Misia—you perhaps even more poignantly than I—that beyond the age of forty, it would be reckless to enter that particular arena. Safer for me to stick to the business I know I can do—not to tie my destiny to the rigged odds on childbearing."

I was astonished at her candor. Nothing ever seemed to embarrass Misia or Coco. That's what I suspect bound them so tightly. For all their fierce rivalry, they understood and respected one another as equals.

"Of course you're right in principle, Coco," Misia said, "but from what I've heard of the Duke, once he sets his heart on acquisition—and his collector's preference has always been for the unusual—he is virtually unstoppable."

"Then, Misia, I only ask that you wish us both the very best of luck."

THREE

*W*e were tied up at the marina in Cannes. It was a bright, cloudless day with a stiff breeze that set the halyards of the hundreds of yachts moored in the small, crescent-shaped harbor to ringing like bells.

Bend'or had swept into Paris after Coco's February triumph to attend the rehearsals of *Le Train bleu* on her invitation and had carried us off for a brief holiday aboard *Flying Cloud*. His strategy seemed to be working. After an initial flurry of objections—her exhaustion after the collection, her meetings with Beaux and the Wertheimers about a possible second fragrance, her commitment to her exporters—Coco had surrendered to the irresistible magnetism of the man.

He had reserved a private car on the Paris-Riviera express and installed us in total comfort. From Paris to Cannes he plied her with caviar, champagne, and a fusillade of gifts, each one more spectacular and ingenious than the last—a Fabergé egg with a miniature golden lion inside, a paperweight that was a pair of crystal shears like the ones she hung around her neck from a scarlet ribbon while she worked, a diamond brooch made of the interlocking ℭℭ's that stood as her trademark.

Coco pretended to be indifferent to this profligate display, but I knew her better. For the first time in her life she was, I think, tempted by the prospect of security. Certainly the fashion house was sufficiently flourishing by now to provide her a handsome income. And the royalties from Parfums Chanel had begun to mount up. But this was different. This was wealth beyond calculating—beyond the most fantastical dreams of a lonely, hungry, orphaned child.

Jean Cocteau, who had come aboard *Flying Cloud* the day before to join us for the weekend, was openly contemptuous of it all. We were sitting on the afterdeck drinking champagne. Bend'or had driven up into the hills to the Château de l'Horizon to see Winston who was visiting his friend Maxine Elliot, the enormously rich, enormously predatory retired actress.

Jean could hardly wait to pounce. " 'Yes, my darling . . . Of course, my darling . . . As you wish, my darling.' " He was a brilliant mimic—he sounded just like her. "Be careful, chère Coco, you're taking on an ominous resemblance to a wife."

"Don't be ridiculous, Jean," she snapped at him. "You know I have no desire to marry. My work and my friends are more than enough to content me. What I can't understand, though, is why you've taken such a deep dislike to Bend'or. He's done nothing but put himself out to be generous to you."

"That's just it, Coco, his aggressive generosity. I read it as arrogance—the sublime confidence that anyone can be bought, if the price is high enough. Even you."

I tried to stop him. "Shut up, Jean. Don't play the bloody fool!" But he was in full flight.

"I watched him last night at the Casino, lording it over the roulette table. He kept insisting that I join the play—pushing piles of ten-thousand-franc chips at me. Do you know what I did, Coco? I pocketed more than half of them and exchanged them when his back was turned. I'll use the money to finance my revisions to the scenario for *Le Train bleu*—and to pay Erik Satie for the score. Last night Bend'or became a patron of the arts in spite of himself."

Coco flushed scarlet under her tan. She was clearly stung. It was the closest I've ever seen them come to a quarrel.

"Don't delude yourself, Jean. You'll use it to buy your opium or a pretty sailorboy to make you forget Raymond. Then, when you've thrown it away, you'll come to me to finance yet one more expensive sanitarium for yet one more very temporary cure."

In all the years I'd known her I'd seen many a Coco tantrum in the fashion house, but I'd never heard her be so overtly cruel. Jean had struck a nerve—her primal terror of being owned.

He was desperately hurt. He leapt to his feet, his wild, curly hair standing on end making him look like an offended cockatoo, and declared that he was leaving the yacht immediately to return to Paris.

I tried to reason with him. I knew very well that he and Coco loved one another dearly, but he stormed down to his stateroom to pack.

"Let him go, Vera. That's the trouble with *pédérastes* like Jean. Their bitchery always gets the better of their fundamental good nature. He'll come back when he needs me—they always do." Her words were cynical but her eyes were infinitely sad. Loss was something Coco couldn't bear.

That afternoon Coco and I were sitting in the yacht's drawing room with its pastel Aubusson carpet, its white baby-grand piano, and the softly lit Renoirs on the wall, waiting for Bend'or to get back from his visit with Winston. Coco was visibly depressed. Cocteau's abrupt, angry departure had darkened her spirits and not even the endless flow of champagne could revive them.

"What in God's name *am* I doing here, Vera?" she asked me. "There are times I don't begin to understand myself. When I told you back at Christmastime that I had no desire for another emotional entanglement, I meant precisely what I said."

Though I was only two years older than Coco, there were times when I felt light years more worldly. "An affair doesn't have to mean an entanglement, Coco. I've taken lovers out of curiosity . . . out of boredom . . . out of pure unadulterated lust . . . even out of exhaustion. Exhaustion was certainly the case with my absentee husband, Fred. American officers are notoriously persistent. He simply wore me down. Now he spends all his time in London."

"But I'm not in love with Bend'or, Vera," she said. "How can I possibly become his mistress?"

"With Benny that's the only way *to* do it. Consider him a *divertissement* . . . a treat, a deluxe vacation from your work. You don't love him. You don't want to marry him—that alone will make you irresistible. You'll be the first woman in his forty-two years of experience who didn't."

"I don't know, Vera." She shivered though there was no chill in the cabin. "There's still something about it that troubles me. Bend'or's a collector—just like Misia. There's something in me that attracts collectors. I tell myself they're drawn to my energy, my creativity. Deep down I'm afraid it's darker than that. My independence tantalizes them. Cocteau was too near the mark for comfort this morning. *That's* what upset me so badly—not our quarrel. Collectors want to own you. I saw it in his eyes the first time Bend'or looked at me in the restaurant. He wants to own me. And ownership is intolerable to me—no matter how comfortable the cage."

Then Benny was back and the gloom immediately lifted. Nobody knew how to raise spirits faster.

"Look what I've brought you, Coco. Your gypsies—the ones from Monte. I found them playing at Maxine's garden party and persuaded them to join us on our cruise. Now we can have dancing on deck every night wherever we go. Won't even have to put into port if the sailing's good." His pleasure in giving was infectious.

"So *you* won't feel neglected, Vera my dear, I've invited a young officer Winston introduced me to to be your partner. Chap name of Alberto Lombardi. Tall, dark eyes, handsome devil. Your classic Roman centurion type. Struck me, Coco, that he might be just the ticket for our Vera. He'll be coming aboard this evening."

I had to laugh. He was incorrigible. "You'll stop at nothing when it comes to the comfort of your guests, will you Benny? Even a little polite pandering. Well, if I end up by divorcing dear old Freddie and marrying this Italian of yours, you'll be entitled to collect the matchmaker's fee."

From the moment Berto walked into the dining saloon that night, I knew I would be indebted to Bend'or for the fee—and more.

For the next seven days we cruised the Mediterranean. The winds were splendid and Bend'or was delighted to find all three of us natural sailors—especially Coco who, to Benny's growing chagrin, could hardly be lured below-decks for a "nap" when the sails were flying.

We only put into port when the breeze flagged or Benny felt the sudden, overpowering urge to buy Coco yet another extravagant gift—a high collar of filigreed silver set with lapis and diamonds from Morocco, a barbaric gold breastplate studded with emeralds and rubies from Capri, and a flame-colored parrot from Ibiza that Benny vowed to teach to say, *"Je t'adore, chère Coco."*

While Coco and Bend'or were playing the elaborate game of hart and huntsman—Coco coming close enough one day to make Benny think she could love him, only to turn cool and elusive the next—Berto and I were falling deeply in love.

His English was limited, and full of fractured idioms that had us all falling about with laughter, but his lean, hard soldier's body and his sensitive hands spoke so eloquently to mine that by the time we returned to Cannes we both knew that Bend'or's spur-of-the-moment pleasure cruise had begun a lifelong voyage for the two of us.

FOUR

S o far, in their intricate mating dance Coco had had one important advantage over Bend'or, one any strategist—and, God knows, the two of them were bloody wizards at manipulation—would immediately recognize. She'd been on her own terrain . . . Paris, where for all the vast difference in the size of their personal fortunes, she reigned just as securely over the realm of couture as Benny did over London's prèmier real estate . . . the Riviera, where her innovative sportswear and championing of the suntan had made just as dramatic an impact on the aristocratic resort scene as the flamboyant arrival of *Flying Cloud* in the harbors of Nice or Cannes or Biarritz.

Now she had agreed to visit him in England for the annual shooting at Eaton Hall and then a trip north to his estate at Lochmore to fish for salmon. She'd had to agree, even though it interfered with her business. There was never really a good time for Coco to leave the fashion house. It was identified so directly with her presence.

"I can't do otherwise, Vera," she confided in me as we began drawing up the elaborate wardrobe list for what amounted for Coco to a royal progress. "You know how single-minded he is. The boyish side of him—the part I actually like best—is dying to show off. He wants to spread all the splendors of his fabled kingdom before me."

"You're right, Coco. I know Benny too well. If you tell him you can't spare a month to come to England now, he'll take it as a personal rejection and be off on the hunt again. Not because he's stopped loving you, but out of a combination of boredom and pique. Benny simply can't bear being denied what he wants. It's the legacy of centuries of Grosvenor gratification."

"That's why I finally accepted his invitation. He absolutely refuses to understand the extent of my personal involvement in the business. *You* certainly do, Vera. You've seen the havoc my announcement caused. The directrices are all in a state of barely controlled panic, and Pierre Wertheimer has visited me three times over the past ten days to attempt to dissuade me from going. I think he's afraid the move might be permanent. And then what of Parfums Chanel?"

"It's more than that, Coco," I told her exasperatedly. "Sometimes you're bloody naive. Wertheimer's your major backer, with a vested interest in your remaining in Paris. But Parfums Chanel is only, forgive me, a pimple on the elephant of Bourjois. Pierre's half in love with you himself. Haven't you noticed the intense way he looks at you with those dark, soulful eyes. The way he hangs on your every word?"

"He's not in love, Vera, he's intrigued by me—finds me exotic. He loves what he calls my 'masculine head for business.' "

"Ironic, isn't it?" I said. "The very thing Pierre finds attractive about you is what threatens Benny. What you need, my dear friend, is a man who appreciates *both* Cocos—the creator and the lover. Surely there's got to be someone out there strong enough to handle both."

"There was, Vera ma chère. There was one man who could entirely afford me, but he's gone now and I have to get on with my life until I can catch up with him again."

Bend'or's opulently appointed private railway car with its soft leather couches and its attentive steward in Grosvenor livery carried the three of us, Coco, Misia, and me, northwest out of London on the last leg of our journey to Chester. The English countryside, rolling by the windows, still green in the chill November mist, seemed to welcome me home.

But Misia was preoccupied and withdrawn, and Coco grew more subdued as the miles passed. The elaborate preparations for the trip—choosing her gowns and sporting clothes and hunting gear and overseeing the packing of her twenty-six leather cases from Hermès—

had only temporarily distracted her from the reality of being in a new country with a new lover, neither of whose ways she fully understood.

Misia had joined us unexpectedly at the eleventh hour, adding her own twenty Vuitton cases to Coco's and mine. It was a good thing Benny *had* his own carriage. We practically needed a separate railcar for our bags.

I couldn't quite make out Misia's motive for coming. Was it simply her ongoing rivalry with Coco for the world's attention? The press was following Coco's first passage across the Channel with excited interest, and there had been a horde of photographers at St. Pancras station. Was it prurient, jealous curiosity about her adored friend's new lover? I'd certainly seen *that* before with Grand Duke Dmitri. Or was it the ostensible reason she gave Coco for virtually inviting herself along—José's enthusiastic flirtation with the young, blonde, self-proclaimed Georgian "Princess" Roussadana Mdivani who had turned up by chance one day in José's studio with her dashing brother, Alexis, and seemed quite determined to stay. Misia was so byzantine in her intrigues it was probably an amalgam of all three.

As if reading my thoughts, Misia suddenly roused herself from her reverie. "It's not a retreat, you understand Coco. My coming along," she said. "I knew— though you'd be too proud ever to admit it—that you'd need an ally against all those envious beauties who want to keep the tiara in English hands."

Was I invisible once again? Not for the first time, I wondered if Misia considered me simply one of the servants—a sort of jumped-up ladies' maid. There were times when her arrogant possessiveness of Coco made my blood boil. If it hadn't been for my introducing Benny to Mademoiselle, this trip would not be taking place at all.

She continued to ignore me. "Besides, Coco, it's a matter of my larger strategy. Jojo's little infatuations are boringly predictable by now. In this first, ardent phase comparisons between the girl's so-called innocence and her nubile, puppy energy and adoration with my more mature . . . more independent style are likely to be invidious. That won't last. Jojo's too absorbed in his work to have the time to play nursemaid to a neurotic, willful child with a weakness for older men that includes her own brother."

What bitchery! Misia really *must* be in pain. Coco knew her so very well . . . knew the secret vulnerability that hid behind the highly lacquered veneer. Knew it as well as she did her own. That "neurotic child" was also an exquisitely lovely one—and thirty years Misia's junior.

"I'm glad you decided to join us, Misia," she said gently, ignoring the situation in Paris. "Vera and I need all the allies we can recruit against the 'Gay Young Things' of the Eaton Hall set. Can you believe the women actually *call* themselves that? Englishwomen have no finesse. Pardon me, Vera, you know I consider you a Frenchwoman by adoption. Then, what can one expect of a nation that nicknames its men after racehorses?"

Coco was trying valiantly to erase the spectre of Jojo and his Georgian princess from Misia's all-too-fertile imagination, but she would not be diverted.

"*You* know Jojo can't do without me, Coco. That girl

won't have the patience I do to listen to his endless boasting about the glories of his work. She's too young to understand that it all comes out of his terrible fear that Picasso and Dali will be the ones to be remembered no matter *how* massive he makes his paintings. She's simply too young and vain to think of anyone but herself. He'll tire quickly enough of that. I'm sure of it." She was agitatedly plucking imaginary specks from the skirt of her smart, navy twill traveling suit.

"Of course he will, Misia ma chère. Jojo depends on you." She took her friend's nervous hands in her own. "And you're right about leaving Paris, too. Making yourself elusive right now is the perfect tactic. It shows you're not threatened by Mademoiselle Mdivani. After a few weeks of playing 'God the artist' to her adoring Muse, Jojo is bound to tire of it. At his age, keeping a heroic façade up—not to mention other even trickier elevations—takes too much energy. He'll be *desperate* for you to come home."

Misia managed the first tremulous smile of the trip, just as we pulled into the Chester station and found Benny himself waiting on the platform, comfortably elegant in his well-worn tweeds and cardigan, surrounded by his band of faithful dachshunds, and with an armada of Rolls-Royces to carry his beautiful conquest home to the Hall.

Our cavalcade made its way down the wide, tree-lined, two-mile drive from the station up to the "golden gates" of wrought iron and gilt, topped by the ducal crest with the Grosvenor motto, VIRTUE NOT LINEAGE, that opened into the courtyard. If you traced "virtue" back to its Norman roots in *vertu*—valor—how very appropriate it seemed to the probable third duchess.

Coco and Bend'or were in the lead car, with Misia and me behind and followed by our luggage.

"Mon dieu, Vera," Misia said in a whisper the liveried chauffeur couldn't hear, startled by the sheer immensity of the Hall into acknowledging me for a change, "how I wish Jojo were here! This incredible pile is built to *his* proportions . . . *his* scale. He'd feel perfectly at home here, which is certainly more than I do."

The vast French-Gothic palace, you'd *have* to call it that really, of Eaton Hall, was originally built in the seventeenth century and wildly elaborated on by generations of architects, flushed with hubris and Grosvenor guineas. Crowned by its steep clock tower, as imposing as Big Ben, it stood before us, reaching on either side of a tall central block into wide wings that swept out toward endless acres of formal gardens in the French style. Then greenhouses, meadows, and the forest, neatly bisected for shooting purposes by the river Dee. The chimes of the Belgian carillon played "Home Sweet Home" to welcome Coco to the heart of Benny's kingdom.

"How can anyone even *attempt* to live in a place this size, Vera?" Misia asked me. " 'Country seat,' Bend'or calls it. It's as big as a French country market *town. Mon dieu . . .*" For the first time since Coco introduced us, Misia was actually awed into silence.

"That's just what I asked Benny the first time I came here as a girl, Misia," I told her. "He just laughed at me. 'Of course we don't live in the big house, Vera. The family stays in the west wing. I save the rest for my houseguests. I can put up a hundred, more or less, depending on the discretion of the thing, in sixty guestrooms. I keep the biggest inn in Cheshire. Lots of latitude for weekend dalliance, too, *if* you're canny, Vera my dear girl, and remember to walk on the outside of the stair treads and not let nerves make you clutch the creaky bannisters on your late-night prowls.' Excellent advice it was, too, Misia. It's stood me in good stead through many a colorful house party!"

Coco who, I'm convinced, Misia expected to be completely nonplussed by it all, took it in her usual stride. What sangfroid! How I admired her. As the four of us walked under the high portico and up the stairs into the great hall, she smiled up at Benny.

"I do favor the simplicity of these black-and-white marble floors, Benny mon cher, and those elegant vaulting arches. How high do they rise . . . seventy . . . eighty feet? It reminds me of the girls' school I attended for the first years after my maman's tragic death."

"Girls' school," indeed. *Orphanage* was more like it, if the widespread rumors of Coco's childhood abandonment were true, as I suspected they were. At that moment I understood something central to her character. Coco could not allow herself to be overawed by the splendors of Eaton Hall with its Rubens room, its dining saloon that easily sat sixty, its seventy-six-foot drawing room, its library bigger than a London lending-library that held more than ten thousand volumes, and its formal ballroom as long as a polo field. No more than she could have let herself be intimidated by the more modest comforts of Royallieu when Balsan first installed her there and introduced her into château Society or by the elegant salons of Édith de Beaumont or Élisabeth Greffulhe when Misia opened the closely guarded doors of the Faubourg St.-Germain to her pre-possessing new protégée a dozen years ago. If she had ever allowed herself to be awed by grandeur, she would never have arrived at this point.

Coco was the ultimate chameleon. Put her in a new environment—however exotic—and she immediately adapted herself to meet it with a naturalness that was positively breathtaking.

It was as if she had been born to stand here at Benny's side, admiring his glowing walls of priceless Gainsboroughs and Reynolds and Turners and looking likely to become the grandest *châtelaine* of them all.

FIVE

riday was the first morning of the shoot, and a hearty English breakfast had been set out in the small dining room of the private wing where Benny's collection of silver tankards glittered down the long table.

We were all up early, with the conspicuous exception of Misia who'd pleaded the first twinges of a migraine headache the night before, assuring Benny she would manage "somehow" to join us at the picnic luncheon in the forest that divided the hours of the day's shooting as precisely as the river Dee did the Friday and Saturday shoots.

If you ask me, Misia's migraine was attributable to jealousy. Ever since we'd arrived at the Hall and she'd experienced firsthand the full magnitude of Coco's good fortune, she'd been simmering with ill-concealed envy. Bad enough that her husband had taken a much much younger woman as mistress, but that her much younger best friend and protégée had fallen into such a golden honey pot had left her suffocating with chagrin.

When she'd retreated to her room the night before, Coco told me she was confident it was nothing more than one of Misia's usual sulks. It would pass like a rainsquall on the water the moment she'd made a conquest of one of Benny's titled, handsome houseguests.

"My wager is that she'll set her cap for Sir Shane Leslie, Vera." She laughed. "Not only is he strikingly good-looking, but he's a published poet—Misia's typical prey."

"She won't make much headway there, Coco. Anita doesn't tolerate poachers."

"Well, Vera, if not a poet, then a statesman. I know he doesn't have the title yet, but Winston certainly qualifies on both counts, as a politician and as a writer. Now I think of it, though, journalism may not be up to Misia's exacting aesthetic standards."

"No chance there either, Coco," I told her, "Winston's deeply devoted to Clemmie. If he's managed to resist the charms of both Maxine Elliot and Daisy Fellowes, I doubt he'll be attracted to Misia. She's *far* too public for his taste. Winston's galaxy, and I say it with affection, has room for only one star—himself. Not to worry, though, Coco. There's bound to be someone she finds worthy of her special attentions."

With the clear, sharp fall air and the crunch of red and gold leaves underfoot as we left the caravan of Rolls-Royces on the roadway and moved off into the forest behind the beaters, dressed in their scarlet wide-brimmed hats, their white smocks, and undergrowth-proof leather leggings, all thought of indoor sport was banished by the pure joy of the real thing.

Benny believed the birds were higher and faster at the end of the season so, while shooting officially began in October, he always held the Eaton Hall shoot in late November.

Coco and I were warmly dressed against the chill in layer upon layer of clothes we'd borrowed—stolen actually—from Benny's wardrobe. Coco loved men's clothes. She was happily lost in Benny's plus-fours and a vintage tweed jacket that hung down well below her knees, like a mischievous child playing grown-up . . . a comic playing the music-hall version of the "Golden Duke."

Coco and Benny stood side by side at the peg marking the first stand. The top of her head was barely even with his shoulder as they passed their shooting sticks back to the efficient loaders and fired volley after volley at the sudden wealth of targets. Benny had the birds bred specifically for the shooting, and they were fast and plentiful.

No matter how comical Coco looked, she was a crack shot. A natural. Her pale cheeks were flushed with excitement. She had her challenge in Benny who pretended indifference to his guests' marksmanship but who had every bird in each individual's bag counted and the number inscribed on their gold-embossed placecard at dinner that evening.

At one point in the morning there were so many birds in the slaty sky that it seemed as though a cloud had covered the pale sun. Then, to the crackle of gunfire, the cloud plummeted to earth—a thousand pheasants bagged by lunchtime.

We arrived at a large clearing in the forest to find a picnic materialized as if by magic. The stewards with their tall wicker hampers had come and gone, leaving trestle tables covered with brightly colored linen cloths, groaning under a hearty feast.

There was wood pigeon pie, game pâté, Cheshire pork-and-apple pie, rabbit with wild mushrooms, cold venison in a Cumberland sauce, and big yellow wheels of Cheshire cheese and pickled walnuts. Out-of-season fruits had been picked in the hothouses. Peaches, nectarines, and mandarin oranges glowed in silver bowls. It was enough to feed three times the number in our party. We fell on the food and the sharp local ale, ravenous after the morning's excitement.

Coco had taken an instantaneous liking to Benny's shy, dark-haired young daughter Mary and had insisted she join us on the cashmere tartan rug to share our food. Mary, who was initially awed by Coco's unorthodox get-up and her accent, quickly warmed to her obviously genuine interest. Before the lunch was over, they were deeply absorbed in the important issues of horses and clothes, like two schoolmates.

Sitting relaxed and happy on the rug, the ale and the cold air combining to bring bright color to her cheeks, Coco looked closer to Mary's eighteen than to her forty-two years. I watched Benny watch them out of the corner of his eye and smile. Mary was his favorite, and he was clearly delighted that she had accepted his mistress so easily, so naturally.

As we were preparing to board Benny's private narrow-gauge railway that would carry us to the afternoon's stands, there was a commotion in the undergrowth. Into the clearing, riding sidesaddle and dressed in a closely fitted black velvet riding habit, intricately frogged in satin, with a high-necked white lace blouse and an elaborately tied ascot, more appropriate to the Grand National than a country shoot, came Misia.

"There you are, Coco, *dieu merci,"* she cried. "I've been wandering in these infernal woods forever. This dratted animal bolted, and I lost the groom who was leading me . . . lost my way completely—lost my new hat . . ." She was flushed and dishevelled and on the point of tears.

Benny, who had no idea of *what* to make of a woman like Misia, tried gallantly nonetheless. He lifted her down from the saddle and ineffectually attempted to brush away the twigs and leaves and brambles that were caught in her hair, on her elegant habit . . . everywhere.

"My dear Madame Sert, how unfortunate." He was all concern. I'll have to reprimand the boy sharply. To have lost a guest as valuable as yourself. How very unfortunate . . ."

Coco couldn't stop herself. She burst out laughing. The sight of a bedraggled Misia and a bemused Benny was too much for her.

"Quel spectacle, Misia. You should see yourself!

Well, perhaps you shouldn't after all. You look as though you've been rolling around on the ground. Are you sure that young groom only *lost* you?"

Misia was in no mood for Coco's wit. "It was only at your insistence, Coco, that I came on this ridiculous shoot at all. I'd have been far happier—and safer—in front of the library fire. At least there are some fine first editions in the Duke's collection."

Coco and I exchanged amused glances. We both knew Misia read books seldom, if ever. Coco told me she didn't even bother to open her mail.

"I'm sorry, Misia. Truly I am," Coco said. "I promise we'll make it up to you this afternoon. The shooting's been glorious—and we've already collected enough pheasant plumage for me to make you a *hundred* new hats."

Coco spoke too soon. Misia's grand entrance was only the beginning. The second half of the shoot was plagued by what I can only describe as "Misia mayhem." Thank God there were only two more stands to cover!

Benny did his damndest to be patient with her. He actually made her his shooting partner which was amazing in itself, since he only liked to partner experienced guns. It hardly mattered. Misia seemed perversely determined to drive him mad, clumsily dropping her shooting stick on every second pass, firing wild at the most obvious birds, and bringing Benny's own tally down dramatically because she required so much attention.

I thought he was going to throttle her. I was tempted to do it myself. Misia was slowing down the stately dance of the shoot and getting on everyone's nerves with her constant complaining—of the chill, of the dampness as the late afternoon mist rolled up from the Dee, of the noise of the guns that aggravated her migraine. Misia was definitely bred for the drawing room not the out-of-doors.

When we reached the last stand, I breathed a sigh of relief. Soon enough Misia would have the consolations of a cheerful fire and an elaborate tea. My relief was short-lived.

By this time she was so impatient to be shut of the whole thing that she neglected to wait until the beaters were well out of range. As a low-flying pheasant rose in the near distance, she impatiently grabbed her shooting stick out of the startled loader's hands, aimed straight and low and fired. There was an astonished yelp from the fringe of the wood.

"Dammit, woman, what mischief have you got up to *this* time?" Benny thundered. "You've probably murdered some poor innocent chap with a wife and little ones. Give me that gun, you silly baggage, before you do any *more* damage." He wrenched it from her hands and hurled it disgustedly off into the undergrowth.

Bend'or was notorious for his sudden rages, but this was the first Coco had seen. She ran over and separated them like prize-fighters. And it did look as though Misia was about to hurl herself at Benny. Her own fiery temperament did not take kindly to being "manhandled by a boor and a bully," as she tearfully put it.

Just then a dark-haired, rosy-cheeked young man in the belted smock and brown leather leggings of the beaters came striding out of the forest and up to our group.

"Amazing shooting, your Grace," he said, smiling

broadly and holding out his wide-brimmed scarlet felt hat. It had been neatly drilled through the crown by a single shot. "Frankly, Milord, I did'na realize the little lady was such a crack shot. Dropped the bird, too, with that very same bullet," he said, handing the bloodied pheasant by its feet to Misia, who finally had the good sense to faint.

SEVEN

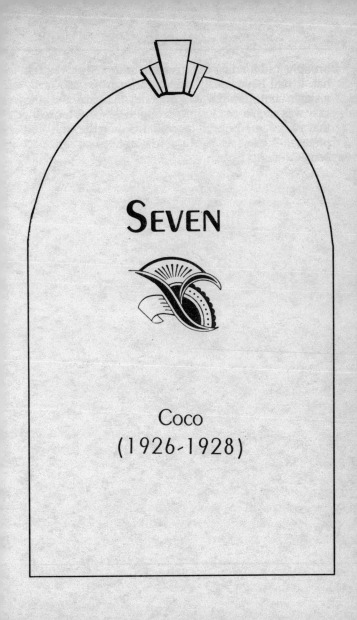

Coco
(1926-1928)

ONE

We were crashing through one more stand of pine. Which was more ferocious, I wondered, our quarry or the terrain? I could hear the pack in full cry up in the distance and Benny's shouted orders to the huntsman.

Mercure needed all his concentration to keep his footing on the loose, sandy soil of the coastal Landes. But it was French soil! *Dieu merci,* how glad I was to be back on my home ground again.

As I broke from the dimness of the pine grove onto a sunlit stretch of land, I could see the huge dark shadow-shape of our quarry, an ancient, battle-scarred wild boar said to be the largest and fiercest the district had ever seen. The patient stalking of lurking salmon in the peaceful pools of Lochmore seemed incalculably distant and hopelessly tame beside the heart-pounding excitement of this wild pursuit.

From the moment of our arrival the day before in Mimizan, Benny could talk of nothing but the coming hunt.

"You fancy yourself a huntress, Coco darling. Until you've gone after boar you haven't been truly blooded. A rogue boar at bay is one part wily, the other deadly. I've seen one go through an entire pack of hounds like a reaper with a double-bladed scythe. Come to think of it, I'm not sure boar-hunting is proper sport for a lady."

"And you know very well by now, Benny mon cher, after Eaton and Lochmore, I'm not *that* kind of a lady— not one of your English hothouse roses. That's precisely why you like me. Because I can bag as many birds and land even more salmon and lake trout than you can. My catch is there in the record book at Lochmore for all to see! Come on, Winston," I turned to Churchill, dreaming over his cognac in front of the fire, "ride with us tomorrow as our tame journalist and you can report which one of us—Benny or me—flinches first."

But Winston had begged off for a painting expedition to the shore, and Vera and Clemmie had simply declared the whole thing barbaric, installed themselves in front of the cheerful fire in the morning room of Benny's isolated, rustic Château Woolsack, and settled in to their needlepoint and gossip.

I tore through one more grove of pines as the distant baying rose to a note of hysteria. The boar must finally have turned to make his stand. I rose to my feet in the stirrups to see how far ahead they were and was rewarded with a stinging slash across the face by a pine bough that laid open my lip. The intense pain made me gasp and tears sprang to my eyes.

Merde, what was the matter with me? Benny would have nothing but justified contempt for an amateur's mistake like that. The heat of the chase had made me reckless. Ignoring the blood dripping onto my white silk shirt, I spurred Mercure in the direction of the mingled cries of dogs and men.

The scene was straight out of one of the medieval

hunting tapestries on the château walls. The giant black boar, his hide a patchwork of the scars of old combats, had his back to a high, sandy dune.

The hounds surrounded him in a frantic semicircle, darting forward to harry him. One came too close, and the boar simply tossed him over his head, swinging him back and forth on his tusks and eviscerating him so that a red mist seemed to hang in the sunlight, while the dog shrieked in agony. A second brave bitch went the way of the first, and in a matter of brief, bloody minutes, the entire pack was decimated.

Now I understood what Benny meant. This was savagery of a sort I'd never witnessed in all my years of hunting, back to my first blooding with Étienne at Royallieu. The huge boar was malevolence itself. When Benny finally got off a shot, it missed the head and struck the shoulder. Instead of felling the boar, it seemed to galvanize him and, grunting wildly, he charged straight at us and brutally gored the huntsman's horse, laying its vulnerable side wide open to the bone.

Time stopped as the boar backed slowly off, apparently oblivious of the blood pouring from the gaping wound in its shoulder, and began pawing the ground as he faced the defenseless huntsman. I sat stock still in the saddle, willing Mercure to immobility, frightened that any sudden movement would trigger the charge.

With a great shout, his red-gold hair burning in the sun, Benny flung himself from his horse onto the boar's back and went for the animal's throat with his hunting knife. Man and beast rolled over and over in deadly embrace.

"Atavistic" Vera had called Bend'or back in the mirrored and carpeted sanctuary of my elegant salon. And atavistic is what he was here, now on this sandy plain somewhere in Les Landes. This was primal combat— one man alone against an adversary with the advantage of size but not ferocity. From some deep reservoir inside himself, Benny summoned the strength to plunge the knife into the boar's neck and drag it across its throat, drenching himself in the fountain of arterial blood. Dying animal and exhausted man lay side by side on the bloody sand.

Half of me was horrified—half of me profoundly stirred. Bend'or was a throwback to his ruthless Norman ancestors. He was right. This was a man who *should* have sons.

When the badly shaken huntsman had taken Benny's horse and galloped off into the pines for help, I knelt at his side and tried to wipe away the gouts of blood from his face with the tail of my shirt.

At my touch he opened his remarkable blue eyes— the eyes that reminded me so of the blue flame of Boy's—and reached up to lightly trace my broken lip with a finger. Had Boy found him for me? There were so many things Boy would have approved about Bend'or—his lion's courage, his strange, compelling combination of strength and gentleness that I had actually begun to believe he had.

"But Coco, my love, your beautiful mouth . . . you've hurt yourself. Whatever happened to you? There's blood on your lip . . . on your shirt . . . blood everywhere." Bewilderedly, he tried to sit up, but I gently pushed him back down onto the sand.

"Lie still, Milord. You've fought your battle for the day." I brushed my fingertips across my aching mouth and touched them lingeringly to his own. "A careless encounter with a pine bough. Not at all in the same league as your boar-baiting. The next time you decide to show off for me, Benny, just promise you won't pick a half-ton antagonist. Even *my* nerves aren't proof against that."

"Then, if that's your condition, Coco, I suppose I'll have to settle for the nearest available featherweight," he said, reaching up to draw me down on top of him, both of us sweated and bloody and laughing under the burning southern sun.

TWO

*A*fter the sunlight and hot sands of Mimizan, the damp London chill seemed to penetrate right to the marrow of my bones. At least the suite I'd taken for Vera and me at the Ritz was cozier than the vast, drafty rooms of Eaton Hall. Besides, though Benny graciously acknowledged me as his official hostess at the Hall, in London I preferred to keep a separate residence. Propriety was part of it, since his divorce from Violet was still not final. More important to me was that I maintain my independence.

From the start I had understood that the moment I

ceded that to Benny, I would be lost—and so, ironically, would he. Mine would be the comfortable fate of his former mistresses. A cash allowance which I would, of course, refuse, and a gradually diminishing flow of important jewels whenever some remembered coastline or the glimpse of a delicate, dark-haired woman with a camellia in her hair reminded him of those delightful months with that "charming little Paris couturière." Unlike the others, I would always have the work to challenge and sustain me. But Benny would be condemned once again to the hunt—the endless search for the perfect consort that had left him the bored, lonely man I had met in Monte Carlo.

Duchess of Westminster. Was it arrogance that made me believe I could play that role? After all, I had already played so many. Nothing in my background and everything in my life had prepared me for it. What was a duchess, after all, but an administrator and an ornament?

I'd certainly had enough duchesses among my customers at the rue Cambon who'd managed to get by nicely with only half the equation. My some two thousand temperamental employees and suppliers, and an equivalent number of equally temperamental clients, and my several salons required the same cool-headed generalship as the army of servants and far-flung residences maintained by the Westminsters. Certainly I qualified on the first count.

As an ornament? Benny obviously thought so. Even Misia, judging as usual by her supremely worldly standards, believed he was serious. "After all," she'd told me, "just look at these extraordinary jewels . . . He treats you like a greedy empress, Coco, ma chère. He *must* be in love with you."

And for two people who'd come from so very far apart we shared so much—hunting, shooting, sailing, fishing, polo, tennis. Benny and I were never happier than we were out under the open sky, using the fine, strong bodies *le bon dieu* gave to both of us. I teased him that there *had* to be a hardy Norman peasant lurking somewhere in his impeccable bloodlines.

Our bodies. That was another point for my side. Benny had an apparently insatiable appetite for me. The funniest—and dearest—thing about it was how very much it surprised *him*. Sometimes when we had finished making love, lying in the vast four-poster in the ducal chamber at Eaton Hall or its smaller replica on *Flying Cloud,* or in the sun-shot pine groves of Mimizan, I would catch him looking at me with genuine bewilderment.

For the first time in his long string of conquests, the unwary huntsman found himself snared by his prey. He needed my embraces more than I did his.

Benny was an ardent, aggressive lover, but he was not sensual. His arousal and his satisfaction were immediate. It was that yearning for the sweet, sustained languor of the sensualist that he saw in me and could never have that constantly enticed him. With me he was the "successful" hunter who lives in fear that his wild captive will tunnel her way under the wire of the cage and make her escape back to her essential difference, her essential independence.

An administrator, an ornament, and an elusive *amie.* What more could be required of Bend'or's perfect consort—the once and forever Duchess of Westminster?

A breeder. How could I—with my sure knowledge of thoroughbreds and the men who worshipped them—have left that out? Because I feared it so.

That's why Vera and I were in London. Not, as I gave out to my friends and the press, to celebrate the success of the newest "Chanel," but in a taxi in the crowded London streets on our way to the offices of an eminent Harley Street gynecologist to consult, as I told her, on the likelihood of my success as a broodmare.

"Aren't you anticipating, Coco darling?" she said gently. "As far as I know, he hasn't proposed. And if he did, why aren't you willing to believe he wants to marry you for love? With all due respect, Coco, if Bend'or wanted to make another dynastic marriage, there would be many reasons—beyond your 'advanced age' as you call it—for him to look elsewhere."

"You're right, he loves me *now,* Vera. I have no doubt of that," I said ruefully. "He loves me because I challenge him at a level no woman ever has and, I'm bold to wager, no woman ever will. That challenge is my independence—the fact that he knows that, for all his incalculable riches, he can't control me. Right now, my identity is every bit as sturdy as his own."

"Well, why ever should that change, Coco?" Vera seemed genuinely perplexed. "I can't imagine it."

"If I agree to become the Duchess of Westminster—that is, of course, should he ask me—and surrender Coco Chanel even partially or temporarily, and then fail to provide him the heir he's so desperate to have, you mark my words, the very things he prizes in me will turn sour . . . bitter—first in his heart, then in his mouth. I can hear it now, Vera, 'What good is making dresses, Coco, if you can't make a son?' "

The elegantly tailored, witty, surprisingly young specialist who examined me made the indignity of the process somehow easier to bear.

"Familiar with stirrups, then, are you Mademoiselle Chanel?" he asked when I jumped up onto the examining table. "You mount with such agility."

"You're right, doctor, most familiar with stirrups and—given the *froideur* of your implements—eager to cross the finish line and dismount as soon as possible."

He laughed and continued his explorations with extraordinary gentleness.

"You know, Monsieur," I told him, "you have splendid hands. What the Society belles of Mayfair and Belgravia have gained has been a decided loss to the practice of veterinary medicine."

His nurse helped me down from the table, assisted me in straightening up my tailleur, and ushered me into the specialist's comfortable, book-lined office.

"Well, Mademoiselle, I probably don't need to tell you that you are in excellent condition. You've obviously led an active, physically challenging life. No serious illnesses?"

"None, doctor, *dieu merci,* not even as a child— though my mother suffered terribly from asthma, I was spared that condition. The worst I can complain of is some mild pain in the joints of my hands—probably from overuse in my profession."

"And your concern now is the possibility of childbearing?"

"Yes, doctor, both the likelihood and safety at my age."

"Forty-three *is* late to begin, Mademoiselle Chanel, but it's hardly unheard-of. Many healthy children are born to women in their forties, and my examination revealed no physical impediment to your becoming pregnant. I assume you still have your monthly flow?"

"Regularly, doctor. In fact, always in the past I've been happily surprised at my failure to conceive. I have taken *some* chances over time." I smiled wryly at him. "Ironically, that's one of the things that worries me now. That I may be barren."

"Or you may not have had the proper partner, Mademoiselle, or the right spirit. You'd be surprised at how great a role emotional readiness seems to play in conception. I'd suggest you continue on in your, ah, conjugal relations. Try not to concentrate too much on success—though I suspect that comes hard to a natural competitor like yourself—and come back to see me again in six months. It would not surprise me to find there was good news for you." He smiled warmly and showed me out of his office.

Back in the cab, Vera was dying of curiosity. "Well, Coco, what did he say? Does he think you should do it? That you can?"

"He was optimistic enough about the odds, Vera, but not very specific. A lot of encouraging talk of 'the proper partner' and the 'right spirit' and 'emotional readiness,' but no advice on technique. Maybe there isn't any science to it after all."

"One of my friends said she'd heard that standing on your head after lovemaking increases the possibility—it seems it gives the little devils a fighting chance."

"Really, Vera. Next you'll suggest I take up kundalini yoga. Boy used to tease me by demonstrating some of

the positions, but he never made me pregnant either. Ah well, I'll just try to approach it philosophically. As far as I'm concerned, with Bend'or it's no pregnancy, no marriage. That's a risk *I'm* not prepared to take. Frankly, Vera, I don't want to be a duchess all that badly."

Of course I was deluding myself. The prospect of the peddler's bastard daughter becoming the wife and consort to the richest man in the world was what Boy would have called a challenge my destiny—my Karma—was throwing down to me . . . a challenge a competitor like me could hardly be expected not to pick up.

THREE

*M*ore than a year had gone by with still no sign of a pregnancy—and not for lack of occasion, believe me. Benny's passion for me was as strong as ever, *dieu merci.* He'd established Vera and me in a handsome town house in Davies Street so that he could keep me virtually at his side without offending the stuffier of the Royals.

Life with Benny was sweet. We went everywhere together—the Grand National, the polo matches, the opera (where Benny could be counted on to be asleep by the second act), dinners and dancing at Ciro's or the Café Royal or the Embassy Club with Benny's regulars—"Benny's brigade" I teased him—Freddy Birkenhead and Shane and Anita Leslie and Valentine and Doris Castlerosse. We were entertained by my new customer and patroness, Lady Cunard, the charming American heiress who'd cleverly changed her name from Maud to Emerald . . . her hair from mouse-brown to platinum . . . and conquered London Society by sheer force of conspicuous spending. Her "arrangement" with Sir Thomas Beecham, the handsome conductor of the London Symphony, was as unconventional as my own.

And I had become far more than social friends with Clementine and Winston Churchill: Clemmie because of our mutual devotion to Vera, and because she knew that, unlike Maxine Elliot or the professional beauty Daisy Fellowes, I had no designs on her husband; Winston because he thought my independent spirit was good for Benny and because the first time I'd caught him cheating flagrantly at bezique at Eaton Hall, I'd agreed to keep it a secret "between rogues like you and me."

Only grudgingly had Benny allowed me to spend collection times in Paris. The press on sides of the Channel, I told him, was having enough sport speculating on the outcome of our affair without our handing them the perfect headline: DAZZLED DESIGNER DESERTS DRESSMAKING TO DALLY WITH DUKE.

Yes, life with Benny was seductively sweet, seductively comfortable, but there was still no visible sign of its outcome. The third of my six-months visits to the

Harley Street specialist had seen even *his* youthful enthusiasm begin to flag. He'd gamely recommended a high-protein diet regimen which he was convinced would energize the entire metabolism and make conception more likely. And, gamely, I'd agreed to follow it, but my monthly flow came on with depressing precision.

With Misia back in Paris, fighting what I gathered from her frantic letters was a losing battle for her marriage, Vera was the only person I could confide in. We were in the taxi returning to Davies Street from the last, futile visit to the specialist when my frustration finally got the better of me.

"Merde, Vera, this pregnancy business is making me *vraiment folle.* It seems to me that all of my seamstresses manage to conceive in the first month of their marriage—*if* not before. I simply can't bear the total lack of control I have over my own body in this."

"You're spoiled, Coco, and I say that with love and affection," she told me. "In everything you've done so far, you've been able to dictate your terms. *You* determine the lines and fabric of each gown. *You* tell Beaux the top-notes and resonances *you* want in a fragrance . . ."

"That's exactly it, Vera. I can expand into new markets or not, depending on my estimate of their potential . . . of the proper timing. I can raise or lower the hems . . . the hairlines . . . my prices."

"And so far, Coco, you haven't put a foot wrong. Your instincts are amazing. All your enterprises are flourishing—the couture, the perfume, the new line of jewelry and accessories you've started in the rue Cambon boutique. If you don't take care, Coco, you're going to become a bloody industry!"

I smiled at her. "You're right, Vera, and that's what makes this business of an heir so tedious." I realized I was nervously twisting the lace handkerchief in my hands into knots. "Suppose I *can't* meet the challenge—can't give Benny the son he's so determined to have. Do you really think I'll still be able to hold onto that quicksilver attention span of his? Two strong-willed wives, and *le bon dieu* knows *how* many mistresses, have already tried and failed. What makes you think I'll be any more successful?"

"Because you endlessly tantalize Bend'or, Coco. You're the only woman he's ever met who refuses to surrender her identity to the force of his gigantic personality. Even someone as domineering as Shelagh couldn't manage him. But you do. Somehow, you've mastered the art of enchanting Bend'or by always doing the unexpected."

"Well, Vera," I said ruefully, "tonight will be a crucial test of that."

That night was the night of his youngest's debut— Mary, eighteen-year-old daughter of Benny's first wife, Constance "Shelagh" Cornwallis-West . . . Mary, the dark, intelligent, watchful young woman I'd calculatedly set out to charm as part of my campaign to conquer Bend'or when I first came to England . . . Mary whose tomboy bravado I'd admired up at Eaton Hall on the shoot, on the Hunt, and on the polo field because it reminded me so very much of my own.

And Mary whom I'd come genuinely to love and whose awkward, coltish beauty I'd contrived to enhance with my simple designs that played to the lean, spare lines of her loveliness, when Benny put her in my hands to dress. In the dowdy discomfort of the shy schoolgirl I saw Adrienne and me in those dreadful grey-and-white uniforms of our convent days so many years ago in Moulins.

It was at Mary's express request that I'd been invited to her coming-out. Certainly not the wish of her jealous, imperious mother who'd clung stubbornly to the title even after the divorce—something his second wife, Violet, had never tried to do. And it was for Mary that I'd decided to give a small dinner for the immediate family and our friends before the formal ball at the Grosvenor Estate offices in Davies Street.

It was an evening the press—and every hungry gossip in London Society—waited for with breath bated. "Constance, the Constant Duchess versus the French Pretender." Who would triumph?

"What do you think, Vera ma chère?" I asked, turning slowly in front of the salon mirror. A shaft of scarlet silk, held up by narrow satin straps, dropped just below the hipline to become a slender tier of horizontal bands of scarlet satin reaching just to the ankle. Incredibly intricate to create—stunningly simple to behold. It *had* to be tonight, if I was to survive the savage tongues of both Constance Shelagh and the more conservative of the Royals.

"A triumph, Coco—perhaps the most spectacular you've ever created. Don't you think scarlet is being a trifle provocative, though?" she asked. "The *'Duchesse manquée'* and all those horrid old Troy biddies will want to pin precisely that color on you anyway."

"That's why I decided on it, Vera. My 'Leo' nature

tells me it's better to enter the arena as a lion than a lamb. I've had the mirror-image of the gown made up in white to wear to the dinner I'm giving for Mary and the family before the ball." I didn't want to admit, not even to Vera, how much trepidation I felt about the evening.

The scarlet had seemed right when I saw the gown in my mind's eye. *Épater les bourgeois* had always been my motto—challenging the proprieties had been the real source of my success. Now, dressing for the dinner in the first, virginal incarnation of the gown, I wondered if I hadn't simply been whistling in the dark in the face of the evening's ordeal.

What was the answer? I knew everyone was watching to see if I could walk the wire of being the Duke's "official" mistress when he had his former wife and daughters in tow. Too many of them were hoping I would lose my footing and plummet headlong from the heights to social oblivion.

As I stood in purest white in front of the cheval glass in my dressing room, pondering my dilemma, Benny came quietly up behind me.

"Exquisite as ever, Coco. You look temptingly like a bride in that dress." He opened the leather jewel case in his hand and took out a high choker of what must have been more than fifty strands of seed pearls. Lingeringly, caressingly, proprietarily, he fastened the collar around my neck with its diamond clasp.

"As luminous and sensuous as the skin of its owner, my darling," he said, turning me in to his embrace. "You do know, Coco, that you were born to be a duchess?"

I laughed up at him. "No, Benny, you were born to be a duke . . . *my* fate was to be a designer. And tonight a designer of occasions. I hope my household is equal to Mary's challenge . . . no one deserves it more. She's a lovely young woman, Benny. You should be very proud."

"Yes. Proud of her and the way she defies her bitch of a mother to be a friend to you, Coco."

I knew I was on treacherous ground here. Shelagh had declared herself my enemy for no more reason, I think, than because she was reluctant to part with the tiara. Violet hadn't made a point of the title—had actually gone into business, after the divorce became final, as owner of a fashionable hair salon in Mayfair. But Duchess of Westminster was Shelagh's identity, and she clung to it tenaciously.

Downstairs I made a final survey of my table. I'd done it all in white in honor of the debutante. Ivory candles in tall Regency candelabra, snow-white, intricately embroidered linens from my Paris embroidery atelier, and centerpieces of my beloved white camellias and sweet-scented gardenias driven down that day from the hothouses of the Hall.

I'd borrowed Benny's French chef for the occasion and spent hours conferring with him over the "all white" menu. Every one of the ingredients from the *Bisque de homard* to the *Oeufs à la neige,* came straight from the lakes and streams and greenhouses and home farms of Benny's vast domain.

I checked the place cards, gold-embossed with the ducal crest, one last time to be sure I had put Shelagh far enough down the table to deflect any assaults from her razor-sharp tongue, but not so far away as to offend her, and that I'd kept Mary and the Castlerosses close at hand for moral support.

Shelagh had been happily remarried for eight years now to John 'Fitz' Fitzpatrick Lewis, a good-looking, charming officer eleven years her junior. But Fitz was a far cry from Benny's level of wealth and influence, and these state occasions always reminded Shelagh of how much she'd lost when she lost Bend'or—and how very much I stood to gain. Especially the title.

As I'd told Vera, the press was right for a change. I'd truly be walking the wire tonight.

Despite all my apprehensions, the dinner looked to be a *succès fou*. Mary, radiant in the ivory crepe de chine gown with its softly tuliped capelet and regal train that I'd created for her, and encouraged by the attention and champagne, had already fulfilled in private the purpose of the evening.

She had come out—out of the prison of her shyness and the shadow of her overbearing mother and her beautiful, blonde older sister, Ursula, who'd inherited Benny's ability to dominate a gathering simply by being there.

Tonight Mary shone for the first time with all the promise of her youth and her fresh, darkly glowing beauty. She captivated the entire table with witty anecdotes of her struggles to become the perfect debutante. And she sweetly and graciously deferred to me as hostess, including me whenever she could in her misadventures.

"Had it not been for Mademoiselle Chanel, Papa, I could never have learned to manage my train. It was a nightmare. I felt as if I'd grown a sort of tail overnight.

It took Mademoiselle absolute hours of walking me back and forth along the runway in the salon to get me to stop fatally tangling it between my legs!"

"How you exaggerate, chérie," I told them. "She's a far quicker study than many of my professional mannequins. Naturally graceful. More patient with the fitters, too. They all adore her."

"Well, *there's* certainly a conquest for you, Mary dear," Shelagh observed acidly. "The *fitters* . . . Perhaps you might even aspire to a career in dressmaking like our Mademoiselle Chanel. It's certainly taken her to great heights."

Completely ignoring her mother's rudeness, Mary went on. "And what about the curtsey, Mademoiselle. I knew you nearly despaired of me after the twentieth attempt. I simply couldn't hold the position without wobbling. What was it you said I resembled?"

" 'One of Diaghilev's baby ballerinas with a flea in her tights,' I think it was, chérie. But eventually you mastered that, too. You're going to be splendid tonight."

"I'll toast that," Benny said from the foot of the table. "My beautiful daughter, Mary—splendid tonight and for nights and years to come."

We all raised our glasses. Then Mary returned the toast.

"To my very indulgent Mama and Papa who have given me a superlative life and their own bold spirit to live it joyously . . . And to my dear new friend, Mademoiselle Chanel, whose originality and style have shown me something more still to aspire to. I thank you all for this evening—I shall never forget it."

As we were getting up from the table, the men to adjourn to the library for their port and cigars, the ladies upstairs to reconnoitre their hair and makeup before the ball, Benny made a surprise announcement.

"To widen the circle of affection before the ball, I've invited a few others—friends and family—to join us, Clementine and Diana Churchill, representing Winston who's unfortunately under the weather from flu, and my former sister-in-law, Diana, and Westmoreland who've driven up from the country and should be arriving at any moment."

As I went up the carpeted staircase to my luxurious bedroom suite with the other ladies, I could not hear a word of their enthusiastic gossip for the pounding of my heart.

Diana, Countess of Westmoreland. Diana, widow of Benny's beloved half-brother, Percy Wyndham, who he told me had died in the fierce hand-to-hand combat in the forest around Château Soupir in the early days of the war. Diana, the ravishing war-widow who'd had the incredible ill-fortune to be twice-widowed before her twenty-fifth birthday when her second husband died in a tragic accident, leaving her with two infant daughters on her hands.

Diana, who'd obviously been rescued once again, this time by the immensely wealthy Earl of Westmoreland. Beautiful Diana, whose second husband had been what they said of Lord Byron—that "mad, bad, and dangerous-to-know" Anglo-French financier Arthur Capel. Arthur "Boy" Capel. *The only man I had ever truly loved.*

Could Benny have known? After all, when we'd first met he'd tried, clumsily, to tease me about Dmitri. No, while I'd confided my passion for Boy to Dmitri in those early days when my grief was still so raw it paralyzed me, I don't think I'd ever mentioned Boy to Benny. This *had* to, be some sort of immense cosmic caprice. Diana . . . here, now, almost ten years later.

I went through the motions of freshening my makeup and paying polite attention to the gossip, with one eye on the bedroom door. Finally it opened and she was there. *Diana.* As breathtaking as she was that first day, ten years ago, when Boy with his reckless heart had brought his new bride to the rue Cambon and asked me to dress her. And I had agreed. What fools passion makes of us all!

"Diana," I said, determined at least to have the advantage of speaking first. "How very lovely you are!"

If she was surprised to see me, she gave no indication of it. Even buried in the country she must have heard rumors of my attachment to Bend'or. The press had been dining out on it for several years now.

"And you, Mademoiselle Chanel," she said with that unaffected warmth that had drawn me to her even then, despite my terrible, gut-wrenching jealousy, "untouched by time. If anything, you're even more remarkable than that rainy afternoon in Paris when you told Boy you might just be able to transform me from dowdy English duckling to swan. I remember how surprised I was at the time that you'd agree to take me on at all. Boy always did manage to get his way."

Boy. How easily his name came from her lips, when I who seldom spoke it had heard it echo daily in my mind and heart for the last ten years. Seeing her brought it all back with such immediacy that I felt weak and dizzy.

"Are you all right, Mademoiselle Chanel," Mary

asked, "you look so very pale. Shall I ask Papa to have his physician called?"

How like her father Mary was. Benny was so quick to call in his army of Harley Street specialists if I so much as sneezed, that I'd taken to hiding even a minor cold. Harley Street would do me no good now.

"Thank you, Mary ma petite, but I'm perfectly fine. Just a trifle too much champagne on top of party nerves. I was determined that everything be perfect for you."

I tried to concentrate on the worried girl, while all my attention was riveted to Diana as she sat at my dressing table, brushing that mane of pale-gold hair. It was as full and shiny now as it had been when we met, and fantasies of that golden waterfall spread out on Boy's pillow and those star-sapphire eyes holding his, had haunted my nights and days.

"How are the children, Diana darling?" Shelagh asked. "They must be growing like weeds. Nothing rivals country air for raising horses and dogs—and children, I always say. I can hardly credit that Ursula's become a smart young matron, and now little Mary's about to leave the nest, too. I don't feel old enough to have grown daughters. Certainly I hope I don't *look* it!"

"Never fear on that score, darling Mother," Ursula said, "there's no better tonic for aging skin than a much younger husband." Ursula had inherited her mother's gift for sarcasm.

"The children are flourishing, Shelagh," Diana ignored Ursula's cattiness. "Ann is almost as tall as I am now, and June looks to be trying to top her sister—and they're both quite mad for horses. They take after their father that way. They've got his striking looks and that

criminally seductive charm. The two of them have had
me firmly in the palm of their hands since they were
infants. Just like he did." She laughed ruefully. "Thank
heavens my marriage to Westmoreland is more stable.
I would *never* have survived another Boy Capel!"

Boy's children. Somehow, I'd managed to block out
their existence. Diana had, at least, a fleshly remem-
brance of him. I wondered if she knew how her casual
family gossip was piercing through me, stripping away
defences slowly, painstakingly built up over a decade.
I doubted it. Diana had no unkindness in her. In her
mind she must long ago have had to rationalize my liaison with Boy as just one of many in the life of a worldly,
wanton Parisienne. After all, here I was with Bend'or.

As the ladies gathered up their cigarette cases and
evening bags and gloves and prepared to rejoin the
gentlemen to depart for the ball, I drew Mary aside.

"Tell your father I've stayed behind to change my
gown, chérie. The debutante must be the *only* one in
white. Benny's used to my frequent costume-changes
by now. Tell him I'll be along shortly." I kissed her on
both cheeks and turned her toward her party.

As soon as the door had closed on Mary, I sank down
on the edge of a chaise longue, my heart still pounding
violently. I felt quite ill. Not even my maid should see
me like this. She'd be bound to alert the housekeeper
and, before I knew it, one of Benny's tame specialists
would be hammering on my bedroom door. By an effort of will I made myself get up and cross the room
to the armoire.

I unfastened the white gown and let it fall to a puddle
of satin and silk at my feet. I took out its scarlet twin

and, moving like one of my mannequins in the frenzy of the *cabine* on collection day, I dropped it over my head and automatically began doing it up. My hands were shaking so I could barely negotiate the dozens of delicate fastenings. When I finally finished, I confronted my image in the cheval glass.

I looked ghastly. My ordinarily pale skin was paper-white and coated with a fine film of perspiration. The stark contrast of my pallor and my jet black hair, with the fever patches on my cheekbones, to the scarlet satin made me look like a badly painted doll.

Quelle débâcle. I couldn't possible face my critics looking like this. In fact, for the first time in my life I couldn't face them at all. Diana's sudden, utterly unexpected reappearance had triggered such an avalanche of images—images of Boy in my arms . . . in hers . . . in his flaming car—that I felt possessed by one of those wracking fever-dreams Dmitri had helped me conquer back in the villa in Garches.

I stumbled to the bed and managed to crawl, fully-dressed, under the duvet. What a cruel joke. Diana had Boy's children and I had none . . . apparently *could* have none. Barren. What a terrible, remorseless word. And how unfair. I who could create so prolifically, so effortlessly from all the fabrics of the earth could not find in the fabric of my body the stuff to shape a son.

What would Benny do when he finally had to acknowledge the truth? He was far too proud to blame himself, though the specialist suspected his two bouts with malaria in Egypt might have left him sterile. No, the fault would have to be mine and—no matter how much he loved me, and I knew he did—he would be away again on the hunt.

I don't know how long I lay in the dark, alternately shivering and burning under the duvet, my gown a sweat-soaked scarlet rag. At one point the door opened and Benny was there, cradling me in his arms, sponging my hot forehead with a cool cloth.

"My darling, why didn't you *tell* me you were ill? When you didn't turn up after two hours, I knew it wasn't simply dithering over a dress. That's not your style. So I told Shelagh to do the honors while I came to get you."

"Oh, well," I managed to say through chattering teeth, "I must have taken a touch of Winston's flu. Besides, we'd already had the best part of the evening here, and I knew I'd find those old fuddy-duddies insufferably boring. I thought you'd like it better this way, too. Make my apologies to Shelagh, will you, darling? I hope she'll understand."

The next morning—or was it noontime—Vera appeared in my bedroom, instead of my maid, with my breakfast tray and the papers. The strange, almost malarial fever that had wracked my entire body was gone, leaving me weak as a kitten.

Vera, *au contraire,* was positively glowing.

"Well, Coco, you've done it again! I should have guessed. Outfoxed them all!"

"Dieu, Vera, what on earth are you talking about? I think I've caught Winston's flu."

"Of course, as you say, Coco. But that's not what the gossips—*or* the press are saying. What a masterstroke. Even your friend Misia would be proud of you."

"Vera, take hold of yourself. What *are* you going on about? My absence from the ball?"

"Precisely, Coco. Pure genius on your part. By giving that lovely dinner here and then not turning up at the ball your absence was *all* that was talked about *all* night long. And that marvelous trick with the powder and mascara. Only *you* would have thought of that!"

I was utterly bewildered. "I'm sorry, Vera ma chère, you may think me simpleminded, but I've no idea what you're talking about."

"It's all over Fleet Street," she said gleefully, unfolding the papers and strewing them gaily on the duvet. She gave a dramatic reading of one of the reigning gossips. " 'And in an inspired act of diplomacy as the art of the possible, Mademoiselle Coco Chanel is said to have avoided any public awkwardness for the Duke and Duchess—and especially for herself—by feigning illness, applying rice powder to her already-ivory cheeks, mascara to simulate dark circles under her already-eloquent dark eyes, and elevating her already-warm temperature to dangerous heights by that old reliable method of thermometer and hot-water bottle. The Duke was seen discreetly brushing rice powder from the shoulder of his evening clothes when he returned to the gala ball at the Grosvenor Estate offices in Davies Street. A triumph of stagecraft that would have done credit to her friend, Diaghilev. A triumph of diplomatic withdrawal that would have done credit to Lord Chesterton.' What did I *tell* you, Coco? You've done it again. You're the talk of the town. No wonder Benny adores you. We *all* do. With you, it's always the unexpected."

I gathered the scattered papers to me and pretended to be sorting them out. *After the agony of last night . . . this sublime foolishness . . .*

"Well, Vera ma chère, as to the unexpected, I simply decided scarlet was not my most flattering color."

FOUR

*E*veryone assumed when I bought La Pausa that Benny had given me the villa, like the important jewels and furs and fabulous trinkets he had lavished on me from the day we met. That was as far from the truth of things as most of what Society says of me. I paid the 1.8 million francs for the perfect piece of land in the olive grove on a hillside between Menton and Monte Carlo, and the six million francs to build it, out of my own earnings. And *my* name was the only one on the deed.

Even as I signed it that February morning in the tiny office of the *notaire* in Roquebrune—and even later, as I decorated the aggressively masculine suite with its Elizabethan bed and its bath of glowing, palest opaline tile that was to be his, adjacent to mine—I knew, with that old intuition which had never given me the luxury of lying to myself, that Benny and I would never really live there together.

Our affair was coming to its close. Not because Benny loved me less. Not because he had tired of me.

If anything, over the years we'd been together, I think he'd come to cherish me even more. No, Benny had no intention of leaving me. It was my reluctant admission to myself that—if today's last, desperate experiment failed and I was forced to acknowledge that I would never conceive—I would have to free him. The hart would have to release the well-loved hunter at last.

So I'd chosen La Pausa to be my sanctuary. It had served that purpose once before, if you believed the locals as I did. It was in the lovely olive grove on the hillside that Mary Magdalene stopped, paralyzed by exhaustion, in her headlong, heartbroken flight from the crucifixion of *her* beloved. A little chapel of weathered stone next to my land commemorated that moment of respite in another woman's history. La Pausa—the pause—like the Villa Bel Respiro before it, a place for me to rest and regather my forces in the headlong progress of my strange, knockabout life.

Of course I kept my fears from Benny. I would have to hurt him—hurt both of us—soon enough. But not until the villa was completed and I had played my last card, could I send him off again on his quest, confident his "little couturière" had her own small fortress against adversity. How appropriate that a peasant's daughter and the grandest landlord of them all shared a passionate regard for the land we stood on and that we knew would ultimately shelter us both.

Benny was wild with enthusiasm for the project from the start. Outside of a fast horse or a high-flying pheasant, nothing interested him more than building. Even when I vetoed Detmar Blow in favor of Robert Streitz, a "baby" architect only twenty-eight whom I'd met one evening at a party on *Flying Cloud* and who'd filled my receptive imagination with visions of Xanadu on the Mediterranean, Benny was all for it.

My house. On my land. Surrounded by my olive trees. More than twenty of them. The number of trunks on each tree indicated its age. Some of them had so many boles they may even have been witness to my neighbor Mary Magdalene's welcome pause in her own journey. Only an "orphan," though I reject that canard to this day . . . only a gypsy child who spent her earliest days and nights traveling from market town to market town, longing for security, for roots, for rest could understand the way I felt now. Here. Safe in my own place, the place I had had designed and built to the precise dimensions of my own dreams.

It was beauty as I knew it—had always known it. Simplicity incarnate. All done in the golden beige that echoed the sandy slope it stood on, with shutters weathered to give the illusion of age and carved tiles of a sun-warmed beige on the floor.

Branching off from a central stone staircase, like one of my graceful olive trees, it had three wings—one private, with two spacious, airy suites looking out over the hillside to the sea; and the others for my guests and my adopted family . . . Misia and . . . please God, Jojo . . . Diaghilev, Serge and Boris, Picasso and Olga, Igor and Vera, Dmitri, Jean . . . even Pierre should he ever decide to venture again beyond the cloistered walls of Solesmes.

Sanctuary for me and whichever of my beloved geniuses might wish—or need—to share it with me. And as a gift for dear Vera who'd brought us together, and for Berto, her handsome Italian whom it had begun to look certain she would marry, I had built a small, private guest house, La Colline, that I hoped would shelter them both in the first celebrations of their love.

First and last . . . beginnings and endings . . . Vera and Berto . . . Misia and Jojo. What of Coco and Benny? How poignant these contrasts seemed to me as I sat beneath my olive trees waiting anxiously for my last hope—the midwife and healer from Roquebrune.

One of the maids, overhearing me confide my anguish to Misia on the telephone, had told me in an awed whisper of Gabrielle, who was famous locally for being able to cause life to quicken in wombs empty for decades.

Gabrielle . . . what a strange coincidence. When I first heard her name, I shivered. Could one Gabrielle really help another? The little maid had assured me that many of the late-born babies in the region were named Gabrielle in her honor.

So I sat on my hillside and waited impatiently for the wise old woman who might just possess the power to unlock my frozen womb and heal my barrenness. It was so sultry in the grove at noontime that I lay back and closed my eyes, letting the after-image of the sun glow scarlet against my eyelids. I must have dozed off in the heat.

When I opened my eyes again, she was standing there at the entrance to the grove with her back to the sun, so that for a moment, with her mass of golden curls lit by its rays, she appeared to be on fire.

Why had I imagined her as an old woman? Tradition, I suppose. Instead, here was a child, really . . . no more than a girl in her late teens. A beautiful young earth goddess blazing against the sun who reminded me of no one so much as Adrienne at the first ripening of her own golden beauty back in Moulins.

"Mademoiselle Chanel?" she asked me now, in a soft, warm resonant voice. "Marie told me I might find you here in the grove. I am Gabrielle . . ."

When I failed to reply, overcome by images of my own sweet, long-ago girlhood with Adrienne, she went on calmly, gently, "You have sent your maid for me, Mademoiselle . . . to the village . . . to consult with me about the question of a child."

I roused myself from my reverie. "Mademoiselle Gabrielle, forgive me. Frankly, I was startled to find you . . . to see someone so young. I had thought you would be . . ."

"Much older, Mademoiselle? An ancient, hunch-backed crone with warts and a moustache—a woman suspected to be a witch—whom the devout but despairing goodwives of Roquebrune slip off to consult in the dark of the moon. Do not be uncomfortable, Mademoiselle. That is what many say at our first meeting."

I laughed at her refreshing candor. "Precisely, Mademoiselle Gabrielle. It's far easier for me to imagine you as one of my young mannequins than as someone with an ability . . . with a mission to heal."

With unstudied grace she dropped to her knees and extended her hand to me.

"Regardez, Mademoiselle, it is clear in my palm. Just as all our destinies are written there. You see, here, in the center where the life-line and the line of destiny intersect . . . the star?"

And I saw it there in the girl's hand—the precise outline, formed by the lines in her palm, of a five-pointed star.

"Very few are given that gift, Mademoiselle, the gift of the healer. The star in the palm is its sign. There are many lonely times when I wonder to myself if it really *is* a gift—or a burden—times when I wish for it to be taken from me. Already it has set me apart from the friends of my schooldays, from the young brides, and frightened away the man I loved who I hoped would marry me and give me children of my own. Roquebrune is a tiny place, Mademoiselle. The people here who seek me out also fear me. I am forced to live alone, apart from society, with only my goat and my cat and the baby owl, whose broken wing I'm mending, for company. And I'm sure the villagers regard *them* as my 'familiars.' I have never seen Paris . . . will never see it in my lifetime, I suppose. But a person with a gift like mine could live there safely . . . unknown . . . unrecognized except by those she chose to reveal herself to."

The girl's honesty and her air of wistfulness touched my heart. I knew loneliness too well. "I suspect you are safer here, Mademoiselle Gabrielle, even in your isolation. Paris is a hard place for the innocent. Once your gift was known, I'm afraid there would be all too many who would try to exploit it—exploit you."

"You are probably right, Mademoiselle," she smiled wryly. "And besides, where on the boulevards of Paris would I be able to find all the herbs and simples I need for my remedies?" She began unpacking jars and jewel-colored bottles from the woven-straw bag she had slung over her shoulder.

"The tools of my trade, Mademoiselle, all made from the flowers of the fields around us—the lavender, the hyacinth, the mimosa—and the soothing herbs and healing aloes. If Mademoiselle will please to remove her clothes, I will begin with a relaxing massage."

Strangely, though it was broad daylight and we were in the open air, I had no sense of false modesty or fear. There was something about the girl's utter simplicity— her naturalness—that inspired utter trust. I took off my clothes and draped them over the low-hanging branch of an olive tree.

I lay on my back, the warmth of the sandy soil pulsing up from the center of the earth, the warmth of the Mediterranean sun filtering down through the silvery leaves, making drops of perspiration bead my body.

Gabrielle sat behind me, her long legs outstretched on either side of me, and lifted my head in her hands.

"Let go, Mademoiselle. Do not try to hold your head up. Let me bear the weight. It's easy for me. You are safe. I am supporting it for you. Breathe very deeply and let go of all your tensions—all your resistance."

When I did as she told me, I was astonished at the sense of release. Gently, strongly she massaged the back of my neck, my head, my shoulders—even cupped my ears in her hands and pulled them lightly. Then she stroked my forehead with her long, slender fingers. I could feel the locked muscles of my neck and shoulders uncoiling.

She moved down to my feet and massaged each of them with a creamy lotion from one of her colored-glass bottles. She pressed hard against my arches with her thumbs, massaging the soles and running her fingers between my toes, tugging them one at a time to release the muscles and then gently kneading the ball of the foot and the heel.

"The head and the feet, Mademoiselle, is where we begin—where most of life's tensions repose. The neck stiff with pride and always guarding against assault . . . the feet bearing us up through days of triumph and pain . . . carrying us toward love and away from loss. My teacher, a very wise, very old nurse-midwife, Mademoiselle, told me the reason she had lived so long was because she gave her feet their proper respect and massaged them every day. And she was a hundred-and-two!" She laughed gaily.

I felt Gabrielle move to straddle my body with her own. I opened my eyes to see her kneeling above me, creaming her hands with a rich, spicy golden unguent from a white alabaster jar.

"And now, Mademoiselle, I shall try to awaken your sleeping womb." She placed both her hands, palms down, on the lower part of my stomach and rotated them slowly on my flesh. "Do you feel anything? Tell me what it is you feel . . ."

How can I describe the sensation? Her palms grew steadily warmer—not the simple warmth of body contact, but a surging heat, radiating from the centers of her hands, spread like stars on my body—stars within stars—a heat that seemed to penetrate right down to my core.

"I don't think I can explain it, *ma fille,*" I told her. "I've never felt anything like it before . . . so intense, like rays of heat pulsing through me . . . like . . ."

"Energy, Mademoiselle Chanel," she said with a radiant smile, her golden hair flaming in the sun. "It is the healing energy that flows through my hands to you from the primal source. If your womb is capable of being quickened, the energy will do it."

Lightly, caressingly she drew her palms down the soft inner flesh of my thighs, kindling them with that same strange, radiant heat, then brought them to rest on the thick dark thatch of my hair.

A climax of shattering force—stronger even than those I'd known with Boy—swept through me. I felt entirely opened up, my whole being unlocked and waiting.

While I lay stunned by its force, the girl got nimbly to her feet and began stowing away the jars of creams and oils and lotions she'd used in her massage. From her bag she gave me three amulets—two crystals, one of amethyst, the other clear, and the third a bouquet of dried herbs tied with a scarlet ribbon.

"Hang these on your bedstead, Mademoiselle. When your lover comes to you tonight, you will be ready to conceive. Your womb is eager for it."

She smoothed down her wild, tangled mane of hair, tucked the envelope bulging with francs I'd given her into the bodice of her dress and was gone, walking lightly out of the grove into the glaring sunshine.

For more than an hour I sat spellbound, turning the crystals over in my hand, breathing in the heady scent of the herbal bouquet. Who was she? *What* was she? Had our encounter really happened, or was it a waking dream brought on by the sultry southern sun and my longing? After all, I did have the amulets as proof that the other Gabrielle existed . . . and that she had touched me with those beautiful healing hands.

That night with the full round pregnant moon sailing in the sky, I called Benny to my bed—called him to the vast wrought-iron Spanish bedstead I'd found with a star as the headboard. A star like the one in Gabrielle's palm. Was it a good omen? I earnestly hoped so.

And there he was, stenciled tall and strong in silver by the moonlight filtering in through the wooden shutters. Silently he came to my bed and silently he took me, sliding the satin shift from my body and repossessing it slowly, not selfishly as he'd used to do, but leisurely, lingeringly as I'd taught him, sensuously, stroking my thighs with his hands hardened by the leather of reins and running his soft, perfectly sculpted lips lightly, teasingly over my sun-warmed skin until he moved suddenly to seek out the very center of my pleasure with his tongue.

Images of Gabrielle bending over me in the grove that morning with her hot, magical hands moving to unlock my womb merged with the reality of Benny rising up from my thighs to mount me.

I arched to him—open fully to him as I had never been before. I surrendered willingly to every sweet demand he made of me and called out his name as he reared above me and drove the strong sure shaft of his manhood deep inside me. I answered his every thrust with my own and we moved with perfect synchrony until the warm liquid of love poured down inside me and mingled with his own.

When I awoke from the deep sleep of fulfillment, the moon was still high in the sky and Gabrielle's amulets, hanging from the bedstead to propitiate the fickle goddess of fertility who had mocked me for so long, sparkled with bright promise.

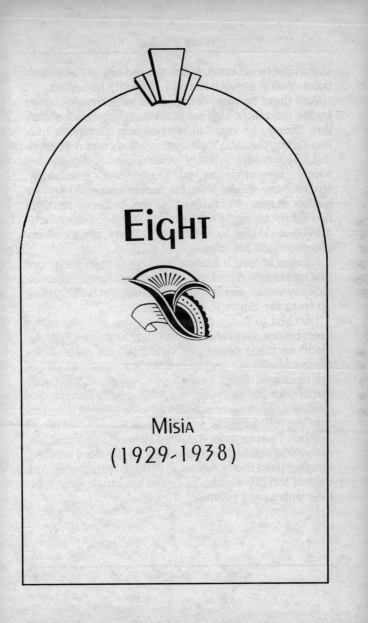

Eight

Misia
(1929-1938)

ONE

*H*ow ironic it seemed to me early on that August morning as I made my way through the labyrinthine alleys and across weathered, silver-stone bridges spanning misty canals, that our roles had utterly reversed.

Ten years before, Jojo and I had roused Coco from her trance of grief at Boy's tragic death on the way to his Christmas rendezvous with Diana. Fearing for Coco's sanity, we had spread the artistic splendors of Venice before her like a dazzling conjurer's trick.

Now, she and Bend'or had plucked me from the equally perilous triangle Jojo had drawn between me and his glorious young wife, Roussy Mdivani—the woman he and I *both* loved with unbridled passion.

Compounding the irony was that third, and in its way equally charged, triangle . . . Coco, myself, and Serge Diaghilev—for whose favor we had fiercely contended for more than a decade, and whose deathbed in the Grand Hôtel des Bains de Mer I had left only moments before.

And *what* a death, one altogether worthy of that master-illusionist who had once commanded Cocteau to "astonish" him. Serge Lifar, Boris Kochno, and I had kept nightlong vigil in that stark white room with its white curtains billowing and its two lonely, narrow white beds.

Alternately sweating and shivering with fever, Serioja raged against his dying, at one moment roaring passages from the *Pathétique* in defiance of his mortal terror, the next crawling desperately from bed to bed in a vain attempt to elude his relentless pursuer, and at the last, exhausted and serene as the morning sun poured in, turning the single tear on his cheek to silver.

Those long, tense hours of waiting told on us all. When they realized that their lover, patron, and surrogate father was *truly* dead, Boris threw Serge to the floor where they fought savagely, biting, tearing at each other's hair, and snarling like animals.

Unable to part them, I simply fled—down the long, sleeping hotel corridors and out into the early morning mist. My own pain and terrible sense of loss was redoubled by practical concerns. Coco and Bend'or, falsely reassured by that smiling Italian quack's hopeful prognosis, had set sail on *Flying Cloud* the day before, confident I would be joining them shortly to resume our cruise. And I had already depleted the small reserve of funds I'd carried from the yacht on the medicines that had failed to save Diaghilev from his deadly diet of drugs, bonbons, and boredom.

All I could think of as I hurried through the bewildering maze of streets was to reach the Jewish quarter where Johanna might be able to direct me to someone to whom I could pawn the three long, spectacular strands of diamonds Jojo had given me in a moment of remorse for Roussy.

Just as I thought I was hopelessly lost in the tangle of cobbled passageways, a figure came hurrying toward me out of the *nebbia*. She was dressed entirely in white—white trousers, white sailor's jersey, white turban—and at first I was convinced she was an apparition brought on in the panicked aftermath of the night's terrors. But no, *dieu merci,* it was Coco.

She embraced me. "The magician is dead, isn't he, ma chère? Last night I told Benny we had to turn back. I'd had a dream of that room and the three of you weeping. I knew in my heart he had left us."

The next morning at dawn, we accompanied Serioja to his grave. Somehow, in those brief hours Coco had managed to organize everything, from the three funeral gondolas to the priest who would officiate at the burial on the Isola di San Michele.

As we were poled across the still mirror of the lagoon, I'm embarrassed to confess that I thought how very theatrical it all was. How much it would have been to Diaghilev's taste—the first black gondola with its gilded swans bearing the catafalque on which he lay in state . . . the second, hung with crepe, carrying the Russian orthodox priest Coco had materialized to perform the rites, and our own black funeral barge.

Boris, Serge, Coco, and I had dressed entirely white—white because it was how Serioja had asked us to remember him, festively, like brides and bridegrooms come to a celebration of new life, not as mourners. I was reminded of that time seven years before when Coco had martialled the white, plumed horses and white hearse to carry another genius, Cocteau's beloved Monsieur Bébé to the Père Lachaise cemetery.

As we crossed the mist-shrouded lagoon, I held tight to her arm.

"Do you know what I see, chère Coco? I see all the beautiful dancers he loved—Nijinsky as the enchanted faun seducing himself with that scarf that caused so much scandal . . . Massine as the Prince in *Schéhérazade* . . . Serge as *Le Spectre de la Rose*—I see them all leading the magician to his rest."

She looked at me skeptically. "You're becoming fanciful, Misia. You always do. You and I know that what Diaghilev would have been considering was the cost of mounting this elaborate production and how to cut the proper corners or to inveigle Astruc or Lady Ripon to put up money one more time, or to find one more impressionable backer to make his extravagant funeral vision a reality. That's what *I'm* doing right now, Misia, and that's what he would certainly respect."

Our gondolas were moored at the pier and we disembarked. The mist had lifted, and it was a glorious August day—a day Diaghilev would surely have insisted that the four of us picnic with him on the Lido.

We followed the coffin to the Russian cemetery. Serge and Boris fell to their knees on the stony path and vowed to do him homage by following him as penitents to his grave. After some fifty yards of this Russian melodrama, Coco lost her patience.

"Boris . . . Serge, *up* off your knees both of you! Didn't he teach you that valiance was the way to confront life and death—valiance not capitulation. Certainly not groveling!"

Abashed, they got to their feet. But when we reached the graveyard, and the box holding the last of Diaghilev's earthly remains was lowered into the ground,

Serge could not control himself. He leapt into the grave and threw himself on the flower-covered coffin, embracing it and weeping bitterly.

Again, Coco intervened. "Serge, mon cher, *je vous en prie,* we all loved him. Perhaps you loved him best—but if you did, you would restrain your excess. Remember the time Cocteau made him a gift of his production of *Oedipe Roi,* and Diaghilev called it *'un cadeau très macabre?'* The last thing he would want now is bad theatre."

Serge allowed Boris to help him clamber out of the grave and brush the dirt and leaves from his white linen suit.

"Pardon, chère Mademoiselle," he said with quiet dignity, "but what he, of all others, would have understood is that there are times when *only* theatre—bad or good—has the power to save us from ourselves."

TWO

As the yacht left Venice and put out to sea again, Bend'or faced a situation even he, certainly one of the most powerful men in the world, could not control . . . could not even influence.

Beneath my agony at the loss of my darling Serioja, and the lacerating pain of the failure of my marriage, and Coco's own grief—valid however much I hated to admit it—at Diaghilev's death, lay Bend'or's inability to communicate with women, especially women in distress. I'd seen it at Eaton Hall. Seen it even when they took me aboard *Flying Cloud,* the cast-off of a ship-wrecked marriage, and tried to cobble me back together again after Roussy. But Bend'or hadn't the slightest notion of how to handle women, surely his first two wives and innumerable mistresses would agree—and certainly not finely tuned, complex mechanisms like Coco and me.

So, of course, he got it all wrong. There was a wistful part of me that wished he'd done it better. Bend'or and I were profoundly foreign to each other at every level of sensibility, except for our love of good paintings and our passion for Coco. Each of us, at least, recognized and respected those central commitments in the other. Then why did he botch this so badly? Because he *was* Bend'or, a man Cocteau would say . . . had said . . . who had outlived his era, a dinosaur left behind by the Edwardians. A man who believed *action* was the answer to any crisis.

Against the strong advice of the harbor-master, he'd had the crew set sail in dangerously foul weather—one of those unexpected August storms that blows across from North Africa with the sirocco. As we were beating our way toward the Riviera, the wind and waves were fierce. I stayed in my stateroom, immobilized by sea-sickness and mourning the deaths of the magician and my marriage.

Not Coco. She donned heavy-weather gear and determined to stay topside with Bend'or and the crew and ride out the storm. If he'd had the slightest notion of her condition--that she was three months pregnant—he would have clapped her in irons sooner than let her risk the fury of such a storm.

The swells were running at nine to ten feet, the worried steward who brought me soothing chamomile tea told me. Even with all her sails, with the exception of the mainsail, tightly reefed, *Flying Cloud* would heel dangerously over and then, because of her sleek lines and Bend'or's inspired seamanship, would somehow right herself just shy of capsizing and battle on.

Spray broke over the bow in loud, cracking explosions of water and drenched everyone on deck, despite their oilskins. Coco should never have dared this storm. But I'd seen her, pale and resolute, as she'd set about staging Serioja's funeral, and I suspect she was counting on the lashing winds and heavy seas to drive the memory of his unnecessary death from her mind.

That he'd died in the very same hotel where Stravinsky, full of hope and youth and promise, had first played him the revolutionary score for *Le Sacre* on the grand piano in the vast, empty ballroom, made it seem all the more poignant . . . and pointless.

Genius was mortal after all. And that Diaghilev, the conjurer who had saved us all so many times, and at such a heavy, but lightly reckoned cost to himself, from the lethal trap of the ordinary—that Diaghilev had not been able to save himself from his own lethal habits tormented me . . . must have tormented her nearly as much.

The Atabrine I'd taken against seasickness, combined with Bend'or's ever-present champagne, had made me drowsy. I drifted in and out of consciousness. Images assailed me, stretching as far back as those enchanted nights when I'd sat on the stairs of the redecorated Théâtre du Châtelet, clutching my knees to my chest in excitement, trying to get closer to him, to the power of his genius, to the amazing awakening of his production of *Boris Godunov* with Chaliapine as the tormented Tsar. And that other time in the near-riot at the Champs-Élysées when I was electrified by Serge and Stravinsky's prophetic double-vision in *Le Sacre* before I ever knew of the existence of Mademoiselle Chanel or the unexpected way she would come to possess me.

At first I thought the low moaning was coming from the ship's timbers themselves, protesting their battering by the force-nine gale. Then I realized that what I was hearing was the sound of someone in terrible pain. I got out of my bed and managed somehow to make my way across the wildly tilting floor, clutching the dresser . . . the nighttable . . . the bedpost for balance. Just outside my door, collapsed in a bright heap of yellow oilskins, was Coco.

"Help me, Misia . . . please help me." Her face was a pale blur in the storm-darkened corridor. "I'm afraid . . . I'm bleeding down there . . . It hurts so very much . . ."

Somehow I managed, half-carrying, half-dragging her unresisting body, to get her inside my stateroom.

"Lock the door, Misia. Benny might come looking for me. He mustn't find me like this," she said, "he mustn't know."

"Oh, Coco, I *told* you you were a fool to go up on deck in this weather. Why won't you ever listen to me?"

"No—it was all right in the beginning, Misia. The yacht's rolling, combined with my morning sickness, was making me terribly ill. I felt much better out in the air. But when the seas started running so high, Benny ordered me below. I couldn't argue with him without revealing my condition—and I was determined not to let him know about the child until the doctor was certain I would keep it."

I had been stripping off the rain-soaked oilskins only to find she was right. She was bleeding heavily, her white cotton trousers scarlet all down the legs. I tried not to let her see my panic.

"Then Misia, just as I reached the top of the stairs, there was a terrific gust. The boom jibed and it shook the whole ship. You must have felt it! I was thrown down the stairs. Dear God, don't let it die. Don't let me have lost our baby."

She was incoherent with the pain, talking at one moment to me . . . then to God . . . then to someone named Gabrielle—or was it herself? I had to use the inadequate scissors from my needlepoint to cut away the bloody trousers. Contractions wracked her slight frame. There was no help for it. She was miscarrying.

"Hold tight to my hands, Coco, and push," I ordered her, what little I knew of midwifery remembered from emergency births of peasant women in the back of my ambulance at the Front during the War. "It will go more quickly if you push."

"No, Misia, I can't. I've *got* to keep our baby. It's the only way. To give him his heir. The way for me to marry Benny. The way for me to be safe at last."

For an agonizing half hour she fought to hold the child, but it was too late. The fall had dislodged the fetus and it would not be denied. When she finally surrendered and expelled it, I cut the cord and wrapped it in a linen pillowcase.

Coco had turned her head to the wall. While she wasn't watching, I opened the porthole into the howling wind and gave the tiny body up to the sea. As I fastened the porthole cover, she heard the click of the brass latch and knew instantly what I had done.

In a voice that was barely a whisper, she asked me, "Well, Misia, you have to tell me. Was it . . . ?"

My heart broke for her. "Yes, Coco, it was a boy."

When we reached safe-harbor in Nice, the killer storm had passed over. Or so it would have seemed to someone who did not know the players. We had moored at the marina so that the crew could give *Flying Cloud* a thorough going-over for any hidden signs of damage.

On the last day of our stay, the yacht having been declared sound and stable and free from any lingering aftereffects of the storm, Bend'or gave a farewell party. The end of August was high noon in the party Season in the south of France, so it was infinitely easy for him to assemble a glittering cross section of friends and hangers-on at the drop of an invitation.

His fellow-rogue, Jimmy, the dashing young Duke of Alba and Berwick, Bend'or's only serious competitor for the title of prince of international playboys, came on board in mid-afternoon with an entourage of his titled friends and their spectacularly lovely, unnervingly young beauties. I think the oldest of them might *just* have achieved twenty. Coco greeted at least three of her own gorgeous mannequins.

The ubiquitous gypsy violinists were playing. The volatile mix of hot sun and icy champagne was raising temperatures dangerously, and dancing and flirtation were the order of the afternoon. Even Benny, after ten days of vainly trying every trick he knew to lift the cloud of gloom that hung over his adored mistress, had finally grown impatient with it all and decided to enjoy himself for a change.

Whirling the loveliest of Alba's decorations, not-so-coincidentally a small, dark-eyed brunette, out onto the afterdeck, he announced a tango contest. Jimmy Alba took the floor with a tall, reed-slim blonde with short-cropped hair.

What Benny couldn't know was how vividly it all evoked for Coco that evening after the premier of *Le Sacre* at Maxim's when she had taunted Boy by dancing the tango with tall, blonde, athletic Charles Dullin, flirting with him outrageously in the dance to enflame Boy's jealousy, just as this child was doing now with Bend'or. I only knew it because she had once confided in me that that was the night Coco understood on her pulses the magnitude of the obsessive passion she and Boy had for each other.

Now, watching her watch this pretty, simple mannequin using all her wiles to attempt to captivate Bend'or, it was as though I was inside Coco's heart and mind. Boy had been lost to her by accident. Now, though so far he had only the smallest notion of it, Bend'or had been, too. I saw Coco turn her back and walk away from the dancers, and I understood the full complexity of her pain.

That night, as I lay in my stateroom, driven out of sleep by dreams of Jojo and Roussy embracing in their marriage bed, there was a light tapping on the door and Coco came in, spectrally pale and lovely, wrapped in an ivory silk shawl, and sat at the foot of my bed.

"You know, Misia, how naive Benny is—and how very good. He thought I'd been jealous of his dancing with that pretty child. He thought *that* was why I left the party. He rushed into Nice before the *joailliers* closed to buy me something to make me forgive him. It was a single perfect pearl—a pearl as big as a dove's egg. We were leaning on the rail when he gave it to me, looking out along the silver track the moon had laid down over the dark . . . dark water. I took the pearl out of its velvet case and dropped it over the side.

" 'More precious things than that have been lost to the sea, Benny my love,' I told him. I'm sure he thought me quite mad. But we know better, Misia, don't we?"

THREE

*I*t must have been well after midnight. I had been lying awake staring into the darkness, acutely conscious of their peaceful breathing, agonizingly aware of their nearness. I ran my hand lightly down the sweet curve of her long, silky back.

Coco and Bend'or had done their very best to provide me with the time and distance to regain my objectivity, but we were no sooner back in Paris than I'd telephoned Jojo to beg him to let me come and stay with them again. I told him I wasn't sleeping . . . was ambushed by night terrors alone in our empty, echoing flat in the Meurice . . . was having dreadful nightmares of Diaghilev's death. I'd abandoned my pride altogether . . . promised I would only stay until I was able to get my bearings, would sleep in the guestroom and not dream of intruding on their privacy. And he had agreed—probably out of an uneasy amalgam of guilt and pity.

How could I have let it come to this? Was it the legacy of my strange relationship with Alfred, my second husband, and his mistress, Geneviève Lantelme? Was I compelled to repeat and repeat, always loving a man who preferred another to me—believing that if I *became* that other woman, my lover would find me equally desirable.

The long-ago days of my obsession with Geneviève Lantelme returned full force. Then it had been as though her wanton spirit possessed me. Without telling anyone I had slipped away, night after night, to the Théâtre Réjane to watch her play her small debut role in *La Savelli*.

I studied her every gesture: the way she moved, the way she inclined her head to one side when she spoke, every inflection of her low, musical voice. Later in my lamplit bedroom I would practice for hours in front of the cheval glass. Were my topaz eyes as gold-flecked

as hers? Was my skin as translucent with that trace of
pink pearl? During the day I would sit for hours in a
closed carriage outside the house Alfred had bought
for her in the rue Fortuny, patiently waiting for her to
go out for a singing lesson or a visit to her dressmaker.

I would order the driver to follow her discreetly, taking careful note of every flamboyant gown she wore.
My own modiste copied the rough sketches I made. I
had my maid dress my long, red-gold hair the way Lantelme did hers. If I looked like her, spoke like her,
dressed as she did—then surely Alfred would turn back
to me.

Now, twenty years later, I had fallen into the same
trap with Jojo and Roussy. But this was far worse. My
rival was a child-woman and I was middle-aged. Oh, my
mirror still showed me to myself as beautiful, but it was
a mature beauty. No dressmaker's art—not even
Coco's—no trick of cosmetics could give me the
weapon Roussy possessed, the absolute loveliness and
freshness of her youth.

So this time I had taken an even more aggressive
tack, courting Roussy as ardently as Jojo, indulging her
every whim and caprice. I took her to Chanel and convinced Coco to dress her like the young Georgian princess she pretended to be. I even persuaded Coco to
allow the girl to bring that filthy monkey she carried
everywhere on her shoulder into the fitting room.

I was reckless enough to suffer the indignity and the
pain of watching my closest friend fall under Roussy's
artlessly seductive spell—her tall, lithe body, her ash-
blonde hair, and slanted tartar eyes. Coco and I had
chosen her trousseau, and I'd even gone so far as to
help Jojo pick out the ruby ring and necklace that were

his wedding gifts to her. Most humiliating of all, I had actually tagged along like an unwanted mother-in-law on their marriage trip to Genoa.

And this is where it ended—the three of us, Roussy, Jojo, and me sharing the vast, ornately carved bed he had designed for his young bride. Where had my pride gone? Suddenly I was suffocating. I had to get away from this insidious, perverse ménage before it consumed me.

I slipped out of the bed without awakening them and dressed quietly. Throwing on a sable cloak, I called for my driver and directed him to the Faubourg St.-Honoré.

The irate concierge, unaccustomed to being roused at four in the morning, reluctantly let me go in to Coco's flat. At my urgent knocking, Joseph came to the door, hastily pulling on his jacket and smoothing sleep-rumpled hair. He suggested I wait in the library while he awakened Mademoiselle.

Frantically I paced the room, still barely able to get my breath, picking up and setting down one after another of the exquisite crystal paperweights and golden lions and the collection of small gold-lined vermillion snuff boxes Bend'or had given her, and blindly turning the pages of the beautiful volumes Hervé Mille had bound for her. Even at this late hour, the embers of a fire still glowed in the grate. Coco was insomniac, too.

She hurried into the room, wearing ivory silk pajamas and a scarlet velvet smoking jacket. She threw her arms around me and I shuddered violently against her.

"Misia, ma chère, what is it? You're trembling."

"I can't seem to get my breath, Coco. My heart is pounding so, I'm afraid I may be having a heart attack.

It's as though I'm being strangled by an invisible garotte. I came to you because I had to get out of that place and I didn't know where else to turn."

She led me to one of the brown suede chaises and settled me on it, pulling my sable cloak up over me like a lap robe.

"Let me get you a cognac. You must be chilled through." She poured amber liquid into a heavy crystal snifter and one for herself as well.

"It's become intolerable, Coco," I told her. "I don't know why I ever thought it *could* work—the three of us together. It's just that I can't bear the prospect of losing either one of them. They're in my blood."

"But Misia, my darling, how do *they* feel about such an unusual arrangement? They must know all Paris is talking."

"That's almost the worst of it, Coco. I don't think it troubles them at all. Jojo is so worldly he fails to see anything seriously irregular in it, while Roussy is so *un* worldly—such a child, really—that she thinks it's all a game. Rather like having Maman and Papa in bed with her and lavishing her with all the kisses and caresses they never gave her. And, of course, like any spoiled child, she loves playing us off against one another." I burst into wrenching sobs. "I don't know what to do, Coco. I simply can't go back there. If I go on this way, it will destroy me."

"There's no question of your returning now, Misia," she said. "You'll stay with me until you're ready to decide what to do. Benny's in London on business. I haven't had the heart yet to tell him it's over between us. I'm waiting until we're back at La Pausa. Somehow,

I always feel stronger there. So I'll be happy for some company, too."

Gently she raised me from the chaise and led me into her bedroom where, since I was incapable of undoing so much as a button, she undressed me, slipped one of her satin nightgowns over my head and tucked me into her bed.

I was so worn out with nerves that I immediately fell into a fitful sleep. At some point when I awakened, I found myself encircled in her arms as she tenderly massaged my forehead and stroked my eyelids and my long hair. For the first time since that afternoon when I saw Roussy Mdivani in Jojo's studio, I felt safe . . . even cherished.

FOUR

I suspect she was actually relieved to have me with her when she went down to La Pausa to meet Bend'or. She needed my support for the confrontation I think they both knew by now was inevitable.

By some strange irony, the weather was spectacular—sapphire-blue, cloudless Mediterranean skies, temperate days, and nights when a light down comforter was welcome against the chill.

Bend'or had brought Churchill with him as if, instinctively, both he and Coco knew they needed their reliable "seconds" in place for the final duel between them.

Coco, who had been told by the specialist she saw in Paris that, after the miscarriage and at her age, there was little likelihood of her ever bearing a child, had determined to emerge from her long involvement with Bend'or with, at least, her pride intact.

Benny, who had been braced by Winston about his obligations to his title, to "the Empire," always a preoccupation of the Westminsters, had determined to emerge from his uncharacteristically long involvement with Coco with, at least, his pride intact.

What both of them needed was an occasion to quarrel.

Our surprise guest provided it. Just as we were being served our dinner out on the moonstruck terrace, the bell at the villa's gate chimed and a servant came out onto the terrace and whispered something into Coco's ear.

"Of course, Juan, ask him to come in. And have a place set for him at the table." She was clearly delighted. "Misia, you can't imagine who it is! You must guess—and I won't put any money on the wager, because you're bound to lose."

"Cocteau? Picasso?" I said. "Igor . . . ?" I suggested any one of the free spirits who might be expected to materialize in the south of France at a moment's notice.

"No, ma chère, it's Reverdy! Don't ask me what he's doing out of the monastery. The last he wrote me, he was firmly ensconced in Solesmes and determined to stay there, far from the temptations of the bottle and wild, wild women."

Bend'or looked genuinely bewildered. "Who is this fellow, Reverdy, Coco? What's he doing turning up here uninvited at this time of night? It's all highly irregular."

Coco was sweet reason itself. "Pierre Reverdy, Benny, a poet and scholar and would-be priest who visits me in Paris and has been helping me polish some maxims on style that the fashion press has asked me to compose for their readers."

"Poet . . . priest . . . expert on style. What sort of a paragon *is* he, Coco?" Benny persisted, just as the butler showed Pierre out onto the terrace. It was immediately clear that he was deep into the brandy. He dropped to his knees in front of Coco, seized her hand and began kissing it ardently, that unruly lock of his shiny black hair falling into his eyes.

"Mademoiselle, at *last*. I thought I would never find you again. I've left Solesmes . . . left Henriette . . . been wandering the streets of Paris looking for you everywhere . . . Le Dôme . . . La Closerie des Lilas . . . Jimmy's . . . until someone told me you were here, at La Pausa, and I managed to make my way to you, begging rides with salesmen . . . market traders . . . anyone heading south. I only *knew* I had to be with you."

Benny was frozen with chagrin.

Somehow, Coco detached herself from Pierre's clumsy embrace, stood up, and turned him toward the company.

"Pierre, you of course know Madame Sert. May I present my dear friends, the Duke of Westminster and

Mr. Winston Churchill. This is Monsieur Pierre Reverdy, one of France's premier poets."

The evening quickly disintegrated. Pierre was impossible, tossing back the strong local red wine and quoting Valéry and Mallarmé and Verlaine, maintaining that England *had* no poets after Shakespeare, never mind those "undisciplined romantics, Keats and Byron and Shelley."

"What would the *clergy* know of romance, Monsieur Reverdy?" Bend'or asked provocatively. "I understand that you are a monastic. A *curé.*"

Pierre was caught up short. "A monastic. Not quite. When the world presses in too closely, I do retreat from it to the monastery. But a monastic, no, I have never taken Holy Orders."

"Precisely what *are* you then, Monsieur Reverdy," Benny demanded. I had never seen him so relentless. For the first time I realized what a dangerous enemy he would make. "You seem to be some sort of chameleon—changing your colors as you change your collar. If not a priest, then are you a lover—of women?"

"I have loved women in my time, Monsieur," Reverdy said with sudden dignity. "In fact, there is a woman I love . . . whom I adore . . . in this company tonight, and she knows very well who she is."

Coco flushed crimson to the roots of her hair. The conversation was careening out of her grasp.

Bend'or had risen to his feet. "And does this woman return your passion, Monsieur? Has she given evidence of it to you?"

"More than once, Monsieur, but not nearly as often as I would have wished it. Only three times. Three nights long ago—short rations on which to exist for a lifetime."

"Well, I have had more than my fill of this conversation—and of that lady." Bend'or was white with barely suppressed rage. "Come on, Winston. Let's drive over to Monte, where at least I can be sure that the *tables* are honest." Without another word to Coco, he turned and left the villa.

I looked at Coco where she sat stranded at the foot of the table. She simply shrugged. We both knew Bend'or had gone for good.

"It was beyond my control," she said quietly.

FIVE

"Hold still, *chérie*. I'll simply never get this train to fall right if you keep twisting around to look in the glass." The exasperation was clear in her voice.

"I know, Coco. It's just that I'm so very excited—and the gown is so incredibly beautiful, I can't resist looking at it. Every time I see myself in it, I imagine how Édouard will feel when he watches me coming down the aisle to meet him. I'm dying of impatience!"

Coco smiled up at her from the platform where she

was kneeling to adjust the eight-foot train of Adrienne's embroidered-silk bridal gown.

"You've managed to be patient for more than fifteen years, Adrienne. You've got to give me another fifteen minutes to be sure this hangs precisely right."

I sat on a chaise in Coco's private apartment above the salon where she was personally fitting Adrienne's wedding dress. Though they were of the same blood, the contrast between them was striking—Adrienne, tall, willowy, and biddable with her white-blonde hair still worn pulled back in a chignon because Édouard forbade her to cut it. Coco, small, dark, and utterly independent, concentrating fiercely now on attaching the small weights that would tether the train to the chapel floor as Adrienne walked at last to become the legal wife of the man whose mistress she had been since the day they met so many years before.

The gown had been a labor of love for both of them. From the moment Adrienne had rushed to the rue Cambon with the news that the old Baron had died and that his widow would consent to the marriage between Édouard and the faithful companion his father had contemptuously dismissed as "that commoner," they had begun the triumphant creation of the perfect gown.

Everything from the choice of the light, silvery silk to the delicate embroidery of the floor-length veil and the appliquéing of thousands upon thousands of seed pearls to cover the bodice and the long, tight sleeves and to pick out the border of the train, was done by hand by the two of them.

They were like giddy young girls, laughing over what some ogre called "Madame Boulanger" would think of the time they spent over the most apparently minor, most intrinsic detail of its architecture, its embellishment. It was the single most exquisite gown Coco had ever created.

I would often stop by in the late afternoon for tea, but really to see how they were progressing and to share the joy that radiated from Adrienne—and from Coco, too, even though she had just firmly closed the door on a marriage of her own.

For all the years I'd known her, Coco had worried about "gentle" Adrienne and what she was afraid was her hopeless passion for the Baron Édouard de Nexon. She needn't have lost sleep over it. Adrienne had that same spine of tungsten as her younger niece, Coco.

Adrienne, the most traditional of all the Chanels, had known what she wanted and never, not for a moment, deviated from it—had been willing to defy convention and live the shadow-life of the unacknowledged mistress. To endure the public slights of his arrogant family. To be denied access to the Nexon box at Longchamp or the Opéra and frigidly cut at every opportunity—at the theatre, in the Bois, at Maxim's, or the Ritz.

Who knows? Perhaps it was the family's intransigeant opposition that made their passion last. Had Édouard set Adrienne up in one of those expensive dollhouses in the Plaine Monceau, with a miniature household, a carriage and pair, and a biweekly visit, he might have tired of her soon enough. *No,* that was just my worldliness talking.

Just because my own emotional involvements were so baroque that I now found myself living in sanctuary with Coco—sanctuary from my own unorthodox desires—didn't mean there couldn't be such a thing as authentic, straightforward love and devotion.

Looking at Adrienne, her golden head bent beside Coco's dark one over the intricate embroidery of the yards and yards of delicate veiling, I recognized that she possessed something rare and beautiful that had somehow been denied to Coco and to me—a true and simple heart and soul.

SIX

"I know you're furious with me, Coco, and I can't blame you. I'm flagrantly abusing your hospitality. But what am I to do? When I'm here with you I feel secure. Whole days go by when I don't even think of her. Then she calls and I seem to have no will. I must go to her—to *both* of them." I was sitting at the dressing table with my back to her.

"Not furious, Misia," she told me, "disappointed. Don't you see that this is as pernicious an addiction as Jean's is to opium? Roussy is quite simply your chosen stimulant."

"You don't understand, Coco. She's the only one who has the power to make me feel young again." Even knowing how cruelly I was wounding her, I continued calmly brushing my thick, lustrous hair. Thank God, so far I'd only had to pluck one or two grey strands from the shimmering red-gold curtain that hung to my waist.

She couldn't resist striking back. "Look at yourself, Misia—that unfashionably long hair. I've told you time and time again to cut it. You're an exquisite woman, but you're still insecure. I see it every day with my mannequins. Otherwise why this unseemly obsession with youth? That's just another kind of self-delusion, like Jean and his passing parade of pretty boys."

She had hit the mark, and I retaliated. "Don't tell me *you* aren't drawn to her yourself. I've seen you with her in the fitting room. In all the hours I've watched you work, Coco, never have I witnessed such prolonged . . . such sensuous attention to detail."

"That's patently untrue and you know it, Misia," she said gently. "Why are we quarreling like this? We've shared so much over the years we mustn't let a spoiled child destroy our closeness." She sat huddled under the white satin comforter, looking nothing so much as a forlorn child herself.

I was thoroughly ashamed. I loved Coco as much as I'd ever loved anyone in my life . . . in so many ways more than I did either Jojo or Roussy. How could I allow myself to abuse her this way? There were times I felt as if I didn't know myself—times when I was as perverse as Roussy.

I went to her and put my arms around her.

"Forgive me, Coco. I'm behaving abominably. It's just that I'm worried about her—the high fever she's been running lately. Jojo took her to his doctor and for all the tests, he can't seem to diagnose or control it.

Since her brother, Alexis, left for America, it's as though she's burning herself up from within."

"That's the whole point, Misia," she said ruefully, "and if we mean to survive as friends, we'd both do better to acknowledge it. Roussy *is* a fever and all her attachments are incendiary and unnatural—to Alexis . . . to Jojo who plays the indulgent father . . . to you. Even to me, the eternal maiden aunt."

That afternoon, as it was Sunday, in an unspoken gesture of peacemaking, Coco came with me to visit them in the studio in the Villa Ségur. It was a dazzlingly sunny day and the bars of light, lancing down from the high windows, lit up the gilt in the mock-up of Jojo's ornate frieze for the Waldorf-Astoria in New York and picked out the glints of true gold in Roussy's long, pale straight hair.

Jojo was in high spirits. Nothing pleased him like the company of lovely women. His black eyes flashed and his flamboyant moustache nearly quivered.

"Now I am surrounded by all the beauty in Paris. No man could wish for more."

"Come now, José my love, admit it," Roussy teased him, "if you had all of us plus Helen of Troy, the Venus de Milo, and Josephine Bonaparte right here in the studio, you would *still* be unsatisfied. 'Always More' should be the Sert motto." She was perched precariously on a tall ladder, working on one of her mammoth, oddly compelling erotic sculptures. The marble dust she was raising seemed to aggravate her perpetual cough.

"Come down from there, child, so we can have a look at you," Coco demanded imperiously.

Roussy climbed lightly down the ladder, followed by the little macaque monkey who went everywhere with her like a witch's familiar. There was no doubt Roussy was bewitching. She fished in the pocket of her blue workman's smock for a packet of Gauloises and lit up.

"Roussy, mon enfant," Coco said, "the only time I ever see you without a cigarette is when you have a hammer in one hand and a chisel in the other. It can't be doing your cough any good."

"Don't scold, please petite Coco. You know I can't bear it when you're cross with me." Roussy was the only one since Boy who'd dared call her *"petite* Coco."

"Let me open a bottle of wine to celebrate your visit," she deftly switched subjects. "José has stashed a case of the most remarkable Pommard in the broom-closet." She dashed about collecting a motley array of glasses and setting them out on a board between two sawhorses covered with a paint-stained drop cloth. She even ran out into the courtyard and picked some blue cornflowers and Queen Anne's lace to put in a turpentine jar as a centerpiece, like a delighted little girl arranging a doll's tea party.

"Open the wine, José my love—let's toast our dearest visitors."

José uncorked the bottle and poured it round with a flourish. "To the superlative day, the superlatively beautiful company . . ." he began.

"And to absent friends," Coco completed the toast for him.

No sooner had we raised our glasses, than Roussy's mood darkened. That was the way with her. Roussy was mercurial, given to plunging precipitately from giddiness to despair.

She raised her glass again and made her own toast. "Quite right, petite Coco, to absent friends." Her grey eyes were granite. "To Alexis across the sea in America—my brother . . . my soul . . . my lover, the only person who ever makes me believe there's the smallest reason for this pointless charade you call existence."

An appalled silence. It's impossible to know which one of us was the most profoundly hurt. Somehow Jojo martialled his Catalan graciousness and got us through the endless minutes until we could make our excuses and retreat to the St.-Honoré. As our driver took us down the twilit Champs-Élysées, Coco turned to me. "You know, Misia, there are moments when I fear for that poor child's sanity."

I took her hand in mine. "I know it all too well, Coco. There are moments when she makes me fear for mine." And of course I slipped away to go back to them—to *her,* really—later that same night.

SEVEN

*C*oco's American "experience" remains for me, as I suspect it must for her, a collage of vivid, discordant images: one part Picasso's cubist skyscrapers from *Parade* seen firsthand on our press-hounded arrival in New York; one part the giddy holi-daymaking mood of *Le Train bleu,* as we sped across an unknown, Depression-strangled land in the gleam-ing luxury of the sleek white parlor car of our private train toward what Cocteau irreverently dubbed "the mecca of tit and tail"; one part the surreal months of shuttling back and forth between our palm-shaded tropical bungalow at the pink stucco Beverly Hills Hotel and the stars' gaudy dressing rooms and vast, echoing soundstages of Sam Goldwyn's personal domain at Santa Monica Boulevard and Formosa Avenue.

It began as farcically as it ended—a match made by the exiled cousin of the Tsar and the self-made Tsar of Hollywood—and it seems somehow appropriate that the only successful picture to emerge from the debacle was a romantic farce, *Tonight or Never,* in which Gloria Swanson wore Coco's gowns to such stunning advan-tage that Coco, as usual, got the lion's share of the press and more raves than anyone else connected with the production.

In a way it was my *own* bedroom farce that triggered the whole eccentric expedition. Right after the Febru-ary collection, Coco, determined to pry me out of the neurotic-erotic triangle that still held me firmly captive to Roussy and Jojo, invited me for a brief holiday in Monte Carlo. I was willing enough to go. The strain of our intense emotional entanglement was wearing me out. I needed a rest from *both* of them.

We were at the *trente et quarante* table in the smoky splendor of the Casino. Coco, shimmering in a silver lamé sheath, was enjoying a spectacular run. She'd picked up Bend'or's preference for the game and al-ways had phenomenal luck at it. The sight of such a beautiful woman winning so aggressively had already drawn a small crowd. A few side bets were being made on the extent of her winnings.

As she retired, flushed with excitement but wise enough to leave the table while her luck held, she quite literally backed into a handsome man who'd been watching her play with fascination.

She turned in surprise. *"Excusez-moi, Monsieur . . ."* Then "Dmitri!" She laughed and flung her arms around his neck. "I had no idea you were here in Monte. What amazing luck!"

"You seem to have the corner on that particular commodity tonight, Mademoiselle," said his companion, a tall, barrel-chested bald man whose curiously high-pitched voice belied the authority—and the hunger—in his intense grey eyes. "I'm a gambling man myself, and I have to tell you it's been one hell of a long time since I've seen such coolness at the tables. What's your secret?"

"Nonchalance, Monsieur," she smiled gaily up at him. "I learned it from an expert. If you don't care too much, you're more likely to win."

"I play it just the opposite." He was looking at her intently. "I'm obsessed with winning. Whenever I see something I want, I go after it—and I usually succeed."

Coco had linked her arm affectionately in Dmitri's. "You must introduce me to your friend, Dmitri. He's so very self-confident he *must* be an American," she said provocatively.

"Forgive my rudeness." Dmitri put his arms around our shoulders. "My very dear friend, Mademoiselle Coco Chanel, and her *amie intime,* Madame Misia Sert, may I present Monsieur Samuel Goldwyn. Monsieur

Goldwyn is in France concluding a distribution agreement for his films."

"And just back from one more wild-goose chase to London to try to land G. B. Shaw. I want him to write movies for me—*class* movies—but the old bluffer stumps me every time, ladies. He tells me, 'Mr. Goldwyn, *you* are interested in art . . . *I* am interested in money.' And then he turns me down every time, no matter how high I up the ante. Come into the bar, dear ladies, Dmitri, and help me drown my frustrations in champagne."

No sooner was the first bottle of Veuve Clicquot nose-down in the wine bucket than Shaw was forgotten and Goldwyn was well-launched on a new venture—the wooing of Coco.

"Just imagine it, Mademoiselle Chanel. Something that's never been done before. Oh, a few of my competitors have hired a high-priced 'name' designer, even from Europe, for a particular picture. But to invite Coco Chanel—the Empress of couture—to travel to America for the very first time . . . to Hollywood to design *all* my costumes—on-screen and off—for *all* my stars, for all the Goldwyn Girls. What a coup!"

His grey eyes were shining. He was completely carried away by his own excitement. And it was infectious. "The women of America will love it! They're *dying* of drabness—starved for glamour by this damned Depression. I'm convinced that's the only reason they go to the movies, even when they *can't* afford to. The press will love it! I can see the headlines: 'GOLDWYN LURES EMPRESS OF LUXE TO L.A.' . . . 'GOLDWYN SIGNS DREAM DESIGNER FOR U.A. STARS . . . FABULOUS SUM UNDISCLOSED . . .'"

"Why not simply: 'COCO CHANEL COMES TO AMERICA,' Monsieur?" Coco said quietly, and I knew that's the way the headlines would eventually read. She had an uncanny knack for self-promotion. "And as for the 'fabulous sum,' would you perhaps consider disclosing it to me?"

"You see, Monsieur Goldwyn," Dmitri laughed. "Mademoiselle is a veteran negotiator who will make your playwright Monsieur G. B. Shaw look like—what is it you Americans say?—like 'a pushover.' "

Dmitri was right. He knew Coco well. Before Goldwyn's dark-browed, barricaded eyes, she was transformed from beautiful flirt to shrewd bargainer.

"If you are serious about this venture, Monsieur Goldwyn, you must understand that an absence of some months' time—which your bold plan would surely require—would put a great strain on my enterprises here in France. Tempted as I am by the challenge, I could not entertain the notion of it for anything less than . . ." Tantalizingly, she let him fill in the numbers. Boy had taught her the formidable power of silence as a negotiating tool.

"Half a million dollars, Mademoiselle?"

She laughed lightly. "I see our notions of the fabulous are uncomfortably far apart."

"A million, then, for four months. A second million when the first season succeeds, for a second four months. *Two* million dollars total. Does that fit your definition of fabulous?"

Inwardly, I gasped. It was an amazing amount of money for less than a year's work. Even for Coco.

She was as cool as she had been at the tables. "With additional expenses for importing and housing my fitters, cutters, and seamstresses, Monsieur, it would be adequate. As a successful producer you *do* know how very important it is to work with trusted people."

"Of course, Mademoiselle." He smiled triumphantly and signaled the captain for another bottle of champagne to seal the bargain.

He raised his glass. "To the inspired marriage of money and art, Mademoiselle," he said.

"Marriage has always had an altogether unnerving sound to it for me, Monsieur. I would prefer to call this the inspired collaboration of creative financing . . . and craft."

By the time we were on the train headed west across the vast continent I had never so much as dreamed of visiting, Coco and Sam—as he insisted we call him—had become the best of friends. Why not? Beneath their elaborate façades—Sam in his Savile Row tailoring, his Sulka ties and handmade shirts, his shoes from Lobb of London, and just the proper hint of Gentleman's Knize Ten cologne; Coco in the spectacularly chic, simple tailleurs the salon had turned out for her at breakneck pace in a frantic ten days' time—they were both rogues. They were both brilliant self-inventors who'd created themselves out of pure genius and that perfect Yiddish word Sam had taught us in Monte—out of *chutzpah.*

After the reporters' barrage when we docked a month later in New York and Sam met us at the Waldorf (a Sam-staged scenario which Coco quickly made her own, admitting to her "wonderful new friend," Carmel Snow of *Harper's Bazaar,* that it was the Americans who had discovered her . . . had validated her vision of the free and independent woman . . . and that, without her allies in America, she would very probably still be embroidering bridal trousseaus in some provincial backwater), Coco managed to put the American fashion press right in the palm of her small, competent hand.

No, she had never seriously considered marriage—not even to Bend'or, the richest man in the world. Why should she? There had already been two Duchesses of Westminster, while there was only one Coco Chanel.

As the miles unfolded beneath the hypnotically clicking metal wheels of the luxury express, Coco and Sam began to let down their guard. She taught him bezique and told him about an abandoned daughter's fantasies of stardom on the *Grands Boulevards*. Of Paris, where a little milliner could become a couturière.

He taught her a game called gin rummy and told her how he'd trekked his way hundreds and hundreds of weary, lonely miles out of Poland across Britain, then a ship's passage to Canada and another illegal trek across the border to make his way to Hollywood, a place where he knew a penniless Jewish immigrant's dreams could come true. Where Samuel Gelbfisz, apprentice glovemaker, could become Sam Goldwyn, millionaire mogul.

She said it was her destiny. He said it was his *chutzpah*. They were both right. I think he was a little in love with her.

Sam never did things on a small scale. When the train pulled into the station there was a full turnout—brass band, banners emblazoned, HOLLYWOOD WELCOMES COCO CHANEL, carried by a bevy of the most beautiful of the Goldwyn Girls, and all his current stars: Gloria Swanson and her handsome husband, the Marquis de la Falaise; Ronald Colman, the suave Britisher who had stolen the hearts of American women and been one of the few to survive the tricky transition to the new talking pictures; Goldwyn's brilliant comedians, Charlie Chaplin and Eddie Cantor. Even Mary Pickford and Douglas Fairbanks, who, with Chaplin, were two of his first partners in United Artists. A bouquet of white camellias almost as big as Coco was presented to her by Sam, and the mayor gave her the keys to the city.

The next ten days were a kaleidoscope of glittering parties and receptions, crowned by Frances Howard Goldwyn's black-tie dinner for a hundred of Hollywood's current royalty at their quasi-Norman farmhouse at 1800 Camino Palmero. Through it, Coco glided effortlessly, making friends and conquests everywhere, though she admitted to me in the privacy of our bungalow that she felt more at ease with the Europeans like Marlene Dietrich, Erich von Stroheim, and Greta Garbo, than with the brash American moguls like Joe Schenck and Harry Cohn. Whenever she found herself cornered by a bore or a boor, she told me, she would plead a slender command of English—a trick she had perfected with the stodgier members of the Eaton Hall set.

Sam was in his element. He adored the press and the press adored Coco—even those lethal dragon-ladies Louella Parsons and Hedda Hopper were charmed by her, especially when she volunteered to design hats for them.

The honeymoon was on. Coco and Sam went everywhere together, accompanied by a watchful Frances who seemed to grow frostier by the evening. I was frankly relieved when Coco had to settle down and get to work on Swanson's wardrobe for *Tonight or Never*.

She had her first "official" meeting with Sam in his private dining room, and he got his first surprise. She did a brilliant imitation of their encounter for me over dinner at the beautiful new Beverly Wilshire Hotel.

"You know my former partner, Florenz Ziegfield, Coco—a *shame* he understood more about women than the business. An ego problem, he had a *big* ego problem—he told me the only reason women go to the pictures is to see the clothes. Clothes they could never afford. Clothes to make them dream. That's what gave me the inspiration of bringing you to Hollywood—to give American women an education in dresses—in the difference between elegance, class, and *schmattes.* So, Coco, now maybe you'll show me the sketches?"

"Sketches, Sam?" She gave him that gypsy grin. "I never *make* sketches. Too stiff, too rigid, confining. They would only hobble me, limit the work."

"No sketches, Coco!" He looked flabbergasted. "If no sketches, so then how do you make the dresses?"

"On the woman, Sam. Preferably on the woman who's going to wear them. My dresses are meant to be a kind of magic—to reveal the essence of the woman who wears them to the world, and to herself. That's what you hired me for, Sam, the magic."

"But no sketches, Coco. How do you make this magic, then?"

"I drape and cut and pin the fabric on the woman direct, through a series of fittings. I *evolve* the dress on her."

" 'Evolve' . . . evolution, Coco? Evolution takes a long

time. I remember it from my science teachers." He laughed nervously. "Evolution takes centuries."

"Sometimes, Sam, you're right. Sometimes the magic happens fast, in the first several fittings. Sometimes it *can* take as many as thirty . . . thirty-five . . . forty fittings until the dress is right."

Sam was looking visibly pale. "Forty fittings—*forty,* Coco. You know I have a budget on this picture . . . forty fittings . . . How many hours? My money man in New York, Jim Mulvey, will tell me I'm putting my head in a moose."

She liked him so much, she decided to put him out of his misery. "Don't worry, Sam, I promise you the dresses will be ready on schedule. Remember, I have to present a collection of four hundred dresses twice a year. And I do. I've already talked to Mademoiselle Swanson and she's eager to work with me. She's the perfect type for my gowns, small, slender, beautiful, and sufficiently distracted by her current Irish lover that she'll hardly notice the time go by in the fittings."

" 'Her current Irish lover'—that's certainly news to me, Coco." Relief made Sam positively generous. "I have a whole public relations department who track every movement of my stars, who monitor every breath they take, and *you* tell me Gloria Swanson has a lover. How do you happen to come by that intriguing piece of information?"

"I'm a dressmaker, Sam. The cliché, as usual, is a universal truth. Women tell everything to their hairdressers—*and* to their dressmaker."

Funny that the romance everyone soon began speculating about—the practiced infidelity between Gloria

Swanson and her very young, very headstrong Irish playboy, Patrick—was not the real romance of *Tonight or Never*. That was the one between the two outsiders, the ultimate dreamers, the two self-inventors—Coco and Sam.

As Coco began the painstaking business of creating Swanson's gowns—the desperate *luxe* of Lili Havatny's down-on-her-luck Hungarian diva, Nella Vago, longing for her chance at the gold ring of starring at New York's Metropolitan Opera—Sam took to turning up on the set with unprecedented regularity. Coco had gotten me a pass to allow me to watch each day's shooting so, sitting in a canvas-backed chair near her own, I was in a position to observe the drama, on-set and off. Everyone was nervous. Everyone listened daily for the charged sound of Sam's footsteps.

It was legend in the industry that, when you heard Sam's hard-heeled walk approaching the set, *somebody* was in dire trouble and had better have a very tough lawyer. This time, though, it was different. This time Sam was on the set every day to see Coco—ostensibly to watch her put the finishing touches to Mademoiselle Swanson's gowns.

They were more than he'd bargained for. From the black velvet afternoon dress with its flowerlike ruff of a collar, lined with silver, to the chinchilla-trimmed bronze satin suit she wore for her final confrontation with her dark, mustached leading man, Melvyn Douglas—the "mystery scout" from New York who would make her the lead soprano at the Met—Coco had designed one simple, striking triumph after another. It was a tour de force. It was as if she'd driven herself to prove to Sam that the million dollars he'd paid her was a bargain.

The critics agreed, raved that Coco had brought "solid gold chic to the world of tinsel and gilt."

The summons to lunch in Sam's private dining room, where they'd begun their collaboration, came as no surprise.

"I think he wants to extend the term of our agreement, Misia," she told me. "Or perhaps this is something more personal." She smiled shyly. "Perhaps he doesn't want me to go back to Paris at all."

Sam's admiration had grown from his daily visits to the set to deliveries of dozens upon dozens of white camellias to our bungalow and discreet dinners *à deux* in obscure restaurants tucked away in the Hollywood hills where they would not be seen by the scandal-sniffing press.

So when I returned to our bungalow from an afternoon of shopping, I was astonished to find the place turned upside down, clothes strewn everywhere, and Coco frantically throwing them into her Hermès steamer trunk. She paused in her furious packing.

"We're leaving, Misia. Immediately. Pack your things. We're going back to Paris."

"Leaving, Coco. What on earth are you talking about? Why now when everything's going so brilliantly?"

"Sam invited me to lunch today to tell me he wouldn't be renewing my contract. He actually had the nerve to say 'A verbal agreement isn't worth the paper it's written on.' His English is even worse than mine. Can you imagine it, Misia? I should have known better than to trust the word of a *glove salesman.*" Her contempt was withering.

"But Coco, ma chère, I don't understand. *Variety* says that every woman in Hollywood is lining up to be dressed by Mademoiselle Chanel."

"That's precisely where you're wrong, Misia," Coco said bitterly. "Sam told me at lunch that he'd had a 'deputation' from his stars who informed him they refused to be dressed by me, refused to be made to look alike—'like automatons in a Busby Berkeley pinwheel,' they told him. As if I *ever* made the same gown twice! You know as well as I do, Misia, that the 'deputation' came straight from the drawing room of Madame Frances Howard Goldwyn. They may have been *his* stars, but they were *her* deputies. Well, it doesn't matter. Sam didn't have the *couilles* to defend me. These American men are all ruled by their women."

Coco slammed down the lid of a bulging suitcase and sat on it to close the clasps. "Our Hollywood adventure is over, Misia. I can hardly wait to get back to Paris."

EIGHT

I never understood what it was she saw in him, even though I was quick enough to spread the rumor that Coco was in love for the first time in her life and likely to marry.

It certainly wasn't his looks. Paul Iribe was no beauty like Boy or Dmitri or Bend'or. A small, pudgy, wrinkled man, he had an unfortunately obvious set of false teeth and wire-rimmed glasses. It wasn't his youth. He and Coco were of an age—one she'd stopped disclosing—and she'd usually preferred younger lovers. It *certainly* wasn't his money. After Bend'or, money was somehow irrelevant.

And, despite his legion of talents, Iribe had had a checkered career, coming up to Paris from the Basque country to Angoulême and joining forces with Cocteau in a failed magazine venture, *Le Témoin,* for which he'd done satirical drawings. He'd illustrated a book of designs for Paul Poiret—vanity publishing for the vainest of them all. His photo-montages had won prizes on exhibit in America over Hoynigen-Huyne and Man Ray. His gifts as a stage and interior designer had brought him to the attention of De Mille who imported him to Hollywood.

Iribe's talents were fatally scattered, though, and his finances were a perpetual roller coaster—yachts and

Mediterranean villas and high-powered motorcars one day, bankruptcy the next. And international female casualties every step of the way.

It may simply have been an accident of timing. We were only just back from our Hollywood misadventure and, despite her brave statement to the press that her intent "was to make a lady look like a lady, while what Sam Goldwyn wanted was for her to look like *two* ladies," Coco was still smarting from the stars' rebellion.

How *could* they have disdained the privilege of being dressed by the Empress of couture?

So when Cocteau brought his old friend and collaborator down to La Pausa for the weekend, Coco's was a willing ear for Iribe's colorful tales of betrayal by the Hollywood "machine." As we sat on the terrace, drinking a flinty Côtes de Provence wine and watching the sun fall into the sea, he certainly was amusing and determined to make a conquest of his hostess.

"I realized quickly enough, Mademoiselle Chanel," he told her, "when he made me scenic and costume designer for the picture, that what C. B. meant by the 'Ten Commandments' was 'Thou shalt spend ten million dollars making sin look deluxe enough to lure the public to the box office in droves. Thou shalt create adulteresses so adorable they cry out for stoning . . . design golden calves so dazzling they make the moviegoers forget the dread word "Depression" . . . make Sodom and Gomorrah look like a posh resort in the Catskills. And, above all, thou shalt never, ever *dream* of contradicting the omniscient . . . the omnipotent Jehovah . . . C. B. De Mille.' "

"Well, if you had the secret of it, Monsieur," Coco asked, laughing, "why didn't you stay? Designing sin de luxe must surely have had its financial compensations."

"It was a conspiracy against the artist, Mademoiselle—an even more popular sport in Hollywood than polo or tennis or illicit love affairs or deal-making, as I suspect you, too, discovered. They're tin gods who create conflicts to relieve their boredom."

His intense earnestness was part of his practiced charm. "Goldwyn knew damned well his stars would mutiny—not at the *idea* of Coco Chanel, but at giving up one iota of their precious individuality. You can be sure he also knew he'd get brilliant press out of it, press well worth the million he paid you for, in effect, that single Swanson picture. Just like C. B. calculatedly had me and Mitchell Leisen at one another's throats on *King of Kings.*"

"How do you mean, Monsieur," I asked him, fascinated. The machinations I'd seen in Hollywood reminded me of nothing so much as the constant jockeying for power and influence I'd witnessed— often gleefully participated in—over the last fifty years in the artistic hothouse of Paris.

"Putting us both on the same picture when our talents were essentially the same, and then billing me as 'Artistic Director,' my dear Madame, made our collision a foregone conclusion. Mitchell was simply the better strategist."

"It seems to me strategy is always the key, Monsieur." This was the first time he had interested me.

"I'd left the Crucifixion to Leisen, so to speak, while he told C. B. that the climactic scene, of course, *had* to be mine. So when there were no preparations for it—no mechanism for dramatically and safely nailing

Harry Warner to the Cross—C. B. had apoplexy, made me the scapegoat, with Mitchell's eager cooperation, fired me from the picture . . . and virtually ran me out of Hollywood. I'll admit I hadn't come up against such treachery since my early days in vaudeville."

"Vaudeville, Monsieur?" Coco, who was actively trying to put Hollywood and Sam behind her, came suddenly alive. "I had no idea you'd had music-hall experience."

"That, Mademoiselle, was my original ambition— even before I came up to Paris. It was a young man's passion, I'll admit. I was determined to be the next Chevalier, to star on the *Grands Boulevards*. But I ran afoul of a corrupt theatre manager in the provinces, a fellow who demanded sexual favors in return for giving me my chance. It soured me on the entire notion, even before I got to Paris and had the great good fortune to meet Jean," he smiled warmly at Cocteau, "though our little review fell sadly short of setting the literary and political worlds afire as we'd hoped."

"In *Vichy*, Monsieur," Coco said—not a question so much as a statement of fact—"at the Élysée Palace. One Alphonse Didier. Short, loud, domineering, with a pronounced paunch and wearing mainly gravy stains. I'm surprised we didn't meet backstage."

"So you had your Didier experience, too, Mademoiselle." He reached out and took Coco's hand. "What did he offer you? Star billing? That was just *one* of the things he had in mind for me."

"Not precisely, Monsieur. While he regretted my unfortunate lack of 'tits or a singing voice,' as he so eloquently put it, he was taken by my style—thought that, under his tutelage, I might *just* have the makings of a designer."

They collapsed in helpless laughter.

I had no idea of who or what they were talking about. No one on the terrace did. But that curious exchange marked the turning point in their relationship. From then on, they were inseparable.

It drove her close friends to near-distraction to watch the arrogant way that arch-opportunist insinuated himself into her life. Jean told me he profoundly regretted ever having introduced them. With growing concern I watched him systematically isolate her from friend after friend. Iribe was Iago reincarnate, planting seeds of suspicion about the handful of people Coco had allowed herself over the years to count on, to trust.

Wasn't it curious that darling Vera had taken to phoning in sick so often? Well, what could you expect when someone was in love? She'd snatch every chance she could to be with Berto, would probably end by marrying him, deserting Coco and modeling altogether, and go to live in Rome, anyway. And Pierre Wertheimer. Was Coco fully satisfied with the distribution deal they'd made on 'Parfums Chanel'? Of course an old friend like Papa Bader would *only* have acted in her best interests. But perhaps he ought to have a look at the documents at this point, just to reassure Coco that she was fully protected against any *sort* of exploitation.

He was amazing, if terrifying, to watch—a great General of disaffection. Having started to undermine her friendships, he moved to her terrain. Her flat in the rue St.-Honoré—which he had been quick enough to move into—was outmoded. Her salon there *had* been spectacular, he admitted. To stay at the head of the pack, though, you always had to understand and capitalize on the irresistible charm of the new. That this ran counter to every one of Coco's best instincts in her own work over the years was utterly lost in the narcosis of her curious infatuation with this master-manipulator.

Besides, though it pained him to admit it, he couldn't bear to sleep in the same bed Cocteau had told him she'd shared with that "other" Basque. He *was* a man, after all—and dangerously jealous when it came to his woman, as only Basques could be. Images of her making love with Reverdy were interfering with his pleasure . . . with the intense pleasure he knew he could give her . . . *owed* it to his manhood to give her, especially since he knew they still corresponded, and that Pierre's impassioned letters from Solesmes showed he remained deeply in love with her. The fact that he'd obviously been reading her mail seemed to trouble Coco, that most fiercely private and secretive of women, not at all.

So the flat must be redone to remove all traces of past perfidious friends . . . past lovers. He personally would design a new bedroom suite for them—one with even greater *luxe* than the Art Deco fantasy he'd created for Mademoiselle Spinelly, the current toast of the *Grands Boulevards.* Or better still, why not give up the rue St.-Honoré entirely and move to a hotel—the Meurice, where she could be close to darling Misia. Or perhaps a suite in the Ritz—so convenient to the work. Where they could be alone together, without the intrusive, overly familiar presence of live-in servants. Like Joseph.

Oh yes, Joseph was part of the purge. I should have been gratified, since Coco had shown no compunction in luring him away from me fifteen years before. But I wasn't. When she dismissed him for no more reason than her intent to relocate to the Ritz, but implying that Iribe believed he was less than discreet, he came to me for a reference. Though deeply wounded, he was still fiercely loyal to her. My heart went out to his injured pride, his natural dignity.

"You *do* know, Madame, that I have never spoken to others of Mademoiselle Chanel's private business as that 'gentleman' suggests I have."

"No need to say so, Joseph," I told him. "Haven't I been there through all the years—all the difficulties? I'm sure Mademoiselle Chanel has given you an excellent reference. I'm fully confident in adding my own."

I had to be particularly careful not to play into Iribe's hands by criticizing him to her. He certainly wasn't above implying my jealousy was sexual. The irony was that this was the single time in my long, complex relationship with Coco that *didn't* come into it. I was so preoccupied with Roussy—and with Roussy and Jojo—I had no energy left over for anyone else.

Iribe aroused nothing in me but contempt, contempt and concern for the blatant way he was exploiting Coco, and for the strangely passive way she was allowing it.

When I heard she'd agreed to lend her salon, and the services of her jewelry designers, including the noble Étienne de Beaumont and Fulco della Verdura, to the Diamond Guild for their international charity exhibition—what a contradiction in terms!—I was genuinely bewildered. Though she sometimes wore diamonds and, God knows, over the years she'd been given yards of them by her lovers and admirers, Coco had never favored them. For very private reasons of her own, she had always made pearls her hallmark.

It wasn't until I arrived at the rue Cambon on the evening of the opening of the exhibit, that I understood it. The salon, usually light and scintillating, with its walls upon walls of floor-to-ceiling mirrors, had been darkened to a velvet blackness—a blackness meant to set off the work of the premier practitioners of the art of diamond-cutting.

As I dutifully walked through the elegant exhibit, crowded with *tout* Paris Society, I was not at all surprised to discover in every second, brilliantly lit case a design credited to *"L'atelier* Iribe." A diamond choker of multiple strands graduated to asphyxiation, a diamond spiderweb, diamond manacles to bind your lover to you, a diamond Cleopatra fringe that not-so-innocently mimicked his mistress' diminishing bangs.

"L'atelier Iribe." As far as I knew, Iribe had no studio, outside of the one I stood in now—the one that belonged to Coco.

NINE

By the time we arrived at La Pausa for our summer holiday, everyone, with the conspicuous exception of Coco, was fed up with him. The nearly four years she'd spent under Iribe's influence seemed longer than the decade she'd been with Bend'or. Seemed to me, at least, a century.

I never thought I'd see the day when I would long for the return of that bluff, emotionally clumsy Edwardian, but now I did. How unfortunate. He'd married one of his own—the Honorable Loelia Ponsonby—and, in the strange tradition of Boy before him, had brought his bride to Coco to dress and, I think secretly, to confirm his own good taste.

She always *had* that effect on the men who loved her. She touched each one of them profoundly. Even if they ultimately could not "afford" her—could not accommodate her power and energy and complexity—they understood how very precious she was, understood the magnitude of her loss. After she was gone from their beds, they still sought her out—for friendship, for approval, for that intensity of being only she possessed. Étienne, Boy, Dmitri, Pierre, Bend'or—all stalwarts in their own right. Now this second-rate Svengali. What *could* Coco be thinking of?

Not only had he infiltrated her business and succeeded in driving a wedge of suspicion between her and Pierre Wertheimer, whom she was now convinced was taking advantage of her, he had persuaded her to invest a great deal of money in his various ventures. "Adventures," if you ask me—Iribe was the classic adventurer.

His avant-garde jewelry designs had, at least, *some* chance of selling, especially out of the Chanel boutique. But he'd even resuscitated that ridiculous rag, *Le Témoin,* to give it a second chance to fail—this time at Coco's expense.

Le Témoin was nothing but a platform for Iribe and the rantings of his rightist friends. Anti-communist . . . anti-Semitic . . . anti-democratic . . . anti-monarchist . . . anti-everything that wasn't French. Somehow he'd even lured Coco into *posing* for the cover of the first edition. Posing as "Marianne"—the French Republic. As France betrayed by Stalin, Hitler, Chamberlain, and FDR.

Enemies, plotters, conspirators, Iribe saw them everywhere, when he could easily have found the most dangerous of them all in his mirror. He was infected with xenophobia like a dog with rabies. And there was only one cure for that! I shuddered. My Eastern soul knew that wishing someone's death only stained your own Karma. I mustn't let my dark suspicions of the man throw a shadow on the beauty and tranquillity of La Pausa.

"Look, Misia!" She was like an excited child. "Thousands and thousands of olives. What a crop! I'll be able to press my own oil this year, I'm sure of it."

How incredibly young she looked. Fifty-two, and in

those blue denim pants—her newest contribution to resort wear—how very like the adolescent daughter of a land-proud peasant.

"The country life suits you, you know, Coco ma chère," I told her. "The moment we arrive at La Pausa, it's as though you throw off all the trappings—and the burdens—of being 'Coco Chanel, couturière to the crowned heads of Europe,' and turn into a carefree girl again."

"You're right, Misia. I was probably meant to be a French housewife, worrying that the hailstorm may have damaged my *flageolets* and whether or not to add more *confit* of goose to my cassoulet."

"I wouldn't carry it quite *that* far, Coco." I laughed at her. "If somehow you'd ended up in the countryside, you'd have found a business in it soon enough. 'First Pressing Virgin Olive Oil, Chanel,' " I teased her.

"You're probably right, Misia, but I *do* love it here. From the moment I set foot on its sandy soil, I felt as if I'd been here . . . lived here before."

"Surely not as Mary Magdalene, Coco. In whatever incarnation, I see you as a leader, not a disciple." I was coming dangerously close now to the truth.

" 'A leader' . . ." She was suddenly over fifty years old again. "I know that was what I was meant to be. Remember, Johanna said so when she read my chart all those years ago in Venice. And she was right. But what she neglected to tell me—probably out of kindness, for I'm sure she saw it as clearly as everything else—was the toll it would take. I'm strong, Misia, you know it very well, but I get tired, too. I need someone to support me, to be there for me, to worry about me, to be a friend to my friends and an enemy to anyone who threatens me."

"Threatens" her. *Mon Dieu,* that was Iribe talking— paranoid Paul. Playing for time to compose my thoughts, I sat down on the low bole of one of her precious olive trees.

"You do know, chère Coco, that genius will always, inevitably attract challengers. You were one yourself when you went up against the giants—Worth, Doucet, Vionnet, Poiret. But challenge isn't threat, Coco, it's inspiration. It keeps you from complacency, from growing old and stale in the work. That you've never done and, I'll wager, will never do."

"It's the endlessness of the pressures, Misia, and my trouble with sleeping."

"Exhaustion I understand, Coco, *and* the need for someone to lean on. It's probably why I cling to Jojo, even when I know in my heart that I've outlived my welcome in that relationship. It's very hard, very expensive to be alone. The fear of that accounts for many curious alliances."

Thwock . . . thwock . . . the sound of tennis balls rebounding off the gut of the players' racquets had its hypnotic quality in the intense midday heat.

Coco and I were sitting comfortably under the shade of a canvas market umbrella next to the court, sipping *pastis* and wondering why on earth men seemed driven to demonstrate their eternal youth and energy in spite of the scalding southern sun.

Paul and Jean had been at it for almost a full set now. "Love . . . love." "Love . . . fifteen." "Love . . . thirty." "Love . . . forty . . . Game." It had begun to sound in my head like a particularly maudlin cabaret song. "Love . . . nothing . . . Love . . . love . . ."

"Come on, Misia," Iribe called from the court. "The two of you look altogether too smug over there in the shade. We've just finished this set, and I've wiped the clay with Jean. I'm ready for new contenders. Coco, Misia, come on! A set of doubles. Losers pay for dinner at the Colombe d'Or!"

Reluctantly, we set our glasses down and reached for our racquets. On the court—in a macabre scene from *Le Train bleu* that Diaghilev never staged—I saw Iribe stagger, clutch his left arm, and then fall backward onto the clay.

"Mon dieu, Misia," Coco's hand was ice in mine. "I think he's ill. Too much sun."

He wasn't ill. He was dead. Dead instantly of a massive heart attack at fifty-two. Dead because his insecurity had goaded him to keep proving his virility over and over again.

That was what killed him, I know. His arrogance. Even as Jean and I made the funeral arrangements for a shell-shocked Coco, I had to keep telling myself that I'd never liked the man, but—*le bon dieu* as my witness—I'd never wished him dead.

TEN

How I hated the dreary furnished flat in the rue de Constantine after the space and light and luxury of the Meurice, but it was all I could afford these days and still keep up a brave front to the gossips with my wardrobe. I spent my sleepless nights there, but my heart and my all-too-vivid imagination were with Roussy and Jojo in their fashionable new home in the rue de Rivoli.

I was so emotionally exhausted, I hadn't even had the energy to do it up, so fragments of my broken life were distributed haphazardly in the three small, cramped rooms—a pink quartz ming tree, forlorn on a battered console table in the drawing room; the little painting Toulouse-Lautrec had made of me in my green velvet, fur-trimmed skating costume for the cover of the winter edition of *Revue Blanche*; and Cocteau's whimsical sketch of Serioja on the wall to remind me of happier days. An ominously empty silver tray for calling cards and invitations. The Russian lacquer box with its fantastical, brightly plumaged Firebird that Nijinsky had given me and that now held the secret of my continued existence. And, on my bedside table, a telephone that rang so seldom these days that, when it did, it startled me.

Coco was uncharacteristically cryptic. "Can you

come to the Ritz right away, Misia? I have a small problem and I need your best advice."

"Of course, Coco, I'll be there in half an hour," I told her, but when I'd put down the receiver I tried to imagine what it could possibly be. Why wasn't she at the rue Cambon this afternoon? Ordinarily, the wild horses of the Camargue couldn't have dragged her away from her dresses.

When the maid let me into the suite, I found her at her writing desk, still in her silk pajamas, frowning over some sort of clumsy, handwritten document. She jumped up to embrace me.

"Misia, you can't imagine how very glad I am to see you. When Papa Bader first telephoned me about what was going on at the Galeries, I didn't pay it much heed. But now, these ridiculous demands."

"Pay *what* much heed, Coco . . . *what* demands? If I'm to be of any help, you'll have to begin at the beginning."

"This rash of strikes, Misia. Since the Front Populaire came to power in April, strikes have become epidemic. First it was the railway men and the construction workers, then the automobile workers and the postmen. Even the bakers. But I never dreamed the organizers would come near the fashion industry. I thought women were much too smart to jeopardize good jobs for these so-called 'concessions.' "

She picked up the paper from the desk and thrust it at me contemptuously, then rushed on without giving me a chance to do more than glance at the heading, IMPROVED CONDITIONS REQUESTED OF MLLE. GABRIELLE CHANEL.

"Two days ago Papa Bader called to say that his girls had mutinied. They were staging something called a 'sit-down strike' for better pay and paid vacations, but he said it was more like a riot. The ones who weren't simply parked behind the display cases were dancing on top of them. They were spraying each other with perfumes, painting one another with cosmetics, and helping themselves to expensive gowns and hats. The damage and looting was out of hand. He finally had to call in the *gendarmes*. Worst of all, he was so unnerved by the experience at his age, he simply surrendered and gave them what they asked."

"Your girls are fiercely loyal to you, Coco. You've done so much for them—paying their medical bills, even buying them that holiday retreat in Mimizan. And they know how hard you drive yourself. They'd *never* do that to you."

"So I believed, Misia, and that's why Papa Bader's story didn't alarm me. Then, early this morning while I was still asleep, a 'delegation' of some dozen of my *own* girls turned up at the hotel, demanding a meeting with me. *My* girls. 'Demanded' was actually the word they used with the doorman. Can you imagine the co-lossal nerve of it, Misia? When Céline wakened me, I instructed her to tell the doorman there would be no meeting. Not this morning—not *any* morning. So they marched back to the rue Cambon, leaving this list of extortionate 'proposals' behind."

She was pacing back and forth in front of the desk.

"I have twenty-four hundred workers in twenty-six sewing ateliers, Misia. If I met even *half* their ridiculous terms, I'd be out of business within the year. They have no notion of the price of doing business—the overhead of maintaining three salons, not to mention the high cost of fabrics, the taxes, and the percentage I pay the

Wertheimers on the perfume. All they see are the high prices I charge for my gowns and the thousands of bottles of Chanel No. 5 that quite literally pour out of the boutiques."

Almost true, Coco. I'd heard enough over the years to know that while, on the one hand, she was an enlightened employer in terms of looking after the emotional and physical well-being of "her girls," she was notoriously tightfisted—like the Auvergnat peasant she was—when it came to short wages and long hours. When the mannequins complained of low pay she told them loftily, "Take lovers. After all, you have the pick of the wealthiest, most elegant men in Paris."

"What shall I do, Misia?" She was truly bewildered. "These 'proposals' make them seem so angry . . . so injured . . . And yet, if I accede to their demands, *all* of us lose."

"You'll have to call their bluff, I'm afraid chère Coco, if accepting their proposals *will* ruin you," I told her. "But you must meet them at the rue Cambon. Bend'or would have told you every great general prefers to fight his battles on his own terrain."

"You're right as usual, Misia. Nor must I go looking like a penitent. Any sign of weakness on my part now will be viewed as an admission of guilt. As I'm only guilty of making a better life for myself—for them—I must admit nothing."

While she was telling me this, she'd rushed into her bedroom, me trailing in her wake, and was ransacking the armoire, frantically pulling out one costume after another and discarding them on the floor, the chaise longue, the bed.

"This is right, Misia." She held up an elegant wool-jersey outfit of midnight blue. "This with my pearls."

"Your pearls, Coco? Don't you think the look of *luxe* will infuriate them?"

"What do you think they're striking *for,* Misia," she asked me, flushed with conviction. "They're striking for the right to look like the women they make my dresses for . . . the right to look like *me.* I won't disappoint them."

We turned the corner into the rue Cambon and, when I saw the number of demonstrators gathered in the misty rain in front of the salon, my heart sank. There had to be more than two hundred of them! Across the rough iron door hung a hand-lettered sign: OCCUPÉ.

As Coco approached, the women began hissing and booing. Raising their fists they hurled insults at her. *"A bas le tyran"* . . . *"Avare"* . . . *"Patronne d'esclaves"* . . . *"Congés payés . . ."* But Coco kept walking apparently oblivious of their abuse, as if this were an ordinary day and she were simply going to *her* salon to begin the work.

The mob in front of the door parted to let her through, but one tall, stout elderly woman with iron-grey hair scraped tightly back into a bun, barred the way. She was clearly the spokeswoman.

"Oh no, Mademoiselle. You may not go in. The workers have taken possession of these premises until you meet their most reasonable demands."

Pale as her pearls, Coco turned to the crowd.

"And you, Mesdames, Mesdemoiselles. Is this your wish, too? Are you turning me out of my house—the house I built over the years from the profits of my vision . . . my energy . . . built with you working beside me. Built for myself *and* for you?"

There was a shuffling of feet and a few murmurs of dissent. The spokeswoman, an organizer trained to take the pulse of a mob, was aware that Coco's courage could turn the tide of sympathy.

"Built for *us*, Mademoiselle," she said coldly. "Then why is it that *you* live in luxury at the Ritz and wear silks and jewels?" Brazenly, she reached out and tugged at Coco's long rope of pearls. "And *we*, your 'collaborators,' have barely enough to feed our children and put cheap dresses—goods you would reject out of hand—on our own backs?"

"I have what I have, Madame," she said with enormous dignity, "because I have always worked for it, from the day more than thirty years ago when I came up to Paris from the provinces, like so many of you, with nothing but a dream and the talent and determination to make it come true."

"And a rich lover to pay the bills, Mademoiselle. We mustn't forget him!" The organizer snickered and the crowd of women snickered, too. Coco was losing them again.

"A rich lover. Yes I had a man I loved very much. And he was rich, that's true. He lent me the money to go into business—to lease my fashion house that you have now denied me." She gestured at the crude sign barring the door. "And I repaid him, including the interest, well before the loan came due. In my fifty-two years of life I have never been kept by a man. I have always made my own way."

"Well, that is all that *we* are trying to do, Mademoiselle, make our own way—make an honest decent living from the work of our hands."

"You must understand," Coco said passionately, "this is not a matter of a handful of additional francs in your weekly pay envelope. If I meet *your* demands, I tell you in all candor *I* will not be able to meet the demands of my suppliers, of my distributors. I will not be able to meet the cost of doing business. My fashion house will go under—and you and I will go with it."

"Merde, Mademoiselle," the spokeswoman spat contemptuously at Coco's feet, "all the lies of the bosses sound the same!"

"All right then, ladies. Listen to *my* proposal. I will give the fashion house to you right now—free and clear. And I will continue to work here with you—*for* you—as a stylist, drawing no salary. Because I must do the work. Then let us see if what I've told you are, as your gracious spokeswoman claims, only 'a boss' lies'! The House of Chanel is yours. You've 'occupied' it. Now let's see if you can run it."

She turned on her heel and walked, spine straight and head held high on that proud swan's neck of hers, through the silent crowd and back in the direction of the Ritz. Never have I seen her so magnificent. But would she prevail?

Three weeks to the day, the Front Populaire called off the strike, the sign on the door was discreetly removed, and Coco's workers—minus the spokeswoman and some three hundred others she had fired for insubordination—climbed the circular stairway to their labyrinth of cutting and sewing and fitting rooms to work against the clock on the collection.

Coco should have been triumphant. Her tactics had succeeded brilliantly.

"Bend'or would have been proud of you, chère Coco, so would Boy," I told her as we sat over a late supper in the Espadon Grill. Dark shadows smudged her eyes. She looked exhausted. The standoff had taken a greater emotional toll on her than either one of us had anticipated.

" 'Proud,' Misia, somehow that's not the emotion I feel. No, if anything it's a sense of sadness—sadness that they didn't share my vision enough to make the necessary sacrifices for it, sadness that they didn't really understand me . . ."

That they didn't love you enough, Coco, I thought to myself, *that they were willing to turn on you. It's happened too many times before.*

ELEVEN

The alarm bells rang as the ancient, battered fire engine rattled at high speed over the pock-marked roadway that passed for the motorway out of Barcelona toward the smoking wreck. "Too late," I cried, "too late!" But the alarm went on ringing . . . ringing . . .

Until I realized it was the telephone on my bedside table, waking me from a recurrent dream of a tragedy I had only heard of, never seen, but whose wreckage was strewn all around me.

"Misia . . ." the hoarse, scratchy voice was little more than a whisper. "Please come. I need you. I can't sleep. It's that dream again. It won't let me rest. *He* won't let me rest. He's calling to me." The whisper trailed off into harsh coughing. Then, "Please Misia, you have to come!" She sounded like the terrified child she was.

Eerie that I knew we were dreaming the very same dream. Not so strange, though, if you understood the amazing rapport that had existed between us almost from the start—that had bound me to her even as she was destroying my life. I picked up the little gold carriage clock and held it under the lamp. Two A.M. It had become a regular occurrence by now. One I dreaded and lived for.

"All right, Roussy, ma toute petite, don't be frightened. I'll be there as quickly as I can." I got up, threw on the first dress that came to hand in my wardrobe, drew a brush through my tangled hair and attempted to pull it into some sort of a chignon.

While I waited for José's car and driver to pick me up to take me to the rue de Rivoli, I used the time to reach for Nijinsky's magical lacquered box, take out the drug and the syringe and inject myself, high on my thigh beneath my concealing skirt, with a sufficient dose of morphine to steady me for the ordeal ahead. Never mind that the necessary dosage was growing.

When I got there Jojo, pale and haggard in the silk paisley dressing robe I remember giving him for some long-ago birthday, opened the door himself.

"Tosche, thank God you're here. You're the only one who can reach her, who seems to do her any good these days. She won't let me hire a nurse, in spite of what the doctor in Switzerland told her, won't let me near her. She still blames me, you know. And sometimes, when the delirium is on her, she almost convinces me that I *am* to blame . . . that I could have saved him. 'You could have done it, José,' she'll tell me. '*You're* the artist. The artist is God, isn't he? You could have put him back together again—painted his beautiful head back on his neck. A small enough job, after all, for someone with such *monumental* talents. Why wouldn't you, José? Were you jealous of him, jealous of how much I loved him?' "

Gone was every vestige of Jojo's bravado. Tears streamed unchecked down his face.

"You know that's just the fever talking, Jojo," I told him, using my lace handkerchief to wipe away his tears. "No one could have saved Alexis. The Rolls turned over and over like a broken top. He went straight through the windshield. You told me yourself, when the *Guardia Civil* brought him to the villa, he'd been virtually decapitated. That the Baroness was thrown clear of the wreck was a miracle. And besides, it was *three years ago.*"

"Three years, Tosche, three minutes. I don't mean to melodramatize, but you know she barely took notice when her other brother, Serge, was killed in that polo accident in America last year. Alexis is her obsession. When he was killed, she simply determined to die with him. And she's doing her damndest to accomplish it."

"Have the test results had no effect on her, then?" I asked him.

"None, Tosche. Even knowing the results, she still smokes four packets of Gauloises every day. She *wants* to die. She wants to go to meet him. I know I was skeptical about the force of a death wish that summer when we took Coco with us to Venice. I promise you, I wouldn't be a skeptic now." The tears had started to fall again down his handsome, tormented face.

There was no way short of lying for me to give Jojo the reassurance he needed so desperately. Bizarre as it may sound, what he'd said was true. That girlish willfulness that had enchanted him, enchanted me, even succeeded in breaking through Coco's reserve when Roussy first came to Paris at nineteen, had hardened now into an iron resolve to accomplish her own destruction so she could be reunited with her dead brother Alexis.

Even the advanced tuberculosis the doctor had diagnosed last summer might have been arrested, if Roussy had only agreed to treatment. She was adamantly against it. The doctor was a quack. What would a Swiss know of a Georgian? Georgians regularly lived past the hundred-year mark. It was just a smoker's cough, aggravated by the marble dust of her work—that's all. She would have no truck with doctors, hospitals, not even a day nurse. Why should she? There was nothing wrong with her.

Except that she was dying.

Except that her dying was killing Jojo and me because neither of us could imagine a life without her.

"Go to bed, Jojo," I told him gently. "Try to get some sleep. If you can't fall asleep, at least rest. You're wearing yourself out. You'll be no good to her if you collapse, too. I'll sit with her." I took him by the hand and led him like a hurt, bewildered child into his study where I collected a scatter of sketches littering the sofa and settled him on it under a warm woolen shawl.

As I went to put them on his drawing table and turn out the lamp, I saw that they were all studies of Roussy—most half-finished. Roussy in her Georgian gypsy finery, dancing with a tall, slender figure who must be Alexis; Roussy on her ladder, fiercely concentrating on her sculpture; Roussy sitting cross-legged on the studio floor, playing with her pet monkey; Roussy, slouched at Jojo's worktable, a glass of wine in front of her and the perpetual cigarette dangling from the corner of her lips. The sketches were delicate, lyrical, loving—totally at odds with Jojo's usual heroic style. He was as obsessed with her as I was.

Lining the sketches up side by side, I could actually trace the progression of the tuberculosis. Roussy was fading, getting steadily more frail, vanishing—vampirized by her disease and her dark fixation. What strange turnings love takes! I lowered the lamp and left Jojo with his agonized memories.

The night-light in the bedroom glowed faintly as I slipped in. Roussy was terrified of the dark. Even in the old days when the three of us had slept happily, lasciviously entwined in that vast, baroque bed, she would never allow it to be extinguished.

Her frail, wasted body barely made an impression in the bedcovers. I sat quietly down on the chair beside her, hoping not to wake her.

"I'm not asleep, Misia," her hoarse voice spoke into the dimness. "I never sleep anymore. Even the drugs don't knock me out, and God knows I take enough of them." She reached for my hand, and I held hers in both of mine. Her strong sculptor's hand was as fragile and insubstantial now as the rest of her, but it burned with the fever that was consuming her.

"You've got to sleep, Roussy. If you won't take any other treatment beyond painkillers, you have to shepherd your energy to fight the disease."

"Disease . . . disease . . . that's all I hear these days. I *have* no disease, Misia—unless you count a broken heart. It *was* my fault, you know Misia, not José's, though there's something dark in me that drives me to torture him by blaming him. Maybe it's simply that he's alive and Alexis is dead."

A spasm of terrible coughing wracked her.

"It was me who insisted that Alexis bring Maude Thyssen down to 'Mas Juny,'" she told me, "and my motives were selfish. That's probably why it happened. Part of me wanted to show off. The villa really *is* beautiful, Misia, though I'm not sure you would like it. It's more to my and Coco's unadorned taste than yours. I've often wondered how I ever got José to agree to it— pure lines, open spaces, soft colors like the Spanish countryside coming awake in May. And no gilt anywhere. No, you wouldn't like it. All our *other* friends think it's stunning. But not to your rococo taste, Misia. That's why I didn't invite you, you know . . ."

Her fevered mind was wandering off into casual cruelties. Roussy could wield candor like a scourge.

"I invited them because I knew I was more beautiful than that cold German—and more intelligent, no matter how rich she is—and I wanted Alexis to see the contrast. In my own setting. I couldn't keep him away from those billionaire man-buyers, Louise van Alen and Barbara Hutton, because Alexis was in America with his fatally expensive tastes, and I was trapped here in Paris with José. But there at 'Mas Juny' on my own ground, I knew I could win out over that icy bitch of a Baroness."

She smiled slyly and her haunted grey eyes blazed almost black. "I saw it in his face the minute he walked into the villa. He wanted *me,* Misia, not her. And she saw it, too. That's why she got him out of there so fast . . . made him take her on that damned drive along the coast. So why didn't *she* die instead? She deserved to for trying to take Alexis from me."

Tears poured down her sunken cheeks and her body shook with another spasm of coughing. Gently, I lowered her back against the linen pillows and sponged her face with a cool cloth.

"Don't think of it now, Roussy chérie. It only makes your coughing worse. Try to sleep."

Suddenly she was an innocent little girl again. "I will if you'll tell me the stories about Valvins . . . about all the artists who painted you . . . about all the poets who loved you . . . the composers who wrote songs for you. I know why they loved you, Misia. You're so beautiful . . . so good. Everyone *has* to love you."

So until she drifted off to sleep, as the first pale light of dawn outlined the heavy velvet curtains, I was Diaghilev's Schéhérazade, retelling her for the thousandth night the springtime of my youth and beauty.

But was it to save her life or mine?

The next day at teatime I hurried to the rue Cambon. My nightlong vigil had taken its toll. When my maid awakened me at noon from my unnatural slumber, it had required a heavier dosage of morphine than usual to arm me against the coming confrontation. But it had to be done. There was one thing those surreal hours in the rue de Rivoli had made annihilatingly clear. Roussy *had* to get treatment. Otherwise, she would be gone in a matter of months, leaving Jojo and me stranded, hopeless, lost in her wake.

And Coco, too, I sensed it. She was nearly as much under Roussy's potent spell as the two of us. But she did at least have *some* distance. She was first and last a brilliant strategist. She could, I prayed to whatever gods directed my destiny, think of some scheme, some tactic to get Roussy into the hands of the medical specialists who might still help her, against all the force of her stubborn will.

Coco, having no idea of the seriousness of my visit, was full of fashion gossip. Had I heard about "that Italian?" She refused to so much as dignify her arch-rival of the moment, Elsa Schiaparelli, with her nickname "Schiap." Had I heard that "the Italian" was cutting bizarre, parachute-shaped dresses in the most *obvious* colors—cerise, magenta, tangerine, aquamarine. Blatant colors Coco would never touch, like that positively offensive "hot pink."

"What do you *expect* of an Italian, Misia," she told me quite gleefully. "Crude colors . . . crude vitality . . . certainly not taste. But Misia, you can be sure I have a few fascinating surprises for La Schiaparelli up my sleeve for February."

She smiled a smile as enigmatic—as catlike—as anything Philippe Berthelot ever unjustly accused me of. Then, suddenly, as if really seeing me for the first time since I came into the office, she got up from her desk and came over to sit beside me on the sofa.

"Misia, you're crying." Gently she brushed the tears from my cheeks with fingertips callused from a million pinpricks. "What is it, my darling? Jojo? I know how hard it is for you without him—living in that depressing little flat. Why don't you move into the Ritz near me? We could be company for each other. You wouldn't feel so alone. God knows, I understand how hard that is. I even considered marrying that parasite Iribe to avoid it."

Somehow, I managed to collect myself. "It's not Jojo, Coco. It's her. Roussy. She's not getting any better. The fever's a constant now, and the effort of that dreadful cough has reduced her to a shadow. Still, she won't stop smoking. You're a heavy smoker, Coco, but I think Roussy must go through more than five packets a day. Jojo and I have to sit up with her all night just to make sure she doesn't drift off and set the bedclothes on fire."

"What do the doctors say, Misia?"

"She refuses any kind of medical treatment. Jojo's at his wits' end, Coco. So am I. We both love that beautiful child so much, we can't bear to sit by and watch her destroy herself. You've got to help."

"But what can *I* do, Misia? If she won't listen to you or Jojo or even the specialists?"

"I don't know, Coco. All I do know is that she's had an adolescent crush on you from the very first time I brought her here to the salon. She talks about you all the time—how strong you are, how steady, how very disciplined, fiercely independent. Everything she's not and longs to be. She laughed when she told Jojo the only weaknesses she has in common with her idol is your mutual passion for beauty—and tobacco."

"Wait a minute, Misia." Her dark eyes were thoughtful. "You've just given me an idea. You say she admires my independence. What if a situation arose in which I needed her? Asked for *her* help?"

"Ill as she is, Coco, I don't believe she could refuse you anything. It's beyond a crush by now. She positively hero-worships you."

"Then I think I may have an answer, Misia. I have to make a few arrangements first. Go back to the rue de Rivoli and wait for my call."

I trusted Coco so completely, would have trusted her with my life—*was* trusting her with the life of the charming, heedless mistress who had made me her slave—that I asked her no questions. I put on my silver-fox coat against the late October chill and went back to Jojo and Roussy.

The call came a few hours later, and Coco asked to speak to Roussy direct. Half an hour went by, while Jojo and I sat in front of the drawing room fire in a silence made noisy by our fears. Then, for the first time in weeks, Roussy appeared in the doorway, pale and fragile in a cashmere wrapper.

"Misia, will you help me? I must pack my things for a short trip."

The tension had been too much for Jojo. He exploded. "Pack your *things*. A *trip*. Have you lost your senses, Roussy? You've been in bed for weeks. You're barely strong enough to stand, never mind travel!"

She was quietly resolute. "I'm sorry, José my darling, but I must go. Coco just telephoned to ask me. It seems her doctor is worried about her cough . . . her smoking . . . her lungs . . . feels the X rays may indicate something more serious . . . the first signs of a condition like my own. She's asked me to go with her to the clinic in Prangins."

Jojo would not be mollified. "Travel to Switzerland now. With winter coming on. With your fever." He turned on me. "Coco *must* know how ill she is, Misia. Surely you've told her. How utterly selfish can she be? Why not ask *you* to go with her?"

"That's just the point, José my beloved," Roussy said patiently, "she's asked for me because we share the same condition and she wants someone to stay with her while she's at the clinic. Someone to go through the treatments with her. Once she's committed herself, the doctors wouldn't let Misia, or anyone who's well, within a mile of her. And though I had to put pressure on her to admit it, she's terribly frightened . . . too frightened even to tell you, Misia. She wants me. She needs me. I understand her terror all too well. I'm going with her. Don't try to stop me, José, you mustn't."

The beseeching look on her exquisite face defeated him. He sank into the wing chair and poured himself a generous double brandy, while I went with Roussy to help her pack.

Oh my brave, deeply beloved friend, Coco. Roussy would get treatment after all. She might still be saved. Only you could have had the brilliance to conceive this ruse—and the courage and stamina to see it through.

For the first weeks while they were at Prangins I telephoned the clinic regularly. Coco gave me good reports of Roussy's progress. The clear, cold mountain air seemed to be doing her good. She was sleeping again, getting her color back and she'd even regained something of an appetite. The doctors were qualifiedly optimistic. X rays had revealed the damage to her lungs was extensive, but she'd stopped smoking altogether, and there was some chance the tissue might begin to repair itself.

She and Coco would go for long walks together in the autumn countryside and Roussy, still believing Coco was the patient and determined to lift her spirits, was full of plans for a new sculpture she meant to make—an equestrian statue commemorating Alexis and his love of sport—and hungry for every detail Coco would give her of the designs for the February collection.

It shames me to admit I was jealous of all that time they spent alone together, jealous that Roussy might transfer her affections from me to Coco. I was even suspicious when Coco discouraged every suggestion of a visit from Jojo and me on the grounds of the doctors' concern that Roussy not be overstimulated. Reluctantly, I stayed behind in Paris with Jojo, counting the days—the hours—till her safe, healthy return would make our strange triumvirate complete again.

In late November, though, she took a turn for the worse. The disease returned full force, and she suffered from night sweats and a dangerously high fever. The doctors told Coco that, sadly, this was often the way when the tuberculosis had progressed too far before treatment—a last false rally, as the body tried valiantly one more time to throw off the invasive disease, then a rapid descent to the end.

"Only a miracle could save her now, Misia. Even the doctors admit it," Coco told me, her own voice choked with barely repressed tears. "She has such a struggle even trying to get her breath. She reminds me so of maman—trying to hide the pain, smiling and laughing and trying to reassure *me* there's nothing to be afraid of—that I can hardly bear it." The tears were loose now, echoing bleakly down the line from Switzerland to Paris.

Only a miracle. Jojo was paralyzed with terror at the news. He spent hours alone in the emptiness of the Villa Ségur, staring blindly at the studies for the Waldorf, unable to so much as lift a brush. Roussy's little monkey restlessly prowled the studio, picking up forgotten traces of her—the blue silk scarf she used to keep her pale gold hair out of her eyes when she was working, a cast-off glove that had protected her slender hand, a half-empty packet of Gauloises—and giving them to Jojo as if to remind him to bring his adored mistress back home.

Only a miracle. Never in my more than sixty years of meddling in the destiny of others, mostly for their own good, I believe, have I felt so powerless.

Only a miracle. If that was what was required, I would try for that, too. Hadn't I successfully mediated time and again between creators? Between Igor and Serioja over *Le Sacre* . . . between Cocteau and Picasso over *Parade.* That was it. I would go to Lourdes to negotiate with God for a miracle—for the life of the woman I loved.

The train that carried me down to Lourdes through the desolate wintry countryside, like one of Picasso's charcoal sketches of bare trees stark against patches of snow, was half-empty. Early December was the quiet time before international Society would set off for the

Christmas and New Year's festivities in the south of France.

Only a handful of fellow pilgrims, making their way to the shrine, filled the occasional compartment with their families, their nurses and physicians, their stretchers and crutches and all the paraphernalia of their various diseases and deformities. Though it was more than seventy-five years since that shy adolescent girl had had her ecstatic encounter with the Virgin Mary in the rocky grotto outside the little village where her indigent family was charitably housed in the empty jail, Bernadette Soubirous had only been officially canonized St. Bernadette five years earlier in 1933.

But for all those years, since Bernadette's inspired touch on the dry, sandy ground had caused a spring to flow into the grotto, word of the healing powers of those waters had spread throughout France—throughout the world. Now thousands of pilgrims made their way every year to ask for healing at the shrine. Lourdes had become the court of last resort for those whom science and medicine had failed. Lourdes was the place of miracles.

When I told Coco I was going there to pray for the miracle of Roussy's recovery and to bring back some of the healing water to Prangins, she encouraged me—didn't laugh at me the bitter, mirthless way that Jojo did.

"Oh, excellent, Tosche my darling. I'm sure an ounce of 'Eau de Bernadette' will do what the specialists at Prangins found impossible, will reverse five years of Roussy's calculated, energetic self-destruction."

I forgave Jojo his cynicism. It was the product, I

knew, of his own intolerable sense of helplessness and fear of the loss of her.

"I have to go, Jojo. I can't just sit here in Paris not knowing how she is—forbidden by Coco, probably for good and valid reasons, to see her, to touch her, to reassure myself that a miracle *can* happen. Even if it's only symbolic, I have to try to do something."

Gently, he took me in his arms and stroked my hair. "I know, Tosche. I'm sorry I was so hard on you. If Lourdes could save her, I'd gladly deed over half my earnings to the Church to help maintain the shrine. But this time I won't go with you. The last thing you need on a genuine pilgrimage is a skeptic!"

So here I was, alone in a small, overpriced, under-furnished room in this tiny village that had sprouted hotels and souvenir shops like mushrooms after a rain. Even in this slow season before the Christmas crush, the streets were crowded, and I was constantly jostled off the roadway as I followed the afternoon's procession of supplicants down toward the grotto under the rocky hillside by the growling torrent.

It was at times like this that I missed Serioja most. Diaghilev would have been the perfect partner for this experience. Despite all our surface worldliness we were both profoundly Eastern in our sense of the mystical, the miraculous. He would have responded to the element of bizarre spectacle, too—the head-on collision of faith and fakery, grace and greed.

Lining the roadway was stall after stall encrusted with layers of cheap, tawdry religious souvenirs and bogus relics—clumsy plaster-of-Paris statuettes of the Blessed Virgin painted garish blue and white, and of Bernadette, looking like nothing so much as a simpleminded village nymphette; papier-mâché replicas of the grotto itself; rosaries in all colors, stones, sizes, and prices; postcards, obviously the work of some local primitive artist, depicting the glorious encounter in the grotto.

And everywhere there were serried ranks of glass bottles in the shape of the Virgin, with her blue crown for a stopper, to be filled with water from the healing spring.

And yet . . . and yet . . . as the steady stream of petitioners wound their way to the grotto, I felt myself beginning to be caught up in the groundswell of their hope, their true belief.

Just outside the entrance to the grotto, I stopped at one of the most opulent of the stalls—its owner clearly having donated heavily to the Church for prime real estate. There I purchased a St. Bernadette candle whose flame would carry my urgent plea for Roussy heavenward—a taper *so* large it required two strapping village boys to carry it into the grotto.

As we followed the winding path toward the spring into darkness, I was forcibly struck by the visible evidence of the miraculous. The grotto was like a *true* version of the gimcrack stalls that had led the way to it. Hung from its sweating walls were crutches, canes, braces, bandages—every corporeal evidence of the triumph of faith over pain. "But not a single wooden leg," I remembered Zola the atheist had said.

With so many people crowded into such a small, dark space—and the mist rising from the spring, beading the rock walls with dampness—I had a moment of claustrophobic panic.

"Light the taper, Philippe," I said to the oldest of the

two boys. "It's so very dark in here." To myself, I said, It's time for you to make your best negotiation, Misia . . . to try to buy her back from God.

As Philippe struck the match and lit the giant candle, it flared up before me. A pain so intense—so excruciating it was like a comet's fiery blaze across the sky— passed behind my eyes. I reeled back and nearly fell.

The smaller of the two boys caught me and supported me back on our fumbling way out of the grotto. When we emerged into the twilight, I could not decide whether the blinding effect of the sudden light in the pitch darkness had affected me . . . or whether it was something more profound. Philippe kindly led me to my hotel and refused to accept the over-generous tip I tried to press on him.

Back in Paris, still uncertain whether the grinding headaches and pain behind the eyes were something worse than the migraines the years had taught me to tolerate, I returned to the rue de Constantine, with my own precious blue glass bottle of spring water packed carefully in my case, only to be handed a cable from Coco by the surly concierge:

Heartbroken to tell you all medical efforts failed. Roussy died today. Will be buried here. Returning Paris soonest. Your Coco.

December 16, 1938. Roussy was thirty-two years old. I was sixty-six, and all my very best negotiating skills had failed to save her. I managed the stairs to my flat and lay down, fully clothed, on my narrow bed.

I thought of the three of us—Roussy, Jojo, and me— lovingly entangled on that vast barque of an explorer's bed in the rue de Rivoli. And I thought of the three of us—Roussy, Coco, and me—laughing heedlessly over the lavishly embroidered nightdress she would wear to Jojo's marriage bed. And I thought how very helpless we all were against the force of the riptides of love and life, wherever they carried us.

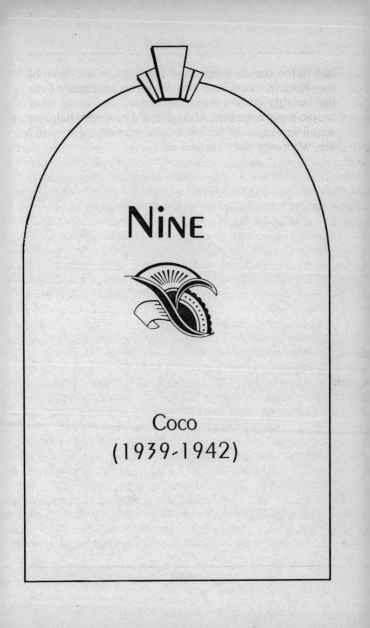

Nine

Coco
(1939-1942)

ONE

*W*hat a strange season that winter of 1939—
the winter of the *"drôle de guerre,"* the
phony war. Though war had been declared
in September and the army mobilized, an army far superior in manpower to the German forces in the west—
augmented by the handful of four divisions which were
all Britain could spare—the indecisive French cabinet
simply failed to act. Sat on their hands like worried old
women while they lost the advantage. Failed to cross
the Rhine and strike what could have been a deathblow
to the Ruhr, the industrial heart of Hitler's Reich.

While the German *blitzkrieg* of fire and steel and terror—of a million and a half warriors and a whirlwind
of stuka fighter planes and death-dealing tanks rolled
over helpless Poland, followed by Hitler's equally ruthless ally, Russia, trampling the prostrate country into
oblivion or "partition" as the diplomats preferred to
put it—France wrung her hands over the fear of disastrous, *expensive* history repeating itself . . . and did
nothing.

No bombs fell on Paris that winter. Only snowflakes
and the propaganda leaflets of the RAF whitened the
cobblestones of the rue Cambon.

Daladier and Pétain and the generals might be dithering, but I was not. This was no time for fashion. My

heart was too heavy. Roussy's death and the heart-break of my dearest friends. My own pain at the point-less quenching of that quicksilver spirit. The darkening-down of the lamps of Europe now twice in my lifetime. Even Reverdy had bricked up the front windows of the barn that was his retreat in Solesmes and turned his back on the world. I sat alone on one of the spindly gilt chairs, staring at the endless repetition of my small figure in the mirrored walls of the empty salon.

No, this was not the hour for fashion. For the first time since Boy and I had stood, spellbound, hand in hand outside No. 21, I would have to put my dreams on hold. I would leave the boutique open. My agree-ment with the Wertheimers required it. And my pride refused to concede to anything less than Luftwaffe fire-bombs obliterating the name "Chanel" from the rue Cambon.

But for now, no more dresses. Only the last collec-tion that would premier tomorrow, February 5th. The collection whose very smallest detail had preoccupied me until midnight, an hour ago, when I sent everyone home—the fitters, seamstresses, and pressers, still complaining that their strike three years ago should have spared them these lunatic hours, spared them my obsession, my *excès de folie;* and the exhausted man-nequins, terrified there weren't enough hours left to re-store the porcelain perfection of their complexions.

The collection that was at once an *adieu* and a pre-diction. The collection I'd infused with my vision of past, present, and future. Johanna would definitely have approved. The press would be surprised and, I hoped for once, *accurately* speculative. Wearily, I shrugged on my sable-lined greatcoat and slipped out my own front door, daring the curfew, to walk the short walk back to one more sleepless night at the Ritz.

It was almost over. I leaned against the mirrored wall at the top of the staircase, watching the *défilé*. Misia and Jojo sat close together at the top of the stairs, along with Édith and Étienne, Fulco, Jean and Christian, Boris and Serge and Marie-Louise de Bousquet (the *enfant prodige* of *Harper's Bazaar* in Paris whose iconoclastic spirit I admired), and my *own* American allies, Carmel Snow of *Bazaar* and Margaret Case of *Vogue*—the privileged few who were allowed to share the catbird's seat, while lesser beings perched expectantly on their gilt chairs below.

It had gone well. The suits with their militarily padded shoulders . . . the cocktail dresses, intentionally simple and elegant in black or white crepe de chine.

Then, my statement. The gowns. There was an audible gasp as the first of the mannequins came down the curved staircase.

"Gypsies . . ." one prominent fashion journalist groped for understanding, "but what *gorgeous* gypsies!"

"Not just gypsies, you fool," her fellow journalist, a notorious *pédéraste* hissed, *"Georgian* gypsies . . . Look at those pouffed sleeves . . . that décolletage. She's never done anything quite like it before."

"Roussy," Misia said in a whisper, reaching up to take my hand. "Roussy's taffeta dance dress. The one she insisted on wearing to all the balls, even when you told her it had outlived its welcome. You did this for Roussy."

"The colors!" Another of the journalists was scribbling furiously on her pad with her small gold pen. "Not Chanel's signature, but the *tricolore—France's* signature. Defiant gypsies flaunting the *tricolore.* Mademoiselle, with her characteristic bravado, has spoken for all of us once again."

TWO

*C*losing the fashion house provoked far more of an uproar than even I would have predicted. Some of my critics seized on the opportunity to call it treason, laying off more than two thousand women. A revenge for their defiance of me in the 1936 strike, they said. I, on the other hand, regarded it as patriotic, freeing them up for essential war work. Uniforms, after all, required the same skilled craftsmanship as ball gowns.

With a pang of nostalgia, I remembered those golden afternoons with Adrienne and me, bent earnestly over the glittering *passementerie* of a chasseur's uniform jacket in the back of Monsieur Redon's tiny shop. The lesson of that first war was that combat was not a thing of dashing uniforms and *élan* and *panache* anymore, if it ever had been. It was a dirty business of mud and sweat and blood and bodies shattered beyond mending. Nameless *poilus* dead in numberless trenches. Hopeful young lives snuffed out by the choking fumes of mustard gas.

Besides, my heart simply wasn't in it. The one thing I would never play false to was my dresses. *They* kept me honest. I knew that anything I tried to do right now—worn-out and heartsick, and for the first time in my memory, bereft of inspiration—would be a betrayal of my vision, myself . . . my dresses.

Instead, I decided on a strategic withdrawal. Like the canny peasant I knew *au fond* that I was, I would go to ground, rest, and husband my energies. I would watch for a while, the way Benny had taught me to watch the direction of the bright ribbons tied to the hal-yards of *Flying Cloud* to see which way the winds were blowing.

I was long overdue, anyway, for a visit to my nephew, André Pallasse, the young man I regarded as a sort of son since those long-ago days when my sister, Julia-Berthe, died and Boy had taken the child up and sponsored him at his own schools in England.

By a strange stroke of irony, I had bought for André and his bride a modest château, the Château Lambeyc, from the agents of its owner—Étienne Balsan. Étienne was most comfortably married by now, as I'd always known he would be, and living nearby.

Of course, by the time I made my way down to Pau, on roads crowded with hordes of aristos, fleeing Paris again in fear of the so-far-invisible *Boches*—as they had once before, down to me and Boy and my profitable beachhead in Deauville—I learned that André had not only been mobilized in the general call-up, but with the inherited ill-luck of his mother had already been captured in the early days of the fighting and interned in a prisoner-of-war camp.

His feckless young wife, Julie, with as pretty a complexion and as high-strung a temperament as my flightiest mannequin, alternated between bouts of weeping that left her red-nosed, watery-eyed and completely spoiled her looks, and feverish knitting of jerseys and warm woolen socks that had about as much chance of reaching André as Hitler did of breaching the Maginot Line.

In the hectic, passionate years I'd spent in Paris, I'd somehow forgotten the original impetus that drove me there—the excruciating boredom of provincial life. The months I spent in Pau seemed to creep by. André had left a passable chestnut hunter in his stables when the rest of his bloodstock was comandeered by the cavalry, so that I could at least escape the claustrophobia of that chilly, smoky drawing room—the army having requisitioned all the seasoned wood, as well—and the endless knitting and local gossip of Julie and her young married friends.

I was racing across the patchwork fields of late spring grass and pale-green hay—easily clearing the low stone fences, the wind in my hair, with a sense of freedom and exhilaration I'd almost forgotten—when I heard the pounding of another horse gaining steadily on me. As the rider drew even, I saw it was Étienne.

"Coco," he cried, "I knew it *had* to be you. No other woman I've ever met has a seat to equal yours!"

I laughed gaily. "That's your old arrogance talking, Étienne. After all it *was* you who taught me to ride."

"The ABCs, perhaps, but no one really teaches a natural, Coco. And that's what you are."

We'd slowed our mounts to a companionable walk. I looked at him out of the corner of my eye. Handsome as ever, perhaps even more so with the streaks of silver at his temple and his stocky body still firm from hours in the saddle.

"What are you doing down here in Pau, Étienne? I'd heard you'd rejoined your regiment."

"I have, but we've been given a brief leave before the serious fighting begins."

"Then there's going to *be* fighting? Weygand and Pétain and those other windbags are finally going to stop talking and act?"

"They'll have no choice, Coco." He was suddenly serious. "Hitler's appetite for territory is insatiable. Czechoslovakia and Poland merely whetted it. His Russian cronies helped him subdue the Finns. Now that he's taken Norway and Denmark to secure sea lanes for the transport of oil, his eye is definitely trained back on the Continent. Holland and Belgium will probably go first, but it's France he wants. It's the old madness that's always burnt between us."

"Will you be going back soon, then?"

"Why do you ask, chère Coco?" His dark eyes looked intently into mine. "I thought my fate was of no concern to you. You made that clear enough in Deauville. If you'd given me even the smallest hope, I would have waited . . . waited just as long as it took for you to get Boy out of your system. I'm waiting still, you know."

It had been an idle question. I knew he was well-married now, with a gracious, loving wife and children. André had told me so. How could I put a stop to the confession I'd innocently provoked, before he compromised himself any further?

"Oh that was just my *ennui* talking, Étienne. With all the eligible men mobilized, it's an infernal regiment of women down here in Pau, and I thought, perhaps, if you were to be here for a week or two, we might find time for a few intimate evenings together." My meaning was unmistakable.

"A fling, Coco." His face flushed dark red as it always had when he was angry or thwarted. "A worldly Parisienne's fling for nostalgia's sake. A convenient antidote to boredom. That's all I am to you, Coco? Even now. Now that he's gone. What a bloody fool I've been!" Without another word, he spurred his big bay hunter, wheeled him around and raced back toward his château—toward the simple, conventional life I'd always understood was the only one he could honestly lead.

Julie was driving me crazy. Not intentionally. She was a good-hearted girl. But André's imprisonment had taken possession of her. She imagined him starved, isolated, tortured by the Gestapo.

The conflict Étienne had predicted had come. It had lasted for exactly six brutal weeks—instead of the four defiant years France had held the *Boches* at bay the last time. And an armistice had been signed in the forests of Compiègne, where Étienne and Boy and I, and the innocent companions of our youth, used to ride to the hounds—signed, humiliatingly, in the *wagon-lit* where a triumphant Marshal Foch had dictated the humiliating terms of Germany's surrender twenty-two years before.

Now, in that same railway car in the summer of 1940, Hitler and his henchmen, Goering, Brauchitsch, Raeder, Ribbentrop, and Hess, had sat down to spell out their revenge.

The country had been neatly cut in half, so that no French government-in-exile could even dream of organizing a serious resistance. The north, including my beloved city of lights, was occupied by the Nazis. The south, where the pusillanimous collaborationist government lodged in Vichy, under that compromiser Pierre Laval, was ostensibly "free."

For a French citizen to move from the free to the occupied zones required an *Ausweis*—a sort of passport. And Julie was determined that I get one . . . that I go back to occupied Paris and use any influence I might still possess to get André repatriated. This was the end of my small respite, my time for rest and regrouping. *Tiens.* It had always been that way with me. Always the unexpected.

THREE

I hardly recognized the city of my heart, as the bizarre gazogene taxi, with its torpedo-shaped gas tank bolted to the boot, drove me to the Ritz. It was twilight, but even the magical *l'heure bleue* failed to disguise the heavy hand of the Occupier.

Instead of the *tricolore,* the swastika hung every-where—even on the Eiffel Tower above a huge sign, DEUTSCHLAND SIEGT AUF ALLEN FRONTEN, which my driver bit-terly translated as "Germany conquers on all Fronts."

The Champs-Élysées, as we drove down it to the hotel, was nearly deserted except for the occasional bi-cyclist and bands of soldiers in field grey lined up at the *Soldatenkino,* the army cinemas, to see the propa-ganda films of Dr. Goebbels.

What waited for me at the Ritz? Would I even be per-mitted to stay there? My driver informed me that the hotel, too, had been taken over by the Nazis. Well, if worse came to worse, I could telephone Misia and ask her to put me up in the rue de Constantine.

I needn't have worried. The doorman, even flanked by two burly German soldiers, greeted me with his usual courtesy. The concierge asked how I'd enjoyed my stay in Pau. There was only one moment of awk-wardness at the desk.

"You do understand, Mademoiselle, that the hotel has been requisitioned by the High Command. Of course, you are welcome to stay. Kommandant von Schaumburg specifically mentioned that Mademoiselle was not to be inconvenienced."

"Then have my bags taken up to the suite, Marcel," I told him.

"That's just it, Mademoiselle Chanel. Your suite has been 'occupied' by General Goering. I personally had your furniture moved to the rue Cambon. There is, nat-urally, still a room for you, but on a slightly higher floor."

I was too tired after the journey even to argue. When I trudged down the seemingly endless corridor and opened the door, I was greeted by a tiny, meagerly furnished, white-painted room, little better than a maid's room and nearly filled by my Hermès trunks marked, "Hold for Mademoiselle Gabrielle Chanel." It was scarcely larger than my room at the orphanage at Aubazine. Its single window looked down from a great height onto the rue Cambon.

At least it had a private bath. I suppose I should be thankful for that. I tipped the bellman and fell, still fully dressed, into the narrow white bed where I was instantly asleep.

The next few weeks were an exercise in futility. I was shuttled, certainly politely enough, from the elegant offices of the second-in-command in Herr Doktor Otto Abetz' German consulate, to the chilly minions of the Gestapo whose gigantic swastika banner fluttered in the breeze above the Hôtel Majestic in the Avenue Foch.

No one knew of the destiny of one André Pallasse, a minor industrialist, interned somewhere in one of the POW camps that mushroomed since war was declared. No one cared to know.

"Look at this," one harried functionary in the Avenue Foch told me, gesturing at a precarious tower of manila folders on his desk. "Every one of them dossiers on men and women who have been found potentially dangerous to the Reich." Then, for a moment, he let down his guard. "Just be thankful, Mademoiselle, that your nephew is not a Jew. We don't trouble ourselves to keep files on *them.*"

Shivering with repugnance and fatigue, I'd returned to the Ritz and telephoned José. Hearing the barely suppressed terror in my voice, he asked, "What is it, Coco? You don't sound yourself at all. What can I do?"

"Nothing, I'm afraid, Jojo. I promised my nephew André's wife that I would try to make inquiries . . . to intervene on his behalf. He's in a POW camp somewhere. But I've been knocking on doors everywhere for the last ten days, and no one's interested. André's simply not important enough for anyone to give a damn."

There was a long silence on the line. Then Jojo said, "Coco, I can't explain the nature of my connections to you right now, but I'd recommend that you go back to the Avenue Foch tomorrow and ask for Baron Spatz. That's the name he's currently using for his work. He's someone I believe might actually be able to help you. There's no need to mention precisely how he came to your attention, Coco. No need to mention my name. He'll know."

Early the next morning I returned to Gestapo headquarters at the Hôtel Majestic and asked the soldier on duty at what used to be the concierge's desk to direct me to Baron Spatz.

After briefly examining my papers, he asked curtly, "And do you have an appointment with the Baron, Fräulein Chanel? He has a crowded calendar."

I'd have to bluff my way in. "Not precisely, but I've just come from the Ritz where you see that I'm living, and I was taking tea with General Goering." It wasn't *entirely* a lie. As I'd sat in the tearoom, too nervous to manage anything more than tea and toast, I saw the obese general and his entourage breakfasting across the room. *Dieu,* he'd had on more makeup than one of my mannequins. I'd swear he was wearing lip-rouge. The diamond and emerald rings on his fat fingers blazed as he pounded the table, demanding service.

I smiled flirtatiously at the lieutenant. "When I told him the nature of my business, the General referred me specifically to Baron Spatz."

The young orderly was suddenly all deference. "General Goering, you say. But of course, Fräulein, why didn't you tell me that in the first place? I'm sure Baron Spatz will be *most* eager to see you. His office is just down the corridor to the right." As I walked away, he picked up the telephone to inform the Baron of his unscheduled visitor.

I nearly laughed out loud when I realized he was housed in the hotel's former beauty salon. How very appropriate! I knocked softly and opened the door.

Quelle surprise! Had I secretly been expecting another Goering? The man who got up from behind the desk to greet me was anything but effeminate. Tall, broad-shouldered, athletic-looking with white-blond hair, he had the warmest smile and the coldest eyes I'd ever seen. He held out his hand and his grip was almost painful.

"Fräulein Chanel, what an unexpected pleasure. I had no idea that you'd remember me."

Remember him. What could he be talking about? Had someone brought him to one of my evenings in the St.-Honoré? He saw my bewilderment and hurried to spare me embarrassment.

"The premiere of *Le Train bleu*. Afterwards, at Diaghilev's party at Maxim's. I was there with my wife."

I still didn't remember, but it made more sense. The party had been jammed and the champagne flowing.

"Of course that was the occasion. And how is your lovely wife?"

A brief frown. "We are no longer married. She has left Paris." No further explanation, either. He sat behind his desk and appraised me so frankly, so fully with those ice-blue eyes that I felt physically assaulted. But his voice when he spoke was all concern.

"And what can I do to help you, Fräulein? To assist you would give me the very greatest pleasure."

I told him briefly about André's imprisonment and the frustrations I'd encountered in even finding him, never mind getting him repatriated.

"His wife is beside herself with worry, you understand. And a mutual friend suggested you might have access to his file . . . know his whereabouts . . . be able to do something for him."

No questions were even asked about the identity of our "mutual friend." Spatz was as circumspect as he was superficially charming.

"It *is* possible, Fräulein," he told me. "You understand, though, that these matters are somewhat delicate. They require time and influence," he hesitated significantly, "and money. Rather a good deal of money."

So it was to be a matter of bribes, then. Well, I could play that game. "Money is not an issue for me, Baron, where my blood relations are concerned, though most of my funds are lodged in Swiss banks."

"All the more convenient." He smiled engagingly. "Let me make some inquiries and get back to you. Perhaps this evening, if you are free. A preliminary report, say, over dinner at the Tour d'Argent. I'm particularly partial to the view of the cathedral by moonlight."

"And I to the roast duckling, Baron Spatz." I had no intention of making things too easy for him. It was clear he was used to dealing in more than one kind of currency. "I will expect you at the Ritz at, shall we say, six o'clock?"

"Six precisely, so that we can have as much time together as possible. To review the possibilities. This *verdammte* nine o'clock curfew will make our evening all too brief as it is." He led me to the door, his strong arm overly familiar around my shoulders. Why did his every gesture speak of conquest?

"I order you not to worry any longer, Fräulein Chanel. Our mutual friend has sent you to the right place. To the right man. I am determined to be of service to you."

FOUR

Having Spatz in my life was a mixed blessing—an *accident de guerre,* I suppose you could say. On the one hand, Jojo was right. He certainly had the necessary connections.

In that single day, before dinner, he had brought André's case to the attention of his superior, Rittmeister Theodor Momm who, fortuitously, was in charge of French textiles for the duration. Not only was Momm able to locate André, but because of Momm's position and my own place in the industry, he might be able to get him released from the prison camp to manage a textile mill near St. Quentin, with me named proprietor. Another irony. Étienne's family had made their fortune manufacturing the sturdy blue twill for Britain's "bobbies." Now, for the first time in my career, I might technically be "making cloth" for the Occupiers.

On the other hand, Spatz was a shrewd negotiator. When he "offered" me André's freedom, in the perfect restaurant, with the perfect moon sailing serenely over Notre-Dame, and the perfect, officially numbered duck in its exquisite orange sauce, he also presented his own numbered account—and the price I would be required to pay for André's rescue. It was a triumph of double billing.

Not only would Spatz count on making me his mistress which, of course, he assured me ardently, was his first desire, but he also had his eye on my company. Parfums Chanel.

"You do know, Mademoiselle Coco," he said earnestly, taking my hand in his, teasing the palm with his practiced fingers and looking deep into my eyes, "that the Wertheimer brothers have been exploiting you for years, making millions from their seventy percent while you—without whom there would be no 'Chanel Numéro Five—receive a trifling ten percent. I don't mean to offend you, Mademoiselle, but you must be aware they are stealing you blind."

Bilked by the Wertheimers. It was an old song. One Iribe had crooned in my ear when he was trying to convince me to marry him—when he had actually convinced me to let him champion me in the first assault on my Longchamp "agreement" with Pierre and Papa Bader.

Why was the ballad of my "exploitation" always sung by men who wished to do precisely the same thing?

Later, lying in my uncomfortably narrow bed in the Ritz, having taken me urgently, roughly, with no thought at all for my own satisfaction, Spatz returned to the subject that obsessed him. The Wertheimers.

"You know, Coco, whenever I pass your salon and see our men lined up there, even in the rain, to buy an ounce of your perfume for their *Liebchen* back in the Fatherland, I'm outraged to think that such opportunists are reaping all the profit."

Those same "opportunists" from Neuilly without whom there would have *been* no mass manufacture . . . no serious profit. Of course, Spatz would never consider that, and perhaps I shouldn't either.

"But Spatz," I tried to divert him, "the Wertheimers are not even *in* Paris. When they got wind of Hitler's intentions toward their people, they had the good sense to leave the country and emigrate to America."

"Exactly, Coco. Their flight provides the perfect opportunity for you to take back what rightfully belongs to you. You know the Commission of Jewish Affairs was established to take responsibility for the businesses of owners who have been spineless enough to abandon them—and abandon their innocent Aryan partners like yourself. You should go to the Commission and demand what's yours. You've been letting yourself be robbed for years."

That simply wasn't true. As Spatz lay beside me, pouring vitriol into the darkness, I could see Pierre's warm, intelligent eyes and his delight as he thought up yet one more ingenious way to market my perfumes. Not just Chanel No. 5, but "Bois des Isles" and "Cuir de Russie." Maybe I wasn't getting a fair percentage of the profits, but neither was I being "robbed blind." Without Pierre Wertheimer, Chanel No. 5 would have been nothing more than a designer's plaything. A gift for my favorite clients. A modest boutique item. Not the industry it had become.

FIVE

Spatz was putting altogether too much pressure on me. Not only had he forsaken what he called the "torments" of my little camp bed in the Ritz for the comfort of my flat above the salon at No. 31 where he'd been quick enough to install himself, but he was at me day and night about going to the Commission to repossess "my" company.

I decided to talk it over with José. After all, he was the one who'd sent me to Spatz in the first place. He must know the man's true colors. If he had any.

When the door to the flat in the rue de Rivoli was

opened, I got a terrible start. The man who stood there might have been young—or ancient—it was impossible to guess. He was tall and spectrally thin, his paleness accentuated by a heavy coating of rice powder, and with dark, burning eyes. This must be José's new secretary, Boulos Ristelheuber, the one the wits were calling "the ectoplasm" because of his extreme height and thinness and eerie pallor. Once you got past that, he was handsome enough, rather like a vampire surprised before prowling hours. And he was courtliness itself.

"Mademoiselle Chanel, please come in. Monsieur Sert is in the study sketching. He's expecting you." He tapped lightly on Jojo's door and ushered me in. "I'll go back to working with Madame Sert now, if you have no need of me, sir," he said to José.

"Of course, Boulos. You're a godsend to her." When Boulos left, Jojo gave his most eloquent shrug. "The boy's thoroughly infatuated with Misia. There she is— easily fifty years his senior, half-blind and almost totally dependent now on morphine. And still he finds her fascinating, can hardly wait for the excuse to be with her . . . spends all his free time helping her make those foolish little ming trees of mother-of-pearl and crystal and coral I know she sells to her friends to support her habit. I simply don't understand it, Coco."

"Of course you do, Jojo. Don't dissemble with me. We know each other too well. Misia is femininity incarnate. She always has been. She will be on the day she dies. She's woman at her most paradoxical and enigmatic. Everyone longs to know the secret of her charm. Everyone falls under her spell. You and I have both been under it for more years than I can count. That's why you keep her near you, even though you're 'officially' parted."

He laughed. "I suppose you're right, Coco. I'm secretly as dependent on her—on her intelligence, her wit, her approval—as she is on the drug." He settled me on the sofa. "But that's not why you're here. You said you needed my advice."

"It's about my company, Parfums Chanel. Spatz is convinced that Pierre Wertheimer and Papa Bader have been taking advantage of me for years, have traded on my innocence at accepting only ten percent of the revenues when, in fact, the original formula is mine."

"It always has seemed an awfully slim profit to me," he said.

"Now, with all the Jewish-owned companies falling under the interdict—and the Wertheimers gone for safety to America—he's convinced I should apply to the authorities to reclaim the company. What do you think I should do, Jojo?"

"It's an extremely tricky situation, Coco ma chère. All depends on the outcome of the conflict, something neither one of us can know. What I've tried to do myself is walk the wire—profess friendliness to both sides, allegiance to neither."

"What Benny would call 'hedging your bets,' Jojo. I suspect that's what I must do, too. I'm just not sure how to go about it."

"If I were you I'd, temporarily, accommodate the Occupier—or Baron Spatz, if you will. I'd go to the Commission and ask for control of the company which, in effect, has been 'abandoned' by its major shareholders, but which still bears your name. If they give it to you,

Spatz will be satisfied for now and, should the wind shift, you can make your peace with the Wertheimers. After all, you were only protecting their own interests *in absentia* by keeping Parfums Chanel out of hostile hands."

Jojo, the ultimate pragmatist, playing both sides against the middle. No wonder his larder was groaning with beef and eggs, white flour and sugar and butter and coffee, while most of Paris stood in line for patient hours, shivering in the cold outside the near-empty *boucheries* and *boulangeries.* They clutched their handsful of coupons, hoping there would be enough to provide food for their family tables and a cup of bitter ersatz chicory coffee in the morning to wash down the grey bread made mainly of straw.

I noticed now that the buttons on his brocade vest were practically popping. This in a time when thinness was no longer a matter of choice by the fashionables. How could I condemn him, though, when I was required to walk that very same wire?

SIX

What a delicious irony! Pierre Wertheimer had beaten me at my own duplicitous game. Of course I could never let on to Spatz—pacing the Savonnerie carpet of "our" flat in a total fury, his face so red I feared he was about to share Iribe's fate—but I was secretly amused. I was even proud of Pierre for being the wily adversary he always had been, since that sunny afternoon in his family box at Longchamp when we shook hands over the formation of Parfums Chanel.

We had just returned from the offices of the Commission of Jewish Affairs where Spatz, my lawyer, and Georges Madoux, the mild-mannered manager who was my choice to administer the company when it was put into my hands as Spatz was confident it would be, had received the disconcerting news.

Even the brown-shirted bureaucrat who explained the situation was offended on my behalf.

"These *verdammte Juden,* Fräulein Chanel, altogether too crafty for their own good. But we're dealing with them in our own way. You may at least be confident of that."

"What do you *mean* Fräulein Chanel can't take possession of her own company—the company that bears her name?" Spatz was incredulous. "The Wertheimers abandoned it when they saved their asses by running to America."

"Not precisely, Baron. When we looked into the case, we discovered that before their hasty 'departure,' Pierre Wertheimer transferred their interest in Parfums Chanel to one Felix Amiot."

"Amiot. Just who the hell is he?" Spatz bellowed. Heads turned all over the busy office. "Another one of *them*, I suppose. That doesn't alter the situation. All Jewish-owned businesses are being conveyed into friendly hands. Fräulein Chanel's lawyer has prepared the appropriate documents." He snatched them out of the briefcase and flung the papers down on the desk. "Just sign these and let's get on with the transfer. We've wasted enough of Fräulein Chanel's valuable time as it is."

The bureaucrat was the soul of sorely tried patience.

"That is what I'm trying to tell you, Baron. There can *be* no transfer. Felix Amiot is an industrialist, an old friend of the Wertheimers, actually an airplane manufacturer who specializes in propellers not perfumes. But he is most definitely an Aryan. Parfums Chanel is legally, firmly in Aryan hands. And, of course, Fräulein Chanel continues to hold her ten percent interest in the company."

Spatz's face was such a study in outraged disbelief that I almost wanted to laugh. Fortunately, I did not. He would have made me pay dearly for it.

Now, back in the rue Cambon, I searched desperately for a way to defuse Spatz before his emotional violence turned physical as I knew too well it could.

"Do stop pacing, mon cher. You're going to wear a path in the carpet."

"To hell with carpets, Coco. Don't you understand what's happened to you? You've been robbed by a conniving Jew!"

But I was still too amused by Pierre's adroit maneuvering to be annoyed. As far as I was concerned, it was better that he continue to maintain a controlling interest in the company through this Amiot. For all his self-righteous indignation, I could see Spatz was the most avaricious conniver of them all. But if I played my cards right, he would also remain a man I could control. A man I could recruit for one of my most daring designs.

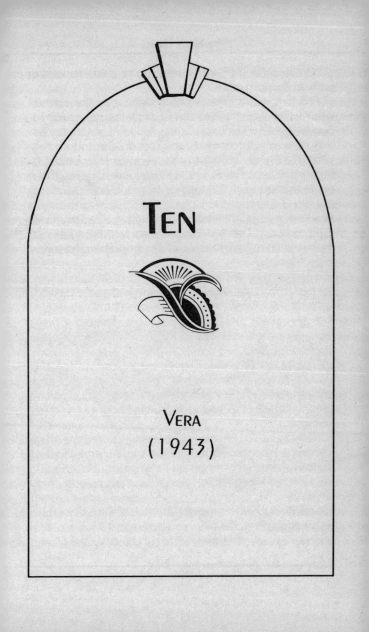

TEN

VERA
(1943)

ONE

Of course I was suspicious from the outset. It had been years since I'd heard from Coco and since those idyllic summers Berto and I had spent with her and Bend'or at La Pausa—in the little villa she'd built for us beyond the main house so that we could enjoy our privacy amidst the perpetual party La Pausa had quickly become.

You never knew *who* would turn up next. It might be Winston, down for a spot of painting in the olive groves; or Max Beaverbrook or, as likely, Dali or Christian Bérard or Cocteau or Georges Auric, asking Misia to play us his latest composition on the grand piano in the salon; or Coco's favorite pretty boy, Serge Lifar, whom I have to admit I'd finally taken a fancy to myself, despite my usual aversion to Nellys.

Berto and I were wonderfully happy there—drunk on one another's bodies in the first blaze of our passion. I look back now on those two golden summers under that burning Mediterranean sky, unclouded by even the hint of war, as a lovely dream inhabited by dreamers blissfully unaware of how very fragile it really was.

Of course, I knew very well that her gift to us of La Colline was her indirect, proud way of thanking me for my introducing her to Bend'or in Monte and making it all possible. Whether she acknowledged it to herself or not, Coco was never "simply" generous. And I suppose that was why I was immediately on my guard when that tall, blond officer turned up on my doorstep with three dozen white camellias and her letter asking me to rejoin her in Occupied Paris to reopen the fashion house.

Whatever it was she was up to was, at that point, immaterial. There could simply be no thought of my leaving Rome while Berto was in hiding from the *Fascisti* on papal lands.

I was watched constantly—either by the Gestapo or by Mussolini's secret police—followed everywhere on those infrequent occasions when I was foolish or desperate enough with boredom to venture out of our house to take Taege for his exercise in the Borghese gardens. If I could not so much as walk my dog unshadowed, how would I ever be allowed to leave Rome? Travel permits for British citizens were infinitely difficult to come by—and for the wife of a hunted man, impossible.

Beyond that, until I was confident Berto was safe from his pursuers, I would consider leaving the country a direct betrayal of our love. No, unlike so many real or imagined crises over the years when I had rushed to Coco's side, this time her summons would have to go unanswered.

The cell door clanged shut and I heard their boots retreating down the long, dark corridor. I sank back on the bare mattress of the single bunk and drew the thin, smelly blanket around me. I was dying for a cigarette, but they had taken my purse and jewels and, ludicrously, my shoelaces when they subjected me to that mortifying body search. Bloody bastards.

I'm not easily frightened. Berto and I had already had our share of run-ins with the *Fascisti* before he went into hiding. But then we were together.

When my terrified maid roused me at midnight to tell me that I was wanted by the Gestapo—that they were waiting downstairs in the library, I thought it must simply be a mistake. I dressed quickly, splashed on cologne, and smoothed my hair into a chignon. Should I put on the Lombardi pearls? Bloody bizarre at midnight—but then, so was this entire situation.

Surely, if the pearls failed to intimidate them, Taege would succeed. Though still only six months old, he was the size of a full-grown pony. Mastiffs are notoriously fierce in defense of their owners, and as I descended the marble stairs with him close at my heels I could see the two men at the library door exchange glances.

"Signora Lombardi, we apologize for this late-night intrusion, but we must ask that you accompany us." The taller of the two, a blond giant with ice-blue eyes, stepped forward. It was the same man who'd brought me flowers the day before. The one who had taken such offense when I told him I was forced by circumstance to decline Mademoiselle Chanel's gracious invitation.

"Accompany you where, gentlemen? And to what purpose in the middle of the night? I'm afraid I must telephone my solicitor before agreeing to accompany you anywhere."

"That will be unnecessary, *Signora* Lombardi." He used the Italian sarcastically. "We have the proper warrant for your arrest." He handed me an official-looking document in German.

"On what charges do you arrest me? What is your jurisdiction? I am a British citizen, living peacefully in Rome, and I demand that I be allowed to see my solicitor."

"Tomorrow . . . tomorrow, Signora—all that can be done tomorrow." The blond giant was actually trying for a semblance of charm. "We are acting in liaison with the local authorities, and we simply wish to interview you on some matters concerning your associates." He stepped forward and grasped my arm tightly, ignoring Taege's low, menacing growl.

The other man, dark and coarse with a ruined complexion, unsnapped his holster and took out an ugly-looking Walther automatic. "Signora, I suggest you silence your dog so that I do not have to do it for you."

I realized he was in dead earnest. He looked just the sort who would find shooting my dog in front of me a source of intense pleasure.

"All right. Maria, take Taege and put him in his kennel. It appears I shall have to go with these men, but I want you to be certain to telephone Signor Ottarini as soon as we are gone and let him know where to contact me. You will, gentlemen, tell me where we are going at this unusual hour?"

"Certainly, Signora," the blond's charm had given way to a chilly courtesy. "You will be confined in the Mantellate Prison until we have completed our inquiries."

The Mantellate. Rome's women's prison. I could not suppress a shudder. How many innocent women since

Mussolini came to power had simply disappeared into its dungeons. The ferocity of the guards was notorious.

Now I was within those stone-deaf walls. But what did they want and what part did the Gestapo play in it? As the last hours of the sleepless night dragged into morning, my mind worked obsessively: Was it Berto they were after? Would they torture me to reveal his hiding place? If they did, could I withstand it? I'd always considered myself a rather brave person—even foolhardy. I could take the highest hedge or the widest ditch, or drive the Rolls at high speed through the serpentine curves of the Italian Alps without a qualm. Berto hated what he called my reckless driving. But physical torture? I wasn't sure.

It must have been morning—I couldn't tell with the bare bulb burning all night—when my cell door opened and a tray was pushed inside. A dreadful, watery broth and stale dark bread, but my terror had made me ravenous and I wolfed it.

Hours passed until the door opened again and a surly guard led me to an empty, white-washed room where I sat uncomfortably on a backless stool. Bloody sadists. I would have killed for a cigarette. I was shaking with weariness before the door opened to admit my colleagues of the previous evening.

"Good morning, Signora. I trust you passed a quiet night," the blond giant said coolly. "I wonder if you would do us the favor of removing your blouse." The request was made as indifferently as though he were asking me to pass the port. But the dark man had his hand on his holster.

When I complied, my hands trembling so I could

barely undo the buttons, he continued, "And now your brassiere, if you please."

"How dare you? I am, as I have repeatedly told you, a British citizen, unjustly detained."

"Justice remains to be determined, Signora. For now, please follow my instructions. It will hasten our interview."

It was his infernal sangfroid that broke me. When I was naked to the waist, he came to me and put his hands on my breasts, looking deep into my eyes. He squeezed painfully, bruisingly. Then he simply turned and left the room. I was alone with the man who had threatened to shoot my dog. He took his gun out of the holster and walked up to me, unbuttoning his flies.

I closed my eyes tight. *Oh God, no.*

"Take it in your lips, Signora. Suck on it."

The cold metal burned my mouth. I knew I was finished. I opened my eyes and watched, mesmerized as he pulled the trigger. A sharp metallic click.

When I came to, I was back in my cell.

TWO

*L*ater that day I heard the sound of footsteps coming down the corridor and my cell door was opened. It was the tall, cold-eyed man.

I tensed involuntarily and moved into the farthest corner of the bunk, my back to the wall.

Again that bloody charm. "Signora Lombardi, here are the documents for your release, all in proper order. We of course regret any inconvenience caused you. I have also prepared a safe-conduct for you from Rome to Madrid, as well as escorts to make sure your journey there is without incident."

"Madrid? But I have no desire to travel to Madrid. I wish to remain in Rome until I have news of the whereabouts and safety of my husband." I could never so much as imply that I knew the location of Berto's sanctuary.

"I must inform you, Signora, that for the time being, the authorities prefer that, so long as Signor Lombardi is at liberty, you leave the country so that you will not be tempted toward any rash activities on his behalf. As our connections with the Spanish intelligence agencies are excellent, we have chosen Madrid as a safe haven for you for the duration of hostilities."

He accompanied me to the administrative office

where my purse and pearls and shoelaces were returned to me.

"A car and driver is waiting to take you to your home, Signora, so that you may pack whatever you require. Your escort will collect you at five for the night train to Milan."

And then I was suddenly outside the prison walls in the hot, lazy Roman afternoon—my release as inexplicable as my arrest. My profound relief at being free and alive was mingled with apprehension. Why Madrid? And Madrid via Milan. Was this another elaborate cover for one more Gestapo abduction?

As soon as I got home and managed to reassure Maria who was on the edge of hysterics that I was unharmed, I telephoned our solicitor, Signor Ottarini, who had been vainly trying to reach me, and tried to explain the curious circumstances of the last forty-eight hours.

He was as suspicious as I was about my destination. When I revealed my fear of being kidnapped, he admitted that he was baffled.

"What would the Gestapo gain by abducting you, Signora, if what they really want is your husband?"

"Perhaps they intend to hold me hostage to draw him out of hiding. But they could do that as easily here in Rome. I did have one other thought, though, Signor Ottarini, however farfetched it may seem to you. They may be aware of my old association with Prime Minister Churchill and the Duke of Westminster."

"What could that have to do with the last two days? I don't understand," Signor Ottarini said.

"Abducting me may be part of some larger scheme with one or both of them as its targets. If that's what this is in aid of, they're *miles* off the mark. Though we

were still in correspondence when the war broke out,
I haven't seen Winston or Bend'or for years."

"Well, my advice to you now, Signora, is to go along
with their plans. Resistance at this point might find you
back in the Mantellate. My unfortunate experience of
yesterday and today is that no civilian can be of help
to you there. As long as you are free, I can use whatever connections I still have to try and protect you—
even at a distance." His "safe journey" sounded not a
little hollow. But I couldn't quarrel with his reasoning.

As the black Mercedes, flying the red-and-black swastika flags on its hood, drew up to the Madrid Ritz, I knew
my Gestapo escort was infinitely relieved to be shut of
me. He'd borne the brunt of my outrage during the
long, lonely journey to Madrid. I suppose I should have
been grateful for the calibre of my lodgings, but I was
simply too weary and emotionally shocked to do anything more than to climb the red-carpeted marble
stairs and follow the bellhop and my bags into the
hotel.

"Vera—at last! You can't possibly imagine the strings
I've had to pull to get you here." Coco's familiar voice
of command penetrated the veil of my exhaustion as
she hurried across the opulent lobby and threw her
arms around me.

THREE

I lay in the blissfully hot, scented water of the bath, a glass of chilled champagne within easy reach, feeling the week's terrible tensions start to ease from my body. What a bizarre contrast. This luxurious, marble-mosaicked bathroom, with its gilt dressing-table and mirror and its sparkling chandelier, was twice the size of my filthy cell in the Mantellate.

Coco perched on the small dressing stool, a glass of champagne in one hand and her perpetual cigarette in the other, tapping her slender foot in its sling-back pump. My prolonged silence was making her visibly nervous.

"All right, Vera, I can't blame you for not speaking to me. But that entire dreadful prison business was not my doing. I had no idea Spatz would take it to that extreme. He was only meant to bring you the flowers and my letter. When you refused to come to Paris, I suspect he simply panicked and decided to try intimidation instead. He's had considerable success using that tactic on women before. I ought to know," she couldn't meet my eyes, "you see, I'm his mistress."

Remembering those ice-blue eyes gazing calmly into mine as he painfully squeezed my breasts, I shuddered. For a moment I felt almost sorry for her. Then my outrage got the better of me.

"And *that* justifies my being dragged from my home at midnight, imprisoned, brutalized—and by the way, darling Coco, your lover *is* rather free with his hands." I let her absorb the significance of that for a moment. "And then to be virtually abducted and told I'm to wait out the duration of the war here, with Berto a thousand miles away in Italy!"

She looked genuinely anguished. "I told you I'm dreadfully sorry for the way Spatz bungled it, Vera. In fact, I had to go over his head in Paris to get you released and brought here. He didn't like it a bit. I suspect he'll make me pay a stiff price when I'm back in the rue Cambon. But it was simply too important."

"All this so you can open another fashion salon to cater to Franco and his Nazi friends? *Fascisti,* whatever the color of their uniform—or their money—are Berto's enemies. And his enemies are mine. I've always been there for you in the past, Coco, but we're on different sides of the fence this time."

"No, we're not, Vera. That's what I'm trying to tell you. That's why I needed you. You see, opening a salon here is just an excuse . . . a cover."

"A cover for what, Coco? Don't tell me you've taken to playing amateur spy. Spying's a dirty, deadly business. Remember what happened to Mata Hari."

"It's not precisely spying, Vera. More a matter of diplomacy. A group of people back in Paris, some of them French, some Germans who are more than a little disillusioned with the conduct of the war—and with their lunatic leader—Germans who never wanted to go to war with Britain in the first place, have approached me about contacting Churchill over the possibility of Anglo-German peace talks."

" 'Peace talks,' Coco, take hold of yourself! You know what Winston said at Casablanca. What he's been saying since he became Prime Minister. *No surrender.* Not while there's an Englishman or woman left alive. I'm sure he's actually quarreled with Benny over it. You know how reluctant Benny was to go to war in the first place."

"This war's gone on for too long now, Vera. Too many millions of lives have been lost. It's time for peace, and Winston is the only one strong enough to negotiate a favorable peace, now that Hitler's experienced such dramatic reversals. El Alamein—the triumph of your own magnificent Montgomery—the disaster of Stalingrad. I believe that if you can just put us back in contact, I can convince Churchill the Reich is finished . . . that it's time to come to the negotiating table."

"But where do I come into it, Coco?"

"That's why I went to all the trouble to bring you here. Because you can convince Samuel Hoare, the ambassador, that my mission is legitimate. Because Winston loves you. Because he likes me and he trusts you. Together, you and I can help save what's left of the old order . . . and beauty as we know it."

She was flushed with her vision. *Another great role.* The couturière as Joan of Arc. I lay back in the rapidly cooling tub, my mind reeling with the audacity, the sheer grandiosity of it. Only Coco. I suppose it's why I loved her. *Always the unexpected.*

"All right, Coco, you win. You know I don't think you have a Chinaman's chance of getting near Winston at this point, never mind convincing him to alter the stance that's kept him—and every loyal Englishman and woman on their feet under the terrible battering they've taken from that madman in Berlin. But I'll go to Sam Hoare for you tomorrow and see what I can do. In my view, the sooner this bloody war is over, the sooner I can be back with Berto again. For me, it comes down to that."

Later that night, lying awake from sheer nervous exhaustion, staring at the elaborately worked plaster ceiling of my luxurious bedroom, I admitted to myself that I planned to use Coco just as calculatedly as she thought she was using me.

I would certainly pay a visit to Sam Hoare and put Coco's consummately romantic scheme to him. Then, when he'd laughed me out of court, then I would ask for what *I* really wanted. Not to go with Coco to London and Winston—certainly not to moulder away here in Madrid till the war's end—but to be sent back to the British-held south of Italy. There I would confidently wait for Berto, a *cinquecento* knight in a Uccello painting, to come back to claim his patient bride.

To my surprise the ambassador did not laugh at what I considered Coco's lunatic "mission."

He had been quick enough to see me and now, sitting opposite me at his vast, polished mahogany desk with the official portrait of King George VI—a hasty replacement for the one of the abdicated Edward—looking down at us, Sam clasped his hands over his considerable paunch and smiled benignly at me.

"I suppose you don't recall it, Vera my dear, but the reason I landed up in this rather minor posting—my three years in exile as I view them—was my original desire for a negotiated peace. A view our mutual friend, Bend'or, certainly shared. When Winston drove Chamberlain out and became Prime Minister, he was quick enough to get rid of all of us who were appeasement-minded. The Mosleys and Archie Ramsay went to prison. Even Bend'or was told by his dear old friend that he would publically frown on his taking part in any active peace efforts. And I was sent out here to my personal Elba."

He gestured at the Spanish sunlight streaming through the fringed-velvet drapes.

"After the abdication, when the Duke and Duchess of Windsor stopped here on their way to the Bahamas, I even had some hope that they might be put in touch with certain peace-minded Germans. I did my damndest to keep the secret service blokes off their backs, so they could have freedom to move, as it were. But Winston was determined to get them across the seas as fast as possible. And he succeeded."

I was thoroughly bewildered. "Then I can't imagine *what* use it would be to try to put Coco Chanel in contact with him, if his 'no surrender' views are so strong. She's only a couturière, after all—hardly a diplomat. And who knows who these 'Germans' are who she says are backing her?"

The ambassador leaned back in his leather chair. "That, my dear Vera, remains to be seen. My viewpoint is clear. I would put myself at the disposal of anyone of influence who favors a negotiated peace. Ask Mademoiselle Chanel to visit me tomorrow afternoon and I'll see what can be done about getting her together with Winston."

I left the embassy with my head spinning. I had fully expected to be ridiculed at the least, severely repri-

manded for Coco's folly at the worst. When I got back
to the Ritz and reported on my meeting with Hoare,
she was delighted.

"Just what I'd hoped for, Vera ma chère. You really
are a darling to intercede for me this way. I know that
once you and I are in London—once I can put my position to dear Winston with all the force of my personality—he'll be bound to see the wisdom of it."

What incredible self-importance. And what self-
delusion! I gave no hint that I had absolutely no intention of leaving the Continent to go to London with her.
For now, until I'd got Sam to agree to guarantee me
safe-conduct back to Italy and Berto, I would appear
to play her game.

FOUR

*J*ust what *was* her game? Was it simply an act of
misguided patriotism on Coco's part? Or was
this a double-blind, played out by two equally
determined, reckless women, acting out of very
personal, very passionate but very different motives?
Will I ever know?

All I do know is that, for the next few weeks, while
Coco played at setting up "Chanel, Madrid," we stayed

on at the Ritz, watching the representatives of every faction in the war pass by us in the tearoom.

It was a darker, shadow-box version of an *Alice in Wonderland* world. One day it would be Prince Alfonso whose "daring" bomber raids on innocent Spanish villages as an ace in Franco's air force probably accounted for the carnage of Picasso's *Guernica*. The next, it was the Marques de Estrella, Don Miguel Primo de Rivera, the civil governor of Madrid who served so many masters it must have made even *him* dizzy. Then the handsome Nazi agent, Prince Max-Egon von Hohenlohe Langenburg, with his retinue of professional beauties.

And then there was the endless parade of international fugitives, making their desperate way with expensively forged papers, via Madrid to Lisbon or Casablanca and, hopefully, in a world gone mad, escaping the *Nacht und Nebel*—the Night and Fog—of Hitler's terror and the communal anonymity of a mass grave.

Nearly every afternoon, Coco went to the embassy to confer with Sam Hoare. She was curiously reticent about these meetings—told me only that Sam had succeeded in putting her in contact with Winston by means of a coded wireless (just the two of them, even Sam banished from the room during their discussions) and that they were attempting to set up a meeting in London.

Then came the ordeal of Winston's face-off with his allies Stalin and Roosevelt, in Tehran, over the carving up of a postwar, post-Hitler world, and Winston's subsequent illness. Was he sick of war? Coco thought so. The press reported that he'd told his daughter, Sarah, in

Tehran that "War is a game played with a smiling face, but do you think there is laughter in my heart?"

Rumors were rampant. Was Churchill dying? Would the lion of England desert her now in her time of utmost need? No. His remarkable resilience—and a case of Napoleon brandy—saw him through to a convalescence in Marrakech. But there could be no meeting between them.

Coco's mission had, for the moment, failed. She was going back to Paris to regroup and, of course, she expected me to join her. Up until the eleventh hour, with the locomotive hissing and steaming in the cavernous Madrid station, she must have waited, leaning out of her compartment window, watching for me down the platform. She had to know I would not be coming. She had to know where my first loyalty lay.

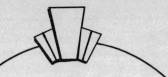

Eleven

Coco
(1943-1950)

ONE

D *ieu merci.* She didn't come, after all. Right up until the moment when the train began to move out of the station, I was afraid her old loyalty to me might still prevail. She'd only have been in my way in Paris. And in danger. She'd served her purpose brilliantly, though, putting me back in touch with Winston through that embittered old conniver, Hoare. And without arousing Spatz's suspicions.

As if I'd *ever* urge Winston to surrender . . . to negotiate with those *sales cochons* in Berlin! I, who all my life have been a fighter against the odds. How I admired his courage and his tenacity—even when Goering's Luftwaffe bombers were raining fire and death so relentlessly down on him and his brave people. That's what made me so determined to get to him—to tell him what I thought I just might be able to give him. How I might help.

But I'd had to do it without tipping my hand, and Vera had seemed the logical route. I only regret the terror and humiliation she'd had to go through in Rome, with Spatz mishandling everything so crudely.

Cocteau was right about me, much as it pains me to admit it, when he told me I was turning into a *"femme pédéraste,"* a woman who acts just like a man—using men and then discarding them. With Iribe, and now with Spatz, I had come to enjoy nothing so much as seducing the seducer. It was a kind of *règlement de comptes,* a settling of scores for all the women they'd abused—whose hearts they'd callously broken in the past.

Now I had the greatest challenge of all. Vera was right when she told me I was playing a reckless game. She just didn't understand how very reckless it was.

From the moment I'd convinced my gullible lover to interest his superiors in German intelligence—especially the target he had unwittingly provided me, Walter Schellenberg—in my proposed "peace mission" to Winston, I knew I had a chance. Schellenberg was one of the most ambitious and most brilliant of Himmler's intellectual gangsters in the RSHA.

And when he laughingly christened my mission "Operation Model Hat," I knew instinctively that I'd piqued not just his genius for intrigue, but his sexual curiosity as well.

I'd first heard about him from Spatz who hero-worshipped him, and Spatz's contact, Rittmeister Theodor Momm, the dead-earnest cavalry officer who'd carried my little scheme to Prinz Albrechtstrasse and managed to interest the head of AMT-VI in it.

Schellenberg was a "young Turk," a university-educated rogue who'd made his reputation with his sinister mentor, S.S. Reichsfuehrer Heinrich Himmler, and risen to the number two position in German intelligence by his bravura moves—his ruthless ousting of Admiral Wilhelm Canaris as head of the Abwehr, his kidnapping of two British intelligence officers in Holland. Then there was his near-success in abducting the Duke and Duchess of Windsor when they were in Sam

Hoare's careless hands in Madrid, and his genius in setting up the deluxe brothel for officers and civil servants, the "Salon Kitty" in Berlin where—thanks to the hundreds of microphones he'd had planted in the Porthault sheets and the champagne coolers—he could keep a close ear to all the baroque internecine plotting of his colleagues at the highest level of the Reich.

Oh, Walter Schellenberg was an interesting challenge indeed.

Suppose I could convince him of what the headlines and battle reports from North Africa and the Russian front were making ominously clear—that the days of Hitler's Thousand-Year-Reich were numbered.

Suppose I could interest him in making a comfortable place for himself in a postwar, post-Hitler world. Just suppose I could "turn" him and make him Winston's spy in place—Churchill's eyes and ears in the very heart of Reich intelligence. Unlikely, I knew—the very longest of long shots—but Winston, over the wireless in Madrid, had put his blessing on my trying it. So as soon as I reached Paris, I would somehow have to contrive a trip to Berlin.

Spatz lay sprawled on one of my brown suede couches in his sanctuary in my flat above the salon. His uniform tunic was half-unbuttoned and he had a snifter of Hennessy in one hand and an excellent cigar in the other. He was looking particularly petulant.

"Momm will think I've gone crazy, Coco—that we *both* have. You know how the Fuehrer hates bad news. It's been known to send him into murderous rages. His hands and feet tremble uncontrollably. He foams at the

mouth. I'm sure the men around him, even Schellenberg, are feeling his wrath. And you want a safe-
conduct to travel all the way to Berlin just to report that
your ridiculous little mission has *failed?* It's already
caused me enough embarrassment with that fiasco in
Rome."

I came to sit close beside him on the couch. "Admit
it, my darling, that 'fiasco' as you call it was entirely of
your own making. If you hadn't terrorized poor Vera
so thoroughly that she refused to budge from Madrid,
she and I might be in Marrakech with Winston at this
moment. And *your* star would be in the ascendant."

He didn't even have the decency to look guilty. "She
was altogether too easy to terrorize, Coco. Like every
woman I've known. Except for you. Your spirit somehow resists domination—that's what makes it . . . makes
you such a damnably endless temptation." He reached
out and pinched my nipple hard.

I smiled and resisted the urge to cry out. "That's why
I must go to Berlin, don't you see? To demonstrate my
spirit—to show Schellenberg that your confidence and
Rittmeister Momm's in me was not misplaced. That this
temporary setback does not mean the failure of 'Model
Hat.' "

"What precisely *does* it mean then, Mademoiselle?"

"The vital thing is that the contact with Churchill has
been re-established. If he recovers from this illness, we
may still manage to meet. Schellenberg can advise me
on how best to proceed. He's a man, after all, Spatz.
He's bound to be flattered that Coco Chanel traveled
all the way to Berlin to declare her loyalty, her willingness to serve."

"Not *too* willing, Coco." Roughly, he pushed me back

on the soft suede and yanked up my skirt. "Schellenberg's twenty-seven years younger than you are. But then, it's almost the same with me, and I'm certainly not immune to your, shall we say, 'mature' charms."

As he raised himself triumphantly above me, I looked steadily into his cold blue eyes. "Then you will arrange things with Momm tomorrow?"

"To satisfy Mademoiselle, of course. Providing she satisfies me."

TWO

As the Daimler limousine that collected me at the airport at Rangsdorf carried me through the outskirts and into Berlin, we passed one bombed-out villa and office building after another. Dr. Goebbels's Paris *propagandastaffel* had, of course, given no indication of the severity of the damage. No reports of the vengeance inflicted by the Allied bombers for Goering's murderous pounding of London had made their way to the pages of the Nazi mouthpiece, the *Pariser Zeitung* which chronicled only one glorious victory after another. But the Adlon Hotel, where I was to stay, was untouched, as were most of the elegant buildings along the Unter den Linden.

The lobby was swarming with officers in field grey or the sinister black of the S.S. Beautiful young, blonde women in couture gowns, sparkling with diamonds and with expensive furs draped casually over the backs of gilt chairs, were drinking cocktails in the lavishly stocked bar, laughing and flirting with their blond escorts. Was I the only brunette in the Adlon? War, a war beginning to go badly sour for the Reich, seemed the very furthest thing from their minds—or, if war, only the perennial one between the sexes.

In the privacy of my suite, as I unpacked the simply cut white crepe suit with its bias-cut, softly flowing skirt that I had designed especially for my encounter with Obergruppenfuehrer Schellenberg the next morning, I'll admit to second thoughts.

I was, after all and as Spatz was never above reminding me, sixty years old to Schellenberg's thirty-three.

Stripping off my creased traveling suit and my delicate lingerie from Odile, I took a hard look at myself in the mirrored armoire—the brutally objective, assessing look even my most exquisite mannequins had learned to dread when it was directed at one of them. Not bad. Not bad at all, considering.

My long, slender neck bore no lines. Probably because I'd carried my head so high for so long. My complexion was, perhaps, a trifle coarsened by the constant smoking I was forever swearing and failing to give up. A light ivory makeup would go far in disguising that. My short, curly hair was still as shiny blue-black as a crow's wing, thanks to Antoine, the young genius hairdresser I'd set up a few doors down on the rue Cambon and promised to make the rage of Paris in return for his discreet ministrations.

My breasts, whose smallness I secretly used to deplore, had survived the dread drooping of the over-endowed. They were as high and firm as they were when Boy first traced them with his sensuous lips that sweet, hot, long-ago afternoon at Royallieu. My stomach was flat and unmarked by childbearing. Barrenness did have that single advantage.

And my legs—well, they had always been the envy of my customers and mannequins alike.

Inventory of my visible assets complete, I felt a good deal more confident about the coming encounter with Herr Himmler's *wunderkind.* I would have a light supper in the suite and make an early night of it in order to be as rested and attractive as I possibly could be.

As I drifted off, considering the long odds on my rash mission's ever succeeding, I suddenly recalled that evening in the Casino at Monte Carlo when I'd confided the secret of my success at the tables to Sam Goldwyn. "Nonchalance," I'd told Sam. "If you don't care too much, you're more likely to win." *Nonchalance.* I'd have to remember that in the morning.

As his adjutant ushered me into Schellenberg's immense, imposing office with its ubiquitous swastika banner and portrait of the Fuehrer, in Himmler's palatial S.S. headquarters in Prinz Albrechtstrasse, I was immediately struck by two things—how handsome he was and how vulnerable. Not insecure—*vulnerable,* a distinction only a woman of my age, experience, and intention could make.

Tall, slim, and elegant in his superbly tailored black cavalry twill S.S. tunic with its menacing death's head insignia, and his high, black, glossily polished jackboots, he was still vulnerable. His extreme youth in his high position made that inevitable.

How did I know it? By remembering my own first days of bluffing haughty, supercilious baronesses and vicomtesses in the Boulevard Malesherbes and still securing them as customers. By seeing the way he leapt up from behind his desk and came forward to greet me and to linger overlong kissing my hand.

"Fräulein, what a pleasure . . . a privilege. Not just to meet you at last, but to think that you have come all this distance in these dangerous times to meet me. And looking so . . . so . . . *ravissante.*" His hungry eyes took in my closely molded white crepe suit—my white lace picture hat flirtatiously shadowing my dark eyes.

"Not to meet you, General," I told him, "though it is a pleasure for me, too. Your reputation for bold maneuvers has certainly reached Paris." I corrected him quickly, in order to tantalize him. "But to report on the unfortunate reversals in the preliminary stage of 'Model Hat.'" Instinctively, I had seized the initiative by confessing my failure before he had the chance to reproach me for it. It put him on the defensive.

"It was hardly *your* fault, Fräulein . . . that Frau Lombardi would refuse to travel with you . . . that Churchill would fall ill after the stress of Tehran. These were variables you could not possibly have anticipated."

He was holding both my hands in his by now, tightly, reassuringly, and looking intently into my eyes. I noticed the faint scar on his perfectly sculpted chin. Another point of vulnerability.

"How very understanding you are, General," I told him. "So you *do* know that one of the main objectives of the mission has been achieved. I am back in contact with Churchill."

"Excellent, Fräulein, excellent. You cannot possibly conceive how impressed I am by your candor, your willingness to come this far to tell me the truth of the situation. Most of my operatives are so self-protective they would never have dared to bring me this report. You couldn't know it, but adverse news is not well-received in the Reich these days. I wish more of my men had your courage."

I drew a deep breath of relief. The first phase of my own mission had been achieved.

Reluctantly, he let go of my hands. "I'm due at a briefing with Reichsfuehrer Himmler, Fräulein, so regretfully I must conclude our interview. But we are far from finished with our ongoing strategy for 'Model Hat.' Is it possible we could meet later on today? Or this evening? Is there anything in Berlin you particularly wish to see? I will, of course, put my driver at your disposal. Perhaps one of our architectural genius Speer's magnificent buildings? The Reichschancellery itself?"

"Actually, General, there *is* one place I would like to visit—a place whose reputation has all Paris talking. Not one of Speer's designs, though. Something of your own . . ."

He actually blushed with pleasure. He was very young. "But I am not an architect, *Gnädiges Fräulein*. Only a theorist and a bureaucrat."

"The 'Salon Kitty.' I know this is an unorthodox request, but I would dearly love to see it. Of course, a respectable woman could never go there unescorted. Perhaps this evening, if you were free."

The desire that flared in his eyes almost made me laugh aloud in triumph.

"The 'Salon Kitty,' not at all a place for a woman of your class, your stature. But in my company, yes, of course! I shall collect you at the Adlon at ten. I cannot tell you how very much I look forward to it."

"And I, who am always fascinated, mon cher General, by the unconventional . . . the risk-takers . . . I will be counting the hours."

After a visit to the Adlon's coiffeur and a long, leisurely soak in a perfumed bath, I took a great deal of trouble over my toilette. A lot depended on the evening's outcome.

I'd brought a long, clinging sheath of black chiffon over satin, with two wings of satin crossed at the bodice and running over my shoulders down to a daringly deep vee at the back. Beneath it I wore only a lacy black garter belt and one of the few pairs of silk stockings left in Paris.

It was rather like one of the gowns I'd done for Gloria Swanson for *Tonight or Never*. That seemed especially appropriate. My only jewelry was the spectacular collar of seed pearls Benny had given me in London. Another talisman.

Promptly at ten, the concierge rang to tell me that Obergruppenfuehrer Schellenberg waited for me in the lobby. His dark eyes lit up as I stepped out of the lift and shrugged my white, glacial fox jacket onto my shoulders.

"*Gnädiges Fräulein*—even more beautiful than this morning. Tell me, how do you achieve it?"

"Beauty is my business, after all, General, just as intelligence is yours. In fact, I'm convinced they have one essential element in common."

"And what is that?" he asked me, clearly amused, taking my arm possessively. Heads turned as we walked through the glittering lobby to his waiting car. He certainly cut a splendid figure, and I felt I had exceeded *his* expectations.

"Instinct, General. An absolute instinct for what is true and for finding out what is false."

He laughed and drew me close to him on the soft leather seat of the limousine. "Not just beautiful and brave, but witty, too. What a paragon. I certainly hope I can persuade you to make your stay in Berlin a long one."

The car pulled up in front of a stately mansion, its tall, narrow windows blinded by the same midnight-blue blackout curtains we used back in Paris. The pitch darkness outside belied the brilliance within. The doorman opened to Schellenberg's command and we stepped into a black-and-white marble foyer lit by a gigantic Lalique chandelier that must have held a thousand candles.

A curved marble staircase swept up into the salon. Up and down it passed officers in their ornate dress uniforms and, on their arms, some of the most gorgeous and gorgeously gowned women that I, in my long professional experience of female beauty and luxe, had ever seen. When I whispered to Schellenberg that they looked more like countesses than courtesans, he laughed and led me up the stairs.

"Some of them are, chère Coco." He used the endearment for the first time. "You'd be surprised at how many aristocratic women came to me when I opened

Salon Kitty and volunteered to work here without pay. 'For the good of the Fatherland, of course,' they'd tell me, but you may be sure it was for the thrill of doing the forbidden while their husbands are away at the Front."

How very hard he sounded at that moment. "You don't have a very high opinion of women, do you General? I hear it in your voice."

"Not of most women. My profession has inevitably made me cynical, I'm afraid. I get to see the very worst of human nature so much of the time, I've even become suspicious of beauty. Life here in Berlin these days is the Salon Kitty in macrocosm. Everyone is treacherous and nothing is quite what it seems."

Again that intent, penetrating look he'd given me that morning in his office. Was he suspicious of me? Probably. He had every reason to be. My motive for coming all the way to Berlin to confess my sins of omission to him could only have perplexed him. But I could also tell that he was profoundly intrigued. He sensed a fellow rogue in me, and he was right.

After an hour of drinking champagne and dancing to the music of an eight-piece orchestra, held so close against him that I could feel the medals on his tunic bruising my skin, as he blew lightly—provocatively— into my ear, he suggested that he take me upstairs and show me the real purpose of the place.

"You *did* say you wanted to see it all. But don't worry, chère Coco," he reassured me, laughingly, "on my honor as an officer, I won't try to take unfair advantage of you."

I replied in kind. "You won't? You disappoint me,

mon General. An evening at Salon Kitty would surely be incomplete without an amorous encounter!"

"*Also*, dangerous liaisons are to your taste, are they? Well, we shall see."

He took me by the hand and led me out of the mirrored salon and up another flight of stairs. At the end of a long, richly carpeted corridor with doors on either side, he took a key out of his pocket and unlocked the last one.

It was a fantasy boudoir that would have dazzled even Iribe. Art Deco in design, it centered on a huge bed with a wrought-silver headboard, obviously the work of Erté, and a white satin comforter. White lilies stood in a tall silver vase, and the dressing table had a complete set of silver Erté toilet articles.

Schellenberg paid absolutely no attention to the decor—or to me. Instead, he prowled the room, removing electronic monitoring devices from the lampstands, the flower vase, the silver hairbrush, the elaborate headboard of the bed, and the bottom of the silver wine bucket where a bottle of Mumm Cordon Rouge was chilling beside a nightstand holding a cut-crystal bowl of beluga caviar. He even found a listening device under that.

"There you are, my darling Mademoiselle. I've swept the room. I ought to know where every one of the bugs are. After all, I had them put there. Now," he took me in his arms and kissed me deeply. "Now . . . afterwards . . . we can finally talk." He picked me up effortlessly and carried me to the bed.

After the brute force of Spatz, more rape than lovemaking, Schellenberg was an artful, tender lover. Surprising to discover such sensual expertise in one so young. He'd obviously been fortunate in his tutors. Where Spatz's style was immediate satisfaction—his—Schellenberg's was to prolong it, and to relish every evidence of my pleasure as much as his own.

He lingered over undressing me, sliding the satin straps of my gown over my shoulders and imprinting a trail of light, burning kisses down my back to the point, just above the base of my spine where the gown ended. Then he slid the black chiffon over my head and turned his close attention to unfastening my garters and slowly drawing my sheer black stockings, one at a time, down my legs, the tips of his fingernails teasing my soft flesh as he did so. He left the lacy belt in place.

He was much quicker about himself. While the silky skin of my inner thighs was still shivering from his touch, he was out of his uniform and boots and standing naked beside the bed, fully erect, obviously proud—as well he might be—to display his superb body to me. It was as though he was making a gift of himself to me. And he was . . . he was that fiercely concentrated on my pleasure.

It seemed to me hours—hours of the most exquisite and delicate sensation, as he celebrated my body with his own—before he allowed himself release. Time and again, as he was clearly on the point of climax, he would withdraw from me—just far enough to calm his arousal and to tantalizingly intensify mine.

In the end it was my patience that broke first, and I reached up, seizing his beautifully firm buttocks and pulling him suddenly, utterly inside me.

"Your hostage, General," I whispered in his ear.

"Your victory, chère Coco," he replied.

I lay cradled in the curve of his shoulder while he smoked a cigarette, the occasional flaring of its tip the only light in the room. How extraordinary. Here in a deluxe German brothel, five hundred miles and twenty-five years distant, with a stranger half my age who I would never see again once my mission was completed, I felt for the first time the same camaraderie and comfort I'd shared so long ago with Boy.

Perhaps it was Schellenberg's natural sensuality, perhaps it was his humor or his roguery, perhaps it was what I'd told Misia in Venice—that for the rest of my restless life I'd be looking for traces of Boy everywhere. Or perhaps it was all just an illusion brought on by the total foreignness of the experience. I felt that we were old—not new—lovers. Enemies, yet for this one night, friends. And he felt it, too. It was a fragile moment out of time, and we were both reluctant to surrender its spell.

Finally, he spoke quietly into the darkness. "You can tell me now, Coco. I won't betray you, and I somehow doubt, whatever the outcome of this evening, that you will me. Why are you here with me tonight? It's not about 'Model Hat.' We both know it never has been."

When I said nothing, he continued. "Your friend, Churchill, has no intention of negotiating peace—especially now he and his allies have our leader on the run. And he knows just as well that the Fuehrer, however diametrically different their world views, will never surrender either. Will die defending his own grandiose dream of *Lebensraum,* of a German master race." He reached for another cigarette and lighted it.

"Hitler knows the handwriting is on the wall. He knows he's surrounded by intriguers. His paranoia is fully justified. Those who aren't actively plotting his death right now are taking out insurance policies against it. Every second general has his own plan for a negotiated peace hidden under the war plans in his safe for the moment he finds prudent to produce it to save his neck. I do. My boss, Himmler, has his own. Goering does, too. Hess actually anticipated us all two years ago by flying *his* across the Channel."

"I'm astonished at your candor, General," I said, but he ignored me, caught up in his vision of a system gone mad.

"I know where all the conspirators are on *both* sides, Coco." He laughed, mirthlessly, harshly. "After all, I'm the one who was assigned to draw up the list of English 'unreliables' for the Fuehrer in those first glory days of the *blitzkrieg* when he was confident his 'Operation Sea Lion' would sweep over Churchill's 'sceptered isle.' "

"I know," I told him softly. "That's why I'm here with you tonight. Churchill reads the same handwriting. It would be infinitely helpful to him to know the lay of the land here now. Who are the serious contenders for succession once Hitler, inevitably, is gone? Which ones are the men with whom a peace will finally be negotiated—after the surrender of the Reich? He needs a man who has access to that intelligence. A man who sees his own future in agreeing to provide it."

He reached out and gently traced the contours of my face with his fingers. "You know, of course, chère Coco," he said, "that I could have you shot for this conversation. After my experts in Prinz Albrechtstrasse had finished amusing themselves with you."

"Yes, I know it."

"Then why in God's name are you here?"

"In the hope of hastening the conclusion, and of bringing the right people together to redesign a world with more *style,* more *douceur.* I'd heard you were a man of daring . . . of imagination . . . of *insouciance.*"

"Redesigning the world. A couturière's dream. How very simple you make it sound." He leaned over and softly, lingeringly kissed me on the lips. "My driver will take you to the airport tomorrow. He will have your safe-conduct to travel back to Paris signed by me."

"And what am I to tell Churchill of our meeting? Your answer?"

"Tell him, Coco, that despite the compelling charms of his ambassadress, I cannot serve two masters and live with myself. But tell him also that, as events unfold, I cannot predict precisely what my response will be."

THREE

I was barely back in my room at the Ritz—the church bells still shouting *"Libération"* all over the city—from Notre Dame to the Sacré-Coeur—when I began to wonder when my summons to judgment would come, as I knew it had to. Nearly two years had passed since my "interview" with Schellenberg in Berlin, as the fortunes of the Reich plummeted and the brilliant surprise Allied "Operation Overlord" at Normandy turned the tide of war in the West once and for all. Spatz, with his infallible instinct for the way the winds blew, had already decamped for neutral Switzerland "on business."

I'd spent the morning at a ridiculous *"fête de la libération"* at the rue de Rivoli. Only José, who'd played a double game nearly as intricate as my own throughout the Occupation, would do something so outrageous.

He'd invited more than fifty people—some half of them *résistants,* the others, *collaborateurs*—to enjoy his black-market Fascist Spanish champagne and his black-market Allied Russian caviar, while they crowded out onto his balcony to watch de Gaulle and Generals Leclerc and the American Omar Bradley march their victorious troops—in a snowstorm of flowers and handkerchiefs and lace-edged panties—from the Place de la Concorde to the Arc de Triomphe where the *tricolore* had at last replaced the hated blood and iron of the swastika.

Misia still loved him, in spite of it all. I'd seen her unquenchable admiration of his Catalan *macho* when he was the only one left on the balcony, after the liberating army had let off a joyful volley of rifle-fire that reduced the tall front windows of the flat to glittering shards. And left the guests of *both* persuasions in panicked retreat.

I'd also seen the very real pain on her face as she watched Jojo link arms intimately with his German mistress, Marie-Ursel, the striking Baroness Stohrer, wife of Germany's ambassador to Spain. He'd probably managed to convince the baroness he could now rescue her from the vengeance of the Free French, just as he'd saved Maurice Goudeket and so many other Jews and intellectuals—but, tragically, not our beloved Max Jacob and his lovely young sister—from Nazi "relocation" into oblivion.

Would old habits, old friendship make him feel obliged—even though I'd made no secret of the contempt I felt at his endless wounding of my endlessly vulnerable friend—to do the same for me when the time came. Would I *need* rescue?

Now, two weeks later, the high price of collaboration was being paid in the heat-shimmering streets and sultry parks of Paris. Kangaroo courts dispensed rough justice to men who'd traded goods and services—or worse, secrets—to the enemy. And to women who'd sometimes done no more than danced and flirted to drive away cold and boredom or to provide food for their hungry children or a frivolous flacon of Chanel No. 5 from my own boutique to restore their flagging spirits.

The men were shot summarily. The women were shaved bald, stripped naked and paraded, shivering with shame in the sweltering August sunshine, to be spat on by their more "virtuous" sisters.

I had done so very much more. As I lay watching the pale dawn light creep across my windowsill after one more sleepless night, I could hear my righteous accusers review my crimes. I had closed the fashion house out of offended pride at my girls' "rebellion," putting more than twenty-five hundred women out of work, yet had left the boutique open throughout the Occupation to capitalize on the German soldiers' endless appetite for souvenir bottles of Chanel No. 5 to send to their lonely wives and sweethearts in the Fatherland.

I had tried to appropriate my own company from my friend and patron, Pierre Wertheimer, when his compromising bloodlines had forced him and his brother to seek asylum in America. Never mind that Pierre's cleverness had neatly foiled what they saw as my rapacious desire to take back my own!

And I had harbored a high-level—oh, to be honest, a very mid-level Nazi in our "love nest" above the aggressively flourishing boutique. In other words, I had compromised. I had survived. *Bien sûr,* I was for the chop. I almost laughed when I remembered Iribe's portraying me as "Marianne," embattled France, on the cover of *Le Témoin* when the war was only a madman's plan and the dilemma of diplomats unprepared to comprehend the full magnitude of Hitler's lethal delusion.

The jangling telephone cut short my reveries. It was the concierge, apologizing for awakening me at the unseemly hour of eight A.M. but announcing that representatives of the Free Forces of the Interior were waiting impatiently for me in the lobby. Only the direct intervention of Monsieur Charles himself, he told me, had prevented their coming direct to my room to "collect" me.

Assuring the anxious concierge that it would only be a matter of minutes, I washed and dressed hastily, then turned to my dressing table to convince myself that I was prepared for whatever this inevitable August morning would hold. As it had for so many years, the mirror calmed me. A trifle pale, but who wasn't among those on whom the jury was still out? A trifle weary, but who wasn't among those who'd played a game of skill and chance far more complex than the bezique that had driven even Winston to cheating on those long-ago golden evenings at the Hall. Who knew what cards the FFI was holding—what they knew and didn't know? What they should and what they shouldn't know?

At least I would be well-dressed. I examined the perfectly pleated, perfectly hung skirt of my cream-colored silk suit. Chanel dressed by Chanel—appropriate to the occasion, as she always had been.

Apparently, though, I had taken too long. There was a loud banging at the door of my room. For luck, I touched the little red-and-gold icon Stravinsky had given me and opened the door to confront what looked like two young hoodlums with revolvers jammed clumsily into their leather belts. Scruffy, bearded, in dirty fatigues and scarred leather sandals, they resembled nothing so much as down-at-the-heels market traders, like the father I'd consigned to legend nearly sixty years ago. If these were typical representatives of de Gaulle's new order, then I was in dire trouble. I mustered all my hard-won dignity.

"Gentlemen, to what am I to attribute this intrusion? I don't believe we have an appointment."

"Perhaps not an appointment, Mademoiselle," the taller, bolder of them said. "Let us call it a rendezvous. A rendezvous with your past. I have a warrant for your arrest." He produced a document signed by de Gaulle himself. "You are to accompany us to FFI headquarters to answer certain questions regarding your wartime activities. Your, shall we say, questionable affiliations."

"Then certainly, Monsieur, my *avocat* should be there to advise me."

"We are not in the hair-splitting or the bargaining business right now, Mademoiselle. We are in the truth business. Whether or not you will require the services of your lawyer will depend entirely on the outcome of these preliminary inquiries."

Inwardly, I shuddered. The cobblestoned courtyard of FFI headquarters had echoed to the rifle-shots of instant executions since the liberation.

"All right then, Messieurs, let's get on with it."

As I left the lift and crossed the lobby, held tightly by the arms by the two disreputable-looking members of the FFI's "Purification Committee" who could do with a purifying bath themselves, I kept my head high.

I would not dream of giving any of my fellow guests, or my customers who lived for gossip—not that any of them would ever be seen up at this ungodly hour— or Monsieur Charles's staff who'd served me so loyally for so long, the slightest indication of my state of mind.

Let them whisper behind my back of my public humiliation. Let them make predictions of my fate. The fate of a suspected collaborator. I'd been proof against malicious gossip for too many years not to be able to handle this strange moment of reckoning.

The dusty *camion* drew up in front of the headquarters building, and my guards accompanied me inside. On wooden benches lining the long corridor sat men and women of all ages and walks of life. The only thing they had in common was their nervousness.

Those who still had watches consulted them every few minutes. Those lucky enough to have American cigarettes, handed out so liberally by the cheerful American GIs, chain-smoked feverishly. They shifted uneasily on the hard benches and read and reread the same paragraph of their tattered copies of *Le Matin* and *Paris Soir,* waiting for their names to be called. I sat at the head of the bench nearest the door to the commander's office.

I practiced the art of meditation Boy had taught me years ago, breathing deeply, concentrating on an image of moonlight silvering a strand of beach, and withdrawing deep inside myself, so that the sights and the sounds of coughing, the rustling of newspapers, the hushed conversations receded into the near distance.

"Chanel, Gabrielle . . . Chanel . . . Mademoiselle Gabrielle Chanel . . ." The orderly had to call my name more than once to reach my calm, still center. I got up, straightened the pleats of my skirt, adjusted my jacket, smoothed the short black curls I hoped very much to keep, and followed him through the mahogany door, where that tall, familiar uniformed figure with the aquiline profile and silver-grey hair sat behind a paper-cluttered desk draped with the *tricolore.* The orderly went out, softly closing the door behind him. We were alone together with the truth.

Three hours later, he rose from his desk and accompanied me to the door.

"See that Mademoiselle Chanel is safely returned to the Ritz," he instructed the orderly in that deep voice that had sustained us all for so long over countless clandestine wirelesses from his rallying-point across the Channel.

When I got back to the hotel, I headed straight for Harry's Bar, paying no heed to the curious glances and whispered comments that followed close at my heels.

Ensconced in a corner banquette with a snifter of

Rémy-Martin to calm my still-vibrating nerves, I wondered to myself at how strangely it had all turned out. No one but the principals would ever know. That was the bargain he and I had struck that afternoon. Highly placed men on both sides of the Channel were best served by my continued silence.

My consolation was the truth itself. The truth that my "ridiculous little mission," as Spatz had called it, had been something more than that. That when the dark dream of the "Thousand-Year Reich" had perished along with its psychotic dreamer, only a little over twelve bitter, blood-drenched years after its conception—when it had died in the towering flames of a Viking funeral for himself and for Eva Braun, his bride of twelve hours, in a shell-hole in the garden of the Reichschancellery—my mission had ultimately borne fruit.

Walter Schellenberg had finally revealed "what his response would be": had influenced Himmler, his boss —*"der treue Heinrich,"* as Hitler used fondly to call him—to betray his master by negotiating with Count Folke Bernadotte of Sweden to surrender the German armies in the West to General Eisenhower.

Remembering the ardency of Schellenberg's kisses and the glint in his eye, I raised my snifter to toast a fellow rogue and nonchalant gambler.

My role in the drama would remain ambiguous. For the rest of my days the shadow of collaborationist would hang over me and I would do nothing to dispel it. I would have to endure the slights and vicious speculation with as much equanimity as I could manage.

I would have the knowledge that Winston had placed me on his "reliables" list—the list of those who could be counted on to come through when high risk was required.

And I would have to bear in mind the wisdom of another independent woman—that remarkable American actress Lily Langtry, who Benny told me had once engraved with the diamond ring the *old* Prince of Wales had given her on the glass windowpane of the villa in Deauville he'd also given her: *"They say . . . let them say!"*

FOUR

Once I'd been officially, if privately, cleared of collaboration, my passport was mine to use at will, so I decided on a temporary relocation to Switzerland.

I wasn't ready yet to reopen the fashion house. The wounds were still too fresh. The diplomacy required to manage the contending social and romantic factions among my customers had been bad enough before the war. It would be impossible now that the political rifts yawned, too, just waiting for the unwary to topple in.

Of course, the boutique was thriving, selling as many if not more ounces of Chanel No. 5 to the fresh-faced American GIs with their "wolf whistles" and their hair cropped *en brosse,* who lined up every day in the rue Cambon to purchase a treasured souvenir of "Gay Paree," just as their adversaries in field grey had done only months before. And Pierre and Paul Wertheimer were still collecting the lion's share of the profit. *Merde.* Perhaps this was the time for me to face that particular hurdle. But to do it I needed the help of my original accomplices.

By now Misia had to be thoroughly tired of the delicate balancing act she performed as Jojo's official hostess, if not his wife—entertaining veteran *résistants* on Tuesdays, veteran *collaborateurs* on Thursdays. It had seemed to me more trouble than it could ever possibly be worth. She only did it in hope of renewing Jojo's old passion for her. I understood.

Her perfect pitch as *intrigante* was failing along with her eyesight. The Baroness Stohrer had been no more than Jojo's wartime insurance policy, quickly dispatched back to her husband when no longer relevant. Passion had died for Jojo with Roussy. I could have told her so, but I couldn't bear to strip away that last illusion.

Against his doctor's warnings of his worsening jaundice, Jojo's distractions were cocaine and absinthe—and that greatest hallucination of all—the mammoth frescoes of the cathedral in Vich. More and more he spent his time there, high on a ladder, lost in their endless perspectives that drew him away from age and loss and death.

Misia prophetically dubbed them the *"fresques fatales"* and waited patiently for him back in Paris—for their "civilized" dinners at Maxim's where, once the wine had unleashed his melancholy, he would reproach her as only a man could do, "All this would never have happened, you know Misia, if *you'd* refused to let me go."

Surely she'd be glad to quit her strange half-life for a holiday in Switzerland. And one last grand scheme for three veteran conspirators. When I sent out my cables, good, loyal Misia was the first to arrive. As she came toward me across the opulent lobby of the Beau Rivage, it was hard for me to disguise my shock at the change in her only two years had wrought. The morphine was taking a dramatically visible toll now. Her beautiful curves had dwindled down to an almost painful thinness. Her beautiful face was drawn, and those superb topaz eyes clouded over. But she was Misia, nonetheless, and I loved her. I hurried to embrace her.

"Misia, ma chère, you can't possibly imagine how glad I am you've come to join us. Never have I needed your genius more than I do now." She must have no suspicion I'd invited her mainly for superstitious reasons—for luck.

She smiled that wonderful, wicked smile. "You know, I've always been yours to command, Coco. Besides, I must admit it's flattering to be needed again. Jojo's so preoccupied with those frescoes *maudites* I barely get to see him. I've come to positively dread the word Vich." She peered over my shoulder around the lobby. "Who is the 'us' you referred to in your cable, Coco? Why all this secrecy? I thought the war was over."

"The global conflict yes, Misia ma chère—the conflict over personal territory, never. You'll recall Spatz's maladroit maneuver to steal Parfums Chanel from the Wertheimers when they were in sanctuary in America. I went along with it for a number of reasons—not the least being that I was counting on Pierre to outfox Spatz, as he proceeded to do. Brilliantly."

Misia looked genuinely perplexed. "Then what has that to do with anything? You got what you wanted, and the Wertheimers are safely back now in Paris."

"That's just it. Their presence in America—and Pierre's marketing wizardry—has only increased the revenues of Parfums Chanel. Dramatically. I know numbers aren't your forté, Misia, but suffice it to say the American earnings alone have more than quadrupled."

"That's *wonderful* news, chérie! We must immediately start thinking of some seriously amusing way to spend your millions." Suddenly, with no warning, she reached into her purse, drew out a syringe and injected herself right through the soft fabric of her skirt, within full view of the typical Swiss amalgam of earnest lovers and earnest businessmen in the bar. I blessed the subdued lighting. From what I could tell, no one had noticed. I was horrified at the flagrancy of what she was doing. But this was neither the time nor place to deal with it.

I continued on as though I'd noticed nothing out of the ordinary.

"That's just it, Misia. Where Spatz's attack on the Wertheimers was motivated by personal greed, there *is* one charge he made that was not altogether false. I did create Chanel Numéro Five, that is, you and I and Ernest Beaux did. Without the three of us, it would never have been born."

"And what a birth, Coco. I'll never forget the look on your face when you unstoppered the fifth vial—transfiguration!"

"True, Misia, but without the Wertheimers possibly a private moment. I needed them to mass-produce the fragrance for me, to give it the international recognition it deserved. The percentages *were* off, though. Ten percent of the profits falls far short of properly reimbursing the effort and the genius that went into creating it."

"Why do I suspect that's why I'm here?"

"You're right, Misia. I devoutly hope the third party you referred to earlier will also respond to my *cri du coeur*. Ernest Beaux. My lawyers have tried twice to correct the financial imbalance between me and the Wertheimers—tried and failed. This time I have a notion that I think might just set it right."

The next morning Beaux turned up right on schedule. *Mon dieu,* he was so very frail. He had to be in his mid-eighties by now, but I was counting on his legendary nose having held up better than Misia's eyesight. After all, he'd led a quiet provincial existence of moderate pleasures and moderate passions. Not the headlong rush Misia made at life. The three of us sat over a long, splendid lunch, accompanied by the light, dry Swiss wines, in the beautiful dining room looking out over the white-capped sapphire of Lake Léman.

We reminisced over the agonizing birth pangs of Chanel Numéro 5, and by the time I had sketched the broad outline of my new strategy, the three of us were laughing like schoolchildren planning an inspired prank.

"You *did* bring the essential oils and aldehydes, Monsieur Beaux?" I asked.

"Mais certainement, Mademoiselle Coco. I have everything necessary to create three splendid frauds."

"Bien. At last. *J'ai tout entendu,"* Misia said. "Heaven knows, I've seen enough counterfeit paintings in my day. Poor Picasso's plagued by the forgers—and he's not even *dead* yet! But forged *fragrances. Quelles délices!"*

"You see, Misia," I told her, "while the Wertheimers have the perfect right to withhold anything more than the ten percent I agreed to when I was an innocent child, and while they refused to allow me to offer a fourth perfume, 'Mademoiselle Chanel,' in the rue Cambon boutique on the grounds of trademark infringement, how dare they imagine they can stop me from creating new fragrances? They can't. Especially if I do it here, outside the country. I'll simply *give* them to my friends."

"And, dear ladies," Monsieur Beaux said, "I will not be required to age ten years in the process. Not that, this time, I have the ten years to hazard." He smiled wryly. "Devising look-alikes, or should we call them 'sniff-alikes?' is child's play compared to creating an original fragrance."

Misia looked at me speculatively. "You've got that old gypsy glint in your eyes again, Coco," she said. "For some reason I feel Pierre Wertheimer had best be on his guard. When you say your 'friends'—the ones you're so generously going to give these new fragrances to—exactly who do you have in mind?"

"Why, my American friends, of course, Misia. Those delightful gentlemen we met in New York and Hollywood. *You* remember. I told you they both reminded me so much of Papa Bader—the same pure retailing genius."

In less than ten days, Beaux had come up with three brilliant "sniff-alikes." Over a champagne celebration, we christened them "Mademoiselle Chanel Numéro 5," "Mademoiselle Chanel Bois des Isles," and "Mademoiselle Chanel 31 rue Cambon."

A hundred of my generous "gifts"—bottled in a new, but subtly reminiscent shape . . . labeled with a new, but subtly reminiscent label—were carefully packed up and sent off. They were addressed to my sympathetic . . . my understanding . . . my *eager* American friends—Bernard Gimbel and Stanley Marcus.

The gambit was played. I dispatched Monsieur Beaux back to his goodwife in Grasse, Misia to her schizophrenic life, shuttling between the rue de Constantine and the rue de Rivoli, and returned to the Ritz myself to wait. I sensed, even with the difficulties of postwar international communications, that my wait would not be a long one.

The first sign my campaign was succeeding was a flurry of "confidential" communiqués between my lawyer and Pierre's:

"How *dare* Mademoiselle believe that she could market new fragrances internationally without the approval of the Board of Directors?" was their thrust.

"What prevented Mademoiselle from allowing her 'friends' to distribute entirely new fragrances created outside France, in entirely new packages created outside France, in a marketplace outside France?" was our parry.

Hours and hours of expensive deliberation, volumes

of lawyerly correspondence, and hundreds of pounds of files later, I knew precisely what would happen. And so did Pierre.

The threat of my entering the international marketplace as, in effect, competition to him—and to myself— was a potent one. I knew it and so did he. Pierre would have to bargain. Knowing his style as I did, I guessed that he would bypass the lawyers and do it himself. Our settlement, should we reach one, would definitely happen out of court.

So I was not at all surprised to receive an invitation to join him at Longchamp for the Saturday races—he had certainly never lacked a sense of irony—and afterward for dinner *à deux* at Maxim's. What *did* surprise and touch me was the little Soutine study, from Pierre's fabled collection, of a pensive, dark-haired, dark-eyed woman bent earnestly over her fine stitchery, that accompanied the invitation.

So that he would understand how completely I shared his recall, I dressed almost exactly as I had the afternoon we met. The only difference was that I had substituted Benny's fabulous pearl collar for the lesser strands of twenty-five years before, and had done away with the gentleman's panama. No need at this late date to pretend to be anything but the woman I was.

The light that kindled in Pierre's eyes as his chauffeur handed me into the metallic-grey Bentley limousine showed that nothing had changed between us. Not the years, not the war and its separation, not its long postponement, had succeeded in snuffing out the flame of mutual attraction that had flared up between us at that first meeting.

"Mademoiselle Coco, unchanged by time, only lovelier," Pierre said, taking my small hand in his. "We have much to resolve between us today."

"We do, Monsieur," I replied, looking straight into his honest, demanding eyes. "And I am confident that we will."

FIVE

*W*hy, after all these years, am I still surprised and frightened by love? Did I think that at sixty-four my caught breath and hammering heart as I waited for the chiming of my telephone was any different from a twenty-year-old mannequin's?

Did I think when I looked into my mirror, which could never lie to someone who had read it so professionally for so many years, that I was *vraiment folle* to imagine a man might still desire me? That I might return his desire? Or was it the fundamental suspicion, running like a secret poison in my blood, that love has only two possible outcomes—ownership or abandonment?

Impatiently, I turned my back on the honest glass of my dressing table and firmly secured the black straw boater in place with the pearl-and-diamond hatpins. What a cosmic joke—the hats that had begun my career as inspired frivolities had now become saving necessities to cover up the bare patches even Antoine's artistry could no longer conceal. To think how recklessly I'd once sheared off whole lengths of its blue-black satin richness to tempt one lover and torment another. How spendthrift I'd always been with my emotions! And how cautious with my money.

Today Pierre and I were going to meet over lunch at Lasserre to review the papers our lawyers had prepared at our instruction after what he laughingly called the "Second Longchamp Accord." He had agreed to agree. Pierre did not want me as a competitor. As the telephone in my small white room jangled, I wondered whether he had come to the Ritz to collect me with intentions larger than the settlement. Part of me hoped he had.

As the town house lift carried us up from the opulent foyer to the dining room, I glanced at Pierre. Perfect tailoring. Perfect barbering. Sartorial splendor. Such studied elegance that it would have been effete had it not been for his splendid physique and the mischievous gleam in his dark grey eyes. He was using the opportunity of our enforced proximity in the tiny lift to openly admire my own ensemble.

I was grateful I'd decided to forego my usual black-and-white simplicity in favor of an emerald shot-silk suit, its sleeves turned up at the cuff to show the amber silk lining, and an amber silk blouse that drew attention to the green-and-gold flecks in my dark eyes. I was wearing the emerald and gold earrings Boy had won for me that long-ago night at the tables of the Casino in Biarritz.

When we stepped out into the restaurant, there was

a perceptible flurry in that room full of wealthy, worldly men and women. It seemed a stage set by Bakst that awaited only our being settled side by side on the blue velvet banquette for the captain to give the order to commence the daily ceremony . . . to order the domed ceiling rolled back to let the dozens of white doves fly free of their cages out into the restaurant's courtyard.

"White doves for peace, Mademoiselle?" Pierre took my hand, looking deep into my eyes.

"For peaceful parlay, Monsieur," I replied. "There *are* one or two points that seem to have suffered something in translation by your lawyer."

I smiled discreetly down into my lap while the captain presented the gold-tasseled *carte du jour* and Pierre selected caviar and *foie gras* to begin and Lasserre's legendary duckling, numbered in a register just as it was at Tour d'Argent. How very different this was, I thought, from that uncomfortable evening with Spatz when I knew I was hostage, not negotiator.

Pierre raised his champagne flute in a toast. "First, to my incomparable partner and to her 'close friends' in New York and Dallas. I only regret depriving them of a new source of revenue."

"Thank you, Pierre, however consider how very much additional revenue these negotiations have provided both our excellent lawyers."

He laughed as we clinked glasses, then turned serious. "I thought we understood each other very well. What are these points that continue to trouble you?"

"Well, Pierre, first about the royalty on the international perfume sales."

"The two percent, of course. It's right here in the document." He drew the papers out of his slim alligator-leather briefcase and indicated the clause.

"But our agreement was two percent of the gross, and somehow your lawyer has mistaken that for two percent of the net."

Pierre took out his gold-rimmed reading glasses and studied the document, then he smiled up at me.

"Quite right, Coco. Obviously an oversight, and one we will correct here and now." With a flourish of his gold and onyx fountain pen, he made the correction and we initialed it.

"Then there's the matter of the compensatory payment for past royalties."

"I'm *quite* certain that's correct."

Did I detect a note of frostiness in his deep voice?

"Five million francs and an additional twenty thousand pounds for the English revenues."

"But, Pierre, what about the sales of my American shares in the company while you were abroad. Remember, I calculated that at an additional 180,000 in American dollars."

"Such a trifling amount, Coco. You *know* we were forced to make the sales by the exigencies of the wartime situation. But if that's your sticking-point, I will, of course, include it." He penned the appropriate amount into the agreement. "Everything is, I surely hope chère Mademoiselle, *finally* in order?" He was distinctly exasperated now, but still just managing to preserve his famous aplomb.

Time for my trump card. "Everything, Pierre. And I was particularly touched by your permitting me, should I ever choose, to make and export my own line of fragrances out of Switzerland. That was characteristically generous of you."

Pierre need never know I had absolutely no intention of developing the line. It had been a hundred-bottle gamble. One even Benny would have admired. One that had succeeded. I had finally gotten my due. Pierre and I had remained friends—perhaps one day soon, more than friends. And, should I ever wish or need to improve the terms of our accord, the spectre of "Mademoiselle Chanel" stood sentinel for me—a fragrant threat.

It was a ruse born of my own peasant cunning, married to more than thirty years of watching one of the most brilliant intriguers of our century, my beloved Misia.

SIX

How did she dare? I'm not sure I can ever forgive her! When I got there she was already gone, her mouth open in surprise as though mortality had ambushed her in the middle of dismantling one last reputation. And to *think* how furious she'd been at Jojo only three years ago for leaving before she could get down to Vich—while she was still in the rue Cambon, tormenting me to put the last touches to the perfect deathbed ensemble, so he could carry her like a Renoir portrait along with him through the "door" Boy had always called death.

Boulos, her friend Denise Mayer, her elderly maid who had accompanied her through her stormy sea changes, the priest summoned just in time for the last rites—they were all gathered around her narrow, nun-like bed in the cramped, cluttered little room at the very back of the grand, echoing flat.

Even after Jojo had left her the rue de Rivoli in his will and she'd moved back three years ago from her dreary exile's purgatory in the rue de Constantine, she had never slept in the splendid master suite.

Just the sight of that fantastically carved and canopied bed, where she and Jojo and Roussy had played their intricate erotic games, would have banished sleep forever. Or so she told me. I think the painful memories of watching Roussy vanish there, and the prospect of the loneliness of her *own* small figure, lost in its vast emptiness, was what really daunted her.

Well, the Empress, my beloved "Madame Verdurinsky," could not possibly lie in state in a maid's room!

And, if Boy was right about group reincarnation, by now the three of them had probably met up again anyway, clothed in brave new forms, to work out their hopelessly tangled Karma. So the master suite it would be.

As usual, it was up to me to take command. Asking the maid to show the good Father out, then go to the fashion house to collect the things I would need for my work, and directing Denise to the Polish Church in the rue Cambon to make arrangements for the funeral the next day, I ordered Boulos to pick up her frail body and carry her for the final time to that significant bed.

Her last conquest was weeping so hard he could barely see his way, with his near-weightless burden, down the dimly lit corridors. I saw clearly enough the paler spots along the parquet floors where Jojo's antique console tables and commodes had stood until she sold them off, one by one, to pay for her increasingly costly addiction.

When Boulos had set her down, as gently as a bridegroom, on the faded pink satin comforter, I led him to the door and sent him out into the blue October twilight to go and tell all of her friends who were left that they could come to make their *adieux* the following morning. I shut the door softly behind him.

Misia . . . lover . . . rival . . . inspiration . . . dearest friend of my heart and soul . . . How could you leave me?

Why did everyone I have ever dared to love leave me? For what seemed to me hours, I sat beside her on the bed, holding her cold hand in mine and stroking her thin, lusterless hair.

Images of her surrounded me. Misia in a cloud of pink chiffon at the Beaumonts' ball, that same hand resting lightly, tantalizingly on my breast . . . Misia in the cloakroom of Restaurant Weber, both of us flown with champagne, her warm, soft lips pressed to mine as I opened mine to hers . . . Misia in white embroidered linen, laughing up at me from under the brim of a straw cartwheel hat, at the impossible beauty of an impossibly young Venetian gondolier, calling me back from the shadow-world of grief I was reluctant to surrender . . . Misia in her red velvet box at the Théâtre des Champs-Élysées, shimmering in ivory satin and ermine and yards and yards of diamonds, her diamond tiara proclaiming her unchallenged ruler of all the arts, unchallenged until I came along to nip at her heels like a determined provincial terrier . . .

Misia, her amazing topaz eyes flashing fire, as Benny lifted her, indignant and disheveled, from her runaway mount . . . Misia, those topaz eyes clouded and almost blind now, feeling her way about the treasured *objets* of my flat with as much instinctive grace as one of Diaghilev's ballerinas . . . Misia, surrounded by prostitutes and pickpockets and fellow addicts, still regal as a monarch, as a surly prison guard opened the cell door to release her into Jojo's and my custody after her arrest for drug possession.

Misia . . . what a strange, spectacular odyssey from the not-so-innocent, exquisite Muse of Valvins to the ruined beauty who lay on the pink satin beside me.

Misia . . . lover . . . rival . . . inspiration . . . dearest friend of my heart and soul. What last gift can I make you in adieu?

As the maid tapped lightly at the door, rousing me from my reverie and bringing me all the necessary tools of my craft, I knew. After all, if I *had* to concede it—now her perfect back was turned once and for all— if she was the undeniable Empress of the arts, then I was surely the Empress of beauty.

Misia was the single most vain woman I had ever known—with, perhaps, one exception—in a business devoted to vanity. How could I allow her to appear less than herself in death?

The next eight hours were a test of all my skills and all my love. I had thought that, with my old horror of mortality, I might not even be able to touch her to do what was required. But Misia and I had shared so much, been through so much together, had laughed and cried over so many dramas—some real, too many only imagined—that our camaraderie allowed me to forget my fears.

Our laughter echoed in my heart. For the very first time in our thirty-four years of friendship I would be able to make Misia shut her beautiful mouth. What was it Denise had told me Misia said when she knew I was hurrying to her deathbed? "Coco! *That* will finish me!"

As I tied the silk bandeau around her head, after deftly inserting strips of cotton to plump out her sunken cheeks, I knew she would forgive me, would even encourage me. By the time I untied the silk, three hours from now, the force of nature—that primal force she and Stravinsky had understood so well—would have closed her mouth in a last, enigmatic smile, one she, of all others, would have approved.

Then there was the matter of her hair. In my mind's eye I could see the paintings of Bonnard, Renoir, Lautrec. Misia with her auburn mane tucked up in a chignon, trailing those seductive, wispy curls, or cascading down her beautifully turned white shoulders in a river of flame.

Finally, in her sixties, I'd induced her, still reluctant, to cut it. And Antoine's genius had chemically—or alchemically, who knows?—maintained its superb color. But now drugs and death had combined to quench its fire and substance. For an hour, first using a henna rinse and fluffing small tendrils down over her brow to mask the deep furrows anxiety and morphine had etched in her high, white forehead, I augmented its thinness with perfectly matched pieces to restore the illusion of that burning waterfall.

Then, using the very best that the Wertheimers' Bourjois had to offer, I had the audacity to delicately repaint the face that had enamored three generations of Paris's premier artists, three husbands, lovers— male and female, confessed and unconfessed—and, of course, myself.

The damage to her body was actually easier to conceal. The needle-marks on her arms and thighs—*Mon dieu,* she still had the most amazing legs! Truly as good as my own—were hidden under a gown of white chiffon, padded underneath with silk tulle to make the dress flow softly as though she were lying in a light breeze.

The high neck of the gown I'd designed and kept in reserve for this inevitable moment, reminiscent of the *belle époque* creations she'd worn before we met, along with the silk pillow I'd slipped beneath her head, fanning out her hair on the pillow the way a lover would—the way I had so many times—would hide the lines time had traced up her soft throat like a cruel choker. And around her neck those three spectacular strands of diamonds Jojo had offered to atone for Roussy and I had saved from the pawnshop the day the Magician left us behind.

Her hands posed a more difficult problem. Woman's ultimate betrayer, they showed her seventy-eight years as nothing else did. But even they could be disguised by a manicure and the artful arrangement of the long sleeves of the gown. I would thread a chiffon scarf through her slender fingers—those agile fingers Fauré had longed to see conquer the concert stage and that had delighted her "captive" composers on so many musical evenings at the Meurice, at the St.-Honoré, at La Pausa. I know that I will never forget their touch.

I looked at the small clock, embedded in one of Misia's collection of crystal obelisks. Five A.M. Strange, I'd lost all sense of time as, like generations of Auvergnat peasants before me, I went about the business of preparing the body to be seen.

Painstakingly, I had used all my skills to restore Misia's legendary beauty—the beauty that had stunned me that first time I'd glimpsed her in her box at the incendiary premiere of *Le Sacre*, before we'd even met. Now was the moment when I needed Diaghilev, or at the very least his resident genius, Léon Bakst. I had to move from costume and cosmetics to stagecraft.

Pretending to be Diaghilev, walking into a new and unexpected theatre when one of his productions had been summarily moved by Astruc in order to meet the astronomical bills, I looked consideringly at the space just as he would have done:

The high ceilings. The tall, narrow windows that, if not properly shuttered, would let in too much merciless morning light—light that would undo all the meticulous work I'd spent the last hours accomplishing. Carefully, I closed and latched the shutters on each of them and drew the heavy, fringed pink velvet drapes. It was, after all, October, and the chill of the room would demand it. Then I ransacked the armoires and—given Misia's lifelong passion for pink—emerged with a sufficient number of silk and gauze scarves and shawls to drape over the lamps.

There was the question of scent. The thrifty French disdained embalming to ensure a fairly timely turnover of available real estate in their family plots. Though she had always teased me quite mercilessly about my obsession with "a little bit of smell-good," Misia was as fastidious about her person as I was.

From my makeup case I took atomizers of Chanel No. 5, whose scent would forever evoke those sweet late-August afternoons, when our work with poor, beleaguered Beaux was done and we would walk the jasmine and lavender-covered hills of Grasse, arm tucked in arm, exchanging confidences like two convent girls on holiday. Liberally—as I had always advised that perfume be worn—I sprayed the draperies, the veils and shawls gentling the lamps, the bedcovers, and, finally, the woman without whom the fragrance would very probably never have existed.

I stepped back to the door of the room to assess the effect. *Almost* perfect. But the small, still figure in the center of the enormous bed was too exposed, too vulnerable.

They would all be here soon, the handful of survivors of our own set—Cocteau, Picasso, Colette, Stravinsky, Serge Lifar, Boris Kochno, Christian Bérard. And the young contenders for her crown she'd diverted herself by taking up. I called them her "muses-in-training." The three Maries: Marie-Blanche de Polignac, Marie-Laure de Noailles, and Marie-Louise de Bousquet—with their ferociously young, ferociously honest eyes that saw with annihilating candor. In this case, the conjurer could simply not afford to invite members of the audience to inspect her legerdemain too closely.

For a moment I was stymied. It would never work!

Then I remembered the yards of silk tulle left over from my arrangement of Misia's gown. *Seen through a veil.* Of course. What a logical solution for me, a woman whose entire life had been hidden behind a veil of invention and artifice.

Standing on one of the last of the Louis XV chairs Misia hadn't sold off to support her morphine habit, I hung a sheer layer of silk tulle, the ultimate disguise, from the canopy around the entire bed. Then I plucked a single pink rose from the bouquet Denise had brought and secured it with a pink sash across Misia's beautiful breasts.

It was done. Until the moment when I would throw open the doors and invite the fortunate to a final glimpse of one of the greatest beauties of our century—looking not a day over thirty, the age she'd decreed she would *always* be—I could rest . . . I could, perhaps, even sleep.

The sun spangled so brilliantly off the Seine that I could barely see—or was it my tears?—as they lowered her coffin into the land.

Only a loyal handful of us—Jean, Igor and Vera, Colette and Maurice, Boulos, Denise, Serge, Boris and I—had made the final pilgrimage from the Polish Church to Valvins and the peaceful little cemetery of Samoreau between the gold satin ribbon of the river and the deep, cool green of the forest. There her loved friend, Mallarmé, had slept for over fifty years, and her beautiful young niece, Mimi, cut off savagely like Boy in a car crash, had lain for only twelve months.

I had never been to Valvins before, but she had told me so many stories of her enchanted young married summers there that, as we passed through the sleepy village, I kept catching glimpses of her out of the corner of my eye. Pedaling madly along the winding country roads, her hair a flaming tail behind her, to try and catch up with Lautrec on his high-seated racer's bicycle . . . sailing by lantern and moonlight with Mallarmé in his little, two-masted yawl under handsful of flung stars, while he told her the magical tales only a poet knows and fell a little bit in love . . . dodging Vuillard's relentless Kodak and his equally insistent passion . . . radiant and laughing in the long summer grass in Thadée's strong arms as they made love in the hay-scented country air. I saw her everywhere. Avid for life. How *could* she be dead?

I wept openly now, as she would have wanted me to do. She had always believed that grief and pain, like love and beauty, should be fully experienced . . . fully expressed. I wept for her gallantry and for the many times she had given her heart so fearlessly to yet another abandoning lover. It was a recklessness we shared. I wept for our fathomless, peerless friendship—the love of two women brave enough to take the risk of true intimacy in which each one of us, inevitably, found the other out.

Misia. How I will miss you! There will be no Venice . . . no remedy for that.

Twelve

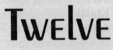

Serge

(1951-1970)

ONE

*A*t first I called her my "artistic godmother" for the delicious reasons I'm about to share. Later, I would come to call her friend, but my first sharp memory of her was at my "christening" on that late afternoon in 1924 when rehearsals for *Le Train bleu* were in stormy progress.

Of course, I'd caught glimpses of her before at Misia's, as she stealthily—and with pure peasant guile—began poaching on our sublime Muse's exclusive preserve. But that April afternoon, perhaps trying to measure the extent of her new powers, she made her influence directly felt for the first time.

The situation was deteriorating alarmingly. From the first day Cocteau and Bronislava Nijinska, scenarist and choreographer, had been at each other's throats.

Never *mind* that Picasso's drop curtain with its two bare-breasted giantesses with streaming hair, running pell-mell along the boiling surf, would raise the pulse of every red-blooded male in the house. Never *mind* that Laurens's cubist décor—especially those adorable beach cabanas—was totally entrancing (I could imagine all *sorts* of mischief taking place in *them*). Never *mind* that Chanel's inspired use of her real bathing costumes and sporting clothes had added a bold and playful new dimension to stage costume.

It was simply that Cocteau's lighthearted approach to the Paris-Riviera express, with its coaches crammed with carefree holidaymakers—its flirts and dandies, its cocottes and gigolos, its sports and their adoring ladies—had come into head-on collision with Nijinska's post-Revolutionary melancholy. With the choreographer in open rebellion, it had begun to look as if *Le Train bleu*'s total derailment was inevitable.

If *that* wasn't enough, well, Serge Diaghilev was at daggers drawn with his lead dancer Massine. Ever since first Nijinsky, and now Massine, had broken his heart by doing the unpardonable—getting married, and to *women* at that—he had been purely impossible to please.

As we stood on the rehearsal stage at virtual impasse, a clear, crisp woman's voice declared in the darkness from the second row center, *"There's* your dancer, cher Diaghilev."

Imagine my astonishment when I realized Coco was pointing at me. Then, miracle of miracles, Picasso, who was sitting beside her, loudly agreed. And of course Misia simply *had* to follow suit. The tension was somehow broken. The very *threat* of me inspired Massine to give the performance of his career. And *I* had been brought to Serge Pavlovich's attention in more ways than one. So you see just how a new star is born and how my long friendship with my guardian angel began.

Twenty-seven years later, when nearly all the rest had gone—some dying of excess, some of ennui, some by accident, and some simply running out of time—she had remained, and we would dine once a week at the Ritz at her table, set right next to the entrance to the

Espadon Grill, where her still-sharp black eyes would miss nothing and no one.

There she sat, Empress in residence, greeting those select few she still deigned to greet, snubbing those she'd broken with, observing those she disdained and making annihilating mock of their pretensions and their offenses against style and taste.

A young beauty swept in, clearly dressed by Christian Dior in an ensemble of rose satin and velvet. How perfectly those colors would set off my dark hair and pale Russian complexion. Serioja had always said it was my looks, certainly not my technique, that made me a star. "Serge Lifar, the Rudolph Valentino of the Ballets Russes," they'd called me.

Coco was less than impressed. "The 'New Look,' Serge, mon cher, that's what they're calling it. *Quelle bêtise!* What, may I ask you, is new about that distorted silhouette?"

"Women seem to like it, chère Coco. I've been seeing those elaborately constructed outfits everywhere, even on the avenues in the afternoon."

"They don't *like* it, Serge," she snapped, "they are told to wear it by those idiots of the press who are always seduced by the extreme . . . who have simply decreed that it's in fashion. Truly, Serge, how could they possibly *like* it? That poor child in the pink has to be in agony. Breasts and waist imprisoned in a tulle corset as stiff and painful as whalebone . . . bodice and sleeves so tightly molded she can barely raise her arms to embrace her lover . . . skirt practically dragging on the floor . . . and three layers of starched, scratchy petticoats. Clothes to imprison you, not to set you free.

That, my dear boy, is the very bastille I liberated women from more than three decades ago!"

For a professional dancer, I had certainly put my foot precisely wrong. How could I atone? "Why don't you set them right, then, Coco? You've stayed out of the game for too long. Your competitors have gotten lazy, or arrogant, or both. Put together a new collection. *Show* them the difference between fashion and style. You're the only one who's *always* made that distinction."

She patted my hand. I had been forgiven. Better that than exiled like poor Jean. Just because of his friendship with Francine Weisweiller, Coco had even burned Cocteau's letters and some irreplaceable drawings. It seemed that as her friends dwindled away, she demanded more and more of the ones who were left. Though I'd never *dream* of saying it, darling, she was becoming rather unnervingly like Misia in her possessiveness.

"Perhaps one day I will, Serge. One day when they've become complacent and counted me out completely. You know me and the lure of the unexpected!"

TWO

_I_ was touched and saddened when she asked me to go down to La Pausa with her for the last time. She had decided to sell it. At first, I was surprised. How many times had she told me how directly she'd identified with the place—with the villa's design and construction, with the olive groves, the land itself?

What glorious holidays we'd all spent there! Coco at La Pausa always reminded me of one of Picasso's earth goddesses, glowing with good health and relaxation, tanned golden and surrounded by her flamboyant friends—an open-handed Ceres, giving welcome and the largesse of the land to her guests.

The tables on the tiled terrace, laden with the glorious food and wines of Provence. The gaiety. The inspired music of Stravinsky and Auric and Satie. The laughter and the unforgettable conversation that only ended when the sun came up over the sea. The flirtation, the illicit love affairs. Serioja and I had spent some of our sweetest moments there—never mind Boris's jealousy. How could she *bear* to give it all up?

Then, I suddenly understood. She couldn't bear to keep it. The news of Bend'or's death—a peaceful death in his sleep with his fourth duchess, Nancy, beside him, had been the catalyst.

"Why is it, Serge mon cher," she asked me, "that it's

always Ia Abdy who brings me bad news from London. I *do* wish she'd stop going there."

Simply too many deaths in too short a time for even her gallant heart to bear. José, then Vera Bate—reunited ever so briefly with Berto—in 1947. Misia . . . insupportable loss . . . three years later. The next year, news of her first lover, Étienne Balsan's death in Rio, ironically in a car crash like Boy, his rival who'd stolen her away.

And now Bend'or—the Golden Duke—the man Coco had come closest to marrying. The man, I believe, she'd thought would share La Pausa with her. Strange that the villa was barely completed when they parted and he was gone.

We sat together on the low-hanging boughs of her olive trees, the golden villa shimmering fantastically in the intense midday sun. Coco voiced my thoughts.

"A mirage, La Pausa. An illusion, Serge. I suppose that's what it is—what it always was. An orphan's dream of land and a home and a family. I thought I could create it single-handedly, the way I do my dresses. Imagine it, then simply *will* it into being."

How very wistful she sounded. "You *had* your family here, chère Coco. We were all of us your family—your spoiled, indulged, pampered, loved family. We knew a secret you didn't know, though. In your heart you're a gypsy. Accuse me of shallowness if you will, but your looks give you away. You're a gypsy—wild as the wind. You don't understand it, but you could never be confined, pinned to one place . . . one time. Even now in Paris you live in two places—the Ritz and the rue Cambon."

She smiled that irresistible smile, jumped down from the olive bough as agilely as a girl, and ran over to hug me.

"Of course you're right, Serge mon cher. I am a gypsy—a *romanichelle.* I carry my house like a caravan with me wherever I go. My Chinese screens . . . my crystals . . . my boxes and my lions . . . and always the dreams of my dresses. The ones I've made . . . the ones I'm going to make . . . *now* back in Paris. Hurry up, Serge, let's go to the *notaire* and sign over the deed. Can you believe it's Winston's literary agent who's buying the villa? I'll wager these olive groves haven't seen the last of his easel! We must hurry. We must get back to Paris. To the dresses. I see them again now. They're waiting there for me." Her eyes were shining. How could she possibly be over seventy? She looked seventeen to me!

THREE

Well, darling, we knew it was going to be bad—just not *how* bad. Sitting there on the staircase with the privileged few as the *défilé* ended, I waited for the usual thunderous applause. Instead, a flutter of perfunctory clapping and a general retreat that stopped just short of a rout. Mademoiselle did not show herself at all.

Unfortunate enough. But this morning's press was venomous: "A fiasco" . . . "A flop" . . . "A melancholy retrospective." "Chanel ees feneesh," Schiap declared. And worse, they were positively vitriolic about her "advanced age" producing her "backward ideas."

As I made my way to the rue Cambon through the light February rain, I tried to calculate what might be salvaged from the debacle. When I thought of the endless hours she'd poured into the new collection—chivying the invaluable old veterans like Madame Lucie and Madame Manon out of the comfortable boredom of retirement with grand visions of at least ten more green years to come, driving the mannequins beyond their young endurance with her inexhaustible fortitude, working until well past midnight, night after night, her poor arthritic hands wracked by pain.

Then, in the grip of her old nemesis, insomnia, she paced her small white room in the Ritz, considering and reconsidering the construction of a jacket or the flow of an evening dress. More than a hundred new creations had emerged from the vital imagination of a woman of seventy-one.

Over dinner at Maxim's, I had tried to warn her that after fifteen years of retirement—a retirement many viewed as a betrayal of France when she closed the house on the eve of war—the fashion journalists would be lying in ambush for her. The Chanel style was so diametrically opposite to that "New Look" of Dior's that had taken both Paris and the export market by storm.

She had just laughed at me. "So I'm to surrender

without a fight, Serge. Simply hand the shears back to the men again—to Jacques Fath and Balenciaga and Pierre Balmain and Hubert de Givenchy, and that up-start, Dior—that reincarnation of Poiret. I'm to tell women to lace themselves back into corsets and waist-cinchers and crinolines that destroy the natural, beau-tiful, *free* lines of their bodies and turn them into *objets*. What do you take me for after all these years, Serge, a quitter?"

No, she was no quitter. She was utterly confident in the rightness of her vision—in the purity and elegance of line that had been her hallmark for so long.

But what now? As I mounted the curved stairway, the house seemed eerily quiet after yesterday's hubbub. The mirrors reflected the empty salon and the empty gilt chairs where the dragons of the fashion establish-ment had perched, making dishearteningly few notes on their little pads of numbers they intended to pur-chase.

Coco's backers had invested sixteen million francs in her "comeback" collection. Would they desert her now . . . accuse her of hurting the sales of the compa-ny's lynchpin, Chanel Numéro 5?

Worse, what of the damage to her fierce pride—pride that I had come to learn over the years disguised the vulnerability of a lonely, orphaned child, an aban-doned lover?

Imagine my astonishment when I found Coco on her knees in one of the fitting rooms. Praying, you imagine. Hardly. She was totally preoccupied pinning and tack-ing the hem of an elaborately pleated, soft pink wool skirt, while a long-suffering red-haired mannequin smiled wanly at me, pale with fatigue.

Coco saw me in the mirror. "How do you like this, Serge? The fabric is as light as eiderdown. Scottish tweeds are always the loveliest. I think it will do nicely for the next collection, don't you?"

I tried to mask my skepticism. "The next collection, Coco darling. There's to *be* an August collection? Somehow I thought the response yesterday was a little less than enthusiastic."

She smiled up at me, almost coyly. "Ah, Serge, mon cher, we must give them time to absorb, to remember—to separate out the timeless from their infatuation with the new. They're bound to understand. And we haven't even heard yet from the American press. You know they've always loved me."

"But Coco, what about the investors? If the orders fall short of their expectations, will they back a second collection?"

"You know my dear old friend, Pierre Wertheimer?"

Dear old friend, indeed. I smiled wryly to myself. Wertheimer and his brother had been the target of lawsuit upon lawsuit during the period Coco now fondly referred to as the "perfume wars." But there was something about Pierre's attachment to Coco—an attachment that had survived their suits and counter-suits—that had always intrigued me. Her beauty and her brilliance fascinated him. He was, after all, a discerning collector. Were they lovers? I wondered.

"Well, Pierre came to see me this afternoon to discuss business. For one moment I was afraid he was going to withdraw his support." Again that girlish smile. "How very foolish of me, Serge. I've always known how much Pierre needs me. As he was leaving, he took my hand and told me, 'Of course, chère Coco, you must go on with the work."

As you see, darling, La Grande Mademoiselle had pulled it off one more time.

FOUR

*I*t was raining again—this time the soft, warm April rain that would cause the pale-green haze flickering over the parks and boulevards of Paris to burst into emerald splendor—on that afternoon when I went to visit her in the hospital in Neuilly.

I would never have known she was there if it hadn't been for her new friend and confidante, Claude Baillen. I'll admit I was suspicious when Coco began telephoning at the last minute to cancel our weekly dinners on one flimsy excuse after another. But I felt it might well be depression after the February fiasco, so I didn't press her. Not even after nearly two months of gentle evasion.

It was Claude who finally telephoned to tell me the truth. Proud, vain, stubborn Coco had indeed suffered a delayed reaction to the rejection of her dresses. Her right hand had become paralyzed. Coco maintained to Claude that it was simply her arthritis acting up under the strain of the collection, but Claude, a brilliant psychoanalyst and sensitive friend, knew better.

"It's a response to the savagery of her critics, Serge, I'm sure of it. Even she doesn't understand," Claude explained to me, "it's a classic pattern for a perfectionist like Coco. An insult to her dresses was an assault on her."

"She went on working, though, Claude. I saw it with my own eyes. She'd started her designs for the August collection. And Pierre was still backing her. She told me so."

"He is now. It was Pierre she turned to. She had gone on working, but she was like a soldier on the battlefield—wounded but refusing to admit it to herself. Fighting on. When the paralysis struck she was terrified—but even more terrified the fashion press would get wind of it and continue to ridicule her, so she went to ground. Pierre brought her to Neuilly where he visits her in the hospital every day."

"But doesn't she *know,* Claude?"

"Know what, Serge? All she knows right now is pain and shame."

"Know that the collection was a triumph, after all. Not here, certainly—the jealousy of those lesser beings was vicious. In *America!* She'd told me her American friends would never let her down, so I've been following the American fashion press and I have dozens of clippings. She was right as usual. The American exports have been brilliantly received. *Vogue, Harper's Bazaar,* all of them heaving a collective sigh of relief at Coco's liberating them from fashion purdah for the *second* time. *Life* did an entire profile on her. I've got it right here, Claude. They said, 'She is creating more than a style: a revolution.'"

The silence on the end of the line was unnerving until I realized Claude was crying. "Get out to Neuilly with them," she ordered me. "She won't believe it until she sees it with her own eyes, I know her. She'll think we're 'humoring the old lady.' That's what she called herself for the very first time when she refused to let me visit her."

So here I was, rushing through the Sunday-quiet streets of Neuilly, the damp envelope of press cuttings clutched in my hand.

I hesitated at the door of her hospital room. Pierre sat in an uncomfortable straight chair beside the bed, holding her good hand, while the right one lay frozen and useless on the white counterpane. Even so, she'd maintained her vanity. A beautifully embroidered white satin bed-jacket . . . a white satin band holding back her hair . . . an air of Chanel Numéro 5 offsetting the antiseptic hospital smells.

She was outraged. "Serge, you naughty boy. However did you find me? Did Claude tell you? Did you, Pierre? You *know* what an incorrigible gossip Serge is. Now *everyone* will find out."

I was too happy to see her to pay attention to her spite.

"I've brought you something, Coco . . . the American fashion reviews of the collection. They're all outright raves. As good as the best notices *I* ever had with Serioja."

At first she looked at me with a kind of frightened wariness. Then she reached out to take the sodden envelope. And Pierre was still holding tight to her good hand.

FIVE

*I*t was as though regaining the use of that hand
gave her a second wind. I understood it. It was
like a dancer passing through the pain barrier—
through agony and exhaustion into a whole new world
of grace and inspiration. There was no more talk of
"old ladies." In fact, if I had the temerity to so much
as try to help her up from her chair after dinner, my
reward would be a hissed, *"imbécile!"*

With only three months to go before the August collection, Coco flung herself into the work with a frenzy.
New designs flowed from her fertile imagination so fast
and furiously her staff could barely keep up her pace.

Mannequins and fitters and seamstresses alike—
working cruelly long hours against the clock—were
dropping with fatigue. But, unlike 1936, and even
though their pay packets hadn't enlarged appreciably,
they were solidly united behind Mademoiselle. They
were determined to show those *cochons de jaloux*
what a *real* designer was made of.

I would visit the rue Cambon now and then, and it
reminded me of nothing so much as the barely controlled madness that preceded the debut of one of
Serioja's new ballets. Little assistants, perspiring in the
July heat in their white smocks, raced up and down the

curving stairway, carrying fabrics, partially finished dresses, silk flowers, hats, shoeboxes . . .

Pale, willowy mannequins stood patiently in half-made gowns, while Coco crouched on her haunches at their feet, like a wrestler ready to spring at an opponent. And when she finally saw the offending excess of fabric, spring she would—attacking the imperturbable mannequin with her flying shears and cutting back, always back toward simplicity, toward perfection.

And the collection *was* perfection. Not that it differed dramatically from February's offering. Chanel hadn't changed. The exquisitely simple elegance of her line was a constant through the most "revolutionary" of the new designs. But the wind had. America and the export market had spoken eloquently and—though they would deny it on Torquemada's rack—the pundits of the French fashion press had had their wrists as severely rapped as Coco did mine on those rare occasions when I lost my dancer's equipoise and offended against elegance.

Reborn, she went from triumph to triumph. To Texas in America, three years later, to accept the fashion "Oscar" from her fellow guerilla-fighter in the perfume wars, Stanley Marcus. And, in her own proud way to say thank you to the brave, independent American women who had vindicated her.

Then, the next year she held out against the all-powerful *Syndicat de la Couture,* resigning over the issue of copies.

"Don't they understand, Serge?" she asked me, "that a copy is an *hommage*—an act of love. True, I dress Madame Pompidou and Grace Kelly, Elizabeth Taylor and Romy Schneider and Marlene Dietrich. But why *shouldn't* a shopgirl or a little *téléphoniste* be able to have a 50-franc Chanel? When I first came up to Paris, I wouldn't have been able to afford the parasol of a Poiret. Why do you think I started designing on my own?"

Coco's sublime snobbery confined itself to fools.

SIX

*W*hen I arrived for our weekly dinner, I found her waiting at our favorite banquette in Harry's Bar, sipping a glass of champagne. She looked stunning, as ever, in an evening suit of blue velvet, with blue silk moire cuffs and a matching blouse. One of Fulco's whimsical ruby hearts, basketed with gold wire and diamonds, was pinned to her jaunty blue beret. And ropes of pearls glowed against the dark velvet. Stunning as ever, but definitely downcast. In all the years of our long friendship, this was a Coco I'd seldom seen.

"What is it, chérie," I asked her. "Forgive the frightful pun, darling, but your mood appears to match your suit—midnight blue."

"Oh Serge, these ridiculous American producers. You won't believe what they've done to me. To imagine

I was actually *flattered* when they approached me about a Broadway musical based on my life! You'd think my experience with Sam Goldwyn would have cured me of that. *Mais non.* I fell into their trap like a green girl straight up from the provinces."

"Come now, Coco, it can't be all *that* bad. You told me they were already famous in America—Alan Jay Lerner who's writing the script, André Previn who's doing the score. And that director, Frederick Brisson's a Frenchman under the skin. What could go wrong?"

She rapped my wrist smartly with her long ivory cigarette-holder like an offended Russian grand duchess.

"Now you sound like *me,* Serge. 'Established' . . . 'Famous' . . . 'What could possibly go wrong?' I don't know how I could have been so naive. I'm reminded of how Reverdy used to warn me about the snares of vanity."

"I still don't understand, Coco. It all sounds on the up-and-up to me. They're only beginning the production. What could be so disastrous? You look like a tragedy queen."

She gave me the cold look—black ice masking green fire—that had brought countless lovers and business rivals to their knees.

"Two things, Serge mon ami, one far worse than the other—and neither of them open to remedy. First, the costumes . . ."

"But of course *you'll* do the costumes, Coco. That's the whole point of it, isn't it? You've done it so many times before. *Antigone, Oedipe Roi, Le Train bleu*—the way we met . . ."

"One would have thought so, Serge. In a rational

world, one would have thought so. But no. I will be doing neither the costumes nor the décor. For that they have contracted with the renowned Monsieur Cecil Beaton. Now, I've nothing against Cecil, Serge. You know what a superb photographer I think he is. He's done all my formal portraits."

"Still, *Coco* costumed by anyone else besides Coco . . ." I was stunned, *complètement bouleversé*. "It's a travesty. A total contradiction in terms. Serioja must be spinning in his grave as we speak—rest his soul. And you say there's something worse . . . ?"

"Far worse, Serge. When they originally came to me about the production, they told me I would be portrayed by the celebrated Mademoiselle Hepburn. That seemed appropriate to me. Well, I have just devoted this afternoon to coaching Mademoiselle Hepburn in the part. I spent four hours simply showing her how I rip out a sleeve and reposition it so that the jacket will hang properly. So that she can pick up on my moves. She *is* a remarkably quick study, I'll admit. We were even able to have tea afterwards. There is only one problem, Serge mon frère . . ."

I was still reeling from the news of Beaton. "And what is that, Coco? It sounds as though at least that part of it went well."

"Well enough. The problem is it's the *wrong* Mademoiselle Hepburn. I was under the clear impression I was to be portrayed by Mademoiselle Audrey Hepburn. After all, our size . . . our coloring . . . we look so very much alike. Now I discover it is to be the undeniably charming, undeniably gifted Mademoiselle Katharine Hepburn. A triumph of miscasting." Her contempt was withering. "She is more than a head taller than me . . . classic American bone structure . . . auburn hair . . . freckles. And besides, Serge, she's sixty years old . . . *sixty,* can you imagine? *Impossible."*

I was speechless. How could I remind La Grande Mademoiselle that she was, in fact, eighty-six.

"Never mind, Serge mon cher. I simply will not travel to New York to attend the premiere."

SEVEN

I know I'm going to sound an alarmist, but I'm becoming genuinely worried about Mademoiselle. She still keeps to her established routines: up at eleven to take her morning coffee and read the papers, then to the fashion house at one for lunch with her favorites of the moment, and to work through the afternoon. Back to the Ritz to dress for dinner with friends, though by now their numbers are sadly diminished, and to gossip endlessly with her captive audience to avoid the nightly duel with her demon, insomnia, for just as long as she can.

But there have been a number of incidents over the past months that make me suspect she's experienced some deep peasant premonition of her own death.

The first was the matter of Michèle. She'd been one

of Coco's pets for years, not just as a star mannequin—though she was so startlingly beautiful she certainly was that—but one of the inner circle who lunched regularly in the private dining room and exchanged confidences with Mademoiselle about their lovers, their abortions, their broken hearts, their bank accounts. I'd even teased Coco by calling them "the young ladies in waiting—waiting impatiently for you to pass the shears of succession."

And in fact she'd recently made Michèle a directrice of the Paris salon, which had her jealous rivals tearing their perfectly sculpted hair with their perfectly manicured fingernails.

Then, one afternoon at tea at the Meurice, she told me Michèle had been dismissed. Frankly, darling, I was flabbergasted.

"But why, Coco chérie? She's always been one of your particular favorites. A perfectly lovely girl. What could she possibly have done to warrant dismissal?"

"It's nothing she's *done,* cher Serge. It's her illness."

"I had no idea Michèle was ill."

"No one did, Serge, until the other afternoon when she collapsed in the salon and had to be taken to the hospital for tests. It turns out she's suffering from heart disease—a fairly advanced stage. She could live for months, years even. She could also have an attack and die at any time, particularly if she's under stress."

"I still don't understand why you felt compelled to dismiss her, Coco. She's a young woman, after all, and surely she's under a doctor's supervision now. And there *is* medication."

She looked at me as though I'd taken leave of my

senses. "What, Serge, you expect me to let her die there in *my* house? *Jamais!*"

There was no adequate response. Only someone who understood Coco's obsession with her mother—with mortality itself—could comprehend what looked on the surface like consummate callousness. But this was no Roussy . . . and, certainly, no Misia.

"Don't be concerned, cher Serge," she continued earnestly. "I've had her sent to a sanitorium and, of course, I'll be paying all her expenses."

And when Michèle did in fact die a few months later, she reported it to me almost smugly. "You see, Serge, I was right. Just *imagine* how dreadful it would have been. She would have died right there in front of all of us."

Then there was her sleepwalking. It had been a life-long problem that had gotten so serious her maid, Céline, had taken to locking her in her room at night or she might be found by the lift-boy wandering the corridors of the Ritz *en déshabillé* at four in the morning.

Even so, when Céline brought her breakfast tray, she would find pieces of fabric—the bedclothes, the bath towels, sometimes even the draperies—strewn all over the room. Coco had been cutting and recutting new designs, all the while deep in sleep.

If that weren't warning enough, there was the new perfume. She'd met in secret with Beaux—he must be in his nineties now—and they'd negotiated their way to yet one more unforgettable fragrance. When I asked her about the derivation of "Chanel Numéro 19," she gave me her most conspiratorial smile.

"Serge, mon ange—'Numéro Nineteen,' the date of

my birth. Now that we're forgetting how many Augusts ago that was, I thought it would be amusing at least to memorialize the day."

She then went on to describe in meticulous detail the arrangements she had made for her burial in Lausanne.

When I asked her why Switzerland, she replied, "I know, Serge, they'll call it another act of treachery. Even you may consider it disloyal. Of all people, you know better, though. You're one of the disenfranchised, too. You must understand that the only place we ever find sanctuary—find real rest—is where we least expect it."

She went on to describe the memorial stele she intended be placed on her grave.

A simple pink marble obelisk—pink for Misia—with five small lions for her birth signs . . . lions for ardor, for valiance, for leadership, for unbreakable resolve, for the one man who taught her the larger resonances of existence.

"It was Boy who led you to the consolations of Eastern thought, wasn't it, chère Coco?"

"It was Boy who led me to myself, Serge—the only one of them all who never tried to own me. The only one to whom I ever truly gave myself."

Epilogue

Paris, January 10, 1971

She lay on the white bed in the white room. She had been too exhausted by her afternoon drive through the Bois to remove her clothes. Céline had gently taken off her pumps and settled her in, still wearing her old favorite green, pink, and beige suit, for a doze before dinner.

The room was austere, almost like the nuns' cells at Aubazine. The only color was the vivid icon Stravinsky had given her for luck so many years before and the cheap, garishly painted plaster statue of St. Anthony of Padua that Misia had bought for her that terrible time in Venice after Boy's death. How very different from the cluttered opulence of the flats on the Quai de Tokyo and the Faubourg St.-Honoré, and the rue Cambon. She had wanted it that way.

They were all gone now—Étienne, Dmitri, Bend'or, Reverdy, Iribe, Pierre—all the bold men who, even when they denied it, had struggled to possess her. Boy, who told her truly she had met her match. And all the brave, beautiful women, too—Adrienne and Vera and Roussy and beloved Misia—impossible now to separate passion out into simple categories.

What was it she had told that brash young television interviewer? Oh, yes, she remembered. "A woman who

is unloved is a lost woman. She can die. It isn't important."

It was cold in the room. The fierce January wind
howled around the corners of the Ritz and rattled the
windows. Just like that sad little room in that provincial
market town so many years before.

"Maman, I know you now. I understand. It's true I
broke my promise. I couldn't help myself—I *always*
loved too much."

A sharp pain ran down her left arm. She fumbled for
the syringe on the bedside table and tried to inject the
nitro. Too late—the syringe fell from her hand.

"So this is the way one dies."

The door is opening, Boy. I'm coming.

*After two decades as an editor, **Patricia B. Soliman** now changes hats to write about one of the most elegant and enigmatic women of the twentieth century. Soliman lives and works in Manhattan.*